W9-CPO-667

CRUSHED

THE HEART OF NAPA SERIES

BOOK ONE

A NOVEL BY

DEBORAH COONTS

Book published by Austin Brown, CheapEbookFormatting.com

Cover Design by Andrew Brown, ClickTwiceDesign.com

Cover photo copyright Marc Volk, Getty Images, 164850828

ISBN-13: 978-0-9965712-9-6

Other Books by Deborah Coonts

The Lucky Series

"Evanovich....with a dose of CSI"
—*Publisher's Weekly* on *Wanna Get Lucky?* A Double RITA(tm)
finalist and NYT Notable crime Novel

WANNA GET LUCKY?
(Book 1)

LUCKY STIFF
(Book 2)

SO DAMN LUCKY
(Book 3)

LUCKY BASTARD
(Book 4)

LUCKY CATCH
(Book 5)

LUCKY BREAK
(Book 6)

Lucky Novellas

LUCKY IN LOVE

LUCKY BANG

LUCKY NOW AND THEN
(PARTS 1 AND 2)

LUCKY FLASH

CHAPTER ONE

SOPHIA STONE KNEW LIFE HELD few absolutes: good wine is art, good Italian cooking is passion, a good child is a gift, and good news never comes in a certified letter.

"You sure this is for me, Tito?" she asked the postman who thrust an envelope toward her. When she tilted her head she could read the word "Certified," stamped in red like a guilty verdict across the front.

A heavy-set man, Tito had a ready smile and an easy, engaging manner. Each day while delivering mail, he also traversed the valley searching for tidbits of gossip with the zeal of an Army battalion scouring the countryside for insurgents. St. Helena was a small community where the denizens believed mining each other's business was an inalienable right granted on the theory that without the titillation everyone would fall over dead from boredom. "Yeah, looks like it's from Charlie. Certified, too." Tito didn't have the decency to hide his interest as he mopped his face with a dirty handkerchief then stuffed it back into his rear pocket. The wiping didn't help—a sheen of sweat still covered his ruddy cheeks. August had been hot with no break in sight.

Sophia eyed him. She wouldn't put it past him to have already steamed open the letter, a thought that made her a bit nauseous. Why had she thought a small town in Napa Valley would be a good place to hide?

"From Charlie, you say?" Keeping her hands in her pockets, Sophia tilted her head further and tried to double-check the sender's address. Then she looked him in the eye. "Any idea what it's about?"

Tito looked like a bully when his bluff was called. He shrugged—an exaggerated movement that seemed like the shifting of a mountain—but a noncommittal answer, leaving Sophia certain whatever was in that letter would be spread around the valley and germinating in imaginations as rapidly as seeds on a spring wind.

At an impasse, Sophia and Tito stood there, the letter between them, Sophia delaying the inevitable.. Unfortunately, with a dinner to cook and a cake in the oven, Sophia didn't have time to see if she could outlast him. So, with a sour downturn to her mouth and a knot in her stomach, Sophia took the letter.

Tito motioned for her to flip the envelope over. "There on the back, that green card? You need to sign that." Handing her a pen, he waited for her to sign, then tore off the return receipt, pocketing it.

Confirming the return address, Sophia gave him a distracted wave as he climbed back into his truck. "Thanks, Tito." A perfunctory nicety.

"Sure thing, Ms. Stone." In a shower of gravel, he gunned the mail truck back through the vineyard down the winding driveway leading to the valley floor. Sophia glanced up as the trees enveloped him and her normal quiet smothered the sound, wiping away all vestiges of his presence.

Except for the letter.

From her landlord.

At least the return address was his—and Sophia was certain he hadn't moved from the corner lot at the bottom of her hill. She could probably throw a bottle and hit his roof, with a little help from the wind.

Charlie had owned this patch of five acres on the top of Howell Mountain since his parents had died in a small plane heading up from L.A. over thirty years ago. Sophia had lived here for fifteen of those years and, through feast and famine, the ups and downs of the wine industry, she'd never received a certified letter from Charlie. In fact, she couldn't remember having received *any* letter from Charlie. Their business dealings were usually hammered out at the kitchen table over a bottle of wine and sealed with a handshake. Napa Valley was a handshake kind of place.

Sophia reached up and rubbed the worn piece of iron Daniel had nailed to one of the porch supports. *Tocco Ferro.* Her family had been steeped in the ways of the Old Country; her husband had become a believer. Touch iron to ward off bad luck. Being a bit too pragmatic, Sophia didn't necessarily believe, but it couldn't hurt. God knew she'd had enough rough patches. With a finger, she traced the initials the four of them had carved in the porch support. Time had whittled their number to one ... almost.

Tapping the white legal-sized envelope on her open palm, she squinted against the sun as she looked out over her small patch of heaven. A rolling hillside with a couple of acres under vine, grapes from the Old Country, grafts of her grandfather's original vines. A small garden flanked the house. Her own private retreat sheltered from prying eyes by a ring of trees.

The farmhouse had been billed as a "fixer-upper." She and Daniel had packed up the kids, moving up valley from the Bay Area, and spent the next several years making the remnants of a house into a home. They'd bribed the kids into helping by letting them paint their own rooms. Dani had picked pink, hot pink. As if the view from his window wasn't enough, Trey had chosen wood paneling and a bucolic scene of vineyards on one wall. When he'd moved away for college, Sophia hadn't had the heart to change it. Perhaps she'd harbored the hope that he would come home someday. He hadn't. Now Dani was poised to fly.

Soon Sophia would be alone, the house emptied of youthful buoyancy. The prospect filled her with dread. Stripped of purpose, she half-feared she would grow brittle like the old vines until the weight of loneliness shattered her into bits and pieces of who she used to be. When Daniel had been killed, she'd had the kids. Now the false friend of sadness stayed ever near, her house echoing with memories. But memories didn't make a life any more than the past made a future. However, the past was her tether. Without it, Sophia felt she would float away like a balloon loosed to the sky, growing ever smaller until vanishing from sight.

While the house cradled her past, the rows of vines just reaching their peak marching down the hill across her two acres held her dreams. Her grapes, started from grafts from her grandfather's stock back in Italy, each juice-filled orb bursting with hope, with promise. Her life's work hanging on the verge of a promise.

Through the screen door, the aroma of a cake on the verge of disaster wafted into Sophia's consciousness, and she turned and bolted for the kitchen, the screen clattering shut behind her. With a dishrag to protect her hand, she opened the oven. The smell of chocolate carried on billows of steam engulfed her. She waved it away, squinting through the heat. She deposited the cake pan on the stainless steel countertop. Pressing her thumb lightly on the cake, she let out her breath in a long rush. Just in time.

Her mother loved chocolate cake. Sophia planned to visit her this afternoon. Perhaps a peace offering would soften her harsh moods of late.

Sophia spied the letter, pristine white and accusing, laying casually on the sideboard where she had tossed it in her haste. Without further thought, she stuffed it in the old cookie jar on the countertop and crammed on the lid. That cookie jar held a lifetime of happiness and heartache—her marriage license, the kids' birth certificates, Daniel's death certificate and obituary—it could handle the letter as well. Whatever problem lurked inside that envelope, it could wait.

Leaving the cake to cool, Sophia strode through the door to the porch, pushing through the screen and down the steps. The grapes, fragrant in the midday sun, neared perfection—harvest a few days away, at best. Sophia had plans for those grapes, unique varietals that would make unusual yet palatable wine ... if she could just figure out the last piece. She was close, though, closer than ever before. Grapes—creating them, growing them, cajoling them to trust her—were her true passion. Unfortunately dreams didn't pay the bills, as her mother never missed a chance to bludgeon her with that little bit or ironic reality. So Sophia had to sell her skills to pay the bills and now found her days consumed with tending to grapes owned by Pinkman Vineyards, one of the vast commercial operations in the valley, which turned her carefully nurtured grapes into mediocre table wine.

She walked the rows testing the scent once more ... the perfume of near perfection as her grandfather called the sweetness of grapes. Memories filtered through the shadows of time like wraiths, translucent, elusive ... fleeting. When she quieted, stilled her mind and opened her heart, Sophia could hear his voice, rich and deep, his laugh, and smell the scent of earth and sun that clung to him, the wine on his breath. But, she couldn't see him anymore. Like sun on paper, time had weathered and faded her mental pictures until only shadows remained, as if the present was slowly erasing the past.

Worry dogged her, the letter and its unknown message on her mind as she tended to each vine, brushing back the canopy, weighing the clusters. This far along in the season not much remained to do; nature would run her course. This year Sophia had planted wildflowers and grasses under the vines to entice the bugs and keep them off the fruit. The plan had worked well, as had her choice to prune more aggressively than normal this past winter. Under her care, her grandfather's grapes flourished, and just now they were beginning to trust her, to give her their best.

This year's wine had the potential to be the stuff of dreams.

At the far end of her property movement across the fence caught Sophia's attention. Shading her eyes with one hand, she still had to squint against the assault of the sun. Her next-door neighbors had sold their property recently to Specter Wines, a new player with new money. Scuttlebutt had it the owner had made a mint somewhere back east. Sophia shook her head as she watched heavy equipment struggle to tame the hillside, prepare it for planting. These days it seemed just about every rich guy wanted a piece of Napa to cultivate his own grapes, make a signature vintage that would rock the world.

As if it was that easy.

CHAPTER TWO

NICO TREVIANI'S MOOD STOOD IN stark contrast to the collegial spirit of the throng gathered at the annual meeting of the Napa Valley Vintners Association. Housed in a LEED-certified, open and airy, steel-and-glass building near the library in St. Helena, the Vintners Association was Mecca to winemakers both experienced and novice—a repository of their collective knowledge and a gathering place to commiserate over the fickle affections of their shared mistress.

Wine.

Had he had a choice, Nico would've done anything other than be a winemaker, but choice was not an option—he'd been born to it, a family heritage so strong that Nico suspected his blood was half Cabernet. As his father's first-born, he was handed the reins to something that was less a business than a calling. On the other hand, his brother, Paolo, had been given the option, and, fool that he was, he chose wine. And the fool had died before he knew the brilliance of the last Cab vintage they'd crafted together. 100 points. Liquid perfection. Not many wines reached those lofty heights—not that it translated into much more than bragging rights, which were a damn poor substitute for food on the table. Without his own land, his own grapes, he was nothing more than the hired help. Oh, he could buy grapes and custom crush, but that wouldn't be the same—he'd have no real control, and folks would take too keen an interest in watching him work his magic ... assuming he had any left without his brother. No, he needed his own space far from prying eyes ... and he needed very special grapes.

Their mother had always said while you'd be hard-pressed to make a good living out of winemaking, you could make a great life. Nico wasn't sure he agreed. And now that he had Paolo's children to house, feed, clothe, chase down, and send to college, he was feeling the pinch. How his brother had done it, he didn't know. Especially after his wife had fled to the city. Preferring a quiet, sophisticated life, she'd turned her back on her family, her children. Nico was sure that was one of the unforgivable sins, the kind that ensured an eternity roasting on a spit over the open fires of Hell. And if it wasn't, when he got there he'd be sure to figure a way to make it so.

As he eased into the back of the large room and leaned against the wall, Nico thought about the price a life of wine exacted. He recognized the back of every head filling the rows in front of him as the speaker droned on. He knew their histories almost as well as they did. One guy was a recovering alcoholic. No longer able to risk tasting his wine, he still made it, slaving over every nuance of the process. One or two had hit a home run and now basked in the ability to make limited batch estate wines that sold for upward of a grand a bottle. Some scratched out an existence on the strength of their wine clubs. Most turned large fortunes into small, proving the old joke. And then there were a very few, like Nico, who had been born to winemaking or grape growing, selling their skills to those who could pay. Despite differing backgrounds, and differing futures, wine glued them together.

Except for Avery Specter, Nico's current employer.

As if thought could conjure flesh, Avery materialized in front of Nico, his usual ruddy complexion flushed hotter than normal. With his eyes at half-mast, his comb-over falling the wrong way in wisps of misplaced hair, exposing his bald pate, he looked like exactly what he was: a self-important prick who'd made a fortune in manufacturing, or textiles, or running a hedge fund, or something, and had bought his way into the wine business.

Specter grabbed Nico by the arm and tugged him into the vestibule as he hissed, "Have you read this report?" Stopping in the center of the open area, Avery turned to face his winemaker and pressed a sheaf of papers into his chest. "And before we get started, you need to learn one thing, Treviani. You come when I call."

Being treated like a dog to be trained was enough to kick up

Nico's simmer to a boil, so he wasn't about to validate Specter's contemptuous attitude by making excuses ... although he did have a good one. He figured talking the sheriff out of turning his twin thirteen-year-old nieces over to the Juvenile authorities would earn him a get-out-of-jail-free card, but ego wouldn't let him play it. The psychologist said the girls were just acting out and they'd get beyond it. Fine for him to say—he didn't have to ride herd on the heathens. Who knew two pint-sized females could bring a grown man to the point of complete surrender? Nico snorted at his own weakness.

"You think this is funny?" Specter's voice rose enough to turn heads as the meeting broke up and Nico's friends filtered out of the meeting room. When Nico ignored the sheaf of papers, Specter pulled them back and began rolling them into a tube, his agitation poorly hidden.

"No, sir." Nico avoided making eye contact as he fought to get his temper under control. "There's a lot more to life than making wine, Mr. Specter."

"Not while you're on my payroll."

Specter had no children of his own, and that thought alone reassured Nico that there was indeed a God. But it also made arguing with the man futile. So he argued with himself. He had sold out. Lowered his standards. And he couldn't shake the feeling it was going to bite him in the ass.

"You wanted to talk to me about a report?" Nico asked even though he knew all about it. Avery Specter might need a report to learn what had been painfully obvious for years, but Nico didn't. Hell, he could've written the damn thing himself—he'd been saying as much for a long time now to anyone who would listen. It didn't take some government expert to know the baby boomers were transitioning to fixed incomes, their penchant for high-end wine taking a hit along with their lifestyle. The next generation, whatever they were referred to as—the Millenials? The Me generation? The Y generation? Nico couldn't remember, but whoever they were, they didn't yet have the disposable incomes or the sophisticated palates to support the high-end wine industry at the current levels. Something had to give.

Wineries had to reposition themselves.

Keeping his eyes lowered, Nico managed to avoid the few

stragglers just now leaving the meeting room. It was bad enough being called to heel by his boss, but having his colleagues witness it threw gasoline on the embers of his foul mood. A few greeted him, and he nodded but didn't invite conversation so they didn't stop. Out of the corner of his eye, Nico caught the looks many flashed at Avery: contempt, thinly veiled if they tried to hide it at all.

Avery wasn't stupid ... anything but. His barely contained frustration and worry pulsed from him like light from a dying star, making his hands shake as he unrolled then re-rolled the sheaf of papers into a tighter tube. "Cult wines are coming under economic pressure and there's nothing we can do about it." His reedy voice screeched like notes played by a fourth-grade clarinetist.

Nico crossed his arms and glowered at his boss. Cocking an eyebrow, he feigned interest.

Avery didn't wilt when he ran headlong into Nico's scowl. "They say that the number of Boomers, the population segment solely responsible for the record profit of the cult wine industry, is shrinking."

"Age attrition. People die, Mr. Specter." Nico's voice was flat, hard.

Avery's mouth pulled into a thin line. His backbone straightened. But at six feet he was still several inches shorter than Nico, so he leaned in closer and lowered his voice. "I like being talked down to about as much as I like tardiness. You're property bought and paid for. You'd be wise not to jerk my chain."

"And you'd be wise to show a bit more respect. You need me, Mr. Specter. Without a winemaker, making wine's damned difficult. And you want high-priced juice, so you need a man with my CV—and, to my knowledge, there is only one."

Heels firmly dug in, both men stared at each other. Neither wavered.

Finally, Specter shrugged as his gaze slithered to the side, focusing over Nico's shoulder. "I know what people think of me around here. You people think I haven't paid my dues. I don't have wine running in my veins, filling my soul." His derision leaked from each word. "You think I'm the worst kind of blight since Phylloxera— a businessman thinking he can buy his way into making great wine. And you know what?" He stepped back and slapped the rolled-up report into Nico's chest. "That's exactly what I am." He shot Nico a grin. "Working pretty good so far, don't you think?"

Nico grabbed the papers before they could unfurl like the white flag of surrender in the heat of battle. A tic worked in his cheek as he watched the bastard saunter away. Avery Specter didn't deserve much, he thought. Perhaps a grisly, lingering, painful death and a pine box, but not much more than that.

Nico felt someone step in next to him, but, wearing the blinders of pride, he resisted looking to see who.

"He's wrong, you know. To me he's more like Pierce's disease. Kill a vine in less than five years and no cure in sight. Phylloxera we got under control." Billy Rodrigues clearly had been eavesdropping, a fact that would make Nico mad if Billy wasn't his best friend.

At the sound of Billy's voice, Nico felt himself relax. "Quatro, you do have a way with words. Let's hope he and his friends don't kill the wine business." Nico called Billy "Quatro" as did many others, because he was William Xavier Rodrigues IV. His father was Tres, same logic. Nico called him "Sir."

Through the years, he and Quatro had witnessed many of each other's indignities; one more wouldn't matter. "But there is another side to all of this. And maybe I'm justifying," Nico said, his temper dissipating. "God, I hate to give the guy any credit, but without money it's damn hard to make a truly great cult wine. When you and I scratched our way up the ranks, making wine was like voodoo, a bunch of wine drinkers relying on folklore and playing around with a kid's chemistry set. And the growers were nothing more than hobby farmers. But now, with property values through the roof, international distribution agreements, hundreds of wineries in this valley alone, it's big damn business." Nico shot his friend a serious look minus the scowl he'd used for Specter.

"I still can't figure whether that's a good thing or a bad thing." Quatro was thick and solid, his hair and skin different shades of brown, his eyes black, and his smile pure mischief. He'd been working the fields so long his hands were a mass of callouses permanently stained from red dirt, and red grape skins, and scarred by the brutal work. As if remembering his manners too late, Quatro swept his sweat-stained broad-brimmed straw hat from his head then raked his fingers through his thick salt-and-pepper hair. When he was done, he set his hat back in place, low over his brow.

"Both. More money to go around, but long-time residents are being priced out of the game." Nico stuck the tube of papers in his back pocket. "All of us are in this together, the whole Valley. If we don't figure out how to distinguish ourselves, the economic contraction is going to squeeze us all back into oenophilic oblivion."

"All your awards—"

"Couldn't save the family vineyard or keep my brother from dying." Nico snarled as his brows snapped into a frown. The emotional tempest dissipated as fast as it had arisen. He squeezed his friend's shoulder. "Sorry. Got a lot on my mind."

"You made a 100-point wine from Beckstoffer grapes. And we all know they are the best."

"I made the wine. My employer makes the money." Nico didn't voice his fear that now, without his brother, his wine wouldn't be as good. They'd been a team. Was half really as good as the whole? And, his worst fear, could he even make wine without his brother? "What I need is something new, something better than Beckstoffer." Nico raised his hand before Quatro could get a word in. "Not better, that was the wrong term—not sure you can grow them any better than they do. I want different, but not too far a reach for the discerning but limited American palate. Something amazing that we can produce at a reasonable price point."

"Amazing yet accessible. The Holy Grail. Well, if anybody can do it, you can. But God knows where you're going to find those grapes. And I know you're a Cab guy, but, if I were you, I'd be thinking about something white or rosé."

"Yeah, short or no aging, quick to market. I got an MBA in the family who's been singing that song for years. We just haven't found the grapes."

"I'm pretty sure if you start making wine on the side, Mr. Specter will have no problem dragging you into court. As I recall his lawyers spent a lot of time crafting your non-compete. He's got you tied up pretty good."

"Given time and conviction all knots can be loosened."

CHAPTER THREE

A SLIGHT CHILL HINTED IN the breeze and the sun dropped toward the horizon when Sophia felt satisfied each of her vines was poised for perfection, or at least as close to it as her skills could bring them. The sun's sharp angle bathed her mountaintop in a soft pink glow. If Heaven were any better, she couldn't imagine how. Life might be shifting like quicksand under her feet, but at least she had her grapes.

Sophia bounded up the porch stairs, pulling her shirttail from her jeans. A shower, then a visit to her mother. The aroma of fresh-brewed coffee hit her the minute she walked through the front door. Coffee? At this time of the day? Nobody Sophia knew could handle caffeine as the sun set. With the doors unlocked, the house stood unprotected from anyone who wanted to wander in. They'd have to get up her hill, though. No cars were parked out front, and she hadn't heard anyone approach as she'd tended the grapes, but she did tend to lose herself when she worked the vines.

She followed the scent back to the kitchen, more curious than alarmed—she didn't figure anyone intent on doing her harm would fix themselves coffee while they waited. Of course, she could be wrong, so she grabbed a poker from the collection of andirons by the fireplace. Holding it like a sword at the ready, she advanced on the kitchen.

With her back to the wall next to the doorway, she eased around, sneaking a peek. "Christ, Charlie. What are you doing here?" She let out a sigh, unaware she'd been holding her breath.

His back to her, Charlie Vespers jumped a little, spilling some of the coffee he was pouring from the carafe into a mug. A nondescript man of indecipherable age—Sophia had pegged him at somewhere around forty—Charlie wore his clothes loose, his light brown hair long, his expression sour. His penchant for always looking on the negative side was his most annoying habit, other than walking in unannounced like he owned the place, which, technically, he did. But, Sophia didn't think that gave him the right to act like it.

Standing at the counter, Charlie glanced at her then refocused on his coffee. "You gonna hit me with that thing?"

"Probably not." Chagrined, she leaned the poker against the wall in the corner, then stepped to the shelf and grabbed a wine glass. She opened the wine fridge, pulling out the shelves one at a time as she perused the offerings. The Turnbull rosé, refreshing, light yet complex, would hit the right finishing note for this day. A blush wine. A whole line of wines that had fallen from favor due in large part to the sweet, syrupy mediocrity of the Beringer brothers' ubiquitous White Zin—the first "woman's" wine. Thankfully, owing to Turnbull and a handful of other local producers as well as some in France, blush wines were carving a niche of respectability for themselves in the U.S., showing their complexity and elegance. And now it was Pinot Grigio being driven into storied mediocrity by mass production, overconsumption and gender marketing.

Unscrewing the top, she poured herself a liberal dose, then proffered the bottle. "Want some?"

"No." Charlie didn't look at her. "I thought there might be a good chance you'd beat me bloody." He sounded serious.

Sophia's face creased in sarcastic disbelief. "You mean since it's so well known that violence is my go-to."

His eyes darted to her, then away, like a wasp embedding his stinger. "I know you got my letter. Tito put the return receipt in my box on the way down the mountain."

The letter! Sophia had forgotten. Her eyes darted to the cookie jar.

Charlie made himself comfortable at the kitchen table. Hands cupped around his mug, he stared into it.

Sophia eased into the chair across from him, her knees and hips creaking with the exertion of the day. "I haven't read it."

Charlie's head snapped up. "What?" His hands shook as he raised the mug to his lips to blow on the steaming liquid.

"Been sort of busy." Still grappling with her upcoming visit with her mother and exhausted by the day with the grapes, that was all the explanation she could muster.

"Tell me about it." Charlie's shoulders slumped. He sighed heavily as he finally met Sophia's gaze. "I'm really sorry, you gotta know that."

Sophia's stomach clenched. This didn't sound like a rent hike. "Sorry about what?"

"You know we got a month-to-month?" He paused for confirmation.

Sophia didn't give him one—she didn't know what they had. They'd always done business with a handshake.

Charlie hung his head, just like one of her grandfather's bloodhounds had done ... right before he took a chunk out of her leg. "Look, man, this is really hard. But you know what you said about life? Well, mine's gone totally in the crapper. My investment advisor lost a bunch of money in the stock market when everything went on the skids. Turns out his advice wasn't worth spit." Charlie's words came out in a tangled jumble, falling over each other like the Niagara River over the falls. "My folks' inheritance is gone. I got nothing left."

"Except your property." Sophia's voice was a whisper as her throat tightened. A cold sweat trickled down her sides. She reached across the table and grabbed his arm. "Charlie, you can't sell this property. My home. My grapes." Words fled as the magnitude of loss hit her like a tsunami, throwing her, rolling her over and over as wave after wave of reality hit her, each successive one larger than the one before, leaving her clawing for breath as the emotional riptide pulled her under. She looked around the kitchen trying to steady herself, to regain her bearings.

"I have to. I can't live on what you pay me in rent."

Buoyed by a thought, Sophia raised her head. "I'll buy it."

"Even if I could break the contract, you couldn't afford it."

"I have a little bit of savings ... the life insurance money from Daniel's policy."

Charlie looked pained. "Daniel wouldn't want you to do that."

"How do you know?" Sophia wrung her hands. Daniel had always made all of these decisions. As he'd told her a thousand times, his job was to keep her grounded, to keep her from being foolish. Was she being foolish? What would Daniel say?

"I don't know what you have, but it wouldn't be enough." Charlie pushed at his coffee cup. "As I said in the letter, they made me an incredible offer, well above market."

"I could get a loan." Sophia felt her panic rising, coiling around her heart. Her home. They were taking her home.

"For what they're paying, the property wouldn't appraise out."

Like a nail popping a tire, reality flattened her until she was coasting on the rim. "My husband." Her lip quivered, she couldn't help it. "His bicycles are still in the garage." Her voice caught. A tear trickled down her cheek. She swiped it away with the back of her hand as she looked out the window. "My grandfather's grapes." When she looked at Charlie, she saw her pain, her fear, mirrored in his eyes. "There are no others like them. These are all that's left." She felt numb.

Charlie squirmed. "Like I said, they made me an offer I can't pass up. Believe me, if I had another choice ..." He left the thought there because they both knew he didn't. "I feel as bad as you do, trust me."

His words ignited a flicker of fight. Sophia's voice hardened and her eyes flashed. "Don't you patronize me, Charlie Vesper. Don't you dare." She tossed back her wine then slammed the glass on the table. The thin stem snapped in her grasp. The pain felt good. She wiped the blood on her jeans. Even though her dreams, her memories, were ephemeral, their loss hit on a visceral, physical level as if she'd lost a limb, and she reverberated with the pain both real and phantom.

"I'm not patronizing you, Sophia." Charlie's lips pulled into a thin line and his face softened, his eyes captured by memories. "I know loss."

His words, the thought of him losing his parents in the plane crash ... he'd been all of ten ... doused her anger. Sophia leaned across the table and squeezed his arm as she marshaled a thin smile. "I know. I'm sorry." Neither of them had much of a past, but at least Charlie still had his dreams. Sophia thought about telling him just that, but he wouldn't understand. "When?" She sucked in air like a floundering swimmer.

"The letter was your thirty-day notice."

Sophia blinked, trying to bring the world into focus, but she couldn't make sense out of any of it. "Thirty days? How do I move a life in thirty days?"

"They want the property real bad. The deal's contingent on time."

Blood finally flooded back into her brain as adrenaline kicked in, anger once again spiking, covering the fear. "Who?" The chair grated across the floor as she stood, pushing it back. With both palms on the table, Sophia leaned toward him. "Who is in such a damn hurry to get my property?"

Charlie cowered back in his chair. "The money man is that new guy, Avery Specter. You know he bought the sixty acres next to this piece."

"Specter?" She'd met the guy once and that had been enough. Brazen, overbearing, arrogant, he was everything that was wrong with the new money flooding into the Valley. "The money man?"

Charlie swallowed hard, his eyes darting toward the door as if gauging a possible escape.

Sophia pushed herself back, out of Charlie's face. She stood tall, shoulders back, sucking in air—which she let out in one long sobering breath. "So there's somebody else? Maybe more than one somebody else?"

"Takes a lot of people to grow grapes and make wine."

Sophia whirled on him and his face closed. "Why now, Charlie? Why are they in such a hurry?" Her eyes drifted to the scene out the window. Sunlight dappling the ground and turning the leaves a light golden green. The vines bowed under their bounty.

And she knew.

She leaned in to Charlie again. This time her voice was hard, her face pinched in anger. "The grapes. Tell me, Charlie, who is the asshole who wants my grapes?"

Charlie eased out of his chair. Pulling it in front of him he used it as a shield. "Butchy Pinkman."

The name hit her like a hot poker to the heart, searing flesh. "Pinkman? My boss? Hell, he wouldn't know good wine if I tied him down and poured it down his throat." Sophia's voice came from some feral place deep inside. But she had to admit the idea of tying him down and torturing him did have some appeal ... too much appeal.

Leaving the cover of the chair, Charlie sidestepped toward the door as he nodded.

Sophia lowered her head, her voice a growl rising like lava from her molten core, hot, angry, deadly. "Get the hell out."

"WHAT ARE YOU DOING SITTING HERE IN THE DARK?"

Dani's voice startled Sophia as she blinked, struggling to make sense of her surroundings. Dani flipped on the under-cabinet indirect lighting, and Sophia looked around, not really seeing. Her kitchen looked the same. Her daughter looked the same, even with worry flattening the curve of her normal smile. With her head of bouncy brown curls and big blue eyes, she was her mother's daughter whether she liked it or not.

"I'm fine. I think I wore myself down working the grapes." Sophia tried to keep her voice calm, natural. "It's been a long day. I just sat to watch the light as it played out across the vineyard." Even to Sophia, her explanation sounded weak.

Dani gave her a look, then a quick shake of her head. She opened her mouth as if to press her mother further. Instead, she clamped her lips shut and puttered with the cake, putting it together with the icing Sophia had left covered in a porcelain bowl. Lightness permeated the gloom in the kitchen as she chattered, masking her concern at finding her mother sitting alone in the dark.

Half-listening, Sophia worked to regain her bearings.

Her kitchen was her heart—the beating center of her family. A large rectangular room with purple walls, a checkerboard floor, butcher-block countertops, some covered with stainless steel, pullout drawers, open cabinets, plates at the ready for an impromptu gathering. The room had weathered time, heartache, hundreds of family meetings, happiness, and more than one culinary disaster. Daniel had built it for her. It was as if his heart was here, too—through the years the family had gravitated to the kitchen and the beat-up round wooden table in the center of it whenever anything needed to be discussed, complained about, resolved, or celebrated.

Standing there, letting her daughter's chatter curl around her like the warmth of a blanket on a chilly fall night, Sophia could hear Daniel as clearly as if he was parked at her shoulder, a beer in hand. "Every pot has its place, Sophie, every pan its hook." He'd tapped the glass-fronted cabinets. "You'll know where everything is." Then, his face alight as he swept his arm in a half circle, "Knives on the wall. A magnetic strip, isn't it cool?" His eyes had danced as he bowed low toward the centerpiece: a commercial gas stove with a vent above it to match. "Now, get to work. Your man is starving." He was the only person Sophia had ever allowed to call her Sophie. Somehow, from Daniel, it had seemed like an endearment, sweet and kind and full of love. They'd laughed and hugged. Sophia had cried. The kitchen was perfect. Daniel was perfect. Life was perfect.

They'd had one more year.

Sophia buried the hurt, but how she wished Daniel could be here to see what an incredible woman their daughter had blossomed into. She pushed herself from the chair. "Tomorrow you start your new job."

Dani didn't answer immediately, her attention focused on the cake. Settling the top layer of the cake on the bottom without breaking it took a keen eye, steady hands, and a plan. "Yep, working with Nico Treviani, who would've believed it?"

"Your father and I."

Dani bit her lip as she inverted the top layer pan onto a plate, then took the handle of a knife and tapped the bottom of the pan to loosen the cake ... in theory. As with life, cakes could come out in pieces, but, unlike life, cake was easier to put back together ... and it tasted just as good no matter how it looked. "What do you think of Mr. Treviani?" Dani's eyes flicked to her mother. "Ever met him?"

"Once or twice. As the most celebrated winemaker in California, he left me with the impression he didn't think highly of Pink's Passion and somehow he blamed me, the grower, in part, for the wine's mediocrity." Actually, Nico had been harsh and dismissive each of the three times she'd met him, but Dani didn't need to hear that. He was formidable enough as it was. "But he sure knows what he's doing. You'll learn a lot, I'm sure."

Dani eased the pan from the cake. No pieces this time. "That's the point." Dani glanced at her mother as she palmed the plate with the top layer in one hand, gauging exactly where and how quickly to invert it over the bottom layer with its coat of frosting. Making her decision, she flipped the layer onto the bottom, then lifted the plate slowly to ensure that nothing stuck when she pulled it away. The layers aligned perfectly. Dani set it down carefully then backed away, hands raised. "Am I good or what?"

"The best," her mother acknowledged. "But I've known that all along."

Dani grabbed the wide-bladed palette knife she'd been using and began slathering frosting. "Nonna's going to love this. Trying to soften her up?" A hint of wicked touched her smile.

"Darn straight. Nothing is beneath me at this point. My emotional armor is wearing thin." Sophia wasn't about to tell Dani about the letter, about Charlie selling her life out from under her to Pinkman the Ass and Avery Specter.

Nico Treviani's boss. Dani's employer.

"Tonight calls for a celebration. How about some of my wine?" Nervous, unsure of her skills, doubting her palate, Sophia had never let anyone try it. But, with the land soon gone, the soil that lent a unique flavor to the grapes no longer hers to plant, now seemed like a good time.

Dani's expression turned serious. "Seriously, Mom? Your wine will blow people's minds."

"Really?" She gave her daughter a narrow-eyed look. "How do you know?"

"I know you. I know what you can do. You just don't see it."

"Oh, I see it alright. The wine isn't ready. Not yet. Something is missing, I'm not sure what. But it's not ready."

Dani pausing in her icing, setting the knife down, then wiping her hands on a towel as she joined her mother at the table. "The wine is ready."

"So you say." Sophia took a deep breath. "Let's put that to the test, then." She grabbed a bottle she had chilling in the wine fridge under the counter. Setting it in the middle of the table, she allowed herself a deep calming breath. "You do the honors?"

Dani picked up the bottle with a reverence that made Sophia smile. "It's just wine, child."

Dani's eyes, dark and serious, met hers. "No, it's so much more than that. It's *your* wine. Bottled dreams." She grabbed a corkscrew.

Sophia nodded toward the corkscrew gripped in Dani's hand. "You won't need that. If you notice, I did this batch with screw caps."

"You're kidding." Dani sounded horrified as she checked the top. "Aren't screw tops for Boone's Farm and Ripple and all those horrible things you guzzled in the back of Dad's Chevy?"

"The elixir of my youth. Call me sentimental."

Dani poured her mother a glass of wine without asking.

It would be Sophia's only glass; one was her limit. A seductive goddess, wine sharpened the colors of life and blunted the pain. But too much dulled all of life and dissipated the magic. Sophia had discovered that the hard way. "Remember, I'm reaching for a wine that is not only sublime but is also one the masses will appreciate and actually be able to enjoy regularly, even on an average salary." Sophia's nerves calmed, her fear fell away. She'd pushed her talent to the limits; she couldn't do any better. Still, though, she knew the wine was lacking something, but what? That she didn't know.

An intensity sharpened Dani's features as she held the glass to the light. A recent graduate from the oenology program at UC-Davis, she'd honed her skills, refined her nose, developed an appreciation for a broad spectrum of wines. "The orange tint is different, but I like it. You left the wine on the skins." It was a statement, not a question. Her focus never wavering, she smiled as if at a private joke. "Old school."

"Old grapes, old methods. Thought I'd give it a try. God knows I've tried everything else."

They both sobered for a moment then Dani held her glass up for a toast. "To dreams."

Sophia took a moment to watch the candlelight as it danced over her daughter's features. Sophia saw Daniel in their daughter. In the flicker of mischief in her eyes. In the one dimple in her left cheek and the way she always lopsided her grin to that side. In the way she stood, shoulders back, chin out, ready. Daniel might be gone, but he lived on in his daughter, and Sophia thought that was the most precious gift of all.

"To dreams." Sophia clinked her glass with her daughter's, but she didn't take a sip. Instead, she lowered her glass and waited, watching her daughter as she tasted, savored, tested the wine.

When finished, the budding vintner spoke first, her face serious, her eyes reflective orbs in the flickering candlelight. "Oh, Mom. This is really good. Acidic, fruit-forward, light..."

"Too light," Sophia added, finishing Dani's thought.

"Really surprising, interesting, but it's so light it makes you feel like it's going to evaporate before you have the chance to swallow. But the finish is lovely, and the flavor layered and complex. You've got primo juice here, but it needs something, some depth without changing the flavor characteristics."

"And therein lies the problem. I need a grape I don't have. Something that will complement, not compete, yet will add body, a richness or fullness so the wine lingers on the mid-palate."

Dani blew a dark curl out of her eyes as she took another sip. "That's a tough one, but this is awesome, so refreshing. Did you put any oak on it?"

"No. I've tried aging it a bit in new oak and neutral. But that doesn't help. It just alters the taste in a way that masks the fruit. I want to taste the grapes, not the oak. Since I don't do any malolactic fermentation, the wine stays crisp. God, how I hate that buttery profile the California Chards are known for."

"So just stainless?"

Sophia took a sip, savoring. Bright, acidic, dry... then gone. "I tried that new concrete egg, but it manifested no discernable difference, so I'll stick with stainless. Some skin fermentation in the old style and not a whole lot else."

"Quick to market." This time her daughter finished Sophia's sentence. "Just one slight nuance to refine."

"Ah, nuance—the difference between a clever rhyme and timeless poetry."

"There you go with the art metaphors again. Just like Mr. Treviani."

Sophia patted her daughter's hand resting lightly on her arm. "One thing these grapes have taught me through the years is winemaking is part chemistry and part voodoo."

"Voodoo" Dani scoffed. "So helpful. Unfortunately, that course wasn't part of my curriculum, but I've got the chemistry part down. It seems all of the blending is done in the lab, trying to hit certain markers, acidity, sweetness, etc."

"Yes, with most of the producers who are running large productions, that's where they work their magic because they have built huge followings in the marketplace and commensurate expectations. Most wine drinkers want the same experience, and they don't understand that each year the grapes are different because the weather varies."

"But you're a voodoo kind of gal," Dani teased.

"The grapes must be seduced, wooed ... they cannot be forced or manipulated—not if you want their true essence. And I'll take what they will give me."

"Mom, you sure sound a lot like Mr. Treviani. More hocus-pocus than science."

"Making great wine is an art—something your Mr. Treviani seems to understand, if your assessment of him is true. And, you have to admit, his success is legendary."

"There's that. And Mr. Pinkman? He's successful as well." Dani's tone changed from reverential and awestruck when talking about Nico to downright disrespectful when talking about her mother's employer.

"Financially, yes." Sophia nudged at her daughter with an elbow. "And no need to goad. You know I'm well aware he uses every chemical trick on the planet to keep his wine consistently over-oaked, buttery and mediocre."

"The Chard grapes you manage for him are capable of so much more."

"Of course they are. I told him so ... once. He thinks his wine is fabulous, and who's to argue? He sells a ton of it. But he doesn't have what he wants the most."

"Respect from his peers." Dani shook her head. "Man, what he would give to have your grapes ... what any of them would give to have your grapes." Dani trailed off.

Sophia sobered. "Don't you breathe a word of what we have up here. These grapes are special, our family legacy." Sophia bit her lip as her new reality hit her heart—Avery Specter would own them, tend them. Would he make bad wine out of them? Would her dream be for nothing? "There aren't any more of these grapes anywhere."

"I know, Mom, it just seems ..." she trailed off as she bit her lip, thinking before she spoke again. "Like a huge waste, an opportunity buried."

"Dani, you know the limitations—we've been through it a thousand times. We only have two acres under vine—not enough to set the world on fire. I don't even own the land," she made a sweeping motion toward the porch and the vineyard beyond, "nor our home." *And now they too will be gone. Sold to idiots posing as winemakers all because they have money.* "The grapes. Oh, they are mine, but not the soil that feeds them, nurtures them, prodding them to their greatest complexity." Sophia took a deep calming breath as she rested her hands in her lap and leaned back, trying not to think of the letter, of Charlie's betrayal. "As your great-grandfather said, *terroir* is everything."

Dani wasn't going to drop the topic. "Don't you think the Californians have burst that European bubble?"

"My grapes are European grapes," Sophia tried for a bit of jaunty but didn't quite succeed. This was an old, emotional topic between them. "Regardless, I'm a grower, not a vintner."

"That's a load. Your wine is sublime," her daughter challenged.

"The wine is good, yes, but not yet what I want. It's close but not quite ready, as you said."

"The wine is ready, Mom, just an easy tweak. It's you who's not."

CHAPTER FOUR

"HOW IS YOUR SISTER?" Quatro kept his voice even, casual as
he and Nico watched their fellow winemakers clustered in the cooling
evening air, trading war stories, gathering and giving information.

Nico knew how much the casual question cost his friend. Quatro
had been in love with his sister, Victoria, since she'd broken his jaw
with a left hook in grade school. "Still single and mean as hell."

Quatro smiled in a wistful sort of way, and Nico felt sad for them
both. A whole lot of education and a set of tracks separated them. It
didn't sound like much to Nico, but apparently it was to them.

"Tell her hey for me."

"Nope. You tell her yourself."

Quatro didn't say anything, but his shoulders drooped just a hint.
"She still commuting to that high-powered job down in San Jose?"

"She's moved up the totem pole so she can work from home. Last
we talked, she goes down there one or two days a week."

"Hell of a drive."

"Yeah, but the money's real good. Good benefits. Great
retirement. All the things wine doesn't give you."

Quatro shrugged a bit. "All the money in the world doesn't mean
much if your heart's not in it."

"Heart not in it?" Nico shot a barb at his friend. "My sister? If
she doesn't like her job, she's free to go. Nobody's holding her here."
Unlike himself, Nico thought with a bit of jealousy. He was the only
family member shackled to his job, this place, at least while his

mother was alive. For a moment he allowed himself the luxury of imagining he could walk away, but only for a moment. The what-ifs were a losing game. "What makes you think Vic doesn't like her job?"

Quatro snorted. "Practically everybody knows that. She's been trying to con my Tia Lou's tamale recipe out of me since high school. And she's taken just about every course at that culinary school in St. Helena."

"Greystone?"

"That's the one." At Nico's startled look, he shrugged. "Common knowledge, my friend. Confirmed by my cousin who's worked there forever. She says your sister is a natural. Word is she's trying to scrape together enough cash to buy the Bucket and Bin in Rutherford."

"She wants to buy a restaurant? Is she bat-shit nuts?" Nico couldn't keep the shock out of his voice. "The only business less stable than the wine biz in this valley is the food biz." But Nico knew that's exactly what his sister would do. If there was a hard way to do anything, trust a Treviani to find it.

"Been talking with your sister a lot, I can tell."

Nico had the decency to look chagrined. "Life's been a bit of a ride lately. But you're right; I should pay her a visit. See what's up. Between the twins and Mother, I'm drowning in estrogen. What could another female hurt?"

Quatro blew out a quick breath and rolled his eyes, then cast a look of pity on his friend. "One more female can hurt a lot, amigo."

Nico didn't detect even a hint of sympathy in Quatro's laugh. Of course, being Catholic and Latin, his family was large and the women strong. Nico made a mental note to take the twins up to the river, rent some kayaks, and bunk at his sister's. He'd need a dog, a quarter horse, and a rope with a good loop to separate them from the teenage pack they ran with—none of which he had. But a day on the river where life seemed to slow to a drifting current would do them all good.

Nico and Quatro watched as Avery Specter finished shaking hands with all those he could corner like a well-oiled politician, then climbed into his McLaren 650S.

"Man, from the way he acts, you'd think he owns the place," Quatro said, sounding a bit awestruck.

Nico didn't fault his friend. Money took on a curious significance when one didn't have any. For as long as he'd known him, Quatro Rodrigues had taken care of half the Valley, and most of those back home in Mexico, leaving his own coffers almost bare. And Avery Specter owned several hundred acres on the top of Howell Mountain—prime cool-grape land. Land that had cost him well over sixty mill. "Own the place? Damn close."

Quatro sighed. "Naw, he just owns you."

Nico bristled. In a moment of weakness and a bit of panic after Paolo died, he'd made a deal with the devil. "For a year. A very long year."

"Come on." Quatro nudged him toward the gathering in front of the building. "You can't avoid your friends for a year."

Nico pasted on a smile he only half felt and let Quatro nudge him out to meet the repercussions of his recent choices. But there were none. Each of his friends and competitors greeted him warmly. They'd all been at his brother's funeral. And they let it be known in subtle ways they were here for him now. Nico found himself humbled, his normal armor of irritation a paltry defense.

After the last goodbyes, Quatro followed him to his truck, an old F-150 with a rusted-out bed and paint so thin it could've been a mirage. Nico'd had his eyes on a new F-350, but there wasn't any money for that now. With his hand on the door handle he gave Quatro a cocked eyebrow. "Need a ride?"

"You need to ask?" The door squealed on worn-out hinges as Quatro wrestled it open.

Both men had settled themselves and Nico fought with the ignition until it finally, grudgingly sparked. The engine turned over and caught in a cloud of smoke. Gears ground as he maneuvered the truck out of the parking lot. "Home?" he asked as he stopped at the stop sign at Highway 29, the main artery bisecting the Valley. As the Valley narrowed at this the north end, four lanes pinched down to two.

Quatro nodded. "I lent my ride to Sal. He picked early this year. Taking a load to the crusher."

Nico took a right, heading further up valley. Quatro had a tiny house in Calistoga. "It's pretty early. Our grapes are still Brixing out too low. Give them some heat in the next few days, they should shape right up."

"Yeah, Sal didn't drop as many clusters as you did. The stress kept the juice down."

"Keeping the junk lowers the quality; he knows that. Is everything okay with Sal?"

Quatro gave a shrug as he looked out the side window at the vineyards as they rolled past. "Life's a crapshoot."

"Every day," Nico agreed and was grateful he didn't have to worry about growing the grapes. Making wine from them was hard enough, but he had a lot more control than the growers, who were at the mercy of Mother Nature's moods.

"Hey." Quatro angled slightly to look at Nico. "I've been meaning to ask you. The rumor mill has it that you hired a new apprentice. A girl."

Nico pulled a breath in through his teeth, then let it out in a sigh and a shake of his head, as if he couldn't believe he'd hired an apprentice either. He'd never had one, male or female. "A tiny slip of a thing with steel balls and one of the best noses I've met."

"Now I'd never thought I'd live to hear the great Nico Treviani compliment another's nose."

"I swear I've never met anybody with her raw talent. She doesn't even know what she has. Of course, she's still green, and cocky as hell. Needs some serious schooling."

"Of course."

Nico didn't have to look at his friend to see his smile. He could hear it in Quatro's voice.

"Does this nose have a name?"

"Dani Stone."

Quatro laughed out loud. "Oh, man, seriously?"

"What?"

"You know that wine you loathe, Pink's Passion?"

Nico gave his friend a look, stopping him cold and wiping the grin off his face. "I know. Her mother is Pinkman's viticulturist. But not all children are tainted with the sin of the parent."

"Very big of you to overlook such a shortcoming in her family tree." Quatro grinned broadly. "You have to admit, Butchy Pinkman makes your boss look like the second coming of the *El Padre* himself.

Remember that guy, about six or seven years ago? What was his name?"

"Paul. Paul Stevens," Nico growled as his mood plummeted. Stevens had lost his grapes, all he'd worked for, after Pinkman put the thumbscrews to the guy who owned the land.

Quatro angled to look at Nico. "I wonder what happened to Stevens. He was a real nice guy."

"He jumped off the Golden Gate bridge." Nico squeezed the steering wheel, wrestling for control and wishing it was Pinkman's neck in his hands.

"Oh." Quatro's grin faded. "Damn."

"Pinkman took everything he had, his life's work."

"Bastard. But you have to think that anybody who can maneuver him and not put a nine-millimeter slug in his back has got some balls."

"Or is just like him." Nico wanted desperately to change the subject. The big money moving in, driving up the property values and taxes and driving out the small farmer, was a huge nut that had been stuck in his craw for a while. His family had been one of the victims. After losing everything he'd worked for, Nico's father had died a broken man. "That kid, Dani? She's going to make some really great wine someday. And I don't care who her mother is or who she works for."

Quatro chuckled as Nico expected him to. "Two primo noses working together. God help the competition."

CHAPTER FIVE

DANI AND SOPHIA BOTH JUMPED at the shrill ring of the phone.

"Nonna?" Dani asked but acted like she knew the answer. "I'm sure she's wondering where her cake is."

"Perhaps." Sophia didn't move to answer the phone. Her mother had been slipping even more lately. Alzheimer's, the doctor had said, but her mother seemed to have forgotten the diagnosis. As the disease took more and more of the woman Sophia once had known, it left behind an angry, unfiltered version that some days Sophia just didn't want to deal with.

Like today.

Instantly she chastised herself. Her mother's burdens were far greater than her own.

"Go get it, Mom." Dani set down her wine glass and grabbed the knife and bowl of frosting. "I'll finish the cake. Then I want more of that wine."

Sophia turned and pushed through the door onto the porch. She let the screen door slam shut behind her as she took a moment to brace herself.

The phone rang again.

"Mom!" Dani called.

"I know," Sophia shot back.

She grabbed the receiver, saying a quick hello, then holding it away from her ear in anticipation of the barrage to come. Even though prepared, she still winced as Regina Otero projected enough energy to propel her voice across several counties.

"Sophia, I have been sitting here all alone stewing."

Sophia had taken her mother's guilt trip so many times, she no longer even got on the train—she just let her mother rant, the words flowing past like scenery outside a window.

"I can't believe you are allowing Dani to do this. She is your daughter. You must do something." Regina's voice held the sharp edge of disapproval and disappointment—disapproval of her granddaughter, disappointment in her daughter. Blades she'd used to hack away at Sophia's emotional fortitude.

Her mother had always been tough, hard, with a razor's edge. Underneath it all there had been sadness and resolve, but where had the anger come from? The doctor had warned of anger, so perhaps that was it. Sophia had been ignoring the whole thing, praying it would go away or the doctor was wrong, so she wasn't prepared for the reality.

"A young woman making wine when she should be making babies. You should be ashamed. It's not right."

"It's right for her." Sophia wiped a tired hand across her eyes. Why her mother had picked this particular knot to worry, she didn't know. When her mother got like this, it was best to just remain quiet. But, when it came to her daughter, Sophia couldn't resist taking the bait. For Dani, she'd walk through the fires of Hell—and it seemed that's exactly what her mother had in mind. "Mother, Dani deserves the life she wants, a shot at her dreams."

Her mother made a rude sound of dismissal. "Like you and your dreams of making wine. The two of you, dreamers just like your grandfather. And look where it got him."

"I know, Mother, penniless and brokenhearted." Like an emotional blacksmith her mother wielded the hammer of history, a litany of disasters and failures, with unrelenting precision.

"You should be grateful I saved you from the same fate. Dreams, bah! A foolish girl you were. You should be on your knees thanking me. And begging the angels to take pity on you. And now Dani. More dreams. You disappoint me, Sophia."

"Mother, the past doesn't dictate the future."

"What a ridiculous thing to say. The past is our teacher. So many lessons, most of which it seems you never learned."

"Let her make her own choices. If they are not the right ones, she will learn."

Her mother rang-off abruptly, without a kind word to knit together the emotional laceration. Apparently she had emptied her verbal quiver of its arrows ... for now. This was just a minor skirmish, and Sophia knew her mother had set in for a long winter siege. If Regina Otero was anything, it was determined.

Sophia sighed and leaned back, letting the worn wooden paneling of the sunroom hold her weight. Her mother was wrong, about many things, but one thing in particular: Sophia had learned the lessons, some of them all too well.

Dani whooped from the kitchen. "I'm done, Mom! This cake looks amazing."

Sophia didn't answer as she slowly re-cradled the phone. The day had pummeled her, her future vanishing like her mother's in a fog of the unknown.

Dani's head appeared through the doorway. "You're awfully quiet. Finding comfort in the ghosts?"

Sophia reached for her daughter, pulling her tight. "The ghosts keep me company. Your great-grandfather, your father who helped me smuggle cuttings to start this vineyard. They're here, you know."

"I don't see them. I sure wish I could." Dani looked out across the vineyard.

"You don't see them with your eyes. Look with your heart."

"You know, sometimes I forget what Dad looked like." Dani crumpled like a small child confessing a horrible transgression. "How could I do that? I loved him so much." Her voice hitched. "I must be an awful person."

"Of course you're not. It happens to me, too."

"It does?" Dani sounded hopeful, but with a hint of disbelief.

"Certain things trigger a memory. A whiff of his cologne in a crowded restaurant. A voice with a similar timbre."

"Yeah, yeah. Or a father scolding his daughter, and trying not to laugh. Or a man scowling over the newspaper at someone making too much noise, but his eyes don't match his frown."

"Exactly. We hold memories in our hearts, not pictures necessarily." Sophia looked out into the darkness, searching. "I don't see him as if he's standing in front of me anymore. I miss that."

"Maybe our memories do that so our hearts can move on."

Sophia gave her daughter a little jostle, still holding her tight. "Where'd you get to be so wise?"

"Nonna says I have the sight. That's just old Italian BS, isn't it?"

Staring up at the stars, Sophia thought about the question for a moment before answering. "The one thing age teaches you is how very little you really know. And Nonna's been spending a good bit of time lately in a world we can't see, listening to voices we can't hear."

"Alzheimer's. Even the word is scary and ugly."

"Everyone's worst nightmare." Sophia didn't want to admit it might be hereditary, so she didn't.

"What I hate the worst about it," Dani continued, "is like one day, I'll go see her and she knows who I am and she asks me all kinds of questions like nothing is wrong. Then the next time, it's almost like when she sees me, she knows she should know who I am, but she doesn't and that scares her." Dani made a rueful noise. "Scares me, too."

"Me, too." Sophia tore her gaze away from the stars and looked at her daughter. "Every time I see her or talk to her, I pray this will be one of the times that she's herself again."

"Even if it means she yells at you?"

"Well, okay, not *every* time."

Dani smiled. "Sometimes, when she's having sort of a bad day, Nonna swears she's talking with her parents and Dad. What do you think? Is she crazy, or do you believe everyone is waiting on the other side and we'll see them again?"

"It's a nice thought." Sophia wanted to ruffle her daughter's hair like she used to do when she was small, but she resisted. Kids grow out of those things, but mothers never do. "But maybe, just maybe, all of Nonna's talk about those who have gone before as if they are standing right in front of her is just her leaving us slowly, transitioning but saying goodbye in a way that will help us let her go."

"That's an interesting observation." Dani's expression showed she gave the comment far more gravitas than her mother intended.

Sophia gave a self-deprecating little laugh. "You know me—I've carefully constructed my belief structure to help me navigate the cruelties of life. Faith as a coping mechanism."

"Whatever brings you to the Lord ..." Dani trailed off, waiting to see if her mother would pick it up.

"Or brings you to your knees." Sophia smiled. She could hear her grandmother say that as she punctuated her points by poking into the air with a wooden spoon stained from generations of tomato sauces. "None of us will know for sure until we get there, but I'd like to think we'll see everyone again. Somehow life would just be too harsh if we didn't."

"I hope Dad's in a good place." Sadness crept into Dani's voice.

Sophia fought against the sad—she had to be strong, now more than ever—if she only knew how. "Me, too. I do know he's watching. And he sees what an incredible young woman you've become."

Dani tilted her head. "You know your wine is really good, don't you? Good and yet, different."

"Different is a good thing."

"The same is what makes them comfortable; different is what keeps them coming back." Dani's voice sounded far away as she snaked an arm around her mother's waist. "So you want some of both."

Sophia leaned away to get a good look at her daughter. "Who said that?"

Dani glanced out of the corner of her eye. "You don't agree?"

"On the contrary. It's quite insightful, actually."

"Mr. Treviani."

"Oh." That was not the answer Sophia expected.

CHAPTER SIX

NICO GRIPPED THE STEERING WHEEL and muttered a few choice comments to the Lexus driver in front of him going ten MPH under the speed limit. Napa had two seasons: winter and tourist. He wasn't really griping—visitors bought wine, kept the multitude of eateries full, and pretty much subsidized his lifestyle—he just wished they'd drive faster.

Fifteen minutes later than he'd promised, he turned into the short drive in front of his mother's one-car garage, but he didn't get far. His mother's ancient Subaru Outback squatted in front of the closed door. She left it out on purpose. Festooned with bumper stickers for a variety of causes and the politicians who supported them, the car was a movable billboard for everything Olivia Treviani believed in: literacy, charity, children, the starving, the disenfranchised, stopping the nukes, stopping war with a hug, saving the whales, saving the missions, saving us all from ourselves, but most of all saving the small farms in the Valley.

Nico parked his truck even though half the bed hung out into the street. This far off the beaten track no one would care—if they noticed at all. His mother's house, a tiny cube tucked out of the way on the road to Geyserville, sported a small porch with two rocking chairs, flower boxes in front of the windows, which his mother kept planted with a riot of color no matter the season, and a bright orange front door. Easy for the paramedics to find, according to his mother. Everything about the place made Nico smile ... except the second rocking chair with the worn cushion and the cigarette stains on the armrests.

Wiping his feet out of habit, he pushed open the door and leaned in. "Anybody home?" No one answered, so he followed the light and laughter back to the kitchen.

A rectangular room running the length of the small house, the kitchen was filled with light and wonderful aromas of something sweet baking. Piles of pots and pans grew from the deep commercial sink, spilling onto the countertops to each side in a landslide of stainless steel. A thick creamy batter dripped from the beaters of his mother's prized Hobart. Thin white powder dusted everything, as if a skiff of snow had blown through when he'd opened the door.

Nico's mother and her two granddaughters kneeling on stools, giggles burbling, clustered around the island. With studied precision, they peeled cookie dough shapes from the butcher-block top and placed the figures carefully on the cookie sheets. Once populated, the cookie sheets disappeared into the maw of the oven. Nico's mother set the timer, then replaced the sheets in front of the girls with trays of baked and cooled cookies. Then she pointed as the girls wielded squeeze bottles of frosting in lieu of piping bags, an old trick of his mother's. Not too long ago the three heads pressed together over cookies had been his, his brother Paolo's, and his sister Victoria's. Time telescoped as he watched, memories flooding back.

After a moment, he couldn't stand it any longer. "Did a flour bomb go off in here, or what?"

"Uncle!" Brooklyn, the eldest of his nieces by two minutes, which she loved to lord over her sister, waved at him with a spatula, flinging batter across the kitchen. Covered in flour, her eyes were dark holes like pieces of coal on a snowman. He thought her shirt was red, but wasn't sure. "We're making cookies."

"Is that what you're doing?" Nico felt a grin lift the corner of his mouth. Thirteen was such an interesting age—one minute the girls balanced on the precipice of adulthood; the next minute, like now, they seemed to slip back into the giddiness of childhood.

"Gingerbread men, to be exact," corrected Taryn, the more pragmatic of the two. She was the only one not wearing a coating of white powder. Remaining relatively unsullied by the culinary activities, she had only a single slash of flour across one cheek like a half-painted Indian brave.

Both of them had wild red hair like his sister's and kind eyes like his brother's. Their smiles? Nico didn't know whose smile they had; he hadn't seen them in a long time. Identical in appearance, yet with personalities as different as the earth and the sky, to Nico they were as beautiful as wild horses and as hard to corral, although his mother didn't seem to be having any trouble—other than the mess.

"Mother?" Nico bit down on his smile as he adopted a scolding tone.

A tall woman, thin despite her truck-driver appetite, with dark eyes and a generous mouth often curled, as now, in a smile, softening her long face, breathed deep, working for control. Usually impeccably turned-out, she looked like she'd taken the worst of the flour war. Covered from head to toe, her gray hair even whiter with the stuff, her normally olive skin was now pasty and pale, except for the tracks tears had scored down her cheeks. Her mouth formed his name, but laughter drowned the words as she dissolved once again, taking her minions down the road with her.

Nico crossed his arms as he braced himself against the doorframe and waited, working not to laugh, but failing. The three women clung to each other laughing, crying, holding on.

Finally, Brooklyn broke free. Slipping off her stool and stepping around the counter, she flung herself at him, her arms circling his waist, a white cloud enveloping them both. "Oh, Uncle." She buried her face in his chest.

Stunned, Nico froze. Uncertain and awkward, first with one hand, then the other, he pulled her into him. "Hey, Knucklehead." When he glanced up, his eyes met his mother's, full of love, tinged with sadness, buoyed by hope. For the first time since his brother had died he felt ... something.

Taryn watched them as her face sobered. She remained rooted to the spot like a princess under a spell, a spell Nico had no idea how to break despite his desperate searching.

He smiled at her, as he gently worked Brooklyn's arms loose. "Gingerbread men? With frosting?"

Taryn smiled, and Brooklyn moved away but grabbed his hand, pulling him with her. "The frosting's the best part. Grandmother taught us how to make it, but my arm is killing me."

Nico smiled at his mother over the girls' heads. Making the children hand-beat the frosting was an old trick of hers. "Takes some of the stuffing out of you little cannibals," she had said so many times he didn't even need to close his eyes to hear her again, to see his brother, full of mischief, and his sister a willing accomplice.

"Your uncle ..." His mother's voice cracked as if she could read his thoughts. She cleared her throat before beginning again. "Your uncle is a bit of a frosting snob."

"You must try my gingerbread man, then." Brooklyn presented him with a one-legged figure, heavily dressed in blue frosting, a big pink smile, and green dots for eyes.

Her father's eyes had been green.

Nico's chest ached as he fought for breath while trying to maintain his smile. "What happened to his leg?"

"Bailey got it," Taryn said.

"Bailey?" Nico glanced around, for the first time focusing on the mess in the rest of the kitchen. Several empty bags of flour, torn and tattered, littered the floor. Huge trails of white powder arced across the linoleum. "Where is that mangy cur?" he asked his mother.

"We locked him in the laundry room," she said, her voice even, her face a mask.

"When we caught him," Brooklyn added.

"Looks like it was one hell of a battle."

"Nico. Your language," his mother admonished.

"Is what it's always been, Mother."

She started to say something, then thought better of it.

"Bailey needs a bath," Taryn added, her eyes wide. "If we wash him, do you think he will turn to glue?"

"That would be the best possible outcome." Nico undercut his comment with a smile.

"He needs a trainer," Brooklyn stated what Nico had been saying since his mother bought the puppy right after Paolo's funeral.

"So does your grandmother." The woman could run roughshod over three children but couldn't raise her voice to a puppy.

This got giggles from the girls, which made Nico's heart light. "Okay," he let go of Brooklyn's hand, then clapped and rubbed his together. "Taste-testing time."

After an hour and more gingerbread men than was good for

anybody, Nico rounded up the girls. "Let's clean this place up. We can't leave your grandmother to tackle it on her own."

His mother stopped him with a hand on his arm. "Just this once, let me do it."

Nico started to argue.

His mother quieted him with a shake of her head. She lowered her voice so the girls who were chattering at the sink as they washed up couldn't hear. "Sometimes it's best to leave the party while you're still having fun."

"But, Mother, it's a mess."

She squared her shoulders. When she did, she could almost meet him eye-to-eye. "I like having children in the house. I like the laughter, the fun, the silliness we somehow forget to allow ourselves as we grow older."

"They are my responsibility now. I don't want to impose."

When his mother shook her head it was with sadness. "You have been our rock, Nico." She reached out and touched his face. "Share the load, my son. It's time you started living."

Living. What did the woman think he'd been doing? "But ..."

She stopped him once again with three fingers to his lips and a shake of her head. "No. No buts. I need to care for someone. Let me. You have lost a brother." She glanced over her shoulder at the girls who still seemed to be occupied with each other and not paying any attention. "They lost their father. And I lost a son. I'm glad your father didn't have to ..." Her voice cracked and she stopped.

Nico pulled his mother into a hug.

THE PHONE SHRILLED AGAIN AS Sophia was just beginning to relax and push the day away while enjoying the comforting presence of her daughter. Charlie's betrayal lurked in the shadows like a hungry wolf licking his lips, salivating ... waiting. And now it seemed her mother was intent on puncturing her bubble. Sophia pushed her worries away. Tonight Dani was here—precious moments in a world often spinning too fast. "Look at the hour. Won't that woman give it a rest?" More than a little bit disgruntled, and not wanting to ruin the perfect hour passed with her daughter, Sophia stared at the phone as if willing it to stop ringing. After the fourth ring, she sighed and reached for the damn thing, pressing the receiver to her ear. "What is it, Mother?"

"Sophia, when is your father coming home?" Regina sounded angry and scared.

The question took Sophia's breath. Reaching behind her, she eased into the chair. "Dad?"

"His car is gone, and he's hasn't been home for ages." Regina breathed heavily into the phone.

Sophia didn't know what to say. She closed her eyes and rubbed them as she searched for the right answer. Her mother was clearly upset, the past holding her captive.

Regina spoke again, this time in a voice tremulous with fear. "Where has he gone?"

Compassion flooded through Sophia. "Would it help if I came over and we could look for him together?"

"Would you, please?"

"Sit tight. I'll be right there." Sophia moved to hang up the phone, but her mother's voice pulled her back.

"Sophia?"

"Yes, Mother"

"I'm scared."

"I know. I'll hurry." Standing, she turned and cradled the receiver. With her hand resting on the receiver, she bowed her head. As life was slipping from him, her father had told her there were worse things than dying. Too young to understand then, Sophia was wise enough to fear that reality now. Losing yourself, your family... your history. Emotion welled inside her, but she tamped it down, stomping on it as she would a match tossed into dry grass.

"Was that Nonna again?" Dani said from the kitchen.

Sophia let her daughter's voice pull her inside. "Yes, she's having one of her spells."

"Bad?"

Sophia glanced at the phone, then back to her daughter's worried face. "This time she asked where my father was and when would he be home."

"Nonno Hank? But he's been gone for years." Dani trailed her mother as she circled the kitchen, collecting her purse and keys, packing up the cake, then held the porch door for her. When she had disappeared into the darkness, Dani snagged a bottle of her wine, then followed her mother out, hiding the bottle behind one leg.

Sophia rarely bothered to even pull the door shut behind her, much less lock the thing. If someone wanted to get in badly enough that they drove all the way up the mountain, she figured they wouldn't let an old door stand in their way.

Dani strode to her truck, then reached for the door handle to the driver's side door. She tucked the bottle out of sight behind the seat. "I'll drive you. I don't want you out driving at this time of night."

Sophia gave her daughter a quick hug, balancing the cake on one hand, her purse over her forearm. "Honey, you have a big day tomorrow." She glanced at her watch—time, impossible to hold, impossible to slow, marching on, unnoticed, like a cloud on the wind. "Not tomorrow. Today. I'll be fine. Besides, you know how agitated she can get. I have no idea how long it will take to calm her down."

Dani hesitated. "Call me if you need me?"

Need you? Oh, Dani, if I called you every time I need to hear your voice, need to know you're safe, need to hear what you think, what you dream, you'd never have a moment's peace. "Sure, honey. Not to worry. I got this. But, I'll hunt you down if you don't call me tomorrow and tell me how your first day went."

CHAPTER SEVEN

TONIGHT CALLED FOR SOME PRIMO JUICE.

Nico Treviani grabbed a bottle of his 100-point Cab, pulled the cork, and decanted the bottle. The wine wouldn't rest long. The twins had exhausted his patience, already worn thin by his run-in with Avery Specter. Their conciliatory moods had lasted as long as the drive from his mother's place to his. Fifteen minutes with one thirteen year-old female generally had a grown man wishing he was trekking across the Sahara with nothing but a canteen and a bandana. Two of them had him swilling brilliant wine, praying for relief ... or answers. He knew they wouldn't be found in the bottom of a bottle of wine, but the wine sure seemed to help—a little pleasure amid chaos.

Damn Paolo. Damn him to hell.

Just like his brother to up and die, leaving him holding the bag.

Nico slammed around the kitchen, putting away pots and pans—the girls had actually done a good job scrubbing the remnants of beans that had scorched to the bottom. Dinner had been an on-the-fly attempt—none of them were hungry, having filled up on gingerbread men. They didn't eat much of the pork and beans, and turned their noses up completely at the vegetables, refusing even to try them. Completely befuddled by the authority of his new position, Nico didn't know how to fight that fight. What exertion of authority was too much, breeding rebellion? His own father had taught him too little would imply a lack of care. But where was the sweet spot? Why didn't teenagers come with an owner's manual? Or at least some instructions? Or perhaps a sign pointing the way? Hell, he'd be happy for a light and a tiny bit of illumination.

And then there was the food thing—he didn't think growing kids would thrive on his staples of something canned, something frozen, and a bottle of Cabernet. One thing he knew for certain: a cook he wasn't, and on-the-job training wasn't panning out so well. The pizza joint in St. Helena was on speed-dial. Could a call to Child Services be far behind?

Completely out of ideas, he'd shooed the girls off to a shower and then bed and now tried to ignore the giggling skittering under the closed bedroom door.

One morning Nico was holding his brother, felled by a massive stroke, as his life leaked away and the light that was Paolo blinked out. That afternoon Nico was painting his study pink, buying bunk beds, and trying to help two sad, frightened, and very young girls cope with a loss he himself hadn't admitted.

After that, time sped to a blur. The axis of his universe had shifted irreparably, throwing the seasons of his life completely out of whack.

So, instead of savoring the life he'd built over several decades, he was struggling with the logistics of living in a tiny house with one bathroom and two hormonally volatile females and trying not to kill every shrub around his house or scandalize the neighbors. Of course, in California, peeing on trees was sort of expected, or at least tolerated, so he didn't worry overmuch about the neighbors. But the shrubs were looking a bit ... stunted.

After finishing the rest of the dinner dishes and putting out clothes and lunch stuff he'd need to get the girls launched in the morning, Nico chose a very good cigar out of the humidor and nipped the ends. Drinking deep of the tobacco aroma as he ran the cigar under his nose, rolling it, he felt himself calm a bit.

The comfort of old routines.

He pocketed the cigar and a lighter in his breast pocket, then grabbed the decanter and full-bowled stemmed glass from behind the bar. If a man was going to smoke and drink wine, then it had to be done right.

When Nico pushed outside, the air was crisp and clean, a cleansing respite from the overheated, aroma-filled air in his kitchen. Night pressed in around him, filling the empty spaces. He left the porch light off. As he settled on the swinging bench hanging from the cross-member at the end of the porch, he breathed deep. People had thought him crazy when he'd hung the swing so he could sit and look out from under the overhang instead of facing across the porch. But he loved the view of the vineyards rolling under the open sky all the way to the mountains to the west—the Myacamas and the boundary between Napa and Sonoma valleys. And he loved watching his feet swing beyond the edge of the porch, the ground below urging him to leap. It reminded him of days past, his brother and sister and a rope swing over the Russian River, when the moments held only adventure and time filled the vastness of the sky.

As he swirled the wine in the decanter then poured himself a glass, he thought about the teacher from the city who had brought a bunch of school kids up to the winery for a tour. He'd told him that most of those kids had never seen the Milky Way, they never knew the billions of stars that peppered the sky with tiny pinpoints of light, light so old that the star it emanated from was most likely gone. That notion had fascinated Nico for as long as he could remember. He was in awe that it was possible to see something that was no longer there.

Maybe Paolo was one of those bright dots. A silly thought, but nevertheless it comforted him.

Tonight a cascade of stars swept across the sky from horizon to horizon. The sliver of moon cast a slight silver hue on the fog just starting to gather in the low places. He thought he heard the melancholy call of a loon, but at this time of night they should be tucked away. Loneliness filtered in to fill the quiet places, and Nico felt the tug of an emptiness he'd not known.

After he'd lit the cigar and pulled the smoke into his mouth several times, he reached for his phone. The time was late, night fully entrenched, but sleep had yet to tease him.

After a moment's hesitation, he flicked his thumb across the screen, and dialed a familiar number.

His sister, Victoria, answered on the first ring, her voice clear, lacking the diffuse softness of sleep. Nico? Are you okay?"

Nico heard her concern and her surprise and felt sorry for having let the distance of time and loss grow between them. They'd barely spoken at the funeral, each of them too constricted by grief to know what needed to be said. "I knew you'd be awake," he said simply. It was both an answer and a bridge across the chasm between now and then, when the Trevianis ran as a pack, inseparable and fiercely loyal.

Once there were three ...

His sister sighed, a tremulous sound like a student facing a particularly onerous exam, resigned and resilient. That should be the Treviani family crest, thought Nico. He closed his eyes, picturing her at the other end of the line. She'd be sitting in her big winged-backed chair by the bay window overlooking the river below. At his time of night, the river would be hidden in the hush of darkness, a random burble the only hint of its resolute meander toward the sea. Her feet would be tucked beneath her, her wild red hair a halo, her peaches-and-cream skin straight from a Botticelli painting, eyes like Paolo's, dark and kind. "I feel like a two-legged dog," she said. "With three legs, I never missed a fourth. Now, with but two, I feel that if I stop running, I'll topple over."

Leave it to Vic to put it perfectly. "That's all I've been doing, running like hell. Of course, instant parenthood has me going in circles, but it seems like life only slows down for moment, gaining strength to run off again. And on my best day I'm at the back of the pack."

"Brother, on your best day, you could conquer the free world with a broadsword and a slingshot."

"Not anymore." Unaccustomed to admitting weakness, Nico lowered his voice as if whispering would keep it a secret. "I feel like a sailor without a sextant. I'm okay if all I have to do is run downwind. But stop and figure out where I am? Forget it."

The Trevianis had been closer than most siblings. Perhaps it was being raised in a small house and being required to work together, alongside their parents, to put food on the table and a roof over their heads. Maybe it was their closeness in age. Barely ten months separated Nico from his brother and Paolo from their sister. Fully expecting more siblings, they'd been shocked when their mother had finally said to hell with the teachings of the Church and she'd taken care of the issue. Their mother had no problem taking on the Pope, and God himself, if necessary. Their father had been smart enough to remain silent. Had he argued, it would have been a hollow gesture—they had a hard enough time feeding three children. More would have impoverished all of them. As it was, Nico was sure there were nights his parents didn't eat so the three of them had had their fill.

"That's understandable, brother. You and Paolo were like music and lyrics, always in time, never a sour note."

"Oh, there were more than a few sour notes. Remember the black eye I gave him?"

"And he loosened one of your front teeth."

"All over a girl."

"Not just any girl. Paolo married her."

"And I dodged that bullet." Nico pulled on his cigar, capturing the smoke in his mouth, savoring the flavor before expelling it on a saved breath. "It's funny..."

"What?"

Nico wasn't used to sharing these sorts of feelings—well, feelings of any sort actually. Yet, finding his sister understood helped him to shift the load to a more manageable place. "You can go through life so sure you've got it all figured out, then something happens, something that pulls the rug out from under you and you realize you don't really have a clue ... about anything."

"You and Paolo always seemed to have a plan."

Nico laughed just a bit and felt his heart lighten, buoyed by the memories. "What Paolo could dream up, I could devise a way to execute."

"Kept things interesting, that's for sure. Even to the end." Nico could hear the sweet notes of shared moments in her voice. "It's bad for me, brother, but it must be living hell for you."

"Yeah." Nico set his cigar down on the metal table next to the swing, the glowing tip hanging over the edge. Holding the stem of the glass in his free hand, he swirled the wine, then inhaled its bouquet even though he could identify this wine blindfolded. He took a sip of the wine he and Paolo had crafted, letting it linger on his tongue. There was more than a little bit of his brother's influence in the dark, rich liquid.

"Tell me," his sister said, her demand a bit unsettling, like a probing light poking into the darkness in his heart.

"He's everywhere, Vic." Nico drew a ragged breath. "Every time I round a corner, I expect to see him. When I'm concentrating in the lab, or I'm at a loss, I swear I can hear him talking to me, telling me to trust my gut, take a risk."

For a moment Victoria didn't say anything. "He lives on in our memories. That's all the legacy we get."

"Yeah. But who knew it could hurt this much?"

"That's what love is. You give the ones you love a part of you, and you get a bit of them in return. When they go, they take that part of you with them."

"But all I'm left with is... is nothing." Nico's anger flared.

"No, you have him with you. Besides, Paolo left to you what he valued most in the world, his children."

"Small comfort." Nico felt he was on the giving end of that equation, constantly.

"Give it time. He asked you to care for the girls for a reason." Vic sounded wistful. She hadn't married. Now the chance for children most likely lay in her past.

Nico had never thought that she might be burdened by her choices—Vic of all people had a clear vision of her life, she always had. But every choice, every path, came with a price, a choice not taken.

"Do you wish you had kids?" Nico's question surprised him. They'd never really talked of such things. Private matters were best kept that way, private—a self-defense mechanism his father had preached to his children, eventually shutting them down, walling them off. Now Nico wanted to breach that wall, restore closeness with his sister. The loss of his brother made Nico realize how close the three of them had been, and how wonderful that was. And now, as adults, he and Vic hardly knew each other, not really.

Vic's voice was measured, as if weighing her words, her emotions. "I guess every woman wants children, or at least feels the primal urge. I'm no different. But I didn't trust myself to be as good a parent as either of ours."

That shocked Nico. "You're the most competent woman I know."

"Book smarts don't equate to common sense."

"Never thought I'd hear you say that, Ms. Wharton MBA."

"School I could do. Life? Not so much." Vic paused. When she began again, her voice, tempered with pragmatism, lacked the wistful edge. "My worst fear is that I would've raised a horrible kid and added to the pain in the universe."

"Paolo's little hellions do enough of that already."

Vic's voice brightened. "How are my nieces?"

"Completely confounding." For a man who had been certain in his course, Nico couldn't believe that the loss of his brother had been like a huge tempest blowing him so far off course he couldn't see a way back. And, in his heart, Nico knew going back was impossible.

The worst part was that the loss of Paolo made Nico realize how little he had of the things that mattered in life. With the love of a good woman, the adoration of a child, and the joy of satisfying work, life is complete, at least that's what his father used to say. And, despite his shortcomings, his father had acquired a certain wisdom through the tempest of time.

Nico had mortgaged the first two for the third and had been left with none.

"In other words, growing into fine young women." Vic laughed.

Nico liked her laugh, a sound like wind chimes heralding a cool fall breeze after the heat of the summer.

The screen door creaked open behind him. Someone closed it gently. Then, soft footfalls, barely discernable, but the groan of the old boards gave her away. Brooklyn stepped into the moonlight, then hovered there like a wraith, ephemeral, distant.

"Hold on, Vic," he said into the phone. Then, "Hey, Knucklehead, you okay?"

Just a wisp of a thing, she practically disappeared beneath the long flannel nightgown. Her hair a rat's nest, her face ghostly white, her eyes worried, she stood, wringing her hands. Then she did the most amazing thing. She sidled in next to Nico on the swing, tucking herself under his shoulder, then pulled her feet up just like her aunt always did when she was that age.

Nico froze. "What are you doing?" Tentatively, he held her shivering body close as her head dropped to his shoulder. She opened the crack in his heart she had started earlier. Emotions coursed through him, raw and visceral, new and frightening. He tried to push them away, but it was too late. And he knew he'd do unimaginable things to anyone who hurt his girls.

"I miss Papa," she whispered.

Nico gazed out at the moon-drenched hills. As children, he and

Paolo, and Victoria too, had ranged far and wide over all of them. Through time, the hills had remained unchanged, but not the three Trevianis. "Me, too, sweetie."

"Nico, you still there?" His sister's voice was muted, muffled.

Nico'd forgotten the phone he still held in his hand. Rational thought had fled when he had wrapped his arm around his niece. He off-loaded the wine glass, setting it on the arm of the swing, then transferred the phone to his other hand. "Sis, I gotta go. Sorry. Can I call you back tomorrow?"

"You okay?"

"Yeah," he leaned down and kissed the top of his niece's head. "Yeah, funny enough."

"You sound surprised."

"Yeah."

"Sounds interesting." Vic almost sounded as if she knew. But she couldn't, could she? "Call me when you can. I've got something I'm working on that I'd like to talk to you about when you have time."

"You got it." He terminated the call, then exchanged the phone for the glass on the arm of the swing and hoped he'd remember where he put it. He felt Brooklyn shiver against him. "Cold?"

"No ... yes, but from the inside." She nestled in, reaching up and pulling his hand so his arm tightened around her. "Crazy, huh?"

"No, not at all. Would some hot chocolate help?"

"You'd have to move?"

"I have my talents, few though they might be, but, unfortunately making hot chocolate from here isn't one of them."

"Then, no. Thanks, though." She shook her head, a motion Nico felt rather than saw, tucked in as she was.

"You don't want me to move?" The thought seemed incredulous to Nico. Wasn't this the child who was screaming at him just this morning because he'd washed her favorite white shirt with her sister's new red shorts? He didn't see the big deal; both of them liked pink. Clearly he had missed the point.

As quiet settled over them, Nico listened for the loon, but it had stopped calling.

The screen door creaked open once again, and this time the footsteps beat a faster rhythm on the old boards. Taryn dove under his available arm, tucking herself in and pulling his arm tight. He was glad his glass was nearly empty, or they all would've been wearing the wine. He placed it safely out of harm's way.

Bookended by the girls, Nico felt a peace, an unexpected stillness.

"Why did the angels take Papa?" Brooklyn asked.

Taryn melted into him as if she wanted to crawl inside.

"I wish I could tell you, but, honestly, I don't know."

"God must've had a reason," Taryn pressed. She was the most like her father, always insisting on a logical answer. Some things in life just weren't logical. And sometimes, there simply were no answers.

"I really hate God," Brooklyn said breathlessly, as if horrified by the thought trying to stifle it, yet compelled to utter it. "Am I going to Hell?"

Nico smiled to himself. "No."

"How can you be so sure?" Taryn asked.

He searched for words. How did you explain the unexplainable, answer the unanswerable? Especially to thirteen-year-olds replete with overblown righteous indignation at the unfairness in the world.

"I don't know why God took your dad. I'm as angry about it as you are, and I hurt just the same. I miss him every moment of every day. It's okay to be mad as hell. We just have to help each other figure out how to go on."

"Will we see him again?" Taryn's tone had lost its fight.

"Close your eyes. That's what I do. He's right there." Nico shut his eyes. Then, cracking one open, he glanced down at the girls, their faces scrunched, their eyes pressed tight. They saw him too. Nico could feel it as they relaxed, the tension easing from their bodies. He left them with their memories for a bit, but not too long. "What do you two say about grabbing the kayaks and heading up river to see your aunt? Maybe a picnic?"

Their eyes snapped open. "When?"

"Soon."

Taryn tensed beside him.

Even though he couldn't see her piercing stare, Nico could feel it. "Okay, okay. Is day after tomorrow soon enough? We can stay, if your aunt will have us, but we have to give her fair warning."

Taryn settled back against him.

"Can we swing on the rope swing?" asked Brooklyn.

"Of course."

"Can we have cake for breakfast?" she pressed.

"Of course not." Nico feigned indignation, and the girls twittered. A good sound, one he hadn't been able to elicit from either one of them. Not since Paolo's funeral.

Maybe, just maybe, the light at the end of the tunnel wasn't an oncoming train.

CHAPTER EIGHT

SOPHIA TURNED INTO THE DRIVEWAY of her mother's house, her headlights arcing across the front of the large Victorian. The house, muted and thinned, as if reflected from the glassy surface of a pond, stood as testament to the cruelty of time and the apathy of age. Several of the shutters sagged on old hinges. The porch buckled in the middle, and the boards on two of the three steps curled up at one end, pulling the nails loose. No matter how many times Sophia hammered them back into place with longer nails, they taunted her, curling anew. Paint peeled and blistered on the western side of the house where the sun punished it in the summer. The rest of the paint remained a pastel hint of its former vibrancy. Old and tired yet defiant to the end.

Like her mother.

After jumping on the steps, using her weight to push them down, and juggling the cake in one hand, Sophia tried the handle. The door was locked. Cupping her face with one hand she peered through the long window to the right of the door. Not a light burned, not even from the kitchen. Alarmed, she fingered through the keys on her ring. On the second pass, she found the one she looked for. The lock stuck; the key wouldn't turn.

"Damn!" Wiggling it a bit more and pulling the door tight to the jamb, Sophia finally cajoled the lock to release. She pushed the door open and flicked on the overhead light.

A figure sat rigid, stoic in the wing-backed chair, which had been pulled around to face the door.

Sophia started and almost dropped the cake, saving it as it wobbled. Her free hand covered her chest, her heart racing. Then she breathed deeply. "Mother! What are you doing?"

"I could ask you the same thing." Regina looked at her daughter with a pragmatic expression, showing no relief at seeing her. A hint of fear slacked her features, as if she knew she should know Sophia but couldn't place her. "Why are you here?" Though it was nearing two a.m., she was perfectly dressed in a St. John suit, probably decades old, appropriate pumps, and a string of pearls at her throat. Her hair a perfect helmet, her face over-done as usual, she looked ready to lunch with her friends at Auberge de Soliel.

Sophia set her purse and keys down on the stool in the foyer, and the cake on the sideboard, then went to squat next to her mother. "You called me. Here, look, I brought you some cake. Chocolate. Your favorite." The fabric on the arms of the chair had worn through, white tuffs of stuffing poking out of the holes.

"I most certainly did not." Regina's eyes shifted to the cake. "Chocolate?"

"Yes." Sophia stroked her mother's arm for a moment, wishing the hands of time to reverse, just for a bit. "I must be mistaken, then." She let her gaze wander around the room. The kids had spent a lot of time here, especially after Daniel had died. Having her mother close had been a godsend. Two lighter squares where paintings had hung over the couch caught her attention. And one of her mother's prized Lladro figurines was gone from the mantle.

When she met her mother's gaze, she smiled. "Has anyone been by to see you lately?"

"Why?" Regina stretched out the words, her tone still guarded.

"Just asking. No reason."

Regina's brows lowered into a frown. "I'm not sure."

"Well," Sophia tried to sound pleasant. "I trust any visitors would have the manners not to show up now. It's late."

"I know." Her mother nodded.

Sophia wasn't at all sure she did know. "Then why aren't you in bed?"

A fleeting look passed across Regina's face. A haunting, upsetting look, one Sophia hadn't seen before. A flash and then it was gone.

She pressed her lips together in a thin line and cocked her chin. "I'm not tired."

From the sagging of her shoulders, the circles under her eyes, Sophia could tell that wasn't the truth. She pushed herself to her feet, her knees crackling in protest. "Why don't we get you in your nightgown, and then would you like it if I fixed you a glass of warm milk to have with a slice of the cake?" When Sophia was young and sleep wouldn't come, her mother would fix her warm milk. She wasn't sure whether the milk helped or whether the comfort of her mother's attention was the panacea. Now the memory alone brought calm and comfort.

"Cake?"

Sophia raised the plate. "Yes. I brought it for you."

"I only like chocolate."

"I know. So how about that milk and cake?"

"I'd like that."

"Great." Sophia rose, set the cake in the kitchen, then returned to help her mother out of the chair. "First, let's get you in your pajamas."

Regina let her daughter lead her upstairs.

NICO PRIDED HIMSELF ON ALWAYS being the first at the winery in the morning. But readying two teens for school then dropping them off played havoc with his punctuality. Today, he arrived to find Dani Stone waiting at the gate. She'd pulled her truck in next to the fence, lowered the tailgate, and now she sat there, her hands under her thighs, her legs swinging. When she saw him, she jumped down. She smoothed her hands down her thighs, rearranging her jeans, then looked up and smiled. Her hair was as he remembered it, a tangle of short, wavy, dark curls, her eyes a pale blue, and one dimple when she smiled, as if she was only half-amused.

All summer she'd worked like a dog as an apprentice, never complaining, not even cringing when she almost dropped a full barrel while regaining her skills on the forklift. But she got the full-time job when she took his check for her services, tore it up, then gave him an invoice for twice the amount. Still, it had been half of what she was worth ... on her worst day. And he'd gladly paid.

Today Nico was sure if she'd had a tail, she would've wagged it. Eager, that's what she was, practically vibrating with enthusiasm. He hoped she wouldn't be disappointed. Wine was like any other love affair—expectations bred resentments, resentments bred dissatisfaction, and dissatisfaction bred loathing.

Nico pulled into the short drive, stopping in front of the newly renovated gate with "Specter Wines" emblazoned in bold iron letters over the entrance. The gate itself was a combination of rustic wood and metal, a bit of tastefulness that stood in stark contrast to everything else about Avery Specter. At least, if he didn't have any class, the man knew how to hire it.

Nico rolled down the window, choking on the oily exhaust fumes that overtook him.

"You're burning oil," she said.

Nico cocked an eyebrow. "Don't give me a problem if you're not offering a solution."

Dani eyed the truck, then the driver. With one hand on her hip and her head tilted to one side, she said, "Your truck's a 2000, like mine." A statement not a question. "You look like a V-8 kind of guy. Do you have the 4.2?"

That got a smile. Either she was a damn good bluffer, or she knew her stuff. "Don't judge."

"Judge? Mine has the 5.4." A cloud passed across her features and her voice quieted. "It was my dad's truck."

"Ah, an inherited gas-guzzler."

Dani jammed her hands in her pockets, looking away for a moment as if she were seeing something he couldn't. When she once again met his eyes, her voice was stronger, confident, and the look was gone. "You're burning oil around the rings. Or maybe it's a valve-stem issue. Either way, I can fix it."

"Good to know. But I hired you to make wine."

She pursed her lips and gave him a curt nod.

Nico tossed her a ring of keys. The truck was long past its point of planned obsolescence, but it had to last a bit longer, just until he got his financial feet back underneath him. However, the minute he could part with the truck for a day, he was going to turn Quatro loose on the engine.

With a quick motion, Dani caught the keys. "What color?"

"Blue." Nico had painted every lock on the place with its own individual color, a bright slash of nail polish, the most indelible paint he could find. Then he'd marked the corresponding keys accordingly. A dozen different bottles of nail polish. The gal at the pharmacy downtown still looked at him like he played for the other team or something.

Dani glanced at the gate, then sifted through the keys. After making short work of the lock and unwinding the chain, she turned to look at him, raising her arms in a questioning gesture.

An electric motor powered the gate when someone typed in the appropriate code on the keypad, which stood at car-window height next to Nico's truck. He punched buttons without looking and the gate swung open on well-oiled hinges, not making a sound.

"You know, the code and whole electric thing should be enough to keep folks out. That's sorta the point." Dani raised her voice so he could hear her over the truck's engine, which had started to clatter.

"So they tell me. I'm an old-school kind of guy." As Nico eased his truck through the gate, he said, "Leave it open. Get your truck and meet me at the lab."

Three separate buildings housed the winery. Peaked steel roofs, weathered wood plank siding, and huge rollback doors gave the impression of rustic, reconfigured barns, which wasn't too far from the truth. The first wineries housed here had been modest operations, building as the Napa wine industry grew. The last one, purchased and transformed by Mr. Specter, had made decent wine; some vintages had even bordered on nuanced, which was a good entry point, at least to hear Mr. Specter talk of it. He intended to make over the winery, resuscitate the wine, then build to greatness—at least that's how he described his plan. The 100-point Cab had been an auspicious start.

First, he'd refurbished and redecorated the two front buildings. The first building housed the tasting room. Beautifully landscaped with flowers blooming year-round and a wrap-around porch invited visitors to stop and stay for a bit. If they wandered around to the back, they were rewarded with a small pond with waterfalls and fountain. Comfortably decorated with low tables surrounded by overstuffed high-backed chairs, and flanked on one side by a wall made entirely of glass, and on the other by a huge open fireplace with stone facing above, the room invited folks to linger over wine, to sample the food, to drink in the incredible view. Specter had staffed the room with friendly and knowledgeable middle-agers who served not only wine but also a changing tasting menu that paired perfectly with the wines being poured that day. The business offices were tastefully hidden behind an upholstered green leather door.

The second, much larger building, tucked behind so as not to interfere with the view, housed the winemaking operation. On pretty days, when there was something to see, the front doors could be pushed back to allow folks to watch as the grapes were sorted, crushed, fermented, and barreled. Aging took place underground in a huge cavernous expanse where temperature could be closely managed.

Housed in the far building, lurking behind the public side of the operation, the lab was the most high-tech part of the winery. Nico believed that winemaking was all about instinct, experience, and a highly trained palate. But Avery Specter thought differently. He preferred to test for a myriad of flavors and various levels from acidity to sulfites that all combined to make a singular wine. Nico considered the process an esoteric bit of alchemy that Avery relied on too much— except for blending. Then the lab was perfect. For the annual ritual, Nico gathered not only the experts on staff but others as well, often inviting members of the marketing staff or the mailroom clerks to offer their opinions as to the amounts of each lot that should go into the final blend. An appreciation for and a love of wine didn't differentiate along formal knowledge nor even socioeconomic boundaries. After all, the consumer's opinion was the most important.

Nico had flicked on the lights and made it as far as his desk in the corner when the girl bounded in, amping up the energy in the room by thousands of ergs. "Kid, throttle it back. Wine takes time, finesse. All that energy is going to cook the juice."

Dani tried to still herself, pausing where she stood, but she didn't stay still for long. "This is my first real job, you know. It's different than being an intern." She moved around the room as she talked, her hand lightly trailing across the stainless lab tables, touching the tubes and equipment as if cataloguing each, measuring, weighing, making the place her own. "Way better."

"You won't like me most days."

Dani shot him a piercing look, her eyes dark and serious. "I'm not here to like you. I'm here to learn from you. Teach me. Treat me like the others, and we'll be cool."

Oh, Nico liked this kid, he really did. And he wondered where she got her moxie. A bottle in her hand caught his attention. "What do you have there?"

Dani glanced at the bottle as if she'd been caught swiping jawbreakers from Giugni's Grocery. "Oh, just something I'm working on."

"I'd like to try it." He pulled out a stool and straddled it, then reached for a couple of glasses. "Bring it here."

Dani glanced at the bottle, her mother's wine, and for the first time had a moment of indecision. Her mother had asked her to keep her secret. And she hadn't noticed Dani tucking the bottle away in her truck last night. She'd probably notice eventually. And she'd be furious. But the wine, it deserved to be perfected then savored. When she looked back up at Nico, her moxie had been dampened a bit. "It's not ready yet."

Nico nodded as he gave her a long look. "Let me give you a heads-up kid. I'm the winemaker, here and what I say goes. You got it?"

Dani nodded. Her chin tilted a bit higher.

Nico fought a grin. "I have no problem with you bringing your own juice in here. But, when you're on the clock, I own you—my wine gets your full attention."

"Got it," Dani said, visibly relaxing.

Dani seemed at war with herself and unusually twitchy all of a sudden, which made him even more curious to taste what was in that bottle. "A word to the wise, kid. Put the bottle away. Don't let Mr. Specter know what you're doing. I might not care what you do here on your own time, but I can't vouch for him."

Dani gave him a quizzical look, then opened the cabinet he pointed to. She spoke to him over her shoulder as she tucked the bottle inside, up high, out of view. "To be honest, I don't know what I'm doing. I'm playing around with a friend's juice." She pulled on the tail of her shirt, straightening it as she turned to face him. "It's funny. I never gave a thought to Mr. Specter. Frankly, I don't know a thing about him. I just wanted to work with you."

"You may regret that."

CHAPTER NINE

ONE FULL DAY WALKING THE vineyards and Nico knew he'd been right about Dani Stone. In her new position, she'd stepped up, challenging, offering an opinion where hers differed from his, asking questions, absorbing. With the sun high in a cloudless sky, the heat, like water set to boil around an unwary lobster, had built slowly, sucking them dry until Nico felt he was little more than a withered carcass. They'd taken water, but not enough—he'd already downed three bottles, resisting the siren call of an ice-cold brew in a frosted glass. A traitorous sacrilege where the juice of the grape ruled supreme.

Winding down now in his office at the back of the lab—he would've preferred the fermentation room, but his boss had insisted on the location—Nico leaned back in his chair and crossed his legs, feet on his desk. He could smell the stench of hard work clinging to him. He liked it. It felt good to get out in the fields. He'd pushed himself, prodded by his youthful apprentice and by the need to just do, to get back to some semblance of the life he had before. Sore muscles, sore feet, a headache, all earned through honest work and hours under the beating sun. A good day.

Closing his eyes, he rested his head as he contemplated the upcoming harvest. A day or two, no more. His vineyard manager had wanted to pick today. But the grapes had told Nico they weren't quite ready. If Dani had thought that odd, she hadn't let on. And she'd agreed with him, except on two lots of Chard he'd contracted for just to play with. She'd been right, but he hadn't told her so.

Taking a deep breath, he felt himself relax, really relax, probably for the first time since Paolo died. He and the twins would find their balance. Life would never be the same, but it would be okay ... maybe even better than okay. Time would tell. Moving his shoulders up and down, backwards and forwards, then swiveling his head around, he managed to cajole his neck muscles into releasing a bit of tension. Where he felt it the most was in the lessening of the throbbing behind his right eye, an almost constant companion these last few months.

He tensed as someone tapped on the doorjamb. He didn't bother to raise his head or open his eyes. "What?" His bark sounded like he had a bite.

"I've finished re-racking last year's Cab." Dani's voice, with a hint of weariness, made Nico grin. "The crusher is clean. Had to take the cylinder apart; the shaft was bent. The motor still doesn't sound right. I can take a look at it tomorrow if you want."

Nico raised a hand and waved her in. "Come on in. Take a load off." When she didn't say anything and he didn't hear her step into the office, Nico lifted his head to look at her. Sunburned, the sleeves of her thin cotton shirt rolled up as far as they would go, mud on the knees of her jeans, she chewed on her lip, her face creased with indecision.

The only other chair in the room was Paolo's desk chair. His desk was still pushed up against the wall in the corner facing out the front windows so Paolo could watch the lab techs. He hadn't trusted them not to ruin his wine. Nico could hear his brother now, "Wine is born in the vineyard, and ruined in the lab." The thought lifted one corner of Nico's mouth. "Go ahead. Give you something to grow into."

Dani pulled the chair out and wheeled it over so it faced Nico's desk. When she sat, it was with reverence as she stroked the worn leather on the arms. When she looked at Nico, her eyes were bright with tears. "It's just not the same without Mr. Paolo here."

Nico slid his feet from his desk, putting his elbows in their place, then steepling his fingers. He was glad Dani had gotten to spend time with his brother. Although the time had been short, she was a fast study and no doubt she'd absorbed more of the Paolo Treviani theories of winemaking than she realized. But Nico was also glad that he didn't have to explain about his brother ... she knew. "He's in each barrel in the barrel room."

Dani brushed at a tear as if embarrassed at her emotion.

Nico lacked the energy to pretend, to play the part. "I miss him, too, kid. Not a second goes by that ..." He shook his head. Emotion he could admit. His fears? Not so much—especially not to his new apprentice. He looked at Paolo's desk, papers strewn, covering the wood in a blanket of inspiration. "How could someone so messy be so precise when it came to wine?"

Dani followed his gaze. "My mother's the same way. Notes stuck all over the place. After she writes them, I don't think she looks at them again. She told me once, writing the idea down is how she gets it into her memory. Once it's there, what does she need the note for?"

"Well, we don't have Paolo's memory, so maybe you could try to make some sense of his notes?"

"Sure thing." She sounded doubtful, as if disturbing his notes would be an affront to the dead.

Nico couldn't argue—there was a finality to straightening Paolo's clutter. "Then file them away." He paused and swallowed hard. "Then I'm thinking you need to make that your desk. You're the Assistant Winemaker, and I don't want to always be shouting for you."

"Okay." Dani let the word linger, stretching it with a hint of hesitation.

While not entirely happy with the thought of Dani at Paolo's desk, Nico knew that's what they all needed. He didn't want to think about it anymore, so he changed the subject. "I've been thinking about what you said about the Chard lots."

Dani's look sharpened.

"You were right. You ever cut grapes before?"

Dani snorted. "Since I was knee-high to a duck. Grapes hang low, in case you haven't noticed."

Nico cocked his head and looked at her. "When would you cut 'em?"

"Tonight after the heat but before the dew. The air is heavy; don't need the water clinging to the fruit messing with the juice."

Nico nodded. "Go home. Get a couple of hours' sleep. I'll have Hector and his crew meet you at Lot 127 at four a.m."

"Midnight would be better."

Nico raised one eyebrow and contemplated her for a moment before he spoke. "Midnight it is. Now beat it."

Dani hesitated. "I've got a favor to ask."

He narrowed his eyes.

Dani shifted in her chair. Feet on the floor, hands on her knees, she met his gaze. "Not really a favor, just an opinion. Say you have a wine. Really light. Super fruity. So acidic it makes your tongue curl, but curiously complex with a serious minerality. It's special, really special. It just needs a bit of body. Right now it's so thin it practically evaporates off the mid-palate so the mouth-feel sucks."

"Oak?"

"Only masks the brilliance."

"Malo?"

"Makes it slimy."

"Slimy." Nico grinned. "A technical term I've not heard before."

Dani shrugged. "I don't like buttery on my whites. I much prefer them crisp."

"A California-style renegade, huh?"

"Who wants to keep making the same stuff? It all tastes the same—like Robert Parker likes it."

"Tickle a few bored palates, is that it?" Nico kept his face passive, but the kid was singing his song. He knew there was a market for unique ... he just couldn't prove it. "Then what you need is a bit of some other juice, one that won't change the characteristics you like but will bring up the ones you find lacking."

"I figured that." Dani sounded exasperated. "But what juice?"

"Kid, I can't tell you that without tasting what you got." Nico watched as Dani fought a battle with herself. "Are we talking about the bottle you hid this morning?"

A quick nod, then she levered herself from her chair, muttering something about being glad she didn't live at home anymore—Nico didn't quite catch all of it. When she returned, she had the bottle in one hand and two glasses from the tasting rack in the other. After unscrewing the top, she placed the glasses on the desk between them. "You can't tell anybody about this stuff. It's between you and me, okay?"

To Nico, the kid had the look of someone about to betray an important trust. He wanted to warn her against it, but curiosity squashed that like a heel on a cockroach. And, as the boss, he needed to know exactly how refined her palate, how discerning her taste—at least that's what he told himself.

Bottle open and ready to pour, Dani waited with raised eyebrows.

"You can trust me, kid."

She appraised him through narrowed eyes as if weighing his words, his manner. Nico hadn't felt this much on the hot seat since he tried to convince Betty sue Warner to let him cop a feel back in middle school. Finally, Dani poured a couple of inches of golden liquid into each glass.

"It really should be cold." Her eyes didn't meet his.

Nico waited. Through the years he'd tasted enough wine to fill the pond behind the winery, very little of it brilliant. Even his own creations often failed to reach such lofty heights.

After setting the bottle on the table, she grabbed one of the glasses, offering it to him. "Go ahead. Tell me what you think ... honestly."

"Aren't you going to taste yours?"

"In a minute. I know what I think to be its strengths and weaknesses. I'm interested in what you think."

He took his time, examining the wine, swirling, smelling, swirling again, holding it to the light. Dani shifted once from one foot to the other, but, besides that, she remained stoic, her arms at her sides, her fingers resting lightly on the edge of the desk. Her eyes, a fraction wide and a bit too bright, too intense, betrayed her.

Nico noticed she had a cat's eye, the pupil of one eye elongated into the iris. He hadn't noticed that before. The wine looked like honey with a bit of an orange tint, unusual but not off-putting. These wines were catching on with the younger crowd, but Nico hadn't seen any made in the valley. He held the glass high with the light behind it. "Extended skin contact?"

"Yeah, a month maybe, not much more but not exactly sure. And a bit of oxidation. No oak, though."

"It's a bit cloudy."

"Intentionally so."

"Any additions? Sulphur? Yeast?"

"Not sure. Doubtful, though. Something about old grapes and old methods, but that's all I know. Winemakers can be a secretive lot."

Nico gave Dani a sideways look.

She seemed nonplussed.

Finally, delicately, he took a sip, rolling the liquid around his mouth, then letting it linger on his tongue before swallowing. Flavors opened, caressed, but didn't overpower. A light touch, a hint of stone fruit, citrus, and a stroke of honey. Acidic and refreshing, complex, tantalizing in its aloofness, it caused the same salivary response of a slightly grapefruity Sauvignon Blanc. Rare, enticing, teasing, luscious. Rolling it around his mouth, savoring, Nico almost groaned. He swallowed. And then it ... disappeared. It was like being on the brink of an orgasm and then ... nothing.

He blinked, coming out of it. Wine to Nico was a lot like sex, fully engulfing. "You're right, this juice is amazing. I can't tell the varietals. Well, other than Ribolla, but even that is lighter than most I've tasted. Lighter by far." He furrowed his brow and took another sip, oblivious to Dani, standing like a statue, brittle, ready to shatter at the first blow of the hammer. "Maybe a hint of Gruner, but that would be a bit odd." This sip, like the other, left him wanting for more. "This wine is like an unskilled lover, good foreplay, but then too quick on the follow-through." Nico shot a quick glance at Dani. "I said that out loud, didn't I? Sorry." For a moment he stammered at a recovery. "No offense meant. Not used to having a ... woman ... underfoot—not real sure how to handle it ... other than with a muzzle." At Dani's narrowing of her eyes, he hastily clarified. "For me. A muzzle for me."

"Treat me like one of the boys and we'll get along fine. Unless, of course, you're in the habit of grabbing the men's asses." Dani grinned. "Then I'll just break your nose."

"No lawyer necessary?"

"My mother taught me to solve my own problems."

"Your mother?" Nico's voice held a note of respect. "She taught you how to inflict bodily harm?" Clearly, he needed a bit of education in the rearing of self-sufficient young women.

"Self-protection runs deep in the Stone family. Sometimes it can run so deep it becomes a place to hide."

"What?" Nico didn't understand. What man would?

Dani lifted her chin toward the glass he still held. "The juice?"

Nico glanced back at the glass in his hand as if it was a grafted appendage, not his own, yet the key to a deficit. "You're right, kid ... mostly. This is seriously good ... bordering on brilliant even. So unique. But the mid-palate and the finish leave you...."

"Unsatisfied?" Dani said, her delivery perfectly deadpan.

"I deserved that. What varietals are in here? I used to think I had a good nose and educated taste, but I'm stumped. Obviously Ribolla, as I've said, but not like any I've had. The rest?" He shook his head. "Could be Welch's for all I can tell."

"Don't feel bad. The grapes are ... unique."

"Where are they sourced?"

Dani waffled a bit, her gaze trickling from Nico's to focus out the window behind him. "Not far."

Nico's eyes widened and he took another sip, once again savoring every nuance. He shook his head. "These aren't Valley grapes."

Dani stared out the window.

Nico pushed himself from his chair, then strode to the window, blocking Dani's view, forcing her to look at him. "The grapes? They aren't Valley grapes, are they?"

"Yes ... and no."

Nico zeroed in. "How many acres?"

"Two."

His mouth dropped open. "Two? You have the elixir of the gods, something so unique yet ... familiar in a way, something you could make a shitload of money off of and you have only two acres?"

"Yeah," the thought deflated Dani. "I guess you can't do very much with just a couple of acres."

Nico lifted one corner of his mouth. "No, only sell out each vintage to a mailing list for a shitload a bottle."

Dani brightened. "That sounds good. But the body and the finish?"

Nico waved her comment away as if swatting at a gnat. "I can fix that." An idea lit his eyes. "That Chard you're dropping tonight might be a good fix. It has a unique lineage. If not that, I've got a tasty little Pinot that's got some body to it, but it's lacking complexity. It might blend nicely."

Dani pursed her lips. "These grapes and pinot, there's something that hasn't been tried. Probably with good reason."

"Kid, it's not the varietal—"

"It's the grape, I know."

Nico's voice dropped. "Who told you that?"

"My moth..." Dani stopped, squeezing her eyes shut and taking a deep breath. When she opened them, she had shut down, retreating behind an inner wall. "Nobody. It's not important."

"I disagree. But it's your juice."

Dani capped the bottle and reached for the glasses.

Nico waved her off. "Let me finish mine. I've still got work yet to do; then I'll take care of the glasses. Now you need to beat it. Time for shut-eye is evaporating and, remember, the grapes—"

"—wait for no one, I know. Believe me, I know." His assistant winemaker finished his sentence then stashed the bottle in the cabinet. With a jaunty wave, she disappeared.

Nico waited until he heard her truck fire up and spit gravel as she accelerated down the drive. No one else was around when he walked over to the cabinet. Reaching up, his hand closed around the bottle of Dani Stone's wine.

THE NIGHT HAD SLIPPED AWAY while Sophia dressed her mother for bed, chatted with her over warm milk, fed her a few bites of cake and delighted in her smile, then sat with her until she drifted off. Thank heavens Mrs. Pettigrew from down the street had agreed to come sit with Regina. Sophia didn't want her mother to awaken alone, but she had a full day at the vineyard ahead of her. As it was, she'd had just enough time to run home, change into work clothes, grab some coffee and a bite of cake from the slice she'd snuck from her mother's, then head back down the mountain to start what promised to be a full day.

Butchy Pinkman's properties stretched the entire length of the valley. If he didn't have the most acreage under vine, then he certainly gave Beckstoffer and the foreign corporations a run for their money. Too bad he didn't have their aspirations to make great wine. At Highway 29 Sophia decided to head south toward Carneros. She'd start at the newest lots: some very nice Chardonnay that was starting to come around.

Sophia pulled her truck in through the open gate. Manny Garza had beaten her by no more than a minute or two, just enough time to unchain the gate. Wiry, with skin the texture of rawhide, an open ageless face and eyes so old they seemed to see everything, Manny gave her a toothy grin. His jeans and shirt were threadbare, and his boots looked so broken in Sophia imagined they were as comfortable as house shoes. He popped some Double Bubble in his mouth and started working it. In a hand a couple of sizes too large for his body, he extended a couple of pieces to her. "Want some?"

"No, thanks." Sophia reached inside her truck and grabbed the light sweater she always kept there for trips to the south end of the valley.

"Gonna be a hot one." Manny chomped on his gum, blew a bubble, then popped it.

Pulling on her sweater, Sophia joined him at the edge of the vineyard and squinted up at the fog that still gauzed the sky. "The temp dropped twenty degrees between St. Helena and here. When the fog burns off, give the grapes an hour or two of sun, then I want the crew in here to start dropping fruit. We'll need to get it before the fog settles in again."

"I got them scheduled for this afternoon, just after lunch."

Sophia smiled. The years they'd been working together had given Manny the ability to read her mind. "Let's walk."

They strolled up the row, each taking mental notes. "Ground cover worked well this year?" Sophia asked.

"Kept the bugs down low, gave them a place to live so they didn't much bother the vines."

They both sampled a few grapes as they walked. Finally, Manny shook his head. "I thought you was nuts the way you trimmed these last spring. Gave 'em a short, short haircut. But damned if they didn't come back stronger than ever. This fruit is ..." He took off his hat and ran his hand across his brow, slapped his hat against his leg, then replaced it.

"Too good for Butchy Pinkman." Sophia turned the tables and

finished his thought. Thinking about these grapes and her own grapes, for the first time she understood the allure of homicide. She swallowed her anger, a practiced habit.

"Yes, ma'am."

They rounded the end of the row and started back down another. A body blocked their path, giving Sophia a start.

Sophia stepped in front of Manny and eyed the stranger. "Can I help you? This is private property."

A man, feet spread, bent at the waist, glared at a cluster of fruit. "I own this property." The man turned but didn't extend his hand.

Not a local, he looked familiar but Sophia couldn't place him. "Really?"

"Well, my partner owns it. I'm Avery Specter."

A modern-day robber baron. Sophia worked to keep her expression bland, her voice cool. "I see. I'm Sophia Stone, head grower. And this is Manny Garza, my right-hand man. What can we do for you?"

"These grapes, these plants, they look so much more robust than the others in the area. You responsible for that, Garza?"

Manny's mitt-sized hands clenched into fists, but his posture remained relaxed. "No, sir. That would be Mrs. Stone."

"Really?" Specter turned his attention to Sophia, letting his eyes run lazily from tip to toe.

So accustomed to the games the good old boys played, Sophia didn't give him the satisfaction of getting a rise out of her.

"I want to know how you did this." He gestured toward the grapes. "Even I can see there's something different going on here."

Sophia would be damned before she gave him her secrets. "Mr. Specter, we're busy right now. And there's nothing different. We're just growing them as best we can. I doubt you would appreciate the nuances."

Specter plucked a grape and popped it in his mouth, seemingly unfazed or oblivious to her jab. "Pretty damned good if you ask me. I'll just walk with you, if you don't mind."

She minded ... a lot. But saying so probably wouldn't help so she didn't bother. As she walked, pulling Manny close to her shoulder, they chatted about the grapes, the various choices they'd made, what had worked, what hadn't. Sophia made mental notes—the more she knew, the better she could school these grapes.

"So how'd you know to do all of that?" Specter asked when they'd finished.

Sophia had forgotten he was there. "The grapes let me know."

The look on Specter's face said he wasn't buying it. "Seriously."

They'd made it through most of the property, at least the part Sophia wanted to see. Manny touched her arm. "Where we going next?"

"Let's do the main sections along the highway. I'll meet you there."

He cast a wary eye at Specter. "You sure?"

"I'll be right behind you."

Sophia turned to Specter, who waited, his cheeks flushed, his eyes flashing his displeasure at being put on hold. "What did you ask?"

"The grapes. How'd you know to make the decisions you did? Nobody else in this end of the Valley trimmed like you did, nor did they leave as many clusters and as much canopy. Why'd you do that?"

"Sometimes you get lucky."

"Luck plays a part in it, for sure. But there's something else, an intangible."

"I've done this a long time, Mr. Specter. I love growing grapes, getting the best out of each plant. Sometimes you just know what they need. And the grapes learn to trust you, but it takes heart, passion, and time."

"I see." He gazed out over the vines. Sunlight thinned the fog and the day had brightened. "This is the screwiest business. In the textile business I could control everything from the quality of the raw material to the brilliance of the finished product. But here, so much is left to chance."

"Not chance really, but we certainly aren't in control. The weather, the grapes, even the bugs and the birds, we can't control any of it. We just mitigate damage and hope to maximize potential and opportunity. It's a work of the heart."

His eyes met hers, and Sophia got the impression he sort of understood the point she was butchering, not that it mattered. If he was in bed with Pinkman, any nuance he developed would be unappreciated.

"Are these grapes going to be an estate vintage? Maybe a Reserve? They're good enough."

"Oh, they're good enough. *All* the grapes I grow for Pinkman are good enough, Mr. Specter." Sophia let her voice take a hard edge. She could handle being unappreciated herself, but for those two idiots to squander such a great harvest, now that was a crime. "But Pinkman will throw them in the hopper with the rest."

"These will end up as Pink's Passion?"

"Yep." Sophia couldn't tell what he was thinking as he stared over her shoulder.

CHAPTER TEN

THE DAYLIGHT WANING, her resolve at an ebb, Sophia eased her truck to a stop at the edge of the forest as the shadow of night slipped across her hilltop. As she'd made the turn off the hard road, Charlie had been drinking beer on his porch. He'd glanced up, wide-eyed as if she'd sicced the Hounds of Hell to nip at his heels, salivating to rip his flesh.

Oh, would that it were so. With her hands gripping the steering wheel, Sophia fought against tears, fought for control in a vain attempt to wrest it from panic and fear. Her body vibrated. Spasms of emotions knifed through her, hacking, cutting, eviscerating.

Weak at the knees and sick with loss, she parked the truck by the house. The sheen of sweat cooled by the evening air had her reaching for the sweater she kept in the truck. Leaving the keys in the ignition and the door open, she fled to the welcoming embrace of her vineyard.

Her grapes.

Blood pounded in her ears. Willing her legs to hold her, running, not seeing, she made it to the middle of the vineyard then sagged to her knees. Pulling her arms into her stomach, she lowered her head as if awaiting the executioner's axe. Despite her sweater, she shivered. Closing her eyes, she turned inward, the only safe place she knew.

Sophia could picture her grandfather wandering among the vines heavy with fruit. Pulling him from the deep recesses of her heart, she sensed his presence. A cool brush against her cheek. A warm flood of comfort, of peace. But a figment, he remained just beyond the probe of her senses. Maybe she imagined him here. Then again, he *had* promised. *Whenever you need me,* cara mia*, close your eyes and I will be right at your elbow.* The deep timbre of his voice, sincere and filled with love, echoed across time. He'd promised. And Sophia had believed. But she'd been a wide-eyed schoolgirl, naïve, trusting of life.

Sophia plunged her hands into the loose dark soil. Lifting handfuls, she let the dirt trickle through her fingers. Dry and rich, the perfect food for her grapes.

Kneeling, sitting back on her heels, connected to the earth, to her past, she leaned her head back. This place. It was a part of her. Her bedrock on which to erect the framework of a future.

Closing her eyes, she lifted her face to catch the cool, damp air as it settled, smothering the lingering warmth of a day long past. Quieting her mind, she listened to the call of a red-shouldered hawk circling high above, using the waning light to shadow his presence, and to the angry buzz of the bees hunting in the wisteria—the cool had yet to drive them back to their hive. Sophia searched the quiet spaces for the peace of her memories.

The earth, warm beneath her, held the late summer heat, reluctant to release it. She breathed deep of the day, the sweetness of the hanging fruit. Ripening dreams, her grandfather had called them.

Dreams. The vessels of hope. Fragile and beautiful, and somehow resilient despite their delicacy, like a porcelain teacup unmarred after a fire when all else around it perished.

Dreams. Like the grapes, each one bursting with promise, filled with the sweetness of life.

She reached up, cradling a cluster of fruit, so heavy, so full, so ... ripe. As she had nurtured her children, Sophia had lavished care on these plants as if feeding her soul. She fingered the canopy—just the right amount of leaves to protect from the sun, but not so much shelter that the fruit was slow to ripen or that too much moisture was allowed to hide, collecting on the fruit. And the cordons like arms branching from the trunks, like arms open inviting an embrace. Each of them had been hand-trimmed after the harvest and guided along the trellis wire to grow strong enough to produce shoots to hold the fruit. Years of decisions, of care, of too much rain, or not enough, of too much heat, or not enough, of over-pruning, or a late bud, of harvesting too late or too soon, of a wrong guess, of a gamble. A game of chance better than any in Las Vegas, but one an oddsmaker would never touch.

And when you got it right, when you beat the odds, that's what made growing grapes so wonderful.

Sophia sank back on her heels. What was she without her dreams? Without her grapes? And Charlie was going to sell them to the highest bidder. And not just any bidder. Butchy Pinkman! Anyone would be better than that man. An ache hot and deep thrummed in her chest. To Sophia selling her grapes would be tantamount to selling her soul.

Behind her, Sophia could hear the clatter of an engine pulling up the grade to her house and she frowned. It sounded like a truck. Dani was the only one of her circle who drove a pickup, but hers hummed with precision and care, unlike this one. This jiggled and clamored like a washing machine with an unbalanced load as it wound up into a high-spin cycle. No one she knew drove a truck that out of whack. And now was most definitely not a good time for company.

Lights speared the encroaching darkness, probing. Sophia crouched down slightly, even though she knew she was sheltered from sight in the vineyard.

The truck eased up to her house, stopping in the dim circle of light cast by the naked bulbs on the porch. Night had doused the lingering light of day. Numb, spent, Sophia watched with a detached curiosity as the driver's door creaked open and one booted and blue-jeaned leg snaked out. The long angular form of a man followed, his back to her as he closed the truck door, then hitched up his pants. His arms at his sides, his posture casual, yet he stood a bit stiff, his shoulders tense and carried a bit too high.

He started toward the house. With one foot on the first step and a hand on the rail, he paused. Leaning slightly to the side, he looked through the window beside the door.

Peeking in her doorway. Who would dare do that? The fact that this man took such liberties set her off a bit. One lone light glowed dimly from the back of the house and Sophia was glad she hadn't turned on the front-room light. The upstairs windows were dark under their dormers. The house appeared as if no one was home.

Hopefully, the man would go away, whoever he was.

Sophia's breath hitched as she caught his profile in the light.

Nico Treviani.

What was he doing showing up here unannounced?

Dani! Sophia bolted to her feet, not pausing to brush the dirt from her knees or hands. Long strides covered the ground between them. "Mr. Treviani. My daughter, she's all right?"

Nico whirled at the voice behind him.

"My daughter?" The lady appeared out of the dark, advancing on him like an avenging angel.

"What?" Nico's thoughts fled, scattering like billiard balls at the break.

"Dani? She's okay? Yes?" Sophia, her maternal instincts on high alert, eyed him with a fierce, protective gaze.

"Dani? His brows pulled together creasing the skin between them. "She's fine, as far as I know. I hope she's home sleeping. She has fruit to drop tonight." Nico hooked a thumb over his shoulder. "After work, I stopped at Cathy Corison's place. She just released the '12. It's stellar, just like the '10. Of course, the '06 is even better. You know her place isn't far."

Cathy's place wasn't close, but Sophia, hands on hips, didn't want to argue so she let him babble. She had no idea why he was here, and he didn't seem in any hurry to tell her, so she took the time to take him in. Tall and broad, with dark black hair which he left long enough to curl over his collar in the back, an angular jaw, high cheekbones and kind eyes, he was ... spectacular... as her friends had said. Sophia really hadn't paid that much attention before, but now that he was standing in front of her... well, she imagined she could feel the pull of masculinity that seemed to ooze from his every pore. Men like Nico Treviani were like pheromone quicksand trapping females, sucking them under until they couldn't breathe. Those kinds of men waded through the world's problems like Moses with his rod parting the Red Sea.

Sophia had no intention of drowning in Nico Treviani. And she knew full well the amazing things Cathy Corison could do with Cabernet, so she didn't need to hear it from Nico Treviani. In fact, she didn't need to hear anything from Nico Treviani. She just wanted him to go away. She couldn't imagine one good reason for him to be standing in her driveway chitchatting about wine.

Nico looked at her as if he could read her thoughts. "I know it's an odd time of day to be dropping in this way."

"Mr. Treviani, the day is long past, thank God. It was a really awful day, and I'm tired." Sophia knew she was being harsh, but really, the man had no right to just appear at her home. But he was here. And he was Dani's boss. Taking a deep breath, Sophia took hold of herself. He clearly was here for a reason, and it must be a good one to wander all this way at this time of night. Dusting off her manners, she swiped a palm on her jeans then stuck out her hand. "Sophia Stone. What can I do for you?"

"I know who you are." Nico took her hand in his. "When I left St. Helena, coming here seemed like a good idea." Nico held her hand a bit longer than a perfunctory introduction required, but he didn't apologize.

"And now?" Sophia eyed him with a jaundiced eye. Nico Treviani's confidence bordered on arrogance, which wasn't an attractive quality. Why would he think it a good idea to drop in unannounced on someone he'd insulted once, maybe twice?

"Now?" Nico sucked in air through his teeth. "Not so much. You look pretty ragged. As you said, it's been a rough day. If you spent it like me and your daughter, then the sun sucked you dry." He lifted his chin, motioning over her shoulder. "And now you're working your own patch."

Sophia half-turned and looked at her vines now softly lit in the moon's glow. "Something to play with. Nothing important."

"As if you don't have enough acreage under vine that you're responsible for."

Sophia pulled her lips into a thin line, then swiped a hand across her forehead, pushing at a few tendrils of hair that had come loose. "Mr. Treviani, why don't you tell me why are you here?"

Nico looked at her for a moment. Chewing on his lip, he clearly warred with himself. Then, decision made, he turned to grab his truck's door handle and wrench it open. Sophia thought he might be leaving, and she felt a twinge of disappointment, which surprised her.

Instead, sliding behind the wheel, Nico leaned across the seat. When he backed out and turned to face her, he had a bottle in his hand, which he thrust toward her. "Because of this. I have to know about this wine." He squinted behind her, taking stock of the vineyard. Two acres, that's what Dani had said. It seemed about right. "It's yours, isn't it?"

A bottle of her wine. The one she and Dani had shared last night. Sophia's façade cracked. Her heart fell. *How could she?* The fatal blow of a deadly day. Sophia wrapped her arms around herself, pulling into herself like a turtle on the highway. "Where did you get that?" Her voice was a choked whisper.

Nico let his hand fall. "I think we both know the answer to that." Sophia looked so stricken he started to reach for her, pull her into a hug—a knee-jerk reaction, ingrained in his Italian upbringing. He stopped himself. Sophia Stone wasn't his sister or his mother or his niece. And he hadn't hugged anyone else in a long time, not with meaning anyway. "Dani's just trying to help you. I'm her boss. I make wine. Some of it's not too bad. It's only natural she asked me."

"She had no right." Sophia almost choked on the words. Swiping at a tear, she turned to gaze over her small vineyard. A lifetime of work. Actually two lifetimes of work. And for what?

Sophia felt Nico put a hand on her shoulder and the warmth of connection bolted through her. She shrugged away.

When he spoke his voice was warm, kind. "It's brilliant wine. Like none I've tasted. Not complete yet, mind you, but really damned awesome."

Sophia turned wide eyes on him. Her lower lip quivered. Then she burst into tears.

This time, Nico went with the hug. Pulling her close, he held her tight, saying nothing. His breath caught as she tucked her face into his shoulder and sobs racked her body. "What's the matter? I don't think you understood. The grapes are amazing. Unique. One of a kind."

Sophia, in a moment of weakness, gave in to the emotions ripping through her. Why did a man's arms have to feel so good around her, so strong, so ... safe? Where was Daniel? She needed him ... and he had died on her. Her father and grandfather as well. All the men she'd counted on, leaned on ... and now they were gone, leaving her alone. Scared. And now two other staggeringly bad men were going to take all she had left. A thought, horrible and traitorous, bolted through her. *Oh they couldn't ....*

She shoved herself off of Nico's chest and out of his grasp, appalled at her own stupidity, staggering back as she used the sleeve of her sweater to wipe her eyes, then her nose. She took large, unsteady steps, like a drunk trying to find her footing. Sweeping her arm in a grand arc toward her grapes, she glared at Nico Treviani, the Golden Boy of the good-ol' boy wine world. "Brilliant, you say!"

Nico reached out a steadying hand as she staggered again. "Yes. Brilliant."

She slapped his hand away and laughed, but it wasn't a happy sound. "Of course, they are. And now the great Nico Treviani comes calling." The look she locked on him was murderous. "Tell me, did your boss send you up here?"

Nico's eyebrows snapped into a frown. "Specter?" He could see the mad in her replacing the hurt.

Sophia pulled her shoulders back, sobering herself, breathing hard with the effort. "That's the one." She took a step, closing the distance between them. "You tell that son of a bitch," she punctuated each word with a poke to his chest, "you tell him I'll die before he makes wine with my grapes. And the same goes for you."

Nico grabbed her hand as she thrust it to hit him again. "Don't. Do. That."

Sophia scoffed. "Or what? You'll take my land, my grapes, my home?"

"What? How would I do that, even assuming I would? You're not making sense," Nico growled.

She shook her head, her lips pulled into a thin line, her eyes hard. "What, do I have 'idiot' tattooed across my forehead? You can't tell me you show up here out of the blue after having insulted my work to any who'll listen." Sophia held up a hand at his wide-eyed expression. "Don't. Whatever you're selling, I'm not buying. I know what you think of Pink's Passion. Well, I gave that ass, Butchy Pinkman, great grapes. And he made swill out of them. *He* made the wine, not me. But," she pointed at the bottle Nico still held, "*I* made that wine."

"I know." Nico waited. One thing his sister had taught him— when a woman got worked up, it was best to let her work herself down. Any other tactic was suicidal.

Sophia took a deep, wracking breath. "Did Charlie call you?"

"I don't know a Charlie."

Sophia put her hands on her hips. "Well, you damn well know

Avery Specter and Butchy Pinkman."

"I can't deny that, even though I'd like to." Nico knew he was being cross-examined and accused of a crime, but he hadn't a clue what it was. "Not that you will believe me, but, I assure you, I hold neither of them in high regard. Do you remember Paul Stevens?"

"Paul?" The single word sounded like a gasp, as if Sophia had the wind knocked out of her. "Oh, poor Paul. He was a good friend."

"Of mine as well." He let her process that a moment then said, "Sophia, why don't you tell me what those two bastards have done?" he asked, although the sinking feeling in the pit of his stomach told him he already knew.

"But you work for Specter Wines." This time when Sophia looked at him, she looked less inclined to bury a knife between his shoulder blades.

"Sometimes necessity makes us crawl into bed with folks we normally wouldn't acknowledge with a nod in passing."

"Tell me about it." Sophia turned inward, weighing her options. She needed an ally. But Nico Treviani? He was probably the last person she should confide in. "Tell me, Mr. Treviani, how can life be so bad for a six-time Vintner of the Year that he has to align with the likes of Avery Specter and Butchy Pinkman?"

"A moment of weakness." Nico's eyes drifted over her shoulder. Emotion pulled the skin tight across the angular planes of his face. "My brother..." He stopped as his voice hitched.

Sophia caught her breath. "Of course." She reached across the distance between them and squeezed his arm, then backed away, retreating again to a safe distance. "I'm so sorry. I remember, now, I apologize. Like I said, it's been one hell of a day. No excuse, though. Paolo, wasn't it?"

Nico, his lips pressed together, nodded. "I'm taking care of his daughters. Do you have any idea how much two females can cost a guy?"

"How old?"

"Thirteen."

Sophia let out a long breath of air through pursed lips. "Oh, Mr. Treviani, they're just getting warmed up."

"Somehow I figured as much. And, if it wouldn't be

presumptuous, would you call me Nico? The only people who call me Mr. Treviani work for me. Besides, you and I are both winemakers."

Sophia still hugged herself and she cocked her head as she thought. "Hardly in the same league."

"Not in the same league?" Nico held up the bottle of her wine. "You're selling yourself short." He glanced over her shoulder, then caught her gaze. "I know it's late and you've had a bad day, so I probably shouldn't ask, but would you mind telling me about your grapes?"

He was a charmer, for sure, Sophia thought as she eyed him. All polished and rehearsed, knowing exactly where her soft spots were. But, as Dani always told her, she needed to trust someone, and he was here, and interested. Besides, what did she have to lose? They were going to take it all anyway. Her arms still crossed, Sophia turned toward her grapes and motioned with a quick hitch of her head for Nico to follow her.

He fell into step as Sophia thought about where to begin. "My grandfather. He and my grandmother had a small vineyard in Friuli. My mother, she hated Italy, hated the grapes, but she sent me every summer to visit."

"Creating another family winemaker."

"Not intentionally. I think she wanted me to hate it all as much as she did. At first, I think she sent me to give herself and my father a break, but then, perhaps she realized my grandfather and I were kindred spirits."

"How did she take your defection?"

Sophia gave him a fleeting wisp of a smile that softened her face. "Not well."

"Families."

"Italian families." Sophia paused, reaching out to cradle a cluster of grapes. "This is the Ribolla, and the basis of all the varietals you see here."

"A noble grape, but somehow lost in history. And very finicky in the vineyard, liking warm days and cool nights."

"Yes, a challenge to grow here in Napa. But up here on the mountain, well, perhaps the grapes think they can see Northern Italy from here. For centuries this grape was protected by Caesar."

"Then it disappeared and was lost."

"First Phylloxera wiped out a lot of it. Then the marketing push to switch to the French varietals like Sauvignon Blanc. And the Italians tend to take their wines far too casually, not wanting to put in the effort to encourage Ribolla to show its many layers and complexity."

"So we end up with Trebbiano."

"Ah, Trebbianno is also a nice grape, good juice, complex and acidic, but it is finicky to grow, like Ribolla. But perhaps both grapes are ready once again to show their brilliance, Mr. Treviani."

"Nico."

"Yes." Sophia ducked her head, then plucked a grape and handed it to him. "With the right encouragement, one can entice history to deliver a gem."

When he bit into the berry, his eyes widened and he gave her a piercing look. Sophia knew that look. And she knew her grapes. For some reason, it pleased her that Nico Treviani did too.

CHAPTER ELEVEN

AS SOPHIA WALKED ON, Nico plucked another grape and popped it into his mouth, then moved to keep abreast. When he bit down on the berry, flavor once again exploded in his mouth. Juice so pure, so simple, yet so subtle in its promise. Like a woman of maturity, battle scarred, but bolder and more challenging, piquing his interest, daring him to drink more deeply.

Like Sophia Stone.

A beautiful woman, with a round, expressive face, she seemed unaware of her effect on him. Of course, tonight her eyes were red, her smile weak, and she looked ... sad, more than a little bit angry, and very much distracted. Yet, even still, she managed to be kind, if a bit cool, although Nico could see it cost her.

As the moonlight danced across her face, her expression changed, softened, the deeper she walked into the vineyard. When he'd held her, she had smelled of the vineyard, ripe grapes, and good juice ... the sweetness of life. This was clearly her place, her heart.

"These grapes are clones of my grandfather's grapes, grafted onto American root stock, as all the grapes in this valley were once European, saved from Phylloxera by combining with American roots. There's something prosaic about that, don't you think?"

"I've tasted at least a thousand different clones. I choose many based on the characteristics inherent to that clone, bouquet and flavor characteristics, berry size, variation within the clusters, or even cluster spacing. But the differences are subtle. Cloning can't explain your grapes."

"In some ways, yes, it can. But not in the fundamental aspects you're referring to." She gave him a challenging look. "When you choose, you are picking among clones of a single varietal: Cabernet, Chardonnay, etc."

The light bulb lit and Nico felt a jolt of excitement. "Your grandfather was a grape breeder."

Sophia smiled. She had a good smile. "Like Pinot and Gouais Blanc are the parents of Chardonnay, these grapes, too, have unique parents."

"So they are new varietals?"

Sophia shrugged slightly. "Perhaps not new. Until two hundred years ago the cross-pollination required to create a new varietal happened as a random act of nature. Then we started getting into the mix. Today, most of the wine is made from perhaps one hundred or fewer varietals with only fifteen of them being popular among the majority of wine drinkers."

"And these are your grandfather's varietals?"

"Each one represents a combination he thought would be interesting. Ribolla cross-pollinated with, well, just about anything, as far as I can tell." Sophia touched each plant, testing a grape, plucking at a dried leaf—gentle caresses a parent would lavish on a child. "Most of them are his original combinations, but I've done a bit myself. I enjoy introducing the grapes, seeing how they get along."

Nico smiled, then felt his face redden when she caught him looking.

Sophia arched a single eyebrow at him. "You think that's funny?"

"Not at all. Your daughter knows you well. I said something similar, or rather I started to and she finished my sentence. I asked her where she learned that. She started to tell me, but then she clammed up."

"She didn't tell you about me and my wine?"

"She told me some other things about you and I connected the dots. But, no, she didn't tell me the wine was yours. Nor did she tell me about these vines." He gave her an imploring look. "Will she be allowed to live? I have a vested interest."

"Jury's still out."

Nico detected less of a sharp edge in Sophia's voice and her shoulders relaxed into a more comfortable posture. "You taught her well."

"Great raw material. She's a bit impetuous." Sophia gave him a sideways glance. "You two should get along just fine."

If Dani was anything like her mother, Nico would enjoy the challenge of their working relationship, not that it would be easy. Of course, that much he'd pretty much figured out already—that's why he hired her; she wasn't afraid of him. He motioned to the plants behind them. "So that section was all Ribolla?"

"Hmmm."

"What's this section?"

"A bit of Erbaluce, of all things, with a Gruner. I've got a real mixture here, Petite Arvine, Fendant, Garganega. I've even messed around with blending some of them with a hint of your hated Trebbiano."

"*My* hated Trebbiano?" Nico feigned insult.

Sophia breezed on. "My grandfather kept poor notes, which really doesn't matter—today we wouldn't be able to find the base stock he used anyway. Nature keeps reinventing itself, with slight variations each time, with or without our help."

"So how do you know the grape's heritage? That's important for making wine."

"I don't, not really. Oh, I had some DNA testing done at UC-Davis, but it was really for curiosity's sake. And a bit for me." She gave him a shy glance. "I thought that if I knew all there was to know about the grapes, I'd understand my grandfather better."

"Do you?"

"It turns out I knew him all along." She touched her heart. "In here. And I knew his grapes here as well. And knowing their origin is not important to making the wine. It's not the varietal ..."

"It's the particular grape each year." Nico finished that thought. "I know. How many different varietals do you have?" He pinched off a grape and popped it into his mouth. This time the response was an instant salivary stimulation on the sides of his tongue. "Wow, so different, yet so fabulous in the ways you would think a raw combination of those grapes would be. How'd you get them from Italy to Napa Valley?"

"My husband, Daniel, it was his idea. For our tenth anniversary he took me to Friuli. We found my grandparents' old vineyard, overgrown and left to ruin. We took cuttings and smuggled them back here."

"No one is farming the old place?"

"No."

"Who owns it? Is it still in the family?"

"I have no idea. I assume, if it was, I'd know it. My mother was an only child, as am I."

"You do know it's illegal to smuggle plants into this country."

Sophia bristled. "That's how every single plant in this entire valley got here. American grapes are only good for grape juice, not wine."

Nico enjoyed the bit of fire in her tone. "What, you don't like Concord or Catawba?"

She shut him down with a slant-eyed sideways look.

"What does your husband do? Is he in the business also?" Nico was surprised that he felt slightly disappointed by the mention of a husband. If she wore a ring, he should've noticed it. Apparently there were plenty of smarter men than he who had snapped up all the interesting women. Not that he was interested. Another woman in his life was the last thing he needed.

"My husband." Sophia's voice tightened down. "No, he was an engineer. He was a bit like my mother. Neither of them took the wine business seriously. I think he rather humored me. But it turned out to be rather important."

"How so?"

"He died." Sophia looked into the distance as if looking back in time. "I needed a way to make a living. It turns out I have a bit of knack for getting the most out of grapevines."

Now Nico felt like a heel. "I'm so sorry."

When Sophia looked at him, her eyes looked stricken. "It's been five years, but it's still hard. For Dani especially. She was Daddy's little girl."

Not just for Dani, Nico thought. It didn't take much insight to see how hard it still was for Sophia. "He was a lucky man to have two wonderful women love him so much."

"You are kind. He made all of this possible, this house, Dani, her brother Trey, these grapes." Sophia hitched as her son's name rolled off her tongue. She hadn't talked to him in a while. When Daniel died, Trey had retreated. And, despite her best efforts, he remained beyond her reach for reasons of his own, something Sophia wrestled with daily. She pulled herself back. "We came back from Italy with twelve different varietals. Two didn't grow well here. Of the remaining ten, I've winnowed them down to the seven best. As you can imagine, nurturing a new varietal from the Old World in the New is a labor of love. That one there was one of the most difficult to convince to give me good fruit." Sophia pulled the band that bound her hair into a tail at the nape of her neck, letting her hair fall free. Casually, as if by rote, and unaware of the effect it was having on him, she ran her fingers through the shoulder-length strands, talking as she smoothed. She raised her face slightly, exposing the soft flesh of her neck, as she re-clipped her hair. "There was this one I tried. It was so bad, when I pulled the vines, I didn't even dare compost them." When she realized Nico had stopped walking she turned and looked at him. "What?"

Nico swallowed hard and tamped down his growing interest in Sophia Stone. No more women. Not ever. "Nothing." He closed the distance quickly. "These grapes are even more special than I thought."

"One of a kind. As I said, I have some idea of what my nonno put together, but not all of it. Besides, you know how grapes are; genetic mutations make it such that you can have two identical clones, and they will behave differently and have different characteristics."

"Like my twins."

"Well, I hadn't really thought of it that way, but yes, like twins." Sophia stopped in front of what looked like the opening of a cave into the hillside. "Are you really having so much trouble with your nieces?"

"I have the sheriff on speed-dial."

Sophia didn't seem surprised. "After Daniel died, Dani gave me holy hell. She was sixteen and more than capable of making my life even more miserable than it was. But teenagers are just big children with the judgment of earthworms. She was grieving and didn't know how to handle it. Your nieces are doing the same. Just love them …

and keep them busy. Don't give them time to get into mischief."

"How'd you keep her busy?"

"I took her to work with me." Sophia stopped in front of an opening in the side of the hill.

"*You* taught her how to drive the forklift." An accusation not a question.

"It was that or have her try it herself. Wait here. This is the part you'll like." Then she disappeared into the opening, swallowed by the darkness.

She was wrong ... he enjoyed all of it.

Light flared and Nico could see the entrance more clearly, so he stepped inside the cave. Flickering light danced across the walls as Sophia lit several candles from the one she held, placing each in holders on the stone walls. His eyes darted over the rudimentary equipment, a crusher/de-stemmer, a siphon system to off-load the juice. Plastic primary fermentation barrels. A handpress to churn the must. Then two stainless steel secondary fermentation vessels. He was surprised to see the sophisticated cooling system on each... not a low-dollar item. "Oh, you got the bug all right."

Sophia blew out the candle she held as she returned to stand in front of him. "I started small. Daniel made fun of me, but my passion for winemaking grew."

"I can see that."

"I do have a confession to make." Sophia stood tall and lifted her chin in challenge. "I'm not trained in any of this. No fancy degrees. Not in winemaking nor in viticulture."

"The grapes don't know that." Nico followed the power cables. "I didn't see any outside lines brought to the cave. What's your power source?"

"Solar." Sophia eyed him as if he was a selection in the freak show with Barnum and Bailey.

"And what do you do with the heat you pull off the tanks during fermentation?"

"Heat the water we use at the house and here to wash dishes, take a bath, clean up." Nico wandered through the equipment, his trained eye missing nothing. "How deep is the cave?"

"A few hundred yards."

"Temperature?"

"Even 55 degrees year 'round."

"Pretty cool."

"Yes, but these grapes don't need a hurried fermentation—the complexity is already there. I do ferment at a higher temp, though. The tunnels will be great for storage, when ..." She trailed off.

Nico kept her focused on her wine. "Any malo?"

"Not too much. I like the tart, the bite. I just want to round the edges."

Nico focused, working through the possibilities. He lifted the bottle he'd been holding all this time. "May I?"

"Sure." Sophia grabbed one glass. Pausing, she then grabbed another and placed them on the worktable in the center of the room.

Nico poured. "Beautiful glasses."

"Cut crystal from the Old Country." Sophia held her glass carefully. She waited for Nico to take the first sip of his.

The brightness and complexity made his mouth water and yearn for more. "You are a romantic, Sophia Stone."

Sophia savored a sip. Nico was wrong—it was not brilliant, but the hint was there, like a tapestry missing only the golden thread. "If wine is about anything it is surely about romance, Mr. Treviani."

"Nico," he scolded. "The grapes must be courted and wooed, is that it?"

"You are making fun of me."

"Not at all." Nico took another sip, swishing and savoring before swallowing. "In fact, I quite agree. The lab is no place to make a great wine."

"No, but if consistency from vintage to vintage is important, then the lab is a place to get it."

"Agreed. Have you tried blending some Trebbiano?"

"Your hated Trebbiano?" Sophia set her glass down. Tonight she felt like slugging down the whole bottle and then not stopping. So one glass would be a step out onto a slippery slope she didn't want to slide down. That kind of coping was in her past.

"While it's rather uninspiring on its own, it has a good mouth feel, a longer finish. And, if you find the right juice, I think it would blend nicely with what you have here, leaving the characteristics you like but bringing up those you don't. And your instincts are good."

"If I have to blend from someone else's vineyard and can't control the quality and annual variation, I want to source locally. At least that way I can keep a hand in. You don't happen to know of any local Trebbiano growers, do you?"

"Not offhand, but I'll ask around. Sometimes what other folks are doing surprises you."

Sophia's face closed into a worried frown. "That much I know."

"May I take another bottle of your wine with me? I'd like to play with some blends."

Sophia shook her head. "It's pointless now."

She looked so defeated—Nico wanted to hurt the men who had done that to her. But he needed the story first. "You never know. You might have a solution. But, regardless, you can make that perfect blend, that perfect wine. And, no matter what, you'll always have that."

"That will take a minor miracle." She looked like she was warming to his enthusiasm.

"I've been told occasionally I have worked a miracle or two with some grapes." Nico didn't know where he was going with all of this or even if he could solve her problems with the wine and whatever the other problem was. He just knew he didn't want to leave. And he didn't want to see her sad.

Sophia eyed him with her head tilted to one side. "You do seem to understand the art. What could it hurt?" She disappeared into the darkness of the cave, returning with a bottle, which she dusted off and handed to him.

"The art, yes. But with blending, sometimes the science helps."

Sophia fingered a locket on a chain at her neck. "I wouldn't know. You're holding the best my art can produce."

"And it is masterful." Nico held out his glass for a bit more wine. When Sophia had filled it, he held it up to the light, admiring. Then his gaze once again captured Sophia's. "So do you trust me enough to tell me what Pinkman and Specter have done to you?"

CHAPTER TWELVE

SOPHIA STRODE INTO GILLWOODS CAFE promptly at five minutes until eight the following morning. Heads swiveled her way when the bells on the door announced her arrival. She nodded to a few acquaintances and greeted a couple of others warmly.

At this hour of the morning, the diner was clearing out, the field hands fortified for a long day in the sun. Harvest was rolling down on them with the speed and ferocity of a winter storm off the sea.

Only a smattering of tourists, conspicuous in their city clothes, dotted the banquet tables against each wall. Sophia claimed the community table in the middle, grateful to find it empty. She had no sooner settled herself than Gracie appeared at her elbow, the fingers of one hand threaded through the handles of three coffee mugs. In the other hand she held a pot of steaming coffee.

A solid woman with a matter-of-fact manner, Gracie had been there as long as the doors had been open. In fact, Sophia didn't think the place would survive without her acerbic wit and seamless competence. "The others joining you?" She didn't wait for an answer. Instead, she placed the mugs at two other places and filled them. "If you don't mind me sayin' so, you look a bit ragged. Been working too hard?"

Sophia gave her a wan smile. "You know me."

"There's always three of ya' but,"—Gracie snaked her hand into the pocket on her apron and pulled out a fourth mug—"I brought a spare in case of Miss Dani and how she might be comin'."

"Not today, but so sweet of you to remember. Thank you."

The screen on the front door banged open as Maggie Tremayne stepped through, her head on a swivel. Sophia waved and Maggie made a beeline, a smile splitting her round face and wrinkling her nose. A mop of short black curls offset her porcelain skin and huge brown eyes that now shone with equal parts mirth and worry. Although fifteen years separated them, Maggie and Sophia had been friends so long neither remembered exactly how they'd met.

As Gracie trundled off toward the kitchen, Maggie jerked out the chair across from Sophia and plopped herself down. "That old battle axe. Isn't she about ready for Social Security or the old folks' home?"

Sophia took a tentative sip of her coffee, cupping the mug in both hands. "If you'd just be a bit nicer to her, I'm sure she'd be the same."

"Yeah, just the same." Maggie eyed Sophia's coffee with ill-disguised lust. With a glance at Gracie's back, Maggie grabbed her mug and went to pour herself some coffee, then returned with a self-satisfied grin.

Sophia watched Gracie work the tables with quiet efficiency. "Mags, you never know what people are dealing with, what secrets they hide behind their smiles. It never hurts to be nice."

"Secrets?" Maggie gave a derisive snort then shook her head, retreating for a moment. Her eyes unfocused, as if peering into the past, she took a gulp of her coffee. Her face turned red and she started spluttering.

Sophia offered her a glass of water.

"Christ Almighty, that's hot." Maggie caught an ice cube in her mouth and sucked on it.

"It's always hot."

Maggie tested her coffee again, this time being a bit more wary, but not much. "You really think anyone can have a secret in this place?" Her tone sounded a bit defensive.

Yes, we all have secrets. As she tried to marshal her thoughts, Sophia caught the defensive undercurrent in Maggie's voice. She knew she had to tread carefully. Lack of sleep worked against her. Most of the night she'd tossed and turned, working through possible solutions only to end where she'd begun—utterly defeated. "Ah, Mags, you know what I'm saying. Nobody gets through life without some dark hours. Sometimes a smile is all it takes to lighten their load, that's all."

Maggie didn't look like she totally accepted Sophia's premise, but, to Sophia's relief, she didn't argue. Instead, she changed the subject. "Man, you look like forty miles of bad road. That ass Pinkman keep you up half the night?"

"I guess you could say that."

"So, spill it. Who died?"

Sophia was grateful for her friends, even though Maggie could be as grating as sandpaper on sunburned skin. Whenever one of them had a problem, all they had to do was put out a call and the others came running. Sophia had dialed that number only once before ... when Daniel died. And, as Maggie had put it at the time, that was "like the top rung of the bad-shit ladder," so it wasn't hard to understand the worry on Maggie's face now.

Nor the pinched look on Annalise's face as well as she eased into the chair next to Maggie. "Maggie, a little bit of grace."

Annalise, with her blonde hair, icy green eyes, and perfectly-put-together appearance always seemed to chafe Maggie like a wool shirt. When Sophia met Annalise, she was dressed as now in Ferragamos, slacks, and a pressed cotton shirt with an Hermes scarf wrapped perfectly at her throat—style the Frenchwoman wore like a birthright. But instead of attending a dinner party, she'd been picking up her yard after her dog. She certainly made a statement in St. Helena where a new pair of jeans passed as high fashion. At some point in the past, Annalise had practiced psychology, but she didn't talk about it much.

Gracie appeared and filled Annalise's mug, then shot Maggie a dirty look as she moved to check on her other tables.

"What is it with everybody?" Maggie complained, her voice on the edge of a whine.

"You're the common denominator," Annalise offered with a smile.

"Thank you, Dr. Phil." Maggie turned her big eyes on Sophia. "Look, I'm sorry. This sorta thing has my heart about to leap out of my chest. I'm dyin' here." She reached across the table and grabbed Sophia's arm. "Just tell me who to shoot. And I didn't mean that dying thing like literally, or anything. That was insensitive, and I'm sorry. And, as usual, you are right." She included Annalise with a look. "You both are right." Maggie leaned back, settling in. "But, I left in the middle of milking to get all the way over here, and if I don't either get back relatively soon or call Devlin to go finish up, I'm gonna have some seriously pissed off heifers and goats. The goats are the worst. When they get upset they'll eat the paint right off your car. Don't ask me how I know that."

Sophia took a deep breath, then motioned for Gracie, who came trotting. "Gracie, can we please have a platter of your best, most decadent muffins and pastries?"

"Which ones?"

"You choose."

Gracie looked pleased. "Yes'um."

Maggie nudged Annalise. "We are about to commit capital-level carb-icide. This must be serious shit."

"It is." Sophia eyed her friends, then told them everything she knew from her visit by Charlie Vespers to Nico Treviani showing up practically in the dark of night, unannounced and uninvited.

Silence fell over the table when she'd finished. Sophia grabbed a chocolate-filled croissant off the top of the pastry pile in the middle of the table. One bite and she knew Gracie had her pegged. She watched with interest as both Maggie and Annalise processed what she'd told them. Knowing them as well as she did, they were working through all the possible solutions. She could've told them short of homicide there weren't any, but she let them get there on their own.

Sophia closed her eyes, anticipating the sugar rush, waiting for it. Pink had painted the eastern horizon when sleep had finally overtaken her. Two hours of sleep was too little to run too far on, but right now she had enough adrenaline to more than compensate for the deficit. Later it would catch up with her. But that was later. Right now she needed to talk and to have somebody listen, the hug of friendship. How men got by with so few intimate friends, she hadn't a clue, and she felt sorry for them. Friends ... life would be impossible without them.

A hurtling body flew around the partition, skidding into the chair next to Sophia. Before she had a chance to react, two arms encircled her, pulling her tight. She knew that hug, and it melted her brave face. Sophia fought the tears as Dani held on.

"Mom! Shit!"

Sophia clung to her daughter, willing this dollop of the sweetness of life to fortify her. "Aren't you supposed to be at work, honey?" she whispered, trying to focus on something else, anything else. "I don't want you to lose your job."

Dani pulled back just enough so Sophia could bring her face into focus. "I got to sleep in a little. We dropped fruit most of the night. When I showed up, Mr. Treviani told me what happened. I about shot him for heading up the mountain with my bottle of your wine and ratting me out. I'm really sorry, Mom. I never meant to break your trust. I was just trying to help."

Sophia looked at her daughter all wide-eyed and apologetic. She should scold her, tell her what a betrayal that was, but she couldn't work herself up to it. Dani had given her the push she needed, too late, but that wasn't Dani's fault. For a moment, she'd felt hope and excitement at what could've been. "I know."

Relief flooded Dani's face, and her words came in quick breaths as if she was sprinting to the finish. "Then he told me what those bastards think they're going to get away with. I had to find you. Your grapes, Mom."

The magnitude of her loss crushed Sophia's voice and she felt small, powerless... insignificant. Was there any worse feeling?

"How'd you find us?"

Dani gave her a look. "Give me some credit."

"Did Mr. Treviani give you permission to leave?"

"Like he could stop me." Dani gave her one of those you-can't-be-serious looks. "But, not to worry, he's the one who told me you would need me and I should go."

"Seriously?" Maggie asked. "Contrary to the vast bulk of local scuttlebutt and hearsay, the great Nico Treviani has a heart?"

Dani threw a look at her. "He's not as bad as you think. He's demanding, autocratic, sharp, and can be an ass when he needs to—"

"—but other than that, he's a peach." Maggie didn't even try to hide the sarcasm.

"Yeah, he is. I think he just doesn't want anybody to know it."

"So now the kid is an expert on men." Maggie rolled her eyes.

"The clear eyes of youth," Annalise said quietly.

Not even Maggie had an answer to that.

Sophia unwrapped her daughter's arms, then motioned for another mug of coffee. "Like I said, he seemed nice, sincere."

Dani grabbed the java, holding it tightly in both hands like it was her caffeine lifeline to functionality. Sophia could so relate. Dani seemed to be weathering the ravages of sleeplessness with aplomb. Youth. Why did only the old fully appreciate its blessings? And, today, numbed by life, if Sophia felt anything, it was old. She worked on her croissant as the other two gave Dani the high points, bringing her up to speed.

When they'd finished, Dani lasered her with eyes that were sharp pinpoints of focus. "Your grapes, Mom. We've got to save those. What did Mr. Treviani say?"

"Not a lot. He listened. He didn't have any answers. But he left me with the impression I don't ever want to be on his bad side." Sophia stared into her coffee. "You guys remember Paul Stevens?"

Silence and sadness fell over the table, a smothering blanket of dissonance. Sophia didn't need to ask; everyone knew Paul's story, even Dani.

"That bastard Pinkman." Sophia felt Paul's loss on some primal, fundamental level, like an ache in her soul.

"And now he's doing it again," Maggie said, her voice growing louder.

Normally, Sophia would be worried that their conversation would get back to her boss, but not anymore. The only thing she worried about was being there to testify against him when he met his Maker. Eternal damnation in the fires of Hell was way too good for Butchy Pinkman. "It's all perfectly legal. I'm the fool for planting my grapes on land I don't own. Apparently, once they are planted they become part of the land. Charlie Vespers can sell all of it to whomever he likes and my vines go with it."

"What you do is what you get." Annalise leaned forward. "There are more important things than a few dollars one way or the other."

"Karma *is* a bitch." Maggie said, looking as if she had personal experience.

"I thought he'd never get in bed with men like those two." Sophia held up her mug and Gracie rushed over with a full pot. "If the commercial growers buy up everything, they explode the property values and everyone, like Paul ..."

"... and us, Mom." Dani sounded more scared and hurt than angry.

She wrapped an arm around her daughter. "Yes, and us. We all will be driven out, not only by the prices, which are stratospheric, but by the taxes as well."

"I was sure you owned your place." Annalise, the non-political one, steered the conversation back to the immediate problem. She was good at that—probably all those years as a psychologist. And, as the newest member of the group, she knew less history than Maggie.

"No, Daniel didn't want to buy. When we made the decision I should stay home with the kids, he didn't want to get buried under a mortgage."

"You mean when *he* made the decision you were to stay home." Maggie's voice hardened.

Maggie and Daniel had never gotten along, something that had surprised Sophia. She shot Maggie a look, shutting her down. "Rents were cheaper back then."

"I don't mean to pry; I'm just problem-solving," Annalise, said, her discomfort obvious.

"Throw it out there. I don't have any secrets. And I need your perspectives and wise counsel. God knows I've thought through everything I can think of."

"Money. You need money," Annalise said.

"Brilliant deduction," Maggie said. Her arms crossed, she slumped like a berated child.

Sophia focused on Annalise. "Ignore her. Stress brings out her worst qualities. Even assuming I could get Charlie to break what he says is an airtight contract, I couldn't even come close to qualifying for a loan. My salary is good, but do you really think my boss would sit still and help me buy the property out from under him? Besides, can't you see the writing on the wall? My job is history. I've given him a great vineyard and taught his guys how to cultivate the grapes for the qualities Pinkman wants."

"So getting fired is the product of competence?" Maggie asked.

"The corporate way," Sophia answered unsure when the wine industry had lost its farmer's values, that sense of shared values and mutual support.

"Pinkman," Dani scoffed. "With that man's nose, a dog couldn't find a bone in broad daylight."

"True." Sophia didn't expound on all the other "qualities" Pinkman lacked, although a verbal evisceration of the pig would be satisfying. "But the fact is I'm now superfluous, especially since he wants my grapes. And, I'm sure he's not too happy with me calling in, not sick, but pissed-off today... and just when the grapes are in the most critical stage."

"You called in pissed-off?" Dani sounded ... proud.

Somehow that made Sophia sit a bit straighter. "I know that's like throwing a dart at a dragon—it made me feel better, but it's only going to irritate the dragon. Not that it really matters." Sophia eyed a second croissant. She resisted for a moment then gave in. But no chocolate this time.

"What about raising the money?" Annalise asked.

"Same problem I have now. It's becoming abundantly clear that, if I don't own my grapes, I can't control them. What happened to the Napa I used to know?"

No one had an answer to that either.

Sophia's cell phone played its normal tune, Colbie Callait's "*Try.*" She didn't recognize the number. "Hello? Yes, this is Sophia Stone." She listened for a moment. "I see. And where are you?" Another moment. "Are you sure?" A pause. "Okay, I'm on my way." She stuffed the phone in her back pocket and took a moment to look around the table. "I've got to go."

CHAPTER THIRTEEN

AMPED ON A CURIOUS MIX of adrenaline, exhaustion, and alcohol—well not so much alcohol itself but the perfection of the blend in front of him—Nico Treviani found it almost impossible to sit still. All night he'd been bent over beakers, engrossed in finding the perfect mixture. Totally absorbed, he vaguely remembered Dani sticking her head in the door, their brief conversation, then the sound of her wheels spinning on the gravel. The passage of time had only just now really registered when he called Sophia Stone.

One butt cheek perched on the three-legged stool, his right leg bracing him, his left foot bouncing on the lowest rung, he fidgeted, waiting for her to come. Would she be pleased? For some odd reason, that was important to him.

At the sound of footsteps approaching, he turned toward the door.

Sophia stopped just inside the doorway as she looked around. "Do you make this much of a mess when you cook at home?"

"A Treviani family trait, I'm afraid." Nico let his gaze travel the room, seeing it through her eyes. Beakers of wine, glasses, test tubes and all the other lab paraphernalia littered virtually every inch of every lab table in the place. He'd been oblivious. "We get pretty focused."

"Apparently. I came as quickly as I could. What's all this about?"

Nico motioned for her to come closer. "I'll show you." He pulled a stool next to his.

"You haven't put Mr. Specter and Mr. Pinkman out of my misery have you?" Sophia took the stool next to Nico, hooking her feet around the legs.

"I'd like to think I'm gallant but not self-destructive."

"Apparently, you have more restraint than I do. Dani has secured all the weapons at the house."

Nico paused. "Seriously?"

She gave him a benign look. "From the looks of things around here, you've been spending time on wine we won't get to make. What's the point?"

Nico moved three beakers, lining them up in front of Sophia. "Sometimes, when problems seem insurmountable, I've found moving forward, accomplishing something helps."

"But ..."

He took her hand in his and the power of the connection warmed through him. She looked so tired and sad, with a hint of wishful homicide. He knew the feeling, but, really, he simply wanted to see her smile. He'd seen hints but not the full wattage, and he'd bet it would touch a spark to a taper in even the darkest heart. "Sophia, I know the problem. And I don't have an answer. I wish I did. You have no idea how much I wish I did. Perhaps in time."

"We have less than thirty days."

"Not much, but it's something. But, in the meantime, I had to see how great your wine could be. Something positive in this whole mess. Don't you want to know?"

Sophia's eyes drifted to the beakers, and she caught her lower lip between her teeth, the skin between her eyes bunched with indecision. "I don't know. Is it a good thing to feel the crushing weight of what could've been?" Sophia pulled her hand free and stared at the beakers.

"Or the lightness of knowing you actually pulled it off." Nico let her think for a moment as he gathered his own thoughts. He hadn't really thought about wine, not like this, at least not in a long time. When had wine become a burden? "You know how when you know you are going to have an amazing meal? My mother's lasagna, let's say. And the anticipation has your mouth watering?"

"Well, never having had your mother's lasagna, I'm not sure it can compare to mine. But, okay, I'll buy in. Anticipation is almost better than realization."

"Exactly. *Especially* with my mother's lasagna." Nico sensed Sophia was relaxing. Her posture loosened, her face softened, some of the angry tension leaving weariness in its stead. "So you sit down, barely able to control yourself as the plates are served."

Sophia smiled, clearly warming to the story. "This is where my mother would make us all bow our heads and she would make up some interminable grace."

"My mother, too." Nico backed off his stool, enthusiasm propelling him. "So, finally, after dragging out the moment of that first taste as long as possible, you fork a bite, lifting it. The aromas make you salivate with anticipation. Delicately, reverently, you slip the cheesy, gooey mess into your mouth. Flavor explodes and you groan in delight."

"I don't groan over food." A smile played with Sophia's lips.

Nico wanted to ask her what exactly would make her groan, but thought that had a bit too much creep factor for the moment, perhaps for forever. Still ... "You haven't had my mother's lasagna. And it's as succulent and satisfying as you could ever dream it to be. Mouthwatering and able to bring aunts, uncles, and lesser cousins to tears."

Sophia grinned. "But not my great Aunt Sophia." At Nico's wide-eyed look, Sophia nodded. "Yes, sad but true, I was named after her, and she would find fault with manna from heaven created by God Almighty herself."

"Herself, is it?"

"Please, do you really think a man could conjure the beauty of the universe?"

Nico had never really thought of God in a gender sort of way, but thinking he might be female did explain a lot. "Point taken. We're more appreciators than conjurers." Sophia rewarded him with a smile, perhaps not full-wattage, but it lit him up inside. "Okay, we'll leave Aunt Sophie out of it."

"Sophie. You'd better watch out for a lightning bolt."

Nico stalked behind his stool, a few steps one direction, then a few steps back, using grand gestures as he told his story. He hadn't felt this free, this much himself, in a long time. "So, this lasagna is so good that all true Italians would be moved to say three Hail Marys and several Our Fathers, then sell their second sons to the Church to get their hands on the recipe."

Sophia leaned back. Lacing her fingers together, she caught her right knee as a counterweight. "A bit of hyperbole, but I'm still with you."

"So you take that first bite, letting it sort of ooze around your mouth, hitting all the sides of your tongue as you savor the rush of flavors. Then you take another bite. Then one more." He stopped in front of Sophia, his arms away from his sides, his palms facing her. "And then what happens?"

"I don't know. You fight a sibling for the last piece?"

"No." Nico let his arms drop and the energy dissipate from his voice. "You don't taste it anymore. After those first couple of incredible, transcendent bites it's not the same, is it?"

Sophia shook her head.

Nico straddled his stool. "Wine's like that. So you see, it's not in the selling, or the producing ..."

"It's the making," Sophia said, finishing his sentence. "And your first introduction, your first sip, is like the blush of young love. While everything that follows can be sublime, it's not the same as that first flutter."

"Exactly." Nico eyed her with new appreciation. "I knew you would understand what I meant. Wine, grapes, they are here." He touched his heart. "Not here." He tapped his forehead.

"Mr. Treviani..."

"Nico."

"Nico, contrary to popular scuttlebutt, you are a softie."

When he laughed, it was a deep rumble of joy that vibrated through Sophia like thunder off of a refreshing fall storm. He was mesmerizing, his passion so apparent. Who could resist? Certainly not Sophia. No one, not Daniel, not even her martyred grandfather, had shared her same deep passion for grapes.

"Don't let it get around; I'll be ruined."

"I can't promise anything." Sophia figured men like Nico Treviani were best kept a bit off balance.

"And here I'd been told you are nothing but sweetness and light."

"I am a woman, Mr...." Sophia dipped her head feeling suddenly shy. "Nico. Dealing with me could hardly be that simple or benign."

"A woman indeed."

Sophia felt her cheeks pinking at the warmth in his eyes. This was nuts! She was about to lose everything and she was mooning around, flirting like a schoolgirl. But it felt good, fun in a not-so-fun world. "Okay, show me what you've come up with."

Nico looked pleased, but he didn't look surprised, as if he'd known she'd capitulate.

"Are you that used to getting your way?" she asked.

"Me?" He sounded genuinely surprised. "Good God, no. Between my mother, my sister, and my two nieces, even with Paolo's help, us men were regularly flattened and left for dead before we even knew what hit us. So, I have learned a bit of ..."

"Manipulation?"

"Harsh," he countered, matching her smile. "I prefer to think of it as persuasion. And you were an easy mark."

"Really." Frost dusted the warmth in her tone, prolonging the banter. Although her skills were rusty, she found a bit of remembered joy.

"No real convincing necessary. One thing I can do is recognize a true winemaker when I meet one."

Sophia flushed at the compliment ... again.

Nico arranged the beakers in front of her, each one filled with a golden liquid. "I tried about a million blends. I ran through every white I had on hand and even a couple of the reds. Pinot Noir came the closest, but it runs thin if not handled just right, so I thought it would be too much of a handful, sort of like a couple of teenagers who try on new personalities by the hour looking for one that fits."

"How long have you been here?" Sophia let go of her knee and leaned forward.

"Since I left you last night."

"You left two thirteen-year-old girls on their own all night?" The thought left Sophia with a cold sweat.

"Good God, no. They'd lay waste to the northern end of the county. They are with my mother." Nico turned back to the beakers. "Like I said, I tried everything, all of it locally sourced as you told me you wanted. These are the three I think are the best." He swept his arm toward a side bar. "I have some others over there you are welcome to try, and you should because they have unique characteristics and unique deficiencies. Blending is an art; it can't be forced. Either the juices meld into something with the major characteristics we are looking for, or they don't."

"Why three? I thought you would narrow it down to the best."

"It is not my wine. And my palate is different from yours. These are your grapes, and the blend should be what you've been imagining it could be."

Sophia was touched. No one had ever acted as if her opinion mattered. No one had let her decide. No, they had just told her what to do. Even Daniel. "I don't know. With choice comes responsibility. I know good grapes, but I'm not sure my expertise extends to their juice."

"You look like the kind of winemaker who can handle the pressure." His voice was warm, kind. Sophia luxuriated as it wrapped around her like a great hug. "Not everyone will love your wine. You aren't making the wine for everyone. Do you know who you are making it for, Sophia?"

She straightened, pushing the hair off her forehead. "I'm making it for myself."

"Exactly!"

"So here are the three. Of course, I'm playing with finished wine here and the blending will be more nuanced, and cleaner with the younger wine, then the blend will have time to finish as a whole. Tell me what you think." He moved a dish with some unleavened crackers toward her, then pushed himself back, out of the way.

Sophia didn't have it in her anymore to remind him that there would be no more young wine, at least not for them, not with these grapes. Taking Nico's little lesson to heart, she decided to be positive. She was willing to try anything, so she smiled—a patch for the hole in her heart—and reached for the first beaker, pouring a bit into one of the wine glasses Nico had gathered to the side. "I feel a bit like Goldilocks."

Nico didn't say anything, leaving her to the business at hand. He pushed a pad of paper and a pen within her reach as Sophia began. She cleaned her palate with a cracker and closed her eyes for a moment, remembering what she wanted from this wine, what she knew it could become. Then she worked through each beaker, analyzing the characteristics of each, cleansing in between. After savoring each sip, she spit the wine out so the alcohol wouldn't dull her senses. Testing, tasting, looking, and smelling, she made notes. The meticulous attention to detail really wasn't necessary. While all three were very good, only one was brilliant, and she'd known it from the first sip. "The last one." She nodded briskly, then turned to meet Nico's intense gaze. "The others are very good and amazingly different. Blending can so enhance certain characteristics until the wine has a distinct personality from the others, although they share a common base."

"But you like the third one best. Why?"

"It's elegant, with that rounded body I was looking for. Yet, the acidity, the freshness, the tart citrus notes shine. And despite the body, the finish is brisk and clean. It's perfect. What did you blend?"

"A hint of Chard, a mountain Chard so with some *terroir* similar to your grapes. And some Chenin-Blanc."

"Really? I wouldn't have thought those would marry well with my grapes."

"You never know. Sometimes the best blends seem at first blush to be the most unlikely."

Sophia thought there was an undercurrent in that comment, but she wasn't sure. Men had always been a bit inscrutable to her. Perhaps that was part of her failure with her son, a hole in her heart. Clearly, he was struggling, but she had no idea how to reach him.

"What are you thinking?" Nico asked.

"Hmmm?"

"You went away."

Sophia slumped, her hands on her knees, her feet braced on the lower rung of the stool. "The last twenty-four hours have pretty much defeated me."

"But you now see what your wine can be." He reached out to touch her, put a hand on her arm, but pulled his hand back. "We need to make this wine. When do you plan to drop your fruit?"

"Soon. But why should we bother? Say it turns out great and really finds a market. Then what?"

"We've shown them what we can do, what your grapes are capable of."

"So someone else can capitalize on our work."

Nico's smile dimmed. "Well, there is that. But I'm not throwing in the towel yet. We'll find a solution, Sophia; I know we will. And that juice will launch a great career for you."

Sophia wasn't sure how they went to being a "we," but she was glad to have an ally, especially one like Nico Treviani. For the first time since Charlie made himself comfortable in her kitchen, she felt hope. "Okay. I'll drop the grapes, and then we'll figure out what to do. Deal?"

Nico extended his hand. When Sophia put hers in his, he closed his other hand over their joined ones. "Deal."

The door behind them burst open. "Mr. Treviani, they're putting the last of the Chard through the crusher. We could use your input." Dani skidded to a stop. She looked amused at her mother's hand in Nico's, but she didn't look surprised. "Oh, hey, Mom. You two bonding over wine?"

Sophia retrieved her hand from Nico's, then handed her the glass of wine.

Dani took a sip and her eyes opened wide. "Righteous juice." Her attention flicked to Nico. "I knew you could do it."

"A lifetime of listening to grapes."

"Jeez, you sound like my mother."

Sophia cocked an eyebrow at her offspring. "Old school?"

"I've got a lot to learn. But," Dani pointed to Nico, "you and I need to have a chat about respect."

"Dani!"

"She's right, Sophia. Dani, I'm sorry. I got carried away by the wine and its potential."

"Don't let it happen again."

Nico eyed Sophia. "She's tough."

"Damn straight."

Just before the pause stretched to awkward, Nico changed the subject. "Look, while I've got you two cornered. I'm taking my girls up to visit my sister on the river. I'd love for you both to come. I don't know about you, but I could use a break. She's got a big house. You're welcome to stay."

"I have work," Sophia said, a knee-jerk response, then she

remembered. Squaring her shoulders she looked at her daughter. "No, no I don't. Butchy Pinkman can go straight to hell."

The three of them reached for the glasses. "From your mouth to God's ear," Nico said. "Here's to that."

They clinked glasses and then drank deeply of the wine that would never be, at least not for them.

Nico was the first to break the silence. "Sophia, my sister has a bunch of experience in the business world, and God knows that woman knows wine. Maybe she can give us an answer to your problem."

"I'm not sure there is a solution. Not a good one anyway."

"If there is, Vic will find it. She's like a tick on a dog when it comes to this sort of thing."

CHAPTER FOURTEEN

SOPHIA HAD NO IDEA WHY she had accepted Nico Treviani's invitation, but she had, surprising herself. And now she had no idea what to pack for a casual day on the river, so she stuffed a little bit of everything into her duffle. At the last minute she put in her swimsuit, the one she hadn't worn in five years. The elastic was probably shot, but it was the only one she had. She had loved to take the kids to the river. Somehow, as they had grown, the trips had become fewer until that life was swallowed by sadness and became the life "before."

A quick glance at the clock confirmed that Dani was indeed late. Her truck was the more reliable of the two they owned, not that that was saying much. But, barring catastrophe, it ought to make it the thirty miles or so to the river.

As she made the last circuit through the house, pretending to not be distracted by the idea of extended time in the company of Nico Treviani in his own environment, she heard Dani whirl to the front and stop in a skid of gravel. *Thank, God!* There was little worse than pent-up excitement with no outlet.

Sophia grabbed her duffle and a hat off the stand then threw open the door. "You're late."

But it wasn't Dani.

Trey, her oldest, grabbed a bag from behind the driver's seat, then slammed both doors on his BMW before looking at her. "In more ways than you can imagine," he said as he trudged up the steps. He didn't look happy, but then he hadn't looked happy in a long time... five years to be exact.

Sophia painted on a smile to cover her concern. Rebecca, his wife, and the twins were nowhere to be seen. And it wasn't like Trey to drive up by himself, unannounced. "What a great surprise." Sophia gave him a hug, but he held his body stiff, his face crumpled in a tight angry bunch.

"Can I bunk here for a bit?"

"Of course." Several days' growth stubbled his face. His eyes, offset by dark circles half-mooned under them, looked hollow and bloodshot. And he hadn't been eating. He'd punched a crude hole in his belt, yet, it still gapped from his waist. "The rest of your family?"

"Won't be coming." He brushed past her and she followed him inside. "We've split, me and Becca. Her idea, not mine."

"Oh, Trey. You can't ..."

His back to her, he held up a hand. "Not now, Mom. I don't need to hear it."

Anger flared. Sophia was tired of being the one with all the responsibility but none of the authority. "Well, maybe you should. You don't walk away from your family. That's not like you at all. What's gotten into you?"

When he looked at her, she almost didn't recognize him. Emotion crevassed his face, deep valleys of cynicism Sophia never thought she'd see in her son. "She left, Mom. Took the kids to her parents' in San Luis Obispo. What'd you want me to do? Chase her down?"

"At the very least. Why are you here when they are there?"

His shoulders dropped a tad, and the Trey she knew peeked through the chinks in his armor of anger. "Because this is the last place I remember being happy."

Sophia wanted so badly to hold her son. But his rigid posture told her that was not what he needed at the moment. "Okay. It's your life; you have to work out how you want it to be. But if you want to talk, I'll listen."

Trey still radiated anger and defensiveness. "I know you're disappointed."

"I'm only disappointed that you're not happy."

He raked a hand through his sandy blond hair. "I'm just going to throw this stuff in my old room. Some of the guys talked about going up to the cabin, you remember the place?"

Sophia nodded.

He looked so much like Daniel, that challenging tilt to his chin, that absolute certainty that he didn't want anyone else's opinion. "I just need to get my head together."

"When will you be back?"

"I don't know."

Sophia knew better than to say any more. She waited at the bottom of the stairs while he put his stuff away then followed him out the door. He didn't wave as he gunned the car back down the driveway.

No sooner had Trey's car disappeared and she heard him turn onto the highway and accelerate toward town, than the growl of Dani's truck sounded as it strained up the hill. The truck had barely stopped when Dani bounded out, leaving the door open. "Was that Trey? He didn't even stop or wave or anything. What's up?"

"I don't know." Sophia handed her bag to Dani. "But, I'm not going to worry about it. Trey's a grown man; maybe he just needs to blow off some steam. Life's got to be a bit of a meat grinder with the twins and school and all."

Dani seemed to buy it. "His loss, he could've come with us. I don't know about you, but it's been too long since we've been in kayaks. I bet I can still kick your ass, Mom."

"No doubt. You and your brother always could paddle circles around me. I miss those days." Sophia settled herself.

"Good memories." Dani tossed her mother's bag in the bed with hers and slid behind the wheel. With a turn of the key, the engine kicked into a smooth hum.

Nervous, Sophia plucked at a string on the cuff of the sweater she'd knotted around her neck. Nights had been cooler lately, with fog gathering in the low places, carrying the hint of fall. "I'm not sure why I came."

"Time to make new memories, Mom. You've been living with ghosts too long."

"You don't think that would be a betrayal to your father?"

Dani looked at her like she'd lost her mind. "It would be a betrayal of the happiness you had together if you didn't try to find it again. Dad wouldn't want you to spend the rest of your life mourning him. Time to get back to the present, let the past go."

Sophia thought that easier to say than to do, but she didn't want to belabor the point. She wished in some ways she could be courageous like her daughter and make a decision and go with it. "I miss him so much. Especially now with life in turmoil and decisions to be made." Sophia pulled at the thread and realized she was unraveling the cuff on her sweater. Rolling the thread between her thumb and forefinger, she knotted it, then pulled the knot tight.

"You don't need Dad to tell you what to do. You know what is right for you."

Dani's confidence surprised her. What did her daughter see in her that she herself could not? "I came to rely on his perspective. I feel somehow exposed without it."

"That's not a bad thing, Mom."

Sophia mulled that over. Regina had always taught her to seek safety, and Sophia was her mother's daughter in many ways. "It's uncomfortable."

"No kidding. But aren't you the one who always preached courage?"

"Did I?"

Dani widened her eyes in disbelief as she glanced at her mother. "Remember that kid at Gott's?"

For a moment Sophia was lost, then the warmth of that day washed over her. "The kid who punched you in the stomach?"

"That's the one. And what did you tell me to do?"

"Hit him back."

"Butchy Pinkman has hit you in the stomach." Dani didn't connect the dots.

Sophia could do that all on her own.

"And Nico?" Sophia hesitated. "What about him?"

"Your turn to really stick your neck out, Mom. Take a flier. Chart your path. Be true to who you want to be." Dani looked like she was relishing the momentary role reversal.

The thought shocked Sophia; making choices, living life, that's what she'd thought she was doing. But Daniel had always led the way. She had never considered the weight of a singular identity and she had no idea how to shoulder it.

But today was too pretty, her escape from life too complete, to worry about the future. Worry would be waiting when she returned home.

Sophia rolled down the window, stuck her elbow out, and savored the wafting sweetness of ripe grapes hanging heavy in the air. On the valley floor heading north, the air warmed as the effects of the cold currents in the San Francisco Bay receded behind them, and she unknotted the sweater, pulling it from behind her and wadding it on the seat next to her. The rest of the ride passed in the comfortable chatter of mother and daughter. Sophia felt herself relaxing into the present.

Rolling vineyards, their vines clotheslined liked resting soldiers, thirsty and beaten under the sun, gave way to low forests and scrub oak. Then the damp canopy of redwoods hugging the river bottom, drawing life from the flowing water and sustenance from the eons of composted forest floor, rose up around them in a protective embrace. Sophia breathed deep, pulling in the moisture, the musty smell of living things. This was a place of regeneration. A relaxing respite from the harsh deprivations when mountains squeezed the water out of the moist air off the ocean, leaving it a dry Socorro to scour the valley floor.

Just outside of Guerneville, Dani slowed, looking for the driveway.

"Treviani?" Sophia helped her peruse the mailboxes.

"Yeah."

They needn't have worried, the place was easy to find, a broad drive leading up the hill on the right and guarded by a heavy wrought-iron gate. As she eased the truck to the intercom and pressed the button, Dani cast a questioning glance her mother.

"Dani and Sophia?" The disembodied female voice projected warmth despite the tininess of the speaker. "Come on up."

Lined with juniper trees, the road leading up the hill was unpaved and in need of grading, the washboard playing every rattle the truck had and perhaps a new one or two. Near the top, the trees thinned and sunlight dappled the large lawn. The word "bucolic" sprang to Sophia's mind and she half-expected a cow to be grazing on the lush greenery. Instead, two yellow labs bounded down the rough-hewn wooden steps leading from the wraparound porch. The rest of the house was constructed of large logs with hand-set mortar. Dormered casement windows bordered in green and filigreed wood triangled from the high-pitched roof ... a three-story man-made edifice with a Tyrolean hunting lodge feel. The red tin roof was the only modern touch. A wisp of cedar smoke, it's scent riding the breeze, curled from the large river-rock-faced chimney on the side of the house.

The dogs raced across the lawn, followed by an energetic but more restrained woman. Lean and lanky with wild red hair and porcelain skin, she bore little resemblance to her darker-skinned brother, but Sophia could see a few shared family traits in her gait and in the way the held herself with quiet confidence. Her light cotton shirt knotted at the waist above a pair of peach pencil-legged capris gave just the right amount of suave to her California rustic.

"Welcome." She greeted Dani first, grabbing her hand in one of hers while trying to fend off the dogs with the other as they lapped and sniffed, darting just beyond her reach. "I'm Victoria, Vic to my friends. Welcome to my home." With a laugh, Victoria clapped twice and called the dogs to heel. "Enough out of you two. Behave or our guests will think none of us has any manners." She stepped around the truck and gave Sophia a brisk hug that managed to be warm and appropriate. "I'm sorry about the slobbering welcome committee. I know I should have a firmer hand, but I find it impossible. They mean no harm. Are you afraid of dogs?" Her flawless skin crinkled into the slight bulge of a frown. Her eyes were a cloudy hazel, like a storm lingering offshore. "I guess I should have asked that before. We aren't used to this many guests. We are all very excited."

Sophia laughed. "Dogs are like children, touchstones—connections to the heart of life."

"Exactly." Victoria eyed Sophia with soft eyes and a kind smile. Freckles dotted her cheeks and the bridge of her nose as if God had wanted to make her perfection palatable. "Nico's told me all about you. I'm so glad you decided to join us for the weekend."

Sophia felt at ease, not what she expected, and not how she had felt as they closed in on their destination, but something about Nico's sister diffused her anxiety ... a peculiar bit of Treviani alchemy she shared with her brother. Dani gathered their things as Sophia fell into step with Victoria. "Thank you so much for inviting us. I'm afraid I won't be staying the whole weekend though—just tonight. With fruit ready any moment, I can't take too much time away." Butchy Pinkman, her job, her contract, Sophia hadn't decided what to do about any of those things. First thing Monday she needed to see a lawyer.

"I understand. It's a hectic time of year."

"Yes, and I needed a break."

"So I heard. I've just gotten the overview, but we'll have to discuss things in a bit more detail later. My mother will be here soon and you'll want her in on it. She wields more power than the Pope."

"I'm not sure that makes me completely comfortable."

"Oh, she's a benevolent despot."

Excited shouts, two female and one male that Sophia instantly recognized on some heightened visceral level, rose from the far side of the property on the other side of the house.

Victoria motioned to the river below, then traced an arc with her arm, following the meandering path the water had etched in the land through the millennia. "The river crosses under the road there—you can just make out the bridge—then it loops back behind our property. We have over six hundred feet of shoreline with several put-ins depending on your choice of craft. But, canoe or kayak, you always have to beware of human missiles."

"Mr. Treviani told me about the rope swing." Dani's voice held a twinge of excitement and a hint of competition.

"Get your suit on and show them how it's done." Vic led them around the house and up the back stairs. "Dani, your room is at the top of the stairs, third floor, second door on the right." Dani bounded up the stairs two at a time.

The older women watched her. Victoria put a hand on Sophia's arm. "You're welcome to join Nico and the girls as well. Whatever mischief they've dreamed up, I'll tell you now the poor man doesn't stand a chance, so he could use an ally."

"What about you?"

Victoria got a gleam in her eye. She lifted one corner of her mouth in a challenging grin. "I learned from my mother, let them wear themselves down a bit, then attack quickly and without mercy."

"And here I was starting to let my guard down about meeting

your mother."

"Ah, with the Trevianis one must remain ever-vigilant." Victoria motioned up the stairs. "Shall we? Your room is on the second floor, first door on the left."

Dani had wasted no time. Clad only in tennis shoes, bathing suit and a smile, a towel thrown over her shoulder, she raced down the stairs, leaping off the third step from the bottom, hitting the ground in stride, looking carefree and happy in a way Sophia hadn't seen in a long time.

Sophia grabbed her bag. *Time to get back in the swing, indeed.*

CHAPTER FIFTEEN

NICO PULLED THE ROPE TAUT, bracing himself on the bank above the river. His arms already shook with fatigue, but he wouldn't let the two heathens win furthest jump honors. If he lost, he would have to wash the dinner dishes and that was not going to happen. "You ready?" He shouted to his two nieces who bobbed in the middle of the river where the water ran the deepest. Dani was just behind them.

All three of them waved. "No way you'll ever beat Dani's jump. She even beat your record, Uncle."

Nico's record had stood for twenty years and he wouldn't relinquish the crown without a fight. The water dripping from their swimsuits had slickened the clay soil. Testing his footing, he dug with his front foot wallowing out a brace for his left heel. Leaning back, testing the rope, he took a deep breath and focused. He shifted his weight as he pushed off with his back foot, launching himself into the short run. Just as he moved to plant his foot for his leap off the bank, he caught movement to his left. Victoria and Sophia stepped out of the tree line. Momentarily distracted, he stepped on a slick patch. Slipping, his push off was weak, leaving him dangling awkwardly behind his leap and trying to recover. As he tugged, trying to pull himself into the arc, his hand burned down the rope, muscles failing. Feet from the apex, he fell, landing on his back in a body-jarring splat. The impact forced the breath from him. With one foot he propelled himself off the soft river bottom. Bursting through the surface, he spluttered, sucking in lungsful of air. Gales of laughter greeted him.

"'You lose, Uncle," Taryn shouted.

He had enough air to argue. "I get a do-over."

"On what basis?" Brooklyn asked. The girls were sticklers for rules and not known for their leniency.

"Infirmity."

"What does that mean?" Taryn asked, her stage whisper carrying easily across the water.

"It means he's a sore loser," Brooklyn said to her sister, then shouted to her uncle, "No way. Rules is rules."

"Ruthless just like your grandmother," Nico groused, pretending to be upset. The girls were wise to their uncle's act. They beamed as he stroked over to the bank. Pushing to his feet, he shook the water from his hair like a puppy. Running his hands down his arms and legs, he squeegeed the rest.

Sophia watched him as she kicked off her sandals. Bending, she hooked them with a forefinger and then picked her way across the rocky bank toward Nico, who was now rubbing himself with a towel. It had been a long time since she'd even looked at a man with interest, much less acted on it.

Nico Treviani changed that. She felt herself drawn to him in ways she remembered and others that were new and exciting. He challenged her, pushed her, and wouldn't accept her self-imposed limits. In a way, he made her see who she could be, which was both exhilarating and terrifying.

Victoria strode ahead of her. "Well done, Brother."

He shot a grin at his sister, but his eyes sought Sophia beyond. "I let them win."

Everyone scoffed, including Sophia. She couldn't help herself.

"Okay, maybe I didn't exactly *let* them win, but, Sophia, my poor performance was your fault, so you shouldn't laugh. You look amazing."

Sophia warmed under his gaze, and she didn't feel sorry at all.

"That's right, blame it on the guests." Victoria laughed. She stepped next to her brother, put a steadying hand on his shoulder and began shucking her clothes, stripping to the tiny bikini underneath. Stepping out of her capris, she flipped her hair and gave him a haughty look. "Let a pro show you how it's done."

When Victoria arced herself from the rope, she timed it perfectly so her lithe body arrowed through the air like it had been shot from a bow.

"Is the water deep enough?" Sophia asked Nico as she moved to stand beside him. She couldn't tell whether the heat she felt radiated off him or was her own.

"There's a natural eddy there that has wallowed out a nice hole." He reached out a hand. "Want to try it?"

After only a moment's hesitation, Sophia lifted her chin. "I'm rusty, but I'll give it a go."

Her first swing was tentative. Nico gave her an encouraging smile but no instruction as he helped her out of the water.

The second time she got it right. That perfect release point, using all the momentum, arcing as if she was an extension of the rope, then cleaving through the water. When she popped to the surface, applause greeted her.

"That was brilliant." Nico pulled her out then handed her a towel. "Not quite as far as Dani, but you gave her a scare."

"I let her win." Sophia gave him a smile and looked at him from under lowered lashes.

"Smart ass."

"A Stone family trait, I must warn you."

"Warning ignored. Challenge accepted. I'll try to keep up." He gave her that arched eyebrow Dani had told her about.

Shivering, Sophia rubbed her arms and legs then squeezed the water out of her hair. The warmth from the brisk rub felt nice, but it didn't help with the shivering. "Where's Victoria?"

"Gone back to the house to work on dinner. She thought she heard Mom's car." Putting two fingers in his mouth, he blew an ear-splitting whistle then motioned to the girls. "Come on you three. KP duty."

As they wandered ahead, Nico took Sophia's elbow. "How'd you learn to swing like that?"

"When the kids were young, Daniel and I used to love to come to the river." Sophia slipped on a slick spot, but Nico's hand on her elbow steadied her.

"Kids?"

"Hmmm. Dani has an older brother, Trey. He and his kid sister were like one of those TV cowboys and his sidekick. Where one went, the other followed, meeting trouble side by side." Sophia felt a momentary longing for life as it used to be when Daniel was alive and Trey was happy.

"Where is Trey now?"

"He's in the engineering program at Berkeley, following in his father's footsteps. It's funny; I always thought he'd be running a winery. He loved the land, the grapes, the business of wine. But everything changed when his father died. I haven't been able to reach him since."

Sophia sensed Nico holding her elbow a bit tighter as they stepped out of the shadow of the trees and into angled shafts of soft light as the sun dropped lower toward the horizon. A hawk turned in lazy circles climbing a thermal. Two rabbits nibbled by the porch steps. As Nico and Sophia approached, the dogs didn't even raise their heads, remaining curled in the last pools of warmth as the sun retreated.

"I wasn't as young as Trey when my father died, but I was profoundly affected. It changed my life, and my mother's ... hell, it changed all of us. We became like soldiers who had fought in the same battle and had survived, but each suffering their own unique wounds."

"Yes," Sophia's voice was soft with wonder and pain. "It's just like that. And now Paolo; I'm so very sorry."

Sophia could see the pull of her words on his face, in the fleeting hollow, lost look in his eyes. "And so what do we do?"

Nico looked at her, his eyes dark fierce pinpoints. "We fight."

THE WARM SHOWER LEFT SOPHIA feeling refreshed and unusually relaxed. Being outside and on the river had certainly helped. So too had watching Dani and the twins laugh and chatter. To Sophia it seemed only a blink since Dani had been thirteen and filled with equal parts angst and silliness, frustrating and delightful like Nico's nieces.

Then there was Nico. Being around him was like touching a live wire—a tingle of excitement, a flush of heat, a spark, and then your heart stops.

Sophia blew once at the soft fringe of bangs that brushed across her forehead as she checked herself once more in the mirror. A familiar face looked back at her as if nothing had changed, as if there hadn't been a seismic shift in her soul. But there had been: her home, her grapes ... she closed her eyes and took a deep breath, willing herself to park that thought and enjoy the day. But she would fight. She didn't know how, but she couldn't let those ... men ... take what was hers, then cover themselves in stolen glory. And somehow, simply in the act of fighting she sensed victory. An intangible one, but perhaps the most important.

Leaving her hair down and her make-up barely there, she headed downstairs to join the others. The soft oriental carpet muffled her steps. Trailing her fingers lightly on the rough-hewn banister smooth with time and touch, she smiled at the stuffed deer head mounted above the landing—made of felt with button eyes and a toothy grin. The paintings marching in file down the stairway marked time and a lineage of farming and growing—a pictorial history of a family that shaped the recent history of Napa. She followed voices through the great room, lorded over by a huge river-rocked fireplace, and the dining room with a table for twelve and a silver service that looked like it had made the journey from the Old Country on the Santa Maria. Pushing through a set of large swinging doors, Sophia landed in the midst of warmth, succulent smells, and a heated conversation. The girls, all three of them, sat with their backs to her at a long, semi-circular counter, their heads turned toward Victoria, who stirred a pot with a long-handled wooden spoon.

The muscles in her arms bunched with each two-handed swipe like she was throwing a punch with each pass. "Mother, they can and they will. You know that, you see it every day."

"Just because I know it and I see it doesn't mean I have to like it." The voice rose from behind the counter, reverberating as if the words bounced around the inside of a kettledrum. A woman stood, tall and lithe, with short-cropped gray hair, Nico's eyes and Victoria's smile. She held a huge roasting pan she had just pulled from the oven. In it, carcasses that looked like some kind of bird—not large enough to be turkeys but too large to be chickens—steamed and sizzled. "That's why I organized everyone. We have to fight. Your geese are cooked, by the way."

"Of course, they are," Victoria added dryly as the girls snickered. She motioned to the counter behind her next to the farmhouse sink. "Put them there, please."

Mrs. Treviani did as she was told, then turning, she gave the girls a wink, spying Sophia behind them. With a mitted hand, she motioned Sophia into the room. "Ah, you must be Sophia. I am Olivia Treviani. Come. Take a seat. We were just talking about you."

Dani patted the seat beside her and Sophia joined the cast at the counter. "That's what happens when you're last to the table, Mom; you get to be the topic of conversation."

Victoria put a bowl down in front of her and began ladling rich red soup. "I've been bringing mother up to speed on what Nico told us about the men trying to take your vineyard." She handed Sophia a spoon. "Here. Try this. Tell me what you think." She raised her voice and shouted through a doorway to the far right. "Nico, how are you coming with the wine? You have four very thirsty women in here. Let us go too much longer and it could get ugly."

As if he'd anticipated his sister's summons, Nico stepped into the room, balancing a silver tray with five glasses of amber liquid.

With her eyes on the wine, Sophia sipped at the red liquid in her bowl expecting it to be hot. It wasn't. She took the whole spoonful. "Oh, my God, what is this?" Then to Nico, "Is that my wine?"

He didn't answer. Instead, he handed a goblet to his mother, one to his sister, and put one in front of Dani. The twins started to whine, but their aunt ladled soup into their bowls and they bowed their heads and busied themselves spooning it in.

"You like the soup?" Victoria said to Sophia. "Watermelon gazpacho."

Sophia took another spoonful. "It's amazing, sweet but with a kick."

"A secret ingredient." Victoria gave her a shy smile. "I like to take a recipe and tweak it."

Nico straddled the stool next to Sophia, pushing one glass toward her, keeping the other for himself. Then he looked at his sister. "I caught a bit of your conversation from the bar. You filled Mother in on Sophia's situation?"

"Yes."

Olivia Treviani had been standing on the sidelines long enough. "We have to fight them, those men who want to take your grapes. New money is moving into the Valley, buying up all the history, squeezing out the small vintner, the boutique wineries, the legacy of Napa. That can't go on."

Nico's tone was calm, rational, as he joined the fray. "Mother, to you, and to me and Sophia, it's passion, it's history, it's the brilliant little wines, not the mediocrity of the conglomerates."

"As it should be."

"Yes, I agree. But ultimately, wine is a business. And, even though all of us here consider wine to be an exalted art, to everyone else it's about money."

"And therein lies the problem," Sophia said. "The property is not mine. I don't have the money to buy it. And, even if I did, apparently a contract has been signed."

"Contracts can be broken." Olivia looked stern, and more than a little bit angry.

Nico concurred. "With some money and a decent attorney you could stonewall them long enough to get other plans in place. But we're back to the first problem—money."

Olivia looked a bit deflated. "That's the problem. Wine is not about money; it is about passion."

"You can't live on passion," Sophia added, surprising herself. "Wine has to be about both. An attempt to drive the conglomerates out of the Valley would be as successful as trying to get rid of Walmart. There are those who want cheap. And there are those who want sublime and unique. The key is balance."

Nico raised his glass. "Well said. Let's toast to the sublime and the unique."

Sophia clinked her glass to his. "And those willing to pay for it."

The room fell silent, except for the slurping of the girls as they eyed the bottom of their empty bowls, looking like dogs ready to lick up the remnants. Sophia took a sip—it was indeed her wine. She looked at Nico with the expression of an executioner eying the condemned. "You made more."

"I had to see if the blend held up. I tweaked it a bit."

Sophia nodded. "Rounder notes. I'm not sure I don't like the hard edge better."

"Perhaps, for a sophisticated palate."

"With two acres under vine, that's our market." Sophia turned to her daughter. "Dani, what do you think?"

"The edge. Totally."

Victoria and Olivia finally caught up. "*This* is your wine, Sophia? It's amazing."

"Tart, acidic, fruit-forward, yet with a rounded, soft, clean finish," Olivia said, as if she was reading tasting notes.

"Perfect for the goose and the gazpacho. Hard gap in flavors for a wine to bridge," Victoria added, clearly impressed.

Nico held his glass to the light and tipped it, letting the liquid flow and swirl around his glass. "This is what those men are after."

EVERYONE HAD DESCENDED ON DINNER like a pack of wolves, reducing the geese to picked-over carcasses, the gazpacho to a memory, and the potatoes and salad to scraps. Sticking to less troublesome topics, the conversation had flowed as the girls chattered about school and boys, causing Nico to pale. And Dani had taken the casual time made warm and inviting by the free-flowing wine to pepper her boss about winemaking. Sophia had nursed her one glass and reveled in the comfort of family. The Trevianis had known loss; yet, they clung fiercely to each other. Loss had fractured her own family, untying the bonds that had held them together until they each were like castaways alone in their life raft bobbing on a limitless ocean of grief. How had that happened?

The conversation ebbed and Victoria seized the opportunity. "I have something I need to tell everyone. And I'd like you to hear me out before you say anything."

All eyes swiveled in her direction as silence fell over the table.

"After a great deal of thought, I've made a decision, a very difficult one. So please don't argue. What I would like is your help."

Victoria took a deep breath, pausing as she looked each one of them in the eye in turn. "I've decided to sell the house."

The twins erupted and started to argue. Nico silenced them with a look.

"I've been thinking about it for a long time." Victoria sounded matter-of-fact, determined—content with her choice. "I guess it was Paolo's death that really focused me and prodded me to action. You see, this house was one dream. I thought I'd get married, have a family, raise my children here. But that dream wasn't meant to be. So, it's time for another one, one I've held in my heart since I was a child, one I lacked the courage to chase."

"Until now." With an encouraging smile and eyes filled with love, her mother reached across the table and gave her daughter's hand a quick squeeze.

Nico, twirling the stem of his wine glass between two fingers, watched the two women with undisguised affection. When he caught Sophia looking, he gave her a smile. The love didn't leave his eyes.

"Selling the house is the first step toward realizing that dream. But there's more." Victoria sat ramrod straight, her hands knotted in her lap, her wine abandoned. "I've learned so much from my brothers. Paolo lived a life of passion and adventure, doing what he loved. I need to honor that legacy by taking it to heart. So, I am trying to put together some money to buy the Bucket and Bin in Rutherford." Victoria looked at her brother. Sophia could see her conflict—she wanted his approval, but didn't want to need it. "You don't seem surprised, Brother."

"Quatro sorta gave me a heads-up."

At the mention of Billy Rodriques, Victoria's cheeks pinked and she fiddled with the stem of her wine glass, keeping her eyes lowered and her emotions hidden. "Billy? How'd he know?"

"A cousin of his works at Greystone. He says you're some sort of savant in the kitchen."

"Billy always had an inflated opinion of my talents."

"He loves you."

Victoria drew a sharp a breath at the simple words. "Perhaps, but he is not *in* love with me, and that makes a huge difference. Besides I scare him."

"You scare me, too, and I still love you." The girls laughed, making their uncle smile. "And how do you know? I think you're wrong."

Mrs. Treviani gave her son a subtle shake of her head.

"So you're looking for investors, then?" Nico asked, dropping into business-mode.

"A few, maybe. I have no idea when this house will sell nor how much it will bring. I have a small mortgage to pay off, but even after that and with my severance and retirement money, it won't be enough to get a new concept up and running and keep it afloat until it can be self-sustaining."

"If dinner was any indication, you won't have to carry the costs very long," Sophia said with a smile of encouragement. "Any idea on how you'd like to position yourself?"

"Approachable food with a flair. I'll leave the high-end stuff to those who like that game. We'll have a happy hour with small plates and wine of quality with a good price point. I want it to be a comfortable place where people can come and hang out."

"With an outdoor fireplace?" the twins chimed in to ask.

Victoria reached for her wine, relaxing with the burden of her announcement lifted. "That is an excellent idea. An outdoor fireplace, and I think we should have the bar open to the patio as well."

"That sounds like an excellent point at which to penetrate the market." Nico sounded pleased but not surprised; he knew his sister well. "Let me know how I can help."

Victoria blushed with Nico's tacit approval.

"Let us all know how we can help," Sophia added.

Olivia raised her glass. "To dreams." She looked at Sophia pointedly. "And to the courage needed to chase them."

CHAPTER SIXTEEN

THE GIRLS CLEARED THE TABLE, leaving the adults to linger over a glass of late-harvest wine while trying to ignore the giggles and shrieks coming from the kitchen.

Dani pushed back from the table. "I'll go referee."

"Try to save as much of the glassware as possible," Victoria added with a smile that lacked the panic Sophia would have been feeling had it been her kitchen.

"And keep them out of the dessert," Olivia said.

Dani acknowledged them both with a wave as she disappeared through the swinging doors.

"Dessert?" Sophia pressed a hand to her stomach. "I couldn't."

"Oh, you will," Nico said. "While many have tried, few have resisted my mother's coconut oatmeal cookies."

"Baking is my therapy," Olivia semi-scolded her son, then turned to Sophia. "When my husband died many years ago, I felt at loose ends."

"So she retreated to the kitchen and didn't reappear until she'd found her smile and perfected some stellar recipes." Nico patted his flat belly. "It's a good thing my job requires me to be on my feet most of the day."

Each of the women gave him a disgruntled look. "No sympathy here, Brother." Victoria stood. "Dani might need a hand if she's to save much of my crystal. Mother, care to help me?"

Olivia started to object. Her daughter cut her off. "Mother, please, I could use your help." With a smile to her brother, she helped their mother to her feet then both women disappeared through the double doors.

Sophia traced the rim of her glass with a forefinger as she gazed at Nico from under lowered lashes, feeling a frisson of excitement at being alone with him. "That was a not so cleverly disguised setup, if I'm not mistaken."

"We Trevianis aren't very long on subtle." He rose and extended his hand. "Let me show you the rest of the house? Bring your drink."

Leaving her wine behind, she put her hand in his—the warmth she'd felt at his first touch was still there.

Nico held on as he led her from the dining room. "I'll show you my favorite room first."

"Aren't you supposed to save the best for last?"

"I've learned it's not wise to delay pleasure." The look he gave her shot straight to her core, leaving her breathless. "Life can be short. Come, this way." He led her through the great room with its overstuffed leather furniture, mounted felt heads. The pink and purple bear with sad eyes was a good touch. Brass lamps spilled pools of soft light, and artwork in an old-school style—most were oils depicting hunting scenes framed in rustic wood—adorned the walls.

Sophia tried to keep up with Nico, but the house captured her. "This place reminds me of a hunting lodge that could've hosted Teddy Roosevelt on his many trips out west."

"Indeed." Nico sounded mysterious.

"Seriously? Teddy Roosevelt slept here?"

"Once or twice." Nico pulled her through a doorway she hadn't noticed. The room was dark. "Hang on." He left her there in the doorway. Within moments, lights flickered on.

To Sophia the lighting was dramatic, carefully designed to render people speechless. It worked. Her jaw fell open as she let her gaze drift around the space. Two stories high, the room was octagonal, with each wall covered in floor-to-ceiling bookshelves. A walkway circumnavigated the second level, which was reached by a wheeled ladder one could push around the walkway to enter where they pleased. With a small table between them, two wing-backed chairs nested in the middle of the room, each with its own curved brass reading lamp.

Nico walked the walls, stopping periodically to touch the spine of a book. He glanced over his shoulder at Sophia, and she caught a hint of the boy he used to be. "All the books I ever read as a child are here, as well as most of my father's lifetime collection. I got my love of reading from him. A shy man, he was a bit of a dreamer. He read and he drank too much, both escapes of a sort. And he could be quite secretive. On our farm, he had a room in the barn that he locked and wouldn't let anyone in."

"Did he tell you what was in it?" Sophia perched on one of the chairs, her gaze following Nico as he wandered, lost in memories.

"No. And I hate secrets."

"Apparently." Sophia took a slight swipe at him for spilling Dani's secret, and hers.

To his credit, Nico took it well. "I can be a bit impetuous. I didn't mean any harm to come by it."

Sophia let it go. "Tell me about your father's room." Nico Treviani was different here in his own environment, with his family. Sophia caught glimpses of the man beneath the public persona, the reputation. And the more she saw, the stronger the attraction, something that scared her a bit but excited her, too.

"When my father would go to bed, and my mother would be upstairs with her nose stuck in a cookbook, I'd sneak out to the barn and try to pick the lock. Took me a while, but I finally got it."

Sophia could picture the small, curious little boy. So much like Trey had been. "What did you do?" Sophia leaned forward, her hands on her knees.

Nico left the books, turning toward her. "The lock gave. I turned the handle; the door opened just a sliver. I couldn't see anything. It was pitch black. My heart hammered in my chest. I could imagine all sorts of horribles my father could've hidden in that room."

Sophia laughed. "An imagination is a scary thing."

"So I'm standing there trying to decide whether to go all the way, or lock it back up and go to bed. I figured either way there would be hell to pay, so I pushed the door open, took a small step inside, then stepped up on my toes to find the light switch. Holding my breath, I flipped it on." He stopped.

"And?"

Pivoting, Nico swept the room with an extended arm, his eyes glassy.

"Oh." Sophia's hand flew to her chest, fisting over her heart.

"He was a simple farmer. He came from nothing. Dropped out of school to help in the family's fields when he was sixteen. These books, they were his window to the world."

"And they're all here?" Sophia felt small and humbled, as if she'd wandered into a shrine to something or someone larger than herself, and she was awed.

"All except for a few that disintegrated with time and too many readings. I've replaced most of them. Google and eBay. I've only a couple left to find and they were in the original Italian."

"Italian?"

"When my father came to this country, he was barely seventeen and could speak only a few words in English." Nico laughed and turned inward for a moment. "He used to tell me he knew how to say all the important things. Please and thank you, you're beautiful, may I have a beer, and where's the bathroom—that's all he could say. He told me those were all he needed because he won my mother with them."

Sophia sighed. "Now that's a love story."

They were two people with one heart, one soul. My mother's been a bit lost without him. She's strong, but ..." He trailed off and shrugged in a self-conscious, shy sort of way. "She's found a passion with her baking."

"And her causes. I saw her car."

"The activism is a way for her to feel socially connected, I think. Not that she doesn't believe in all the things she supports, but I think they are a way to belong, to get out of her loneliness."

"And to feel needed."

Nico speared her with an intense look. "Yes."

Sophia heard a question. "An empty nest gives one a bit of perspective. But, back to the books. Tell me more."

"Yes. Where was I? Victoria, the smart one, went to fancy schools back east and ended up with a lucrative Silicon Valley job. She bought this house and we moved all of Father's books here after he died and we lost the farm to a land-grab scheme much like the one being played for your land."

"It's not my land."

Nico's anger flared. Sophia knew it wasn't directed at her. "No, it's your heart. As our farm was ours." Nico strode across the room then pulled out a few books, tilting them outward. He didn't have to look; he knew these by heart. "These books—my father spent long days in the fields, a common laborer, and then long nights reading, teaching himself English and viticulture at the same time." From a small table in the corner, he picked up a book too large to fit on the shelves. "This is his dictionary. Someone told him the Oxford dictionary was the best, so he had to have one. Bound in leather, embossed in gold, I don't know how many weeks he saved for it." Nico flipped the pages. "Look. He made notes. Almost every page has at least one."

Sophia leaned over for a peek. "Clearly, he believed in the American Dream."

"And he lived it. We all did. At first, he could only rent his acreage and a small house."

"And the barn."

"The barn came later. My mother said we would not be true successes without cows and a horse, and to have that, we needed a barn."

"So your father built the barn for her."

"Board by board."

Sophia swiped at a tear, suddenly self-conscious.

"He slaved in the fields to pay the rent, but without my mother we never would have had anything else. She went to the landowner and negotiated a purchase price and strong-armed him into financing the deal. She was a formidable woman, still is. The poor man didn't have a chance."

"What did your father say?"

"He was apoplectic. Twelve to fourteen hours a day he spent in the fields—the work eventually broke him. With all that, they could barely make ends meet. He had two boys who were bottomless pits." Nico chuckled. "Even with logic on his side, he didn't stand a chance, not against my mother."

He was milking the story and Sophia relished every moment. Held in the embrace of history and time, she felt an intimate connection with this interesting and complex man. A man with a big heart and a hint of sadness each time he smiled. "And why not?"

"Mother held the trump card." One corner of Nico's mouth ticked up into an appreciative grin. His eyes turned dusty blue when he smiled. "She told him she would give him the daughter he had always wanted."

"And she did." Sophia allowed herself a satisfied sigh. Stories with happy endings filled her heart, especially love stories.

Nico shook his head. "Even God couldn't say no to that woman."

"It has been written that God is wise."

"Or a coward." Nico gave her an interesting look, one she couldn't interpret, but one that left her with the impression that Nico Treviani and the Almighty didn't exactly see eye-to-eye. "And Victoria is proof."

Sophia clapped once. "Victoria! Victory! Of course."

Nico reached out. "Come, I'll show you my second favorite part of the house."

Sophia let him pull her out of the deep cushions. She was surprised when he let his arm drape across her shoulders.

Nico must've felt her tense slightly. "Am I presuming too much?" He stopped and turned her to face him. "I'm very drawn to you, Sophia; I won't lie. As a colleague. As a friend. As a woman. The mixture that is you is intoxicating."

With a hand on his chest, Sophia felt the rush of heat through the thin shirt he wore. Like an electrical charge it surged through her, incinerating doubt, short-circuiting clear thought. A nervous rush of breath escaped before she could pull it back. "It's been a long time since I've allowed myself ... to feel. Everything is coming at me in a rush, like a rogue wave knocking me off my feet."

Nico kept his arm around her shoulder, easing her closer to him. "I think I like that."

He pushed aside the ladder, exposing a set of double French doors. The night had turned cool and tendrils of fog filtered through the trees, giving the lights hidden high in their branches ghostly halos.

"I do love the fog, don't you?" His voice was soft, his breath a caress.

Picturing her mountaintop, bathed in moonlight under a star-filled sky, the heat of the day just tempering, Sophia let him pull her close, delighting in his nearness. Her spot in the universe was a world away from this flagstone porch and the grassy slope beyond that rolled to the woods and the river hidden in the darkness. Sophia heard a bit of melancholy in the call of an owl and the silence that answered. She shivered, and she didn't know whether it was the chill in the air or the pull of ghosts.

Nico pulled a cashmere throw from the back of one of the Adirondack chairs clustered around a fire pit and draped the soft cloth around her shoulders.

"The coast isn't far. And the effects of the cold currents can be dramatic."

Sophia pulled it tighter, binding herself in its warmth. The ghosts felt close tonight.

"Here, why don't you sit?" Nico motioned to one of the chairs closest to the pit. "I'll build a fire."

As she took the chair he indicated, he pulled another to join it and then set about making a fire. This wasn't the push a button and a gas fire springs through fake logs. No, this was the real thing. Nico pulled logs from the stand at the edge of the porch, eyeing each one, putting some back and keeping others, until he had an armful. As Sophia watched him, she wondered if he was the real thing, too.

"What do you think of your sister's decision?"

He organized a bit of kindling on and elevated wire mesh in the bottom of the pit before he answered. His brows furrowed in concentration, his mouth serious when he looked up at her. "I don't see how it matters what I think. Her house, her dreams, her life." He shrugged and his expression softened. "I want her to be happy." He lit a match and touched it to the bits of dry wood which erupted in flames. Then he carefully arranged the logs so they would burn and not smother the fire.

"What about the memories?" Sophia loved the way the light played over the angular planes of his face as the fire took hold.

"Memories. Perhaps they'll be comfort when our future is short, when age no longer lets us see the possibilities and all we have is what has been. But right now?" When he looked at her, Sophia could see the intensity in his eyes. "Right now, I see too many people heading for crashes because they're spending too much time looking in the rearview mirror."

"Perhaps. But the past is our tether to ourselves."

Nico sat back on his heels. "Do you really believe that?"

"We are a product of all our experiences."

"Exactly." Nico touched his chest. "So the past it is here. And and our eyes should be forward."

Sophia smiled at his earnestness. "You are quite the philosopher, Mr. Treviani."

"Now you are making fun."

"Not at all. I've never met a man who thought as deeply, as profoundly as you apparently do. Maybe my grandfather, but I didn't know him well as an adult."

"I've had a lot of time keeping my own company. My mother would tell you too much." Nico moved the chair closer still to hers, then sat, stretching his long legs out in front of him and laying his head back. Almost instinctively, he put his hand over hers where it rested on the wide arm of the chair.

"You never married?" The question seemed easier to ask under the cover of darkness, in the light of the fire, with Nico's eyes closed and not measuring every inch of her face.

"Came close once. But no." He sounded wistful, but not sad, at least Sophia didn't think so.

"What happened?" Sophia surprised herself. Normally she didn't pry this way.

"I wanted a love story like my parents."

"A fairy tale?"

"No. I'm not that much of a fool. That would be way too much pressure on a relationship. I simply wanted someone who loved me for the right reasons."

"And those would be?"

He let out a long sigh. "Someone who loved me for me, not for what I could do for them. Like it seems you had with Daniel."

Sophia leaned her head back. Even through the glow of the fire the stars were bright, and she could just make out the Big Dipper. She traced the line formed by its upper cup to the North Star, the guide star that would help you find your bearings. "I used to think we had that, but now I'm not so sure. My friend, Maggie, loves to remind me of all of Daniel's shortcomings. We both had our issues, but it was a good marriage, I think."

Nico turned his head and cocked an eye open. "But?"

"But lately I've realized I capitulated a lot."

"I can't see you doing that."

"I'm not as brave as you think. Besides, I was busy raising the kids, so it didn't seem to matter. I was a mom. I kept life together for everyone. There wasn't time for anything else. And I was happy." Sophia paused, searching for the words. "But somehow, I lost me.

"That's what happens when the 'shoulds' drown out the 'want tos.' I know, sometimes responsibilities force us not to be self-indulgent. I understand. Responsibility can snuff out that spark of individuality, and we become people we never meant to be."

"You don't want to be a winemaker?" Sophia thought that a travesty considering the wine he made, but competence didn't always dictate the heart.

"Oh, I wanted to make wine. I couldn't have escaped it even had I truly set my mind to it, so I didn't try. And I'm glad I didn't ... most days." Nico opened his eyes and stared up at the sky. "But, in addition, what I wanted was a farm like we had, with grapes that I bred growing on the hillside, and a couple of kids running around like heathens. Like your grandparents, actually."

"They had a good life, I think. Not perfect, but what life is? Sometimes I think, when we are old and we look back on our lives, they will seem perfect from that perspective. What we needed to learn, life taught us. What we needed, life gave us. Maybe that's not what we wanted, but time shows us it's what we needed." Although, she wondered, right now, how could losing my grapes be the thing I need?

"Now look who's being profound," Nico teased. "As I get closer to the end than to the beginning, I suspect you're right."

"Right or wrong, it makes me feel better. But you didn't get your farm?"

"No. My father died; I was the oldest. I'm sure you can fill it in from there. I never wanted to use my passion, my father's wisdom, to line someone else's pockets. Especially someone who didn't value the art in the product."

Sophia moved her hand underneath Nico's, turning it so she could give his a squeeze. "Sounds like both you and I have spent far too long, have given too much, chasing other people's dreams."

They sat there for a bit longer, savoring the night and the comfort they found in each other. Sophia never wanted the night to end. Like a great book, she turned the pages slower and slower as the end drew near. The fire had burned down to embers before either one of them could break the spell.

The kitchen was empty, the dishes cleaned and put away, the glassware washed and turned over onto towels to dry, when they finally wandered inside.

"We never got dessert." Nico pulled open one side of the double refrigerator and peered inside.

"You can't be hungry."

"When I was young, my mother thought I had a tapeworm. Not much has changed." His voice was muffled as he stuck his head inside. He backed out, holding a platter of cookies. "I knew I'd find them in here. Mother has this annoying habit of putting cookies in the fridge. Who likes cold cookies?" He put several on a plate and popped them in the microwave, then poured two glasses of milk while the cookies were heating. "Come on. You have to have at least one."

Sophia joined him at the counter. "You are going to be bad for my waistline. I hate shopping and if I have to move up a size in my jeans because of you, I'm going to be most unhappy."

"Men don't like skinny women." Nico held a cookie between his thumb and forefinger, cupping his other hand underneath. "Here. Take a bite. But I warn you, these things are like culinary crack."

The cookie melted in her mouth, the chewiness of the oatmeal, the sweetness of the coconut and brown sugar, and the savory deliciousness of sweet cream butter, and Sophia believed Nico ... culinary crack. "God, these are ... well, if the Girl Scouts ever find out about them, Olivia needs to be prepared to see her face on the side of a gazillion cookie boxes."

"She'd probably like that, but I'm not sure the Girl Scouts would. In no time, she'd reorganize the whole cookie-selling thing, making it run like German machinery. Their cookie sales would skyrocket."

Nico popped a whole cookie into his mouth and groaned in delight. He washed it down with a swig of milk. When he put the glass down, he turned serious eyes on her. "I want to ask you something."

A frisson of nervousness arced through her. "Okay."

"May I kiss you?"

Sophia thought for a moment, she didn't know why. She'd been unable to think of much more than kissing Nico Treviani for the better part of the last couple of hours. "I'd like that."

He didn't give her a chance to change her mind. Nico stepped into her, sliding one arm around her waist, holding her close. With the other hand he gently swept her bangs out of her eyes, then brushed his thumb lightly over her lips. His touch was warm, leaving a trail of heat where he touched her. His hand slipped to the nape of her neck. He murmured her name as his lips closed over hers.

Fire shot through her as need exploded in her core. Sophia stood on her toes; arching her body she molded it to his. He groaned and pulled her tighter to him until she thought she'd melt into him and there would be nothing left of her. She couldn't breathe—she didn't need to—as sensation engulfed her.

Finally he released her, leaving his forehead pressed to hers and keeping her body on his. "You're not going anywhere, Sophia Stone, are you?" His voice was husky with need.

"No." Sophia's voice sounded small and filled with wonder. She couldn't remember a kiss like Nico's, not ever.

"You'll be here in the morning?"

She wondered what it would be like to spend the night wrapped in his arms. She wasn't ready, that she knew. But, still, it was hard not to think about it. "I'll be here. Where else would I be?"

CHAPTER SEVENTEEN

NIGGLING WORRIES TORMENTED SOPHIA. She tossed and turned, haunted by dreams of grapes and her grandfather and Nico Treviani. She fought with sleep until, the battle lost, she finally surrendered. Only an hour had passed since she slipped under the covers, the night barely begun, yet deepening. It had seemed much longer.

Swinging her legs over the side of the big four-poster bed, she dropped to the floor and strode to the window. Like a flame pulled a moth, the light of a waxing crescent moon drew her.

A restless moon.

Sophia's grandmother had been a simple woman, a country woman used to hard work and well-schooled in the old ways. When Sophia had visited the farmhouse in Friuli with its outdoor plumbing, dirt floors, vegetable cellar, and brick fireplace with a constant fire banked in the back, it had been easy to believe her grandmother when she said the Oteros had the gift of foresight inherited from Romani ancestors who had drifted south from their ancestral home. To a young child it all sounded wonderfully exotic, and gave Sophia a spark of feeling special.

Back in the world of modern conveniences, science, and the pragmatism of her mother, such a thing as being able to see into the future sounded like a silly child's tale, like Peter Pan and his gift of everlasting youth. Regardless, through the years Sophia had learned to trust her gut. Whether it was the gift of sight or simple intuition, when it told her something was wrong, she listened.

Like now.

Of course, Nico Treviani sleeping in the room next to hers was like a jamming signal, muddling clarity and making it impossible to gather her thoughts in any meaningful order. *Men.* A bit disgusted with herself, Sophia shook her head.

She turned the lock and eased the window open. The sounds of the forest had quieted. Every now and then a bat whispered past on silent wings. Breathing deeply she thought she caught a hint of the salty ocean breezes. The Pacific wasn't far, not more than thirty miles. The fog had thickened, cocooning the house and muffling any outside sound. Maybe a truck rumbled past on the highway below, but she wasn't sure.

Home.

The thought hit her hard in the chest, hitching her breath. She closed her eyes, deepened her breathing, pushing her jumbled thoughts and tangled emotions aside.

Home. Stronger now. Her eyes flew open. She had to go home. Now.

Groggy and confused but used to her mother's ways, Dani had relinquished her keys before burrowing back under the covers. After stuffing her hastily gathered things into her duffle, Sophia had tossed it in the passenger seat and said a silent prayer before turning the key. The engine caught on the first spark—a prayer answered. Now out on the highway, she shifted into a higher gear and let the big truck go. Compelled by surety, if not complete clarity, she pressed the accelerator and flew through the curves, oblivious to the redwoods bracketing the road. She really opened it up when she hit the highway back into Napa. A straight shot, she coaxed every MPH out of the old truck ... Daniel's truck. *Take me home, Babà.*

Calistoga and the jog over to Silverado Trail passed in a blur. Every vibration of the truck reverberated through her white-knuckled grip on the steering wheel and up her arms until she thought they would stop her heart. *Let me be in time.* The thought, vague and ominous, propelled her. Wind whipped at her through the open window. She didn't care. Focused, intense ... scared.

Finally, the turn toward the lake, climbing higher. Then slowing. Just around the second curve, her driveway, unmarked and obscure, branched off to the right. Nobody just wandered in. One had to find

CRUSHED

the turn then follow the arrows painted on boards nailed to the occasional tree. Dense forest canopy blotted out the night sky, and the truck bounced over the uneven road. Charlie hadn't graded it in several years. Soon, it would be impassable to anything other than a four-wheel drive, high-clearance vehicle. Of course, that wouldn't be Sophia's problem.

Reality dropped back on her shoulders with the weight of the world.

This wasn't home. At least not for much longer.

As the trees thinned, Sophia slowed. At the tree line she killed the lights, negotiating the rest of the way on moonlight and memory. Idling, letting the big engine pull her, Sophia scanned for anything amiss. But nothing moved; no lights shone in the windows, not even a glow from the kitchen.

That's odd. I was so sure.

Relaxing, but still wary, she eased the truck around the house and parked in the back. Before heading inside, she made a quick tour of the vineyard. No matter how askew, the world righted when she was there among her grapes. She plucked one and popped it between her teeth. *Tomorrow. Yes, tomorrow would be the day to drop the fruit. The day after at the latest.*

An act of defiance, harvesting was the only way Sophia knew how to fight back, to keep going, to claim her grapes. Hadn't Nico said they should keep moving forward and an answer would present itself? While she didn't exactly share his enthusiasm, she needed that bit of carrying on, that bit of normalcy, to keep her grounded ... to keep her whole.

Having walked each row, she was turning toward the house when she heard the first truck start up the grade to her house. A diesel. Heavy. A vineyard truck. She stopped, hidden among the vines. Listening, she waited. Below her one set of headlights poked through the fortress of trees. Two other trucks followed, each flatbeds with fenced sides holding a small army of grape hands. Enemies ghostly and pale in the thin moonlight. The trucks were unmarked, the faces she could make out, unfamiliar.

Running low, bent over, she darted up the porch stairs. Grabbing the shotgun she kept by the door, an old Mossberg pump action her father had bought for her years ago, she retreated once again into the

137

cover of her vines as the first truck reached the top of the hill, its lights probing, a violation she felt in her core.

Eight rounds ... that should be enough. She could hear her father's voice, calm, sure. "Sophia, there is no value in a gun that isn't loaded. But once you point it, you better be ready for what happens next."

Shaking and terrified, she watched the men spill out of the trucks. They weren't even trying to be quiet.

Like thieves and cowards under the cover of darkness, they had come to take her grapes.

She was ready. Oh, yes, she was very ready. But she was scared. She'd never had to stand up before, to defend what was hers, what she wanted. She'd always had Daniel to do that for her. And, while the fires of passion burned hot, acting on them took courage. She didn't know if she could do it.

As she crouched there, she squeezed her eyes shut and prayed to all that was good and holy that the men would get back in their trucks and go home.

The foreman motioned to men and barked orders. "Okay, listen up. You know how this is done. Grab your baskets and get to work. We've got two acres and not much time. We want to pick by section, mark the harvest, keeping everything separate. Now go."

The men started to murmur among themselves as they pulled baskets from the back of the first truck.

Sophia stood, stepped out into the open, and took a wide stance, the gun held in front of her across her body, its weight a comfortable friend in her hands. Anger, cold and deadly, slithered through her, coiling in her gut.

With a quick jerk on the pump, she chambered a round—an unmistakable sound.

The men whirled.

"Can I help you?" Sophia's voice held a tone of brashness she didn't feel. Her palms sweaty, her heart beating a staccato rhythm, she was thankful her voice remained steady. She prayed her knees wouldn't buckle. A bead of sweat trickled in a cold slide down her side.

Trying to hide his surprise, the man who had given the orders stepped forward. After swiping his palms down his jeans, he held his hands open, his arms wide. "Put the gun down, Mrs. Stone." He advanced on her.

Sophia shook her head. "Don't," she ordered, her voice cold and hard. "You boys need to leave. Now."

The expression on his face said he didn't believe she'd follow through on the threat in her voice. His stride hitched, then he continued toward her.

Men. They took what they wanted. They pushed. They intimidated. They demanded. Not anymore. Anger burned through her. Lowering the barrel a fraction so that it was aimed at the ground in front of the foreman, she pulled the trigger. Perhaps it was her father guiding her, but she remembered not to close her eyes or to flinch against the kick.

The report echoed off the trees. Dirt kicked up no more than a foot in front of the foreman. He froze. "Shit."

Sophia held the gun steady and leveled her gaze. "Now, let's start over. What are you doing here?" Behind him Sophia caught one man reaching into the truck. A pistol in the glove compartment, she bet. So this was how it was going to be. She chambered another round, a heart-stopping sound. "You there. Leave it."

He backed away, his hands open, palms facing her.

"All of you, if you doubt that I have the resolve to protect what is mine, you will regret it." She kept her eyes moving over the small band in front of her. "Now, I will ask it one more time. What are you doing here?"

A sneer twisted the foreman's thin lips. Clearly, he didn't like being on the business end of a shotgun, especially one held by a woman. "We were sent to harvest the grapes."

"Believe it or not, I figured that much out myself."

That drew a few snickers from the men.

"On whose authority?"

The man dug the toe of his boot in the sand, testing the hole the buckshot had made. When he looked back up, the look of resolve in his eyes had weakened. "Look, this isn't our fight. We were just told to come get the grapes. I don't know or care who they belong to or why we were sent."

"You should care. By coming here you made it your fight."

One of the workers stepped to the foreman's shoulder. "Mr. Pinkman didn't say nothing about her showing up."

"Shut up," the foreman hissed out of the side of his mouth.

Murderous intent flooded through Sophia, tunneling her vision and making her trigger finger tighten. "Pinkman sent you here?"

The foreman stalled. "We'll leave your grapes alone, okay? We're just going to go now." He started backing away.

Sophia aimed to the right of his left knee and pulled the trigger.

He yelped and looked down at his thigh. "Jesus Christ woman, you hit me."

She was sure he was well outside the buckshot pattern at this close range, but perhaps not. Shotguns were not so much about precision as brute force. But she couldn't have hit him with more than one or two tiny pellets. She didn't feel in the mood to apologize and he seemed to be more surprised than anything, so she ignored him. "You all are trespassing on my land," she said to the crowd. "And I'm vastly outnumbered. If you want to, you can go cry to the sheriff, but that might bring up a few other interesting felonies. You there," she motioned to the man who had spoken with the foreman, "Everyone in the valley knows this is my place. Why did you think I wouldn't be here?"

"Look, lady, I'll lose my job if I tell you."

"You should've thought of that before."

The foreman stepped forward. When Sophia swiveled toward him, he stopped, putting his hands up, waist-high. "I'll tell you."

When he'd stepped forward, he'd caught just a bit of light on his face. The left side of his face looked drawn upward, his eyebrow arcing too high, as if a wound above it had been closed with too little skin to cover it. And he was missing the last digit on his left forefinger, not that unusual considering the sharp tools and heavy machinery used in the vineyards and the wineries. But, his hands weren't calloused and stained like a true field hand's would be.

Sophia was sure she hadn't seen him around, and she knew most of the regulars in the fields, Pinkman's and the other growers'. "Okay."

He looked at her, a steady gaze full of meanness that made

Sophia shiver. "I heard it from Mr. Treviani."

The world stopped turning, and, for a moment, life as it was stopped. "What?" Sophia whispered. "Nico told you?"

The man's eyes darted to the foreman, who stepped in. "Like he said. We're here cuz of Mr. Treviani."

A few simple words. That's all it took to transform happy into homicide. Sophia lowered her voice. "You'd better leave. Now."

The men dove for their trucks. Amazingly, Sophia watched them go without killing even one of them or falling apart herself. Rooted, she watched, transfixed long after they had disappeared and the sound of their trucks had faded into the night.

Nico had told them?

She thought of him, the glimpse she'd seen this evening. Traversing the memories, she wondered what she had missed. How could she have been so wrong? Finally, the cold, of night and of betrayal, seeped through the cracks of her resilience, shaking her to the core and she headed toward the house ... her haven, her home.

The kitchen and its warmth welcomed her, but she found little comfort there.

Nico.

At first, she didn't believe it; her heart refused to believe it. But who else had known she would be gone, that she would be with Nico and his family at the river? Dani? She wouldn't have said anything. The only other person who had known was Nico.

His betrayal cut like a cold-tempered steel blade, eviscerating, carving out her heart and dicing it into tiny bits. Placing the gun at the ready in the corner, she paced around the kitchen as her thoughts stormed through her head, first denying it could be true, then castigating herself for being such a fool, buying a handsome man's line. She should know better. Her emotions swung wildly from heartbreak to anger, hitting every low point in between.

The river had been a setup. A well-acted play with her as the butt of the joke.

After wearing a track across the kitchen and weak from the emotional beating, Sophia succumbed to exhaustion. Stopping in the middle of the room, light-headed, she swayed on unsteady legs. Defeat panted at her shoulder. Anger cooled to a simmer.

Had she really been that stupid? Nico hadn't seemed like that kind of guy. That kind of subterfuge took a special kind of ugly. Most folks could be capable of it, she guessed, given the right kind of motivation. But what did Nico need from her? He was the toast of Napa, the top of the winemaker heap. Did he really want more? Could she have been so wrong about him? None of it made sense.

Sophia sank into one of the chairs at the table, her hands molded around a mug of hot coffee. Calming herself with caffeine spoke volumes about her day. A bone weariness leaked in around the edges of her resolve. She had no answers, yet she was worse off than before. Completely stymied, a bit broken, she sat there, her mind dead, her nerves numb.

The sound of a truck fishtailing up her drive caught her attention but took a moment to fully register. Pushing herself to her feet, she grabbed the gun. Stepping onto the front porch, she stared into the lights of the oncoming truck that headed for her, then braked, skidding to the side in a shower of gravel.

CHAPTER EIGHTEEN

DANI BOUNDED OUT OF THE passenger side. "Mom! What the hell is going on? Some guys stopped us at the turn-off. They were babbling that you shot someone." She arrived breathless to stand in front of her mother. Bed hair, still in her nightshirt but with a pair of jeans underneath, she looked like the child Sophia remembered from many Christmas mornings—well, if you substituted happiness for the worry now clouding her face.

"I just scared him a bit." Sophia didn't recognize her own voice. It sounded odd, with a new tone of don't-mess-with-me.

"So you *did* shoot someone?" Dani sounded almost pleased.

"If she did, I'm sure he deserved it." Nico stepped around the truck and headed toward her. "Are you all right? What the hell went on up here?"

Sophia felt nothing. Then aching sadness and need unfurled in her belly. Her knees weakened; anger kept them from buckling. "Stay right there." She swiveled the gun toward his feet. "I mean it."

"What?" he stammered, a look of stunned disbelief on his face. But he did as she asked.

"Mom?" Dani, too sounded incredulous.

"The men, I hadn't seen them around, which was unusual, but not unheard of. They came to pick my grapes."

"What?" Nico's face clouded, his mouth drew into an angry slash.

"They said Pinkman sent them."

"That son of a bitch," Nico growled.

"They said you told them I wouldn't be here."

"You aren't serious?" Now, as reality dawned across his face, Nico looked hurt. "You think I ..."

"I don't know what to think."

"You can't think I had anything to do with this." He held his hands out, waist-high, imploring. "Even assuming I'm capable of what you are accusing me of, why would I do such a thing?"

"I don't know? To keep your job? You are the Devil's minion, you know."

His face clouded with anger. "No matter what, I would never sell my soul like that." A lock of dark hair had fallen across his forehead. Come to think of it, his normally well-kept hair was a mess and Sophia fought the urge to comb it into place with her fingers.

"But you have. You said so yourself."

Nico took a deep, steadying breath. "True. Look, Sophia, the river, the invitation, I know how it looks. But I swear I had nothing to do with this."

"Then how did they know? Why did they say you told them I wouldn't be here?"

Nico, letting his arms drop to his sides, looked at a loss, his shoulders slumped in defeat, or weariness ... or both. But Sophia saw no righteous indignation, the ruse often used to cover guilt, and her heart opened just a little. She so wanted to believe him.

Sophia hadn't had much sleep, and she figured Nico couldn't have had much more. From the looks of him, he could use a cup of coffee and a hug, one she ached to give him, but couldn't.

Dani reached out and touched her mother's arm. "Why don't we go inside and you can tell us exactly what was said and we can try to piece this together, okay?"

Sophia looked at Nico, remembered the stories he'd told, the dreams they'd shared. He couldn't be behind this; he just couldn't. She lowered the gun and stepped aside, inviting them in. "Even an accused gets his day in court."

The kitchen, warm and bright with the smell of fresh coffee hanging in the air, welcomed them and soothed Sophia's jangled nerves. Buoyed by memories and the sense of belonging, she once again rested the gun in the corner by the door. Wiping her fear-slicked palms on her jeans, she searched for balance in the routine of the mundane. "Coffee?"

Nico nodded as he took a place at the table—the same place Charlie Vespers had chosen. Dani pulled three mugs from the cupboard, leaving them on the counter for her mother to fill.

"The coffee is fresh."

Dani grabbed cream from the fridge—none of them took sugar—placing it within reach as she took the chair next to Nico.

With the three mugs clutched by the "c" handles, Sophia joined them at the table, putting Dani between her and Nico as she dispensed the coffee. Overtaken by a weariness that seeped through her bones and hollowed her heart, Sophia started to shake. She cupped her mug, anchoring herself to something solid, something real, as thoughts and fears hacked at the last threads of her strength. "I don't know what got into me."

"What do you mean?" Dani asked as she poured enough cream into her coffee to turn it a slight sandy color.

"Taking your grandfather's gun. Shooting at that man." Sophia ran a hand through her hair. "I've never done anything like that before."

"I bet you scared the shit out of them." Dani grinned.

Her daughter's grin warmed the coldness Sophia felt inside. Neither of them seemed to think she had done anything wrong. She gave a tentative smile. "I scared the shit out of me, too."

Dani's grin faded, her eyes turned serious. "What made you leave like that, in the middle of the night and come home?"

"I couldn't sleep. Something was nagging at me. And I just knew."

Dani's voice dropped to a whisper. "Like Great-grandmother used to say."

"What did she say?" Nico asked.

Reverence painted Dani's face as she looked at him with bright eyes. "That the women in the family have the gift of sight."

"There is no such thing," Sophia said, trying to shut down the topic with her tone.

Nico started to disagree; she could read it on his face. She shut him down with a look. "It was fun, I bet." Nico looked at her over the lip of the mug as he blew on his coffee. "Taking back a bit of power."

"A rush, I admit." She leveled a strong look at Nico. "These grapes. This house." She looked around for a moment, lingering on the whispers she heard in the corners. "Well, they're mine for a little bit longer."

"Hopefully more than a little while," Nico said but with a little less conviction than Sophia had noticed before.

Sophia looked between her tablemates. "Okay, who's going to start?"

Nico leaned forward. "I'll tell you what I know. I was asleep when the sound of a truck engine woke me up. I couldn't see who was driving, so I checked your room and you were gone. Worried, I went and woke up Dani. She told me some silly story about you having some premonition or something that you needed to get home."

"Not so silly now, is it?" Dani jumped to her mother's defense.

"No." Nico set his mug on the table and pushed it away. "Sophia, how did you really know to come home?"

Sophia waved that away. "The better question is how did the men know I wouldn't be here?"

"I didn't tell anyone," Nico stated, as if that was enough. "I don't share my personal life. The only people who knew you were coming for the weekend are my mother, my sister, and the people sitting at this table. I didn't even tell Taryn and Brookly until we were in the truck. Took some ribbing all the way to Vic's." He didn't look displeased.

Sophia's gaze shifted to her daughter. She didn't need to ask.

Dani looked thoughtful, a serious look making her appear older than she was. "I've been going back over the scenario, and the only time someone could've overheard was in the vineyard." She turned to Nico. "Remember? You came to find me. You wanted my help in grabbing a few bottles more of Mother's wine? I asked you why."

Nico's eyes grew larger, harder. "Of course!" He punctuated the statement with an open hand slap on the table, making the mugs jump. "We spoke of it in detail." When his eyes turned to Sophia, there was a plea in them. "Someone had to have heard us. Believe me, if I had any idea those two asses would pull such a shady stunt, I would've been more careful." He launched himself to his feet. His chair flew back. "And I would've been up here with a goddamn gun myself."

Sophia was too tired to be startled. "Where are you going?"

He pulled his cell from his pocket and began dialing, then glanced up as the call connected. "The men might be back. We need some help." He strode through the door.

Sophia watched him pace back and forth across the porch door opening as he barked into his phone, only half-paying attention to what he said or who he was talking to.

"Mom, you have to believe him. He wouldn't do this—try to steal your grapes in the darkness. That's a coward's way. If Nico Treviani wanted what was yours, I guarantee you would know it. He would tell you."

Sophia's mind drifted back to the house on the river, the heat of Nico's presence, his touch. The fire in his kiss. He'd murmured, his breath hot against her cheek, "I want you, Sophia Otero Stone. I want you in a way I've never wanted anybody." He'd pressed his hand over his heart. "I saw your tear at my parents' story. You feel deeply. You understand."

Yes, he'd told her what he wanted.

"So, who told Pinkman and Specter about the grapes? Who showed them what I have?"

"Well, it wasn't Mr. Treviani. The deal was inked before he had any idea what you have up here."

Before Sophia could fully grasp that idea, Nico stepped back into the kitchen, energy radiating off of him. "Okay, I've got Billy Rodrigues rounding up some guys. They're going to hang out at the bottom of the road up here. Billy will join me up here first, then I'll probably post him somewhere down the hill and we'll keep watch until morning."

"You're not staying here." The thought of having Nico Treviani this close all night was both a fear and a temptation Sophia worried she couldn't resist.

He slid into the chair next to hers and took her hands in his. "Let me do this. I won't sleep thinking of you up here all by yourself."

"I can stay," Dani offered.

Both Nico and Sophia turned and said, "No!" in unison.

F

"Well, okay." She sounded a bit amused.

"Honey." Sophia squeezed her arm. "If those men come back, I don't want you here."

Dani started to argue but quieted at her mother's look. "Yes, ma'am." She rose, gave her mother a peck on the cheek, a smile to Nico. "You take good care of her. If anything happens to her ..."

"It won't."

With a curt nod, she turned, swiped her keys from where Sophia had thrown them on the counter, and disappeared into the night. Within moments her truck fired up and eased into gear.

Both Sophia and Nico watched until her red tail lights blinked at the forest edge then were swallowed.

A companionable silence filled the space between them, each of them lost in their own thoughts.

"You really don't have to do this, Nico. This isn't your fight."

"Yes, I do. And, yes, it is." He raised a hand to quell her argument. "It's my fight because I choose it to be."

They talked a bit over several mugs of coffee, working for the words, each trying to re-find their once solid footing. The ease between them was returning when Billy Rodrigues tapped at the back door then walked in. "I saw you sitting in here. Hope you don't mind."

Sophia started to stand as Nico made the introductions, but Billy motioned her back down. "Don't stand on my account. You've had one hell of an evening, I'd say. And call me Quatro." He flashed her a bright smile that was both friendly and sympathetic.

Put at ease by his manner, disarmed by his smile, Sophia liked Billy Rodrigues on sight. And the obvious affection he had for Nico soothed her jangled nerves and diffused her doubts. Sophia's grandmother had always believed one could tell the character of a man by the friends he kept. And Sophia didn't think a man like Billy would have a scoundrel for a friend.

Billy hooked his thumb, gesturing over his shoulder. "Most of the men followed me. We're waiting on a few stragglers. Nico, why don't you come and tell them what you have in mind?"

"Did they bring their guns?"

Billy raised an eyebrow. "They keep them in their trucks all the time. Hell, you know that."

"Give me a minute. I'll be right there."

Billy touched the brim of his hat and dipped his head slightly toward Sophia. "Ma'am."

"Call me Sophia. And thank you." When Billy had gone and she was sure he was out of hearing, she turned to Nico. "Is that Victoria's Billy?"

"Yes."

Sophia stared after Billy, lost in thought. "Why aren't they together?"

A cloud passed across Nico's face. "You'd have to ask them."

NICO HAD ORGANIZED THE MEN, leaving Billy to stand guard at the back while he took a position in the front room, in Sophia's reading chair by the bay window, her shotgun across his knees. Specter had surprised him with his end-run around not only the unwritten rules of business but the legalities as well. Underestimating his opponent was a great way to be left out in the cold without any clothes. Nico had done that once before. He wouldn't make that mistake twice.

Curiously, even with amazing grapes and brilliant wine, all he could think about was Sophia asleep upstairs. It had taken all of his powers of persuasion and self-control to convince her to get some rest and then to watch her climb the stairs and turn to wave wearily from the landing.

He leaned his head back and closed his eyes. He swore, years ago, no more women other than the occasional gratuitous, no-strings-attached kind. He'd stuck to his deal, but now, with just a couple of times in her presence, he was ready to throw caution out the window and his heart into the fray.

Women. They always wanted something, and he could never figure out what it was. Except Sophia. Guileless, upfront, she seemed capable, yet unsure ... perhaps even a little afraid. He wasn't quite sure of what. She'd been hurt badly by the loss of her husband; that part was easy to figure out. But the wine part, the grape part, less so. She had that dream in the palm of her hand, right there, ready for the picking … literally. Why couldn't she see it?

The combination of maturity and the calm that comes with it, tempered with a need to hang onto dreams, her kindness, defined by her ability to draw a line and not let anyone step over... and then be so surprised at her ability to enforce those boundaries—the curious combination that was Sophia Stone had him turned in circles.

And, he liked it. She made him feel alive in a way he thought had died years ago.

But the grapes and the wine presented complications, complications he had no idea how to navigate. He'd lost at precisely that game before. Caught in the vise of work and reputation, responsibility and confidence, life tugged him in conflicting directions. Sophia's grapes, their wine could solve a lot of his problems and give him what he so desperately needed. And there was Sophia. No matter what he did, how hard he tried, the mere sight of her cracked the shell around his heart and reminded him what feeling and connection really did for one's soul.

No doubt about it, he had some difficult choices to make.

CHAPTER NINETEEN

SOPHIA HEARD THE STAIRS CREAK as someone hit the old board, third from the top. Her heartbeat quickened. She wasn't afraid. The door eased open. Moonlight streaming through the window at the top of the landing silhouetted a figure in the doorway. A man, long and lean. She knew him.

Nico.

He whispered her name.

She eased to the far side of the bed, folding back a corner of the covers, inviting him in. He unbuttoned his shirt, letting it slough off, then stepped out of his jeans, letting them fall to the floor. He wore nothing else. He lay next to her, wrapping her in an embrace, pulling her close, working his hands under the light shirt she wore to sleep in. Raising her arms she let him shimmy the thin cloth over her head. Curling into him, she bowed her body to his, skin on skin, until the heat consumed her thoughts, leaving only white-hot desire.

His mouth took hers, his tongue plundering. Pleasure bolted through her.

He traced her body, singeing her skin with need. He smelled of wine, of dreams, musky and elemental. Bending her back, his lips found her neck. Nipping, teasing, he branded her with desire as he kissed the hollow of her collarbone. A moan, low and primal, escaped as his mouth closed over her breast, nipping, his tongue teasing, sending flashes of desire deeper, a warmth spreading lower. His fingers brushed down her belly. Soft flesh, a nub of pure pleasure. His strokes slow and sure. Pleasure curling, tightening.

She rolled slightly, pulling him, encouraging, his mouth again finding hers. With his knees he moved her legs apart. As he moved over her, he held himself above her, looking into her eyes. Her eyes locked with his, her breath fast, her body at the edge of shattering, she reached for him, guiding.

His breath hitched at her touch.

"Please, Nico."

He plunged inside her. Deeper. Then pulling back, then once more. Pleasure building, clutching around him ... Her nails dug into his back. Riding higher and higher ... until she shattered.

Spent, she uncoiled and lay back as the waves of her orgasm pulsed through her, weakening her legs, leaving a ball of warmth that huddled in her core that radiated outward in frissons of ecstasy.

Breathing fast, she laughed and opened her eyes.

She was alone. The room empty.

Raising on her elbow, Sophia looked around. A soft breeze billowed the sheer curtains. Moonlight softened the harsh pull of loneliness.

She pressed a hand to her stomach. Sweat dampened her nightshirt. The visceral memory of his touch, the heat of his skin, the burn of his lips, the fullness of him as he filled her assaulted her.

But it wasn't real.

THE DAY DAWNED HEAVY WITH the promise of heat. Sophia felt profoundly unsettled, an imagined connection somehow making her feel disconnected, out of synch. The smell of fresh coffee brewing wafted in through her open bedroom window. Nico must have the door open downstairs.

Nico.

In her kitchen.

The thought of him there, using her things—the chipped mug Daniel had bought on their honeymoon or the painted one Trey had made for her in summer camp when he was ten—felt like a violation and an impossible dream at the same time. Suddenly she felt a bit shy, nervous really, and oddly irritated. No. Not irritated ... disquieted. Encountering Nico on neutral ground was hard enough. The intimacy of his presence in her home awakened feelings, hopes, she wasn't sure she was ready to risk.

The bang of the screen door, then a truck firing up. Sophia stepped to the window, hiding behind the gather of the sheers. She caught the blink of Nico's tail lights, then his truck disappeared into the trees. The sound of its engine misfiring lingered, then faded.

Silence. Her home was hers, which did little to calm her fluttered feelings. Nico took them with him, or at least removed them from the immediate, surrendering them to another problem with no resolution—something of which she had an abundance.

She had no idea what to do about Nico, but she sure as hell knew where to start with the property problem.

Back to the beginning. Back to Charlie Vespers.

Grabbing her clothes, Sophia hit the bathroom, spending as little time as possible pulling herself together. Hopping on one foot as she pulled on a shoe, then she switched feet doing the same thing with the other shoe, and headed downstairs. The kitchen was empty, but she thought she could just catch the lingering scent of Nico Treviani.

Pushing thoughts of him away, she poured some coffee into her insulated mug and slapped on the top, bypassing cream. Nothing to sweeten the day. No pleasure until she'd inflicted some pain. That sounded good to Sophia, but made her laugh at herself a bit. Pain was something she was used to enduring, not inflicting.

She grabbed her keys from the hook, took a sip of coffee and grimaced. Nico had found the Starbucks, the most undrinkable coffee on the planet. Bitter and burnt, bad for a normal day, but just the tonic for a showdown.

He'd also left a message stuck to the screen door. After arranging for a different crew to guard the entrance to her property, he'd headed off to work and would "see her later." Anticipation loosed a swarm of butterflies in her stomach, but at the thought of the day ahead, they settled. First pain then pleasure. Her truck started easily, a horse ready to carry her to battle. She didn't have far to go.

Charlie's house squatted at the bottom of the mountain. His truck was out front, and she pulled hers in next to it. Sophia found Charlie in the kitchen huddling over a plate of runny scrambled eggs that smelled a bit past their prime, or maybe that was garlic powder, something every good Italian found offensive.

When she stepped through the screen door, letting it clatter closed behind her, Charlie's eyes flicked to her then back to his meal. He didn't look surprised. "I thought I heard your truck. You haven't fixed that muffler yet."

Sophia placed both hands on the table and leaned down until she was close enough to Charlie to make him lean back slightly. He reeked of stale beer, late nights, and bad choices. "I want copies of everything you've signed with Specter and Pinkman."

Charlie focused on his plate as he forked in a bite of egg then tore off a piece of burnt toast. He parked the whole mess in his cheek. "Those won't help you."

"I'll be the judge."

He focused on his eggs, refusing to keep her gaze. "Why should I show them to you? None of your business, really." He chewed a few times then swallowed, washing everything down with a cup of coffee that had a film on it. Yesterday's batch, Sophia guessed.

"You told them about my grapes, didn't you?" Sophia had underestimated Charlie Vespers. Outwardly he'd never shown any interest in wine or grapes, but, she should've known. Living in the Valley one couldn't avoid wine or grapes, the lust and lore permeated the air and infected every hill and hollow.

Charlie's eyes darted to hers then back to his plate, and she had her answer.

"You are profiting from my labor. You are selling my soul. You owe me." The tone in her voice surprised her, and it seemed to galvanize Charlie Vespers.

His tone turned solicitous. "It's all legal."

"Legal doesn't make it right." Sophia held out a hand. "Give me the papers, Charlie."

He waffled, but the fight had left him. "They'll have my ass."

"Who're you more afraid of? Men who slink around, hiding like coyotes looking for easy prey or the woman in your kitchen with a case of red-ass and nothing to lose?"

Charlie might be lacking in character and of questionable moral fiber, but he wasn't stupid. He dabbed at his lips with an oily paper towel, then pushed back from the table.

Sophia followed him to a small office in the front of the house. His parents' original artwork was gone. So was the gun collection in the gun case against the far wall and most of the pieces of nice furniture. The few chairs and sofa that remained were threadbare and forlorn. Charlie grabbed a sheaf of papers from the desk—at least he'd kept his father's burled walnut desk—then fed them into the slot on the printer/copier. When a second set kicked out, he gathered them and thrust them at her. His eyes were hollow, unfocused, as if he didn't see her, but instead stared, mesmerized by an untethered future. Sophia could almost sympathize ... almost. But Charlie had brought this upon not only himself but both of them, something she couldn't forgive.

Pausing, Sophia glanced through the papers. When she looked up, her eyes were hard. "*This* is what you got for my home? *This* is the offer you couldn't refuse?"

"They have me over a barrel. Like I said, life has taken a wrong turn lately. I need the money."

"If I can break this, I just might be doing us both a favor. You didn't even give me a chance, Charlie. Not even the decency of a heads-up. If Daniel were alive, you wouldn't have had the balls to pull a fast one like this." Sophia turned on her heel. She felt, weak, overlooked ... and bullied. Not an unusual feeling, still it chafed.

Charlie's voice followed her out the door. "It's not personal."

That's where he was wrong.

CHAPTER TWENTY

TO HEAR HIS FATHER TELL IT, Beck Silver was a local boy gone bad. Instead of riding his father's coattails into the wine business, Beck had defected and had become something worse than his father imagined—Beck had become a lawyer.

After editing the *Law Review* at Berkeley, he'd clerked for the Ninth Circuit, then turned his back on the partnership track at some fancy firm in San Francisco. Returning home, he'd hung his shingle in front of one of the Victorians in the old residential part of St. Helena on the east side of the highway close to the Safeway. Most of the old homes now housed businesses of one sort or the other. A massage parlor flanked his on one side, a homeopath's office on the other. He'd opened his doors ten years ago and had been unraveling the myriad legal knots the locals managed to tie ever since. His mother was delighted, but his father had never gotten over it, at least not that he stated publicly. To him, being a member of the Bar was akin to joining the Communist Party. Beck's father had died last year. Sophia hoped he'd patched things up with his son—that was too large a burden, too unbearable a legacy to leave.

With battered briefcase in hand, Beck was just turning up the front walkway as Sophia pulled the truck next to the curb and killed the engine. A smile creased his face at the sight of her, and he stopped and waited, both hands on the handle of his briefcase, which he held in front of him and bounced off his knees. Short, with wavy brown hair just showing a hint of distinguished gray, bright blue eyes that held a perpetual twinkle, he wore a work shirt, creased jeans, scuffed boots, and a welcoming smile. "Sophia, it's so good to see you."

"Beck, it's been awhile." Beck had handled everything when Daniel had died. Sophia had never forgotten his kindness and consideration, giving her time to grieve before hitting her with the tidal wave of details to be handled when someone dies unexpectedly. More recently, maybe two years ago—the time had just flown and Sophia couldn't be sure—he'd worked up an estate plan for her mother.

They walked shoulder-to-shoulder up the walkway and the stairs to the porch. Beck opened the door, then stepped back, allowing Sophia to precede him. "If you don't mind me saying so, you look loaded for bear. What's going on?"

"Do you have time now or should I make an appointment? It's a bit much to explain."

Beck glanced at the watch on his wrist, the leather band dark and worn through years of service to his father. "I've got time before my first appointment, and it's just a will execution. Mrs. Martinez can organize all of that." Beck laughed. "And far better than I, I'm afraid. She could do most of what I do in her sleep." Mrs. Martinez was his assistant, and she'd been with first his grandfather before him and now Beck for more years than anyone wanted to admit. Beck motioned Sophia to a chair. He stepped around his desk and heaved his briefcase onto the polished mahogany, making Sophia cringe. He gave her a lopsided smile as if he knew what she was thinking, then he fell into his chair and leaned back.

Sophia slid the papers across to him. After donning a pair of round wire-rims, he scanned through each sheet then tilted his head, looking at her over the top of the rims. "I'll need a bit of time to go through these in more detail. I'm assuming you want to find a loophole, a way for you to keep the land?"

Sophia leaned back, grabbing the wooden balls at the end to the arms of the chair in a strong grip. "I want to know if I have any options. Quite frankly, I don't know how I'd come up with the money, even if Charlie could and would break this contract. He needs to sell."

"I'm not surprised." Beck sounded as if he knew more, but Sophia didn't ask. At this point, she no longer cared.

She leaned forward. "I need to tell you what happened last night."

Beck steepled his fingers as he rocked back and let Sophia talk, his eyes widening in surprise as she got into the story. "They came to steal your grapes?"

"*Are* they my grapes? Do I still own them?"

"Well," Beck fingered the papers, "that's a good question. You say you and Charlie don't have a written lease?"

Sophia shook her head. "Not that I remember."

"Transfers of real property need to be in writing. And a lease is a transfer of an interest, the interest to occupy and inhabit the property and use it for the stated purpose. Are you sure you and Daniel didn't have a lease? You must have. Daniel was a stickler for details."

He didn't say it, but Sophia knew what he was thinking. Details she'd let slide. "I'm sure we did, Beck, but that was a lifetime ago. I couldn't remember to save my soul."

"How about to save your home?"

That hit Sophia like a knife between her ribs. "I'll try, but any physical agreement, well, that would've been in Daniel's papers. After the accident ..." She raked her fingers through her hair as she stared out the front window trying to go back, but resisting the pain, the deep, soul-numbing pain she knew she'd find there. After a moment, she pulled herself back. "The first few months I lived by rote. My mother helped me make sure the basics were covered. Other than that, I pretty much checked out, I retreated.... somewhere. It's possible we have some paperwork, an old lease or something. But you remember this place back then. A handshake sealed most deals, and paperwork, if any, was spotty."

Beck looked at her with kind eyes. Sophia appreciated that. God knew she'd let a bunch slip through the cracks back then.

"If there was a lease, do you have any idea where it might be?"

"In a box in the attic or in the garage. I kept most everything. Of course, I haven't looked at any of it in a long time. Mother and I cleaned out the desk and threw all of it in boxes." She wasn't going to admit that Daniel's clothes still hung in his closet, which hadn't been opened since she'd chosen the pants and shirt to bury him in.

"Take a look. I know it won't be easy, but, Sophia, it's important." He waited until she nodded. "And ask your mother if she might know where a lease would be. If we have one, then there should've been a holdover provision. That would give us some solid legal ground." Looking out the front window, Beck thought for a moment. When he looked at her, Sophia felt like a rabbit being eyed by a fox. "What about Charlie? I'm sure he has a copy of the original lease."

Sophia gave him a look. "Charlie? He wants the deal to go through as quickly as possible. Do you really think he'd give me legal ammunition to delay if not totally derail the sale?"

"If he had any honor," Beck started, then quit. He knew Charlie even better than Sophia did.

"So, if we can't find a lease, they could come back and take my grapes?"

Beck gave her a grin. "Oh, don't sell me so short. We'll stall them. We can file for a protective order and we can subpoena the lease from Charlie. Of course, I'm not sure it'll fly with old Judge Caruthers; he's a crusty old salt who's gotten used to making the law as he goes—but it'll buy a little bit of time."

SUNLIGHT HIT HER LIKE THE harsh light of an interrogation, leaving her stranded for a moment on Beck Silver's porch as her eyes adjusted. Unsure of the next step, Sophia left her truck and walked over to Main Street. Annalise's bakery was on the corner. Her stomach growled in anticipation, surprising her. She'd eaten her weight at the river last night, each dish irresistible. But an overload of adrenaline had evaporated any calorie reserve, and hunger gnawed anew.

Slaying demons was hard work.

The smell of warm croissants seduced her the minute she walked through the door. Sophia was in luck; the line was only ten-deep. Annalise, trim in her pale blue apron, ubiquitous cotton blouse, her hair piled on her head and an efficient look on her face, helped each patron in turn, thanking them with a wisp of a smile and only a hint of warmth as she hurried them through.

Even still, the line moved slowly, and Sophia was worried about getting her chocolate-filled croissant as hungry shoppers snatched up the pastries. Like moviegoers at the Cameo counted patrons in front of them and measured the number against the tickets that remained, Sophia eyed the dwindling supply and wondered what the man in front of her would order. Would he take them all? Was he counting croissants, too? He was noticeably fidgety. Short, with wavy grey hair he wore in wispy curls just long enough to be attractive. He carried a small paunch, and when he turned, catching Sophia looking, a shy smile curled his lips and lit his eyes, which crinkled at the corners. Round and cherubic he looked nice, but distracted, even a little nervous.

When he reached the front of the line, he stammered out his order. Annalise smiled and her cheeks pinked as she dipped her head shyly. Flirting. Annalise was flirting. Sophia watched the two of them do the verbal two-step. She couldn't hear the conversation, but it clearly extended beyond croissants and *café Américain*. Sophia leaned in, trying to hear. The man conversed in halting French, French with a decided American inflection. Annalise, her eyes warm, her expression kind and interested, waited patiently as he bumbled through. She replied in the same tongue. Was there any word in the English language that didn't sound magical when lilted on a French accent? Sophia thought not.

Finally, Annalise cast a look over the man's shoulder and caught Sophia's amusement. She didn't seem bothered by it, but she finished the man's transaction and muttered a few indecipherable words to him as he picked up his tray and sought a table. Whatever she'd said, the man seemed pleased as he slid past Sophia.

"Well, well. *Who* was that?"

Anticipating Sophia's order, Annalise dove into the case, wax paper in one hand a plate in the other and began to pile the remaining croissants on the plate. When she reemerged, she once again wore a semblance of regal composure. "What do you mean?"

"Oh, come on, give it up. Others might be afraid of the haughty, icy stare, but not me."

Annalise crumpled a bit, relaxing into happiness, which warmed her skin to a glow. She looked furtively over Sophia's shoulder and from side-to-side, then leaned forward. "Anthony West," she said, her voice modulated to just above a whisper.

"What?" Sophia's head snapped around.

Annalise grabbed her arm. "Don't look. Christ, he'll see you. I'm not supposed to tell, but I know his secret is safe with you."

Sophia tore her gaze from the sweet-looking man in the corner busy slathering his croissant with unsalted butter. "He's like the most feared food critic in the Bay area. Restaurateurs and chefs alike practically faint at the mention of his name. He can be quite ..."

"Cruel? Yes, he leaves them quaking in their boots." Annalise nodded once, looking pleased. "He considers that to be his job."

"He's not what I would've imagined."

"That's what makes it perfect. No one knows what he looks like, and no one would suspect."

"Wow." Sophia chewed on the inside of her cheek. "And he comes here for pastries?"

"For some time now."

"I gathered that since you two are sharing ... confidences."

Annalise smiled and gave a Gallic shrug. "He's nice."

"He better not hurt you or I'll cut out his heart."

Annalise didn't look worried. "Take the booth in the corner. I'll join you in a minute."

"You're not going to join your friend?"

"He's got to be in the city by noon."

Sophia took the plate of croissants and a large mug from the stack by the register. "I don't know how many you piled on here, but it's definitely over my limit. Don't tell me you're going to risk that incredible figure and help me with these."

"No." Annalise reached behind her, untying her apron, then eased it over her head without disturbing a hair. "Maggie will be here in a few."

Annalise didn't waste time handing over the reins to her register. Sophia barely had time to take a breath before Annalise slid into the booth across from her. "So, how are you doing, really?"

Sophia played with her empty mug. "Too numb to know."

Annalise took Sophia's mug and eased out of the booth. Returning with two mugs of steaming coffee, she pushed one toward Sophia. "Cream, no sugar." It was a statement, not a question, and she'd remembered correctly. "I know something about loss," she began quietly. "Years ago my life served up a maelstrom much as yours is doing to you now. First Daniel, then Trey—oh, I know he's not lost, he's just gone, but in many ways it can feel the same."

Sophia nodded, her chest starting to hurt.

"Now Dani."

Sophia pulled an end off the croissant, hoping the buttery middle came with it. She wasn't disappointed. As she savored the delicacy, she wished Annalise would get to the point. Rehashing wasn't going to provide any answers, nor would it make her feel better. "You forgot my mother."

"Yes. But that is a loss our souls are prepared for. The others alter us in ways we can't comprehend." Annalise took a croissant for herself, surprising Sophia. "I lost a child once. Well, I didn't lose him. I was responsible for his death."

"What?" The word escaped on a rush of surprise and horror. "I'm so sorry." *Secrets.*

Annalise's struggle to give voice to hers was painful to watch. "I was young. My first car. The boy ran between two parked cars—you know how Paris streets can be. I never saw him."

"Oh!" Sophia flinched at the visceral horror. "But surely you know it was an accident."

"Yes, but the burden is still mine. I'll never forget, the boy... his parents ..." She shivered and visibly worked to pull herself together.

"Is that why you never had children of your own?"

"And why I don't drive." Annalise cocked her head and gave a slight shrug. "I've not spoken of it in a very long time. I just wanted to let you know that I'm here to help. I understand what loss can do to you, how hard it is to start fighting your way back."

"Thank you." She could see how hard it had been for her friend to share. Annalise's story had had one effect, perhaps one she had intended. But her experience put Sophia's in perspective. She'd been passive far too long. It was time to fight for what she could save—her grapes, her family... herself. If only she knew how.

The young girl at the counter seemed overwhelmed as the line now stretched out the door. Annalise put a hand on Sophia's arm. "You will find a way to put the past where it belongs. And now, you must find the future you want." With an apologetic smile, she excused herself to go help.

Sophia was filling her mug with fresh coffee when Maggie burst through the door.

"Hey, everybody!" She waved liked she'd been voted Rodeo Queen. Most of the patrons waved back. She stopped to talk with a few as she worked her way back to the booth. Sophia retook her former position in the booth, careful not to spill her fresh mug of coffee. She arranged the forks around the table. Maggie positioned herself in the seat Annalise had vacated. "Hey. I didn't know you were going to be here. What's the latest?"

Maggie's question jolted Sophia back to reality, her reality, and her heart fell. She filled Maggie in.

"Are you shitting me?" Maggie leaned forward, her eyes wide.

"Don't breathe on the food, Maggie," Annalise admonished as she eased in after Sophia had moved over making room. She'd opened a second register, and things flowed more smoothly now.

Maggie gave her a look. "I'm up to date on all of my shots."

"Yes, but that doesn't account for any animals you've kissed recently."

Maggie laughed a throaty, bawdy laugh. "True." She sobered and looked back at Sophia. "But Devlin isn't an animal—well, not much of one. Being British, he's all very proper, you know."

That got both Annalise's and Sophia's attention. "Devlin?" they both asked.

Maggie preened in the limelight. "He bought the farm over the hill—the old Franklin place."

"A dairy farmer?" Sophia asked. Sonoma County had been discovered by the organic, artisanal folks—refugees from high-powered jobs looking for some hippie happiness.

"Horses. One of the British Olympic team—show jumping, eventing, all of that." She waved away any more questions. "More on that another time. Sophia, why don't you give Annalise the skinny, then we'll plot who to kill first and where to bury the bodies."

Toying with her mug and not wanting to make eye contact, Sophia started in again on the story she didn't want to tell.

Annalise listened, her expression remaining passive. "The loss is now compounded. Trying to steal your grapes? For once I agree with Maggie. Which one do we kill first?"

Sophia grabbed a croissant and bit into it. "I love you guys, but those two asses aren't worth the jail time. I've got to think of another way."

"Like what? Even if we sold everything we have, coming up with a cool two mill would still be impossible. And that wouldn't even get you a long-term lease."

"Have you spoken with Beck?" Annalise asked.

Sophia nodded. "He's working on it, but he wasn't very encouraging."

"We'll think of something." Maggie forced an upbeat tone.

"That's what Nico said." Sophia took another bite. "Annalise, these are amazing. Something is different. Not that your stuff isn't always brilliant, but these are better than normal, just a hint."

"I made them myself. I fired my baker; she didn't have her heart in it. And, as you know, without the heart..."

"The food has no soul," Sophia finished. "Are you looking for a replacement?"

Annalise shrugged with a less-than optimistic lift to her shoulders. "It is hard work. And they must be passionate. Impossible to find."

"Maybe." A thought tickled at Sophia, and the more the itch bloomed, the better the idea looked.

Annalise gave her a sharp look. "Why? Do you know someone?"

"I might. I'll have to ask first."

"Does the someone know what it is like to work for a baker?"

"You mean someone who is exacting, demanding, and hard to get along with?"

Annalise seemed unperturbed by Sophia's assessment. "Yes."

"I'm pretty sure she can handle whatever you throw at her." The bigger question was would Annalise wilt in the glare of the formidable personality of Olivia Treviani. The two of them in kitchen would either be a symphony or a discordant cacophony—there would be no middle ground.

"So," Maggie inserted herself into the middle of the conversation. "Nico, now, is it? Give it up. Inquiring minds want to know."

As if her thinking about him drew him to her, Nico stepped through the bakery door and scanned the room. He smiled when his eyes found Sophia's, and her heart tripped. The two other women fell silent as he loomed over the table, their eyes taking him in.

"I thought I would find you here."

Maggie and Annalise looked at Sophia like tennis fans awaiting her return. "Really?" Sophia felt a flush of pleasure that he was looking for her. "These are my friends, Annalise who owns this bakery, and Maggie ..."

"Who loves your wine," Maggie injected.

Annalise narrowed her eyes.

"Thank you." His eyes flicked to Maggie, then back to Sophia. "Actually, Dani helped me find you."

Maggie scooted over then patted the seat next to her. "Join us?"

Annalise shot her a look. "Said the spider to the fly." She rose and offered her seat to Nico. "Sit here. Trust me."

"Thank you. Actually, I just need Sophia for a moment, if that would be all right." He extended his hand.

With only a moment of hesitation, Sophia took it and let him help her from the depths of the booth. Her hand felt good in his. She avoided Maggie's eyes, turning instead to Annalise. "I'll be right back."

The Frenchwoman gave her a knowing look.

Nico guided her by the elbow out to the street.

"What's this about?" Sophia asked; there was something about the way he gripped her elbow, a tension that triggered concern. Maybe she was overreacting.

"Your wine." Nico turned and faced her, stepping just a bit too close. "You ... we need to make it. The grapes are ready, aren't they?"

For the first time, she was aware of how intimidating his size could be. Sophia crossed her arms and stepped back, putting a bit of space between them. "Mr. Pinkman and your boss seemed to think so."

"I'm not asking them, I'm asking you. Are the grapes ready?" He looked bothered, distracted, intensity radiating off him like water shimmering off hot concrete.

Sophia didn't like the way he pressed her. "They're close.

Depends on the heat."

Nico looked up, his eyes fixed on something in the distance over her shoulder. A tic worked in his cheek. His eyes looked intense, his expression, focused. "Okay, I can clear out some press time. I've got a whole tank we can use. The chard juice is already pressed and ready to blend."

Sophia put a hand on his chest. While her touch was soft, her voice was not. "So let me get this straight. What I stopped them from taking last night, you now want to deliver to them?"

"The grapes and the juice will be under my control."

"Really? Don't fool yourself; your control, as you say, is by fiat from Mr. Specter. You are an employee, nothing more than a chess piece to men like that. The land, the winery, all of it is his. You deliver my grapes to him, and they are his."

"He wouldn't do that."

Sophia's anger boiled over like lava breaking through a cool crust, unleashing steaming heat. Yet, even though she seethed, she kept her voice level and hard. How she summoned the strength, she didn't know. "What you're saying is, he'll take grapes from a nobody like me, but he would never dare step on the toes of the great Nico Treviani?"

Nico refocused, his eyes meeting hers. He sighed. "That's not what I meant."

"The implication was clear." Sophia waited for him to stop digging the hole deeper.

Nico's struggle for control was visible in the taut lines of his face, the clench of his jaw. Something bothered him; that much was clear. "We need to make that wine."

The plural wasn't lost on Sophia—now it had become their wine. "Those grapes, at least for now, are mine. And I have no intention of pressing them or fermenting them at Specter Wines. I'd rather be dead."

"But ..."

She dropped her hand from his chest and stepped back. His nearness weakened her resolve. She wanted to give the grapes to him, to let him do what he wanted, to make him happy. Sophia had spent a lifetime making others happy; she was good at it. But to do that now?

She'd have to sell her soul. "I still don't know why you want to make that wine anyway."

"So everyone will know what you have, what you can do. It's your ticket out of the vineyard and into the wine room."

Her voice was quiet. "I've never said that's what I want."

Nico looked surprised. "Well, if you don't want that, you should."

"Who are you to tell me what I should want, what I should think, who I should be? I'm sick of people doing that." Sophia vibrated with emotions welling up, words she'd never voiced but always felt. Even toward Daniel, although she'd never admitted it while he was alive. Her vehemence shocked her, but she didn't try to mute it. "The only person to benefit from making that wine is you. After all, with me out of the way, you'll be the one in charge, as you put it. Your boss will own my grapes, and you will make my wine. Works out well for you." Sophia turned to go.

Nico grabbed her arm. "You can't think that."

"Let me go." A hint of her power taunted her. It felt good.

He dropped his hand. "Sophia, please."

Sophia turned her back and walked away.

Conversation stopped when she sat back down, this time next to Maggie.

"We saved you one." Annalise pushed the plate of croissants toward Sophia as her eyes scanned her face, reading and absorbing. "You look upset. Want to talk about it?"

Sophia raised her hand and shook her head, choosing her now lukewarm coffee instead. "Not right now."

Annalise didn't push. Maggie wasn't so easy to deflect. Next to Sophia, she twitched like a kid in Church. Sophia ignored her.

Maggie finally erupted. "Seriously, that walking god strolls in here asking for a moment of your time and you're not going to tell us what it was all about?"

"I don't know what it was about."

Maggie slapped the table and leaned back. "Oh, like I believe that."

"Sarcasm will not help." Annalise shut Maggie down with a cutting stare.

"It seems everybody wants my grapes, including Nico Treviani."

"And how do you feel about that?" Annalise trotted out her analyst mode, and for once, Sophia welcomed her ability and interest.

"Angry. Rushed."

"Is that all?"

Sophia moved her mug, turning it in her hands as it rested on the table. "No. I'm tired of everyone wanting something from me."

Annalise cocked her head slightly. "Perhaps you are more tired of giving it to them?"

Sophia leaned back, closing her eyes for a moment and breathing deeply. Sucked dry—that was how she felt. Emotionally parched, burnt, like an arroyo in August. Her anger toward Nico had shocked her with its fire, its flash, its depth. Why was she so angry? The grapes? She pondered that. No, it wasn't the grapes. Not that that didn't make her mad. But they were just a symptom. Something else ate away at her emotions like disease debilitated the flesh until she was tired, wrung out, and ready to level both barrels on anyone who crossed her.

Everyone around her expected her to do whatever made their lives easier or fulfilled their expectations. She'd been happy to do that for Daniel, or at least she told herself that. And, of course, for the kids. But now it was time she figured out what she wanted to do for herself. After years of giving everyone else what they needed, it was time to say no. "Tired of giving. Tired of doing what someone else thinks I should do. Yes, that's exactly it."

"Mad as hell and not going to take it anymore?" said Maggie with a hint of smile, quoting one of their favorite movie lines.

"Damn straight." She might lose everything in the fight, well worth it if she regained her self-respect.

Feeling oddly more herself than she had for decades, Sophia left her friends, forgetting even to offer to pay for the breakfast and the coffee. Annalise never let her, but she always made the gesture.

Sophia had one destination in mind. Somewhere she had to go. Something she had to do.

It was time to go to work.

CHAPTER TWENTY-ONE

BUTCHY PINKMAN'S WINERY STRETCHED FOR almost a mile on either side of Highway 29 south of Napa. A huge Hollywood showcase, Sophia loathed the place and everything it stood for. But she loved the grapes.

Her confidence in need of bolstering, she headed into the fields first. The workers, bent over the vines, nodded and smiled, then averted their eyes. Sophia wasn't surprised. Napa was a small valley and word traveled fast—especially if Tito the postman had caught Charlie in a weak moment and he'd spilled it. If so, everyone in the Valley probably knew more about Sophia's current problems than she did, which did little to improve her mood. But tilting at windmills wasn't on her agenda this morning, so she ignored the knowing looks and took heart from those of sympathy.

Lost in her world, focusing on the grapes, Sophia fondled the clusters, heavy with fruit, as she worked her way up and down the rows. Pausing, she brushed back the canopy with a gentle motherly touch. The berries were full, homogeneous in size. Periodically, Sophia would pull the refractometer from her back pocket, squint at the sun, then pluck a berry, pinching it, like squeezing venom from a snake. The juice was Brixing out near perfect. This harvest might be as good as 2010.

She found Manny Garza exactly where she knew he'd be—Lot 32-577. Standing feet spread, hands on his hips, straw hat pulled low on his head, he glowered at the grapes.

"Scaring them isn't going to make them any sweeter any sooner."

A grin split his face. "'Where you been? The boss man has been ... well, he ain't been all sweetness and light, let me put it that way."

"Is he ever?" Sophia snorted. "You can handle these grapes without me. All we can do at this point is wait. He knows that. Besides, I needed some personal time."

"You're the only person I know who would take PTO when the grapes are just coming up like this." Giving a squinty-eyed look at the sun, he swiped his hat from his head and mopped his brow with an old square of cloth that looked a lot like a shirt he used to wear last year. His face turned serious. "Look, I heard what went down last night. I want you to know it wasn't me or any of your crew here. You know we're on your side, right?"

Sophia nodded once. "I know that, but thank you." Her handpicked team had worked together for years. She knew they were loyal to her, but she also was wise enough to know they needed their jobs and she didn't write their paychecks.

"What those men tried to do, well, it was flat wrong. I sure hope they get what's coming to them."

"I hope I can give it to them." Sophia's voice was flat, hard, her resolve unwavering. She eyed the vines. "How are our problem children? They're looking better, although still the runts of the litter."

"Brixing a bit low, a point, some less. But they're coming along." Manny cocked his head toward the rest of the field. "What do you think?"

"Tonight?"

He nodded. "Yeah, me, too. I got the team lined up; they're just waiting for the word."

Sophia looked at the sun, the cloudless sky, felt the heat. "Not any moisture lurking under the canopies. And tonight isn't going to cool off too quickly. How about midnight?"

"You got it."

"If I'm not here, you know what to do."

WHEN SOPHIA PUSHED THROUGH HER boss's door,

dragging his secretary with her, Butchy Pinkman sat dwarfed behind his massive desk, looking like a child pretending to be important.

"You can't go in there," the woman mewled as she tugged on Sophia's arm, to little effect. In a show of futility, she turned to her boss. "Mr. Pinkman, I'm so sorry."

"Miss Wilde. If you can't do better ..." He left the threat hanging for a heartbeat. "There are many panting to take your place." Butchy gave Sophia a lascivious grin that made her skin crawl.

At her boss's bark, the young woman cowered back like a scolded dog. "Yes, Mr. Pinkman." She scurried out, closing the heavy wooden doors behind her.

Sophia chose the chair on her right. Leaning back, settling herself, she adopted a casual pose.

Pinkman, tiny and trim, with a mean mouth and small, close-set eyes, looked at her like a wolf eyeing a rabbit. "How dare you?" His voice was hard, feral.

"How dare *I*?" Sophia had to admit it: the man was good. Hadn't Daniel always told her the best defense was offense?

Pinkman pushed some papers across the desk. They fluttered to the floor.

Sophia bent to pick them up. As she arranged them she scanned the type and smiled. Beck Silver had come through, or at least he'd fired a salvo, and pretty darn quickly—a couple of hours. He must've chased down Judge Caruthers on the golf course and caught him in a rare good mood and sober moment. She tossed the papers back at Pinkman. "You think you can push everybody around, that nobody's going to do anything. It's about time somebody pushed back."

"Push all you want; there's nothing you can do."

"We'll see." Sophia smiled and let her gaze linger on the papers on the desk, making a point. "And, according to those papers, there's nothing you can do. Not until this mess is sorted out."

"I don't know what Horace thought he was doing signing off on that. My lawyer will burn right through it, whether you got that old windbag to sign it or not. He's half-senile and the other half stupid."

"But he's smart enough to smell a rat, or, to be more precise, two rats."

"We've got the law on our side." Pinkman seemed pretty sure of himself.

"Maybe. Maybe not. All I know is you can't set a toe across my property line until we have this sorted out to the satisfaction of the court." Sophia matched his confidence, surprising herself. Bluffing had never been one of her strong suits. Having her back against the wall had taught her more about herself than perhaps she was truly comfortable with. She rose to go. Halfway to the door, she turned. "Oh, one other thing. I quit." As soon as she said the words, a feeling of peace and of power settled over her like a shield.

Pinkman reddened. "You can't quit. We have a contract." He spit when he got angry.

Sophia had never noticed that before. Of course, she hadn't made him angry before either. She'd just given him what he wanted and soldiered on. Those days were over. That version of Sophia Otero Stone was gone. "I don't care."

"I'll sue you." His eyes narrowed into little evil slits.

"And take ... what? My home? My land?" She took a menacing step toward him. "My grapes?"

Pinkman retreated, cowering into the back of his chair. "Don't you touch those grapes. They're mine."

"Not yet, they're not."

"I told you. That deal with Charlie Vespers is rock-solid. All the legal i's and t's dotted and crossed."

"What about the moral ones?" Sophia knew the man didn't have a conscience. He probably didn't have a soul either, but she fired that shot anyway, because it made her feel good.

Pinkman gave a derisive snort. "I can't afford those kinds of considerations."

"Karma's a bitch, Mr. Pinkman." Sophia returned his stare, holding his gaze until she felt he got her message: she wasn't afraid, not anymore.

"I'm going to make that wine. Nico Treviani tells me he's got it all figured out. He's just waiting for the juice." Pinkman's voice was low, smooth, the luring cadence of a cobra's dance.

His bite tore into a soft spot, but Sophia didn't let Pinkman see it—she'd rather die before giving him the satisfaction. "You'll have to wait. *He'll* have to wait." Even though she vibrated with indignation and loathing, she turned and sauntered out of his office as if she hadn't a care in the world.

After a few minutes sitting in her truck, the engine humming, the adrenaline-fueled anger had dissipated enough for rational thought to worm its way in. Taking anything Pinkman said on faith was unwise. When he had something to gain, accepting his word as gospel was the quickest way to seal your fate. He'd sell his own mother if he could benefit by it.

Getting to the heart of Nico Treviani was another matter. He had a lot to be gained by siding with his boss and Pinkman. Trusting him would be difficult ... although she wanted to more than she'd wanted anything in a very long time. There was something about him. Something in his manner. A dignity. A kindness... even when he was being overbearing. Surely he wouldn't throw his lot in with the swine. As Dani said over and over, at some point she had to trust someone. And Dani trusted him. Sophia filed that worry for another moment.

She was stopped waiting to turn out onto the highway, feeling that first niggling what-have-you-done-feeling, when her cell rang. She heard it, but she couldn't find it. Finally, she located it between the front seats. She swiped her thumb across the face and pressed it to her ear. "Sophia Stone."

"Oh, Ms. Stone. I'm so glad I caught you. I was about to give up—I've called several times."

"I'm sorry. I was in a meeting." Holding the phone to her ear with her shoulder, she timed a gap in the traffic and joined the flow, heading back up-valley. "What can I do for you?"

"This is Kimberly Preston; I went to school with Dani."

"Yes, Kimberly, I remember. How are you?"

"Fine—well, actually, not so fine." Kimberly took a steadying breath. "I'm the dispatcher at St. Helena Fire Department, the one on Railroad."

A surge of adrenaline jolted Sophia's heart. She mentally tried to catalogue where all of her loved ones were, then realized she didn't really know. Her children were adults, her mother erratic. "Yes?"

"I have your mother here. At least I think she's your mother. Small, red hair, drives an old Cadillac?"

"My mother? Yes, that sounds like her."

"Oh, good." Kimberly's relief sounded in each syllable. "I wasn't sure, and she wasn't ... helpful. Anyway, I think she's lost."

"Lost? She's lived here forever."

"I know, but I don't think she knows how to get home."

CENTRAL TO THE NORTHERN PART of the Valley, the fire station sat on a nice street near the Safeway and Beck Silver's office. Glass and steel, the station still sparkled with newness. Sophia pushed through the doors into a small vestibule. Her mother, in a nice St. John's jacket, silk blouse, and her pajama bottoms and slippers, sat, knees pressed together as she perched on the edge of a plastic chair against the wall. She cupped her hands around a paper cup filled with steaming liquid—Sophia suspected tea—it smelled like mint. Watching four firemen playing cards at a table in the back, Regina didn't notice Sophia until she put a gentle hand on her shoulder. "Mother."

Her mother's face collapsed with disappointment. "Oh, not you. You always spoil the fun."

That rocked Sophia. She'd never thought of herself as a wet blanket. "I don't mean to. If you're having fun, perhaps you wouldn't mind if I joined in?"

Regina looked at her a moment, and Sophia wasn't sure her mother was certain of their relationship. The look on her mother's face hinted at recognition, but there were questions lurking there as well, as if she couldn't quite place her. "Okay. But don't be bossy. I hate it when you're bossy."

Unsure of exactly what to do, how to handle the moment, Sophia pulled another molded plastic chair next to her mother's.

"My father plays scopa with his friends. My mother won't let me watch." Regina's eyes were alight with memories when she looked at Sophia. "I think they use bad words. And probably they drink too much wine."

"No doubt." Sophia remembered her grandfather's games as well—spirited and hotly contested. His neighbors brought wine, and her grandmother cooked. Sophia had been allowed to stay, sitting on her grandfather's knee as he explained the game.

"Do you know them?"

"Yes."

Regina's face brightened, then crumpled. "Do you think they might be coming to get me soon? They told me they would come."

"They did? When did they tell you?"

"When I left earlier." Regina again turned to watch the card game, which was getting louder by the minute. When one of the firemen jumped up, fists raised, Regina clapped. The fireman turned and bowed dramatically in her direction. Regina ducked her head shyly and gave Sophia a sideways glance. "Did you know my father makes very good wine?"

"Really?" Sophia hid her surprise. That's not the version of her grandfather's story she'd been raised on.

"Everyone says so."

"Why doesn't he sell it, then?"

Regina's face clouded. "He keeps thinking it could be better. He says it's not ready. So we don't have a car, like the Fratellis. Mother makes my clothes. My shoes have holes. The other girls laugh." Regina's lips quivered. "And Babbo is sad."

Sophia's voice constricted. "I never knew."

"I don't like wine. It makes people sad and poor."

"Sometimes." Sophia put her arm around her mother. Perpetually thin, Regina felt skeletal, as if with each day, life whittled her away a bit more. "You must be tired. Would you like to go home?"

Regina gasped and looked at her wide-eyed. "You know where I live?"

Sophia blinked back a tear. "I do."

The look of relief on her mother's face broke Sophia's heart.

CHAPTER TWENTY-TWO

THE SUN HOVERED ON THE horizon when Sophia turned up her drive. Her nerves shot, her emotions barely tethered, she wheeled to a stop and killed the engine. Leaving the keys in the ignition and the door open, she bolted into her vineyard.

She'd made arrangements for her mother and had gotten her settled. The crisis over, for now, the adrenaline abating, emotions too long held in check tumbled through her like rocks carried by a swollen river.

Sophia breathed deep, fighting tears, pushing down panic, stuffing it deep. Panic wouldn't help her now—it wouldn't help any of them. Surrounded by vines, covered by darkness, she dropped to her knees. Sweetness and promise hung in the night air. Her grandfather wandered among the vines heavy with fruit. Sophia could feel his presence. A cool brush against her cheek. A warm flood of comfort, of peace. But, a figment of her memories, he remained just beyond the probe of her senses. Maybe she imagined him here. Then again, he *had* promised. *Whenever you need me,* cara mia, *close your eyes and I will be right at your elbow.* The deep timbre of his voice, sincere and filled with love, echoed across time. He'd promised. And Sophia had believed. Some things one just had to take on faith.

Faith.

Is it true, Nonno? Your wine was good?

What had he told her about the wine? Sophia searched the quiet spaces for the peace of her memories. She had been a child, unburdened by the economic aspects of life, filled only with the magic of dreams. They hadn't talked of selling the wine, of that she was sure.

Memories. Soon they would be all she had left. But their comfort wouldn't soften the harshness of her mother's last years. Anger, like a viper ready to strike, coiled in her stomach. Crumpling into the earth, she quivered with emotion. Tears ran hot down her cheeks as she sobbed.

The earth, warm beneath her, held the heat of late summer, reluctant to release it. Finally, emotion spent, tears run dry, Sophia breathed deeply of the day, the sweetness of the hanging fruit. Ripening dreams, her grandfather had called them.

Dreams.

Sophia took a deep ragged breath then opened her eyes. Dreams were just that ... the fancies of youth, as her mother often reminded her. There's no place in the real world for such silliness, she'd said so often that, had her voice been a recording, that tape would have worn clear through. Remember what happened to Daniel? Her mother also never missed an opportunity to callously hurl that at her as if it were absolute proof that hope hadn't been the last thing in Pandora's box.

How could she forget?

Daniel had died. A part of her heart died that day, and the last vestiges of youthful optimism had been lost.

But, the distracted child in the SUV hadn't killed everything. No, Sophia had kept her children ... and her grapes ... even if she had already lost herself.

Sophia absorbed the magic of the rays of the setting sun, arrows of pinks and oranges piercing the darkening sky as if trying to keep their grasp on the earth a bit longer. Ten years in the ground, the vines were teenagers, just on the cusp of blossoming into their fullest potential. She cupped her hand under a cluster of golden fruit, taking its weight. With her other hand, she plucked a grape from the bunch, quickly, like extracting a tooth. Letting the vine once again hold the weight of the grapes, she broke one grape between her forefinger and thumb, then placed it in the receptacle of the refractometer. Holding it to her eye at an angle that caught the sun, she took the reading. Twenty-four.

She wanted an alcohol content of thirteen percent. That would mean roughly a twenty-five. She could live with a twenty-four. She was going to have to. Succulent vessels, the grapes hung low, shaded by the leaves of the canopy, browning slightly at the edges, crying out for water. But, as her grandfather said, the vines were like families; the more the stress, the better the fruit. There'd be no water. This year, as most, Sophia dry-farmed her small plot. Carefully pruning for the perfect balance—too much fruit left on the vine often reduced the quality.

Anybody could grow grapes. But growing good grapes was an art.

Sophia frowned. Could her mother be right? Did these grapes really cause so much sorrow? Or was that just a child's hurt finding a cause? Were dreams really the province of a silly child with no place in reality?

Sophia couldn't imagine life without dreams. They'd been a lantern of hope in her darkest hours.

How would she find her way without the light of dreams to guide her?

"Sophia?" A voice, Nico's voice, called to her. "Sophia, where are you?"

She hadn't heard him drive up. "Go away!" she shouted as she swiped at her face, wiping away the tears with the sleeve of her sweater. She peered through the vines but couldn't see him. Daylight had surrendered and dusk deepened, casting the world in the shadow of advancing night.

"We need to talk."

"I've nothing to say to you." Sophia sniveled then wiped her nose.

"Okay. Then just listen. Please." Nico's voice sounded closer as he searched for her.

Sophia, constricted by indecision and completely spent, knelt there, not hiding, but not helping. And she listened as he talked, hearing his words and charting his progress through the vineyard.

"I've been beating myself up since this morning, going over and over our conversation, wondering how we got so off track. How I somehow had you believing the exact opposite of what I feel."

"Nico, this really isn't a good time. Please go away."

"Not until I've said what I came to say."

From the sound of his voice, Sophia figured he was two rows over and working his way closer.

"Look, I'll be the first to admit, I got a bit excited about your grapes and the wine. And then when the blending turned out so well ..."

Sophia could hear his footsteps now.

He materialized out of the haze of half-light and growing darkness, a shadow backlit by the brilliant sunset, he dropped to his knees beside her. "I won't lie, Sophia." He took her hands in his, easing her around, forcing her to look at him. "I want to make that wine. I want to rub their noses in it. I want to show them what we can do, how great your grapes are."

"But ..."

He put a finger to her lips. "I know. It'll bite us on the ass, I'm sure you're right. It just would feel so ... great." He paused, like a child on the edge of a confession. "After Paolo died, I wondered if I could make great wine again. The wine we made needed us both—he was passion."

Her lips tingled with heat where he'd brushed his fingers to them, the attraction to him so strong. Sophia was raw, wounded, vulnerable and she didn't want to muster the energy to fight it. God, how she wanted to believe him, needed to believe him. "And you were pragmatism." Sophia knew that doubt; she lived with it.

"But you and your grapes showed me I can still make good wine. You and I are a perfecting pairing."

"But I don't want to be a perfect pairing. I want to be me."

Nico looked perplexed. "Why would you not be you? Who else would you be?"

"Spoken like a man. Men are never asked to be anything other than who they are. Women are not so lucky. But, your point is well taken. Who, indeed?"

Perhaps he sensed her weakening. His voice took on a note of urgency. "I remember what it felt like when they took our farm from us, my father's dreams, his hard work ... gone. And I had nothing to show for it. No legacy to give him. I know you feel it, too. I saw how you responded to my parents' story. I've tasted your wine." He let go of one of her hands and reached up, plucking a grape. "I see your grapes. I've tasted their juice. If we don't show them what we can do, if we don't prove to them that passion wins over money, that you can't buy brilliance, then what was all of this for?"

"Pinkman said you told him the wine was ready to go; you were on board and had it all under control."

"And you believe him? I haven't seen the ass—I'd probably break his jaw if I did."

"Then how did he know?"

"How does he know?" Nico gave her a look.

Right, St. Helena was a small town with a very efficient town crier. "Tito." Sophia didn't need Nico's confirmation.

"Or any number of Specter Wine employees. Sophia, the man is lying out his ass. He's trying to drive a wedge between you and me. Divide and obliterate, isn't that his M.O.?"

He had Pinkman pegged. "Okay, but that doesn't change the fact that if we do this, we'll just be handing it to them. And, worse, making a market for them."

"Perhaps, but everyone will know those two clowns had nothing to do with the wine. You and your grandfather created this perfection."

"With a very important bit of brilliance added by you."

Nico dismissed that with a shake of his head. "We could steal their thunder," Nico said, his voice low with a conspiratorial tone. "How would that feel?"

Even though she couldn't see him clearly, his features shadowed by night and only partially illuminated by the hint of the rising moon, she could picture his intensity as it played across his face, sharpening his features, lighting his eyes.

"Almost as good as shooting them both." Sophia laughed, a small choked sound, but a positive one, one that gave her hope.

Still holding her hands, Nico sat back on his heels. "You'd do it, too. I've seen you and that pump-action shotgun in action."

"No I'd just scare them a little." Sophia pulled one hand free, and despite the dirt that still clung to it, swiped a stray lock, anchoring it behind her ear. "My grandfather always told me money comes from doing what you love. That didn't exactly pan out now, did it?"

"We're not done." Nico rocked back, then rose, pulling Sophia to her feet. "Come on. You got some coffee? We've got a long night ahead if we are to plan this out. These grapes are close, a day or two, no more?"

Sophia understood the question. "Depends on the heat tomorrow."

"The sooner, the better." Nico threw an arm around her shoulders and steered her toward the house.

With Nico comfortable at the kitchen table, his long legs stretched in front of him, Sophia busied herself pulling things from the fridge. Normally done without thought, tonight Sophia felt uncomfortably self-aware as she felt his eyes following her every move. Not one to take pains with her appearance, tonight she wished she had a bit more of the prissy in her. But she was a woman who'd seen her share of heartache and happiness through the years, each one etched in her face ... and her figure, which flared in ways that would've alarmed her as a teenager. No amount of primping would change that. An amalgam of experience, she'd been told she wore her life well.

After loading her arms with plates from the fridge, Sophia turned and kicked the door shut. "You hungry?"

"Famished."

Tonight, short on time, Sophia warmed some leftover lasagna in the microwave even though it toughened the pasta.

Nico sniffed the air like a bear hunting for dinner. "Good God, what is that?"

"Lasagna."

"You made that?" Nico sat up, snapping the checkered napkin then laying it across his lap.

Sophia shot him a disgusted look. "Don't you know better than to insult an Italian woman in her own kitchen? The alchemy of food can nurture you ... or cause you great pain."

He laughed as he took up his fork and knife, preparing to dive into the plate of steaming pasta Sophia set in front of him. "Smart, competent, challenging, beautiful, and you can cook too? Sophia Stone, you would terrify lesser men."

"No doubt." Sophia turned away, pretending to be busy tonging salad, mixing the greens with dressing. It wouldn't do to have Nico see his effect on her. No it wouldn't do at all. Wasn't she the one hell-bent on keeping him off balance? *And how's that working for you, Sophia?* She shook her head at her own inadequacies, although she'd never excelled at games. After fixing a small plate for herself, Sophia added salad to the plate in front of Nico and joined him at the table.

Clearly unconcerned that his mouth was full of salad, Nico waved his fork and said, "What would it take to get a glass of decent wine in this joint?"

Sophia laughed. It was hard not to share his fun. "The price is high, but the juice is worth it."

"I'll gladly pay the freight, but make it the good stuff." Nico blew on his plate of steaming lasagna.

Sophia complied, pouring them both a healthy dose of her last vintage. Nico's eyes narrowed as he watched her pour. "We need a name."

"A name?"

"For the wine and the winery. And a label. I'll have to see about scrounging up some bottles—all the orders for glass have been placed months ago."

"I've got bottles."

He raised one eyebrow at her. "Really? You thought of everything for wine you weren't going to make."

"I'm sort of like a Boy Scout."

"If the scouts in my troop had been anything like you, I would've made Eagle easy."

"I'm not sure flattery is a merit badge, but, if it were, you'd have that one ten times over."

He gave her a smile. "My skills are rusty, but they're coming back."

They both fell to eating their salads while the lasagna cooled a bit. Sophia was surprised at her hunger.

His salad a memory, Nico took a sip of wine. "Great juice. I have yet to find any food this wine doesn't make better. I'm thinking we need to drop your fruit tomorrow night."

Sophia didn't disagree, letting him forge ahead.

"I'll round up the best guys. They'll make short work of two acres. Say, just after dark?"

"That should work." Sophia surprised herself with her easy acquiescence. She paused. Was she agreeing because that's what Nico would want, what he expected her to do? No, she thought as she nestled the wine bottle in a cooler. If they were going to make the wine, they had to get after it. "I'd thought about calling the wine S.O.S., but that was before you became involved."

"Your initials." Nico nodded, a smile playing with his lips. "I love it. Given the circumstances it actually works on a bunch of levels. And the winery?"

"I'd leave them guessing. Since this will be our one and only vintage, I'm not sure it's important."

"Okay. For now. But I'm not convinced this will be our swan song, Sophia. We have a brilliant future."

His gaze fanned the embers of desire, warming her from the inside. She wanted to read more into his words, but ...

Only after Sophia started in on the lasagna did Nico take a bite. He groaned in pleasure. "Man, you picked the wrong path. Your wine is nectar of the gods, but this! This is sex on a plate."

Sophia met his eyes. "Food is passion."

Nico smiled as he forked in several bites, swallowing them with healthy sips of wine. Finishing the lasagna, he left the cake untouched and the light in his eyes turned dark and smoky. He didn't say anything; he didn't need to. Sophia felt a shift in the clenching in her core, in the pulsing of her heart as blood pounded through her.

Suddenly, acutely aware of the charged air around her, Sophia felt small and open, alive and fearful, shuddering on the brink of something greater than herself—a fire that would consume her, and yet bring her alive.

Nico rose, his empty plate in his hand. "Let me do the dishes."

Sophia had taken a few bites, but, for some reason, now she didn't want food. She joined him in front of the sink, taking his plate from him. "Guests don't do dishes."

He didn't let go. "Is that what I am? A guest?" He stepped in close, his body pressing against her.

Sophia relinquished the plate.

With measured care, Nico set it on the sideboard. Then he turned to her. Capturing her face in both hands, he ran his fingers through her hair, pulling it loose until it cascaded in waves over her shoulders.

Sophia could hardly breathe, coiled, ready, awaiting a sign. At his touch, she closed her eyes, leaning her head back, pressing her body into his. Craving the connection, needing this touch, his strength, she pushed aside her fears, her doubts.

His mouth closed over hers, hot, demanding, plundering with his tongue, igniting a need so strong, so hot, it surprised her. She surrendered herself.

His hands found her breasts, kneading, teasing as he thumbed a nipple hard with desire. Shivers of pleasure coursed through her, coalescing in her core, hot, liquid desire.

Pulling at his shirt, she popped the buttons, her hands finding flesh.

He groaned as he struggled for control. Bending, he scooped her up, one arm behind her back, the other cradling her knees.

"Upstairs," Sophia murmured into his kisses.

At the top of the stairs, Nico kneed the door to her bedroom open. A soft breeze billowed the sheers. Letting her feet go, he kept her close to him, sliding her body down his. Breathing hard, he fumbled with the buttons on her shirt. She knocked his hands out of the way. Both of them shucked their shirts, then stepped out of their pants, leaving them pooled on the floor.

Desire whipping them, driving them, they fell on the bed. Nico rolled on top, capturing Sophia's mouth. Sophia's nails dug in his back, her body arcing in pleasure as he moved from her lips, capturing a nipple between his teeth. Sophia found the hard heat of him. Guiding, insisting, she opened her body to him.

Levering his weight on an elbow, Nico paused, looking intently at her as if asking. Her eyes bright, her face pinched with need, Sophia nodded once.

Nico plunged inside. Slick with desire, she welcomed him, enveloped him. Pleasure built as he filled her, his need fueling her want. Nico moved, slowly at first, then quickening. Sophia matched his pace, clutching him to her, her legs wrapped around him, her hands pulling him deeper into her.

Lost. Falling, then riding a wave, building, tossed. Time, place, disappeared, only pleasure.

Nico, his voice tight, full, managed one word. "Sophia."

The wave broke, pleasure exploded. Both of them tumbled then were lost.

CHAPTER TWENTY-THREE

NICO TREVIANI AWOKE SLOWLY, allowing each of his senses to unfurl fully into the new day. He couldn't immediately place where he was, but he wasn't alarmed. No, this wasn't his room; nor was it his bed—softer, silky sheets. He ran his hand over the fabric next to his thigh, sensual in its silkiness. The room smelled of grapes and roses, with a hint of honeysuckle. Breathing deeply, he caught the hint of something else: earthy, musky, yet pleasingly sweet. The scent of a woman, of sex. Then it all came flooding back to him in a warm, intense pulse of pleasure.

Sunlight, soft and new, greyed the darkness. Sophia Stone nestled tight against him, curled into his embrace. For the first time in a long time, Nico felt at peace. And he had slept, unmolested by the nightmares of loss, the heavy weight of responsibility—the crushing doubt of the future.

Sophia stirred, rubbing her hand casually across his stomach and chest. Nico clenched his jaw. If she only knew what she did to him. A woman hadn't wormed her way under his skin in a very long time. And he hadn't wanted then like he wanted now. Steeling himself, trying not to react to her touch, he watched her face. Her eyes closed, a smile tickled her lips, curving them, inviting a kiss, as her hand trailed over his skin.

Her hand drifted, lingering on his stomach, her skin singeing his. He sucked in a sharp breath when her hand drifted lower. Sophia smiled when her hand closed over the hot, hard heat of him.

He thought she purred.

Grabbing her hand, he moved it as he struggled for control. "No."
Her eyes snapped open.

He softened his tone. "No. Now, it's my turn." He pushed her shoulder, rolling her gently away, opening her body to his gaze... and his touch.

This time she did purr, moaning under his touch as he teased, nibbling, nipping. Her breathing changed as her desire rose, pleasing him and driving his own. Nico liked hearing the effect he had on her, measuring her response.

When his fingers found her sweet wetness, stroking, then plunging inside her, she moaned, pressing into him. When he curled his finger inside her, she clenched around him.

He shuddered, fighting for control as his desire threatened to boil over. She reached for him, but he dodged her hand. "Wait."

His mouth closed over hers. She clung to him as his tongue teased her mouth, as he nibbled, biting her lip. Her breath hitched when he found her pleasure nub once again. He kept the pressure. As he stroked, her body arced, her muscles tensed tighter, tighter. Her breathing caught. Her body tensed. A moment of sweet tightness. Then she groaned as pleasure pulsed through her in pounding release. Nico plunged his fingers back inside, feeling the rhythmic clench. Holding her tight as she clutched him, he let the waves subside, let her wallow in the aftermath of pleasure until she relaxed.

There'd be time for him later, but right now her pleasure pleased him more than his own.

Sophia rolled into him, tucking her head into the crook of his neck. She smelled of musky sex and sweet lasagna. "I'm hungry," Nico spoke low as he twirled a strand of her hair around a finger. "I'm thinking I need some dessert."

Sophia giggled, a low happy sound that curled around his heart. "Worked up an appetite, have you?"

"I'm Italian. Food is a part of every pleasure."

"I'll remember that, but if you break out the whipped cream or chocolate body paint, I might have a problem with that."

"Might?" Nico pulled her close. No matter how tight he held her, he wanted more.

"I've heard a bit of mystery is attractive."

"If you were any more attractive, I'd never get anything done, sacrificing my life to just bask in your presence."

"Oh, you are Italian." Sophia went quiet for a moment. "I could get used to that," she whispered.

Nico closed his eyes as he kissed her forehead, letting emotion filter into all his hidden places, filling them with hope. "Me, too."

Sophia stiffened slightly. "But you work for the bad guys."

Nico countered by pulling her tighter. "So do you."

"Not anymore."

Nico loosened his hold, leaning back to look at her. "No?"

Sophia shook her head and told him about her visit to Butchy Pinkman.

FOR THE FIRST TIME IN a long time, Sophia hummed as she cleaned the kitchen, washing the dishes that she and Nico had abandoned. Some of the dried lasagna would take more than a scrubbing to remove so she set the crusty dishes to soak and tried not think about Nico in her shower upstairs. But the sound of the running water drew her imagination. Closing her eyes, leaning on the counter, she pictured the water cascading over his chest, the flat surface of his stomach, the curve of his hip, tangling in ... with a visible shake, she took control of her galloping imagination. The image dissipated leaving the heat of a remembered touch and the furtive flutter of need deep inside her. A man once again in the house gave Sophia a sense of safety, of peace. A remembered connection, yet so distant a memory it seemed translucent, fragile, like a hummingbird's wings beating a staccato rhythm to sustain their load.

The kitchen back in some order, the sound of running water thankfully silenced, Sophia grabbed a bar towel to dry her hands as she thought about her day ahead—a vast expanse of time to fill as she saw fit. She tossed the towel across one shoulder and stood looking out at her grapes. Tomorrow night. Although she kept her equipment in good order, it could use a going-over. The de-stemmer and crusher had been balky last year, the gears wearing out. She'd replaced them, but the whole thing needed to be greased and timed.

Movement along the tree line grew her attention. A black sedan eased out of the shadows. Sophia squinted against the light. Trey's BMW.

She hadn't known when he'd come back. Part of her was glad he had; the other part hoped she had the strength left to be the mother he needed.

Nervously she rolled her eyes upward. Nico's footsteps hard and heavy. A man upstairs. Her son driving up the drive. As she stepped onto the porch, she pulled the bar towel from her shoulder, folding it to give her hands something to do and to hide their nervous flutter.

Trey wheeled the car to a stop and stepped out. He paused, staring over the vineyard and Sophia caught her breath. There, in the sunlight, his sandy hair a tad long, curling over his collar, his jaw lifted slightly as if challenging the future, he looked so much like his father. But Daniel's shoulders never slumped in defeat, nor had his expression ever been quite so guarded, so angry. What had happened to the happy little boy who wanted nothing more than to grow grapes, make wine, and paint beautiful pictures?

When Trey turned and caught his mother standing there, smiling, he didn't smile in return. Nor did he rush to greet her, preferring to look out over the vineyard for a moment longer. "Some guys at the gate stopped me. What's that about?"

"It's been an interesting few days. I'll fill you in later."

Sophia gave him his time and space. As a boy, he'd been captured by this hilltop, the vines, the way the light played through the trees in the forest. When he ambled over to give her a perfunctory kiss on her cheek, he sighed, "I love this place. I feel different here."

Ah, there was a hint of the Trey she knew. Sophia's heart constricted, but she kept her bright smile. "I'm so happy to see you. How was the cabin?" He seemed distant, distracted, his manner making Sophia nervous, awkward, as if unsure how to act toward her own son. But the son she'd known was gone, hidden, swallowed by the man in front of her.

"We didn't go. A couple of the guys couldn't get away."

"Oh."

Trey glanced at her. "I just drove around. Ended up out at

Jenner. I love watching the river mix with the ocean. They come together, dance around each other, and then seem to clash and boil as they try to blend." He gave her the hint of a smile. "Even nature has a hard time making two into one."

"But is that the goal?" Sophia asked.

When Trey looked at her, his eyes seemed less troubled. "Why do I feel a mother moment coming on?"

"I take them where I can find them; that's my job. Anyway, it seems to me the goal might be to make a partnership, a team that is better and stronger than the two separately. A partnership that enhances each partner but doesn't destroy their individuality."

Trey gave her a hug, lingering in it. "How are you so smart?"

"Mistakes."

He let her go and stepped back. "Grandmother called. She said something about someone stealing her car?"

"Ah, your grandmother. We need to talk, so perhaps it's good that you are here. She seems to listen to you." As she turned toward the house, Sophia hooked her arm through his. They used to walk that way all the time, even after he'd reached the age where his mother should've become an embarrassment. "I was just putting some coffee on."

Trey retrieved a knapsack from the passenger seat and followed her to the kitchen. "I'll do it." He set his things in the corner. "One scoop for every cup." He looked at her with the hint of a smile. "Not too weak, not too strong, I remember. So, Grandmother says you've hired someone to keep her prisoner in her house and now her car is missing." Trey glanced at his mother. This time the smile was weak but real. "She thinks you sold it." He handed her a mug of coffee, the mug he'd made at camp all those years ago.

Sophia needed something to do. "Do you want some eggs?"

Trey shook his head. "That bad, huh?"

Even though she felt she didn't know her son at all, he knew her better than she'd like. "Sit. I could use your help."

Trey listened, his face pinched, his eyes haunted as Sophia told him what she knew.

"You hired Mrs. Pettigrew to help out, keep an eye on grandmother?"

"For now. But that's a short-term solution. She's doing it out of the kindness of her heart and, quite frankly, your grandmother can be..."

"Forceful?"

"I don't want Mrs. Pettigrew in the line of fire when your grandmother gets good and mad."

"What do you plan on doing with her car?"

"I'm not letting her back behind the wheel. This place is small; she's lived here forever. And now she's forgotten how to get home."

Trey leaned back, kicking out his feet. "She's got to go to a home where they know how to deal with this sort of decline."

"You want to tell her that?"

He gave a derisive snort.

"Didn't think so."

"While you're thinking about solutions, I could use your help fetching her car from the fire station. We could park it here until we decide what to do with it." Sophia had made short work of her coffee—hoping the caffeine would offset her lack of sleep. She rose to fill her mug. "You're going to stay the weekend, I hope?"

"I'm all yours."

Heavy footfalls sounded on the stairs, a quick rhythm. Sophia had only a moment of panic before Nico stepped through the door.

His hair wet, cleanly shaven, and just buttoning his shirt, he didn't even hitch when he saw Trey at the table. He stuck out a hand. "Nico Treviani."

Trey's eyes widened as he gave Nico's hand a single pump.

"Nico, this is my son, Trey." Sophia managed not to stammer, which was a victory, all things considered. Heat climbed her face as she worked hard to adopt a casual attitude, as if it was normal for a handsome man, fresh out of the shower, to appear in her kitchen before breakfast.

Nico gave him a grin. "Nice to meet you." He turned to Sophia. Hooking an arm around her waist, he pulled her in for a kiss, appropriately short given the audience, at least that's how Sophia looked at it. "I'll be at the winery most of the day. We dropped a bunch of fruit last night; they'll be shouting for me. I'll see you later."

With that he was gone.

Trey stared at his mother, a flood of emotions playing across his face, humor lighting his eyes. If she was the butt of the joke that made him smile, she'd gladly play the fool. Ignoring his look, Sophia turned back to the coffee.

"That was interesting," Trey said.

Sophia couldn't read his tone. She snuck a look at him, but his face remained passive.

"Nico has been helping me with ... the grapes."

"A hands-on kind of guy, huh?"

Sophia whirled on her son as he threw his head back and laughed—a good sound that warmed her heart—and she heard a hint of the boy inside. When he sobered, he looked at her. "Good for you, it's about time. But why aren't you at Pinkman's? I thought I'd just be dropping my stuff off then heading to the fields to track you down."

"I quit."

That wiped the grin off his face. "No way."

"Yes, way. You up for some work? I need to test the equipment. The grapes will be ready soon."

He rolled up his sleeves. "Sure. As long as there's some of your lasagna in it when we're done. And you tell me what went down with that ass, Pinkman. Good riddance, by the way."

"It'll have to be leftovers. And, while I'm glad Mr. Pinkman is gone, I can't say the same for my paycheck."

"Maybe it's time to make some wine. This vineyard is like your rainy-day fund. The cash cow lying in the barn, I think Dad used to say. One he thought would have to earn its keep one day." He held the door for her, then joined her, striding shoulder to shoulder toward the cave. Sophia took his arm, looping hers through his. She didn't care whether he liked it or not. She was a mom, and no matter how old, how distant and withdrawn, how secretive he became, nothing would change that.

"Cash cow." Sophia felt her heart clench as she gave him a wan smile. "A lot has happened in that last day or two. I'll tell you about it while we work."

The sun was long over the yardarm when they finally finished up. Trey had actually used some of his mechanical engineering knowledge in helping Sophia troubleshoot a problem with the fermentation tank.

Technology she could handle. Green technology, not so much. As they'd talked and worked and sweated through the heat of the day, Sophia began to see more of the son she used to know.

Trey actually looked calm, more himself, covered with dirt, his faced creased with a frown, but not a sad frown, an angry one. "Those assholes. I never knew Dad wouldn't buy the place. It was so obvious how much it meant to you."

Sophia was touched. The quiet, sensitive boy who had seen so much, felt so much. Daniel's death had hit him the hardest. And, through the haze of her own pain, Sophia had lost him.

"And now it's all going to be gone." Trey looked around the cave slowly, his eyes resting on each piece of equipment as if cataloging memories. "I always thought... " Trey looked at his mother and shrugged.

"What?"

"It doesn't matter now."

"Oh, Trey." Sophia sank onto a stool at the wooden table in the middle of the cave, her legs shaking under the strain of a busy day and the weight of old emotions. "It matters a great deal."

He leaned up against the tank, a tower of stainless steel. "I was always the happiest here." He shrugged slightly. "Or out in the fields with my pencils and sketch pad."

"Yes, we all loved to be outdoors, to work under the sun. Still do, I guess."

"All of us except Dad."

"Yes, he fed on fluorescent light." Sophia eyed her son. "Is that why you left the fields and turned to engineering?"

Trey cast a look toward the fermenter. "I can be pretty handy."

"You can't be your father. Nor should you."

Trey scoffed. "Thanks."

"Trey, that wasn't an insult; it was an invitation. Stop trying to be your father. Stop trying to do what you think he would have wanted for you. You need to be yourself. If you're not, if you let others define your dreams and expectations, you will live a life of quiet desperation that will end badly. Being someone we're not is a façade we can wear for only a short period of time." Sophia looked down and her hands fisted against her legs.

"You seem to do it just fine."

The words sliced through her like a hot blade. "Life sometimes makes choices for you."

Trey stared over her shoulder, looking slightly lost and a bit helpless, surprising his mother.

Sophia knew she was justifying, but she felt compelled at least to offer an explanation. Not an excuse, she knew that. But now that she'd realized some of her mistakes, some of the easy paths she had taken when the difficult ones would've been more fulfilling, she found it hard to forgive herself. "With two kids to raise, I didn't have a lot of choice when your father died. I had responsibilities."

"Responsibilities." The way he said that single word sounded as if he was Atlas shrugging under the weight of the world.

Sophia reached out a hand, her heart seizing at his pain. Perhaps she'd been too quick to step back, too afraid of shutting him off altogether. She wasn't sure if shutting him off entirely would be worse than this limbo—seeing him unhappy but powerless to reach him. "Stop doing that."

"What?" He tried to shut her down with a closed look.

When he didn't take her hand, Sophia let it drop. "That. Shutting me out. I'm your mother. I get it that you're a grown man and need to make your own choices. But you're not happy—you haven't been happy for a long time. And it worries me... you worry me. Life is too precious to waste. By your own words, I should know."

Trey's shoulders sagged. He grabbed a bottle of wine from the rack then joined her at the table. "May I?"

Sophia nodded and waited. Trey's opinion of her wine would be interesting. His nose rivaled Dani's. He poured himself a glass, a look of concentration and joy lit his face. Holding the wine to the light, he swirled, then sniffed, then swirled again.

Watching him with a mother's eyes, Sophia could see that time and heartache had tempered the boy into a man as he lifted the glass to his lips. She held her breath as he tasted, swishing the wine around his mouth, then letting it linger on his tongue before swallowing.

A soft smile lifted the corners of his lips, relaxing his face. "Nice. Acidic, stone fruit, crisp, clean, but with an interesting hint of cinnamon, I think. A bit thin on the feel and the finish, but that should be easy to fix. Unique, yet accessible. And bold enough to pair well across the flavor palate from poached fish to a rare steak. By far your best yet. What are you calling it?"

"My initials, S.O.S."

"I love it!" He slapped his hand on the wooden table. "Show those assholes the Stones don't go down without a fight. What about the label?"

"Nico and I didn't get that far. It's all a bit of a rush—we are under the gun, you know."

When his face clouded, Sophia held up her hand.

"Don't go there. For now we have the grapes. And Nico has the blend. We can make one grand vintage."

Trey's shoulders slumped as the fight left him. "This is all great fun, but I don't see the purpose in it, not really. Oh, giving them the finger is great; you'll steal a bit of their bragging rights down the road. But won't you be creating a market for their wine?"

"Maybe. They still have to make it."

"Your Mr. Treviani is under contract to Mr. Specter, right?" Trey kept his face bland, his eyes steady.

"For a year—less than that now. By next harvest he'll be free of them—if he doesn't do something rash before then." Sophia held her glass up in a toast to her grandfather, his dreams, Napa and the passion that drives it. "We're doing it because we can. I've always wanted to finish your grandfather's dream."

He looked at her in the way Daniel used to, head tilted slightly, eyes narrowed. But his words were not his father's. "Then will you have time for your dreams, Mom?"

Sophia's brow crinkled. "These grapes, the wine, they are my dreams, and too long in coming to fruition. It's so easy to lose oneself to life's responsibilities."

He looked at her through old eyes that hid his thoughts. "Tell me about it." Trey savored another sip, swishing it around his mouth before savoring the swallow. "Rebecca wants to take the twins down to Los Gatos to live closer to her parents. She can get a good job down there with her EE degree. Don't tell Dani, okay? I've disappointed myself enough as it is; I don't want to let her down, too."

His words, the reality, knocked the wind out of Sophia. "Oh." The sound was more a gasp than a word and breath rushed from her. Her grandbabies would be so far away. They were only two now and on the cusp of becoming interesting.

Trey twirled the stem of the glass between his fingers as he talked, staring into the wine. "I don't blame Rebecca, actually. Being married to me is no cakewalk. As you said, I haven't been happy for a long time, so no surprise to you. But I can tell you it came as a hell of a shock to me. I thought I was doing what I was supposed to. I thought that would be enough. It isn't." When he looked at her, tears glistened in his eyes. "I want to come home. I want to bring my family home. I want..." —he let his gaze travel around the room— "this." He shook his head. "Now there's no home to come home to."

CHAPTER TWENTY-FOUR

NOISE REVERBERATED AROUND THE LARGE crushing room at Specter Wines. Machines whined, people shouted, trucks backed into the bays, dumping their precious cargo handpicked last night. They were down to the last load of Chardonnay dropping into the de-stemmer. Rubber blades turned, separating grape from stem. A tangle of vine and stem spiraled out of one end as the grapes passed into the crusher. Nico stepped back and watched his young winemaker crack the whip. Dani was proving to be an able assistant with an intuitive feel for the grapes and the juice. She was her mother's daughter all right, and the thought made Nico smile.

The juice siphoned into the large stainless steel fermentation tanks. Dani readied Nico's recipe of cultivated yeasts, carefully weighing and measuring. This batch of Chard was new, so mixture of yeasts was Nico's best guess. So many of the traits appreciated in the final product came not from the grapes, as most thought, but from the yeast, so the choice was not a casual one. Sulphur dioxide went in as well. Nico wanted tight control on fermentation. Years ago, when his lots were small, he'd been an avid proponent of native yeasts and temperature to control fermentation, both alcohol and malolactic. Now, with larger lots and higher stakes, Nico didn't leave much to chance, although that confounding element always remained. Despite the most well-thought-out plans and exacting execution, many variables remained beyond control, so anything could happen and often did.

When Dani looked his direction, he gave her a thumbs-up, then a sign to wrap it up. Tennis practice would be over; the girls would be waiting.

Amazingly, Brooklyn and Taryn both were ready as promised, chattering as they climbed into the truck, red hair flying, cheeks flushed pink, and mouths running full-tilt.

"Hey, Knuckleheads." Nico got their attention, although he knew only briefly. "What new thing did you learn today?"

"I learned Billy Schumacher wears pink underwear," Brooklyn announced, while Taryn twittered behind her hand.

Nico gave himself a full thirty seconds and was still not exactly sure how to respond. "Well, I ought to teach him not to wash his Jockeys with anything red."

That got big smiles and some good-natured ribbing out of the girls. When they'd quieted, Nico turned to Taryn. "What about you? What new thing did you learn today?"

Her face sobered, and her eyes grew round. "I learned that Carla Edmond's mom thinks you're hot, which is like the most disgusting thing ever."

Nico wracked his brain. "Edmonds. Edmonds." His eyes grew big like his niece's. "That *is* the most disgusting thing ever." Then he remembered who he was talking to. "But you breathe a word I just said that, and I'll turn your entire wardrobe pink. Got it?"

Brooklyn elbowed her way into the conversation. "As Nonno taught us, you don't screw family." She nudged her sister. "Right?" Taryn nodded, her eyes serious.

"Good." Nico wheeled out of the parking lot. "I'm thinking ice cream at Gott's then maybe we could stop by the Bucket and Bin. I'd like to try to picture what your aunt has in mind, and I'd like your opinions. What do you say? You got the time?"

"Totally," the two girls said in unison.

"Nobody's ever asked our opinion before," Taryn added, her voice quiet with a hint of awe.

"Kids eat, right? Though it's hard to tell by you two." Nico grinned as he caught their surprised looks out of the corner of his eye. "You eat; it's a restaurant. Seems to me your opinions are just as good as mine."

Brooklyn put a hand on his leg. Her smile put a song in his heart.

Ice cream consumed, appetites sated—Nico had given in to the siren call of a burger and fries—the three of them tumbled out of the truck at the Bucket and Bin. A California casual kind of place with a fire pit, lots of glass and weird grasses growing from gaps in the siding, the Bucket and Bin had been an outpost of a popular national restaurant chain. None of the other restaurants in the chain bore the same name, and with good reason: this was how most of them got around the ban on chains in upper Napa Valley.

In Rutherford, a bit south of St. Helena, the restaurant had long been a prime location for vintners to meet over food and wine, generally after the lunch crowd but before happy hour, to discuss anything pertinent to the business, and some things not so pertinent—a business meeting masquerading as a coffee klatch. Nico came as often as he could. He never knew what pearls might pass his way. Familiar as he was with the establishment, he'd never thought of it as anything other than a good place to meet. Now he tried to look at it through his sister's eyes.

The girls sauntered up the walkway leading to double glass doors, then opened both sides for him with a flourish. A comfortable, inviting place with lots of wood and warm colors, with a U-shaped bar and an open kitchen behind, the Bucket and Bin was exactly the sort of place Victoria would be drawn to—simple, refined, elegant yet casual. With her steady hand on the helm, and her food on the menu, the restaurant would quickly be the toughest table in town.

The three of them clustered at a high-top table in the bar area and perused the menu. The girls ordered apple juice, Nico, a flute of Schramsberg Mirabelle. Deep into a heated discussion with two thirteen-year-olds as to the merits of the menu, Nico felt a tap on his shoulder. The girls stopped talking as Nico turned.

Butchy Pinkman, his face a mask of barely controlled anger, hissed, "I need to talk with you, outside."

Nico turned back to his girls and his wine. "I'm with my family."

"You want me to do it right here?" Pinkman raised his voice, turning heads.

Knowing he had to acquiesce to avoid a scene, Nico pushed off his stool. "I'll be right back," he said to the girls, careful to keep his anger out of his voice. "You two don't burn down the place, okay?"

Taryn gave him a sly grin while Brooklyn just looked scared.

Nico gave her a wink then strode through the bar and out onto the patio, staking out a position where he could converse in relative privacy and could still keep an eye on the girls—while he trusted them, sometimes mischief was a mighty calling. "Make it quick, Pinkman."

The little man got up in Nico's face. "Don't you let that woman do anything with my grapes; I'm warning you."

Nico ground his teeth. "As I see it, you'll have them soon enough. But you keep pushing, you keep doing your underhanded shit like you always do, and you're going to queer the deal. Nobody likes their backs against the wall."

"She's gotten under your skin, hasn't she?" Pinkman sneered. "You always were the weak link."

"You'll take those grapes and turn them into mediocre table wine like that Pink's Passion crap you pass off as wine. That's about as good as you can do."

"We own you. And soon we'll own those grapes, all of them. It's a little late to be getting all righteous."

Nico didn't like Pinkman's tone; there was something there, some subtext he was missing.

"You made your deal, Treviani. Your contract is bullet-proof." Pinkman preened.

With one swift movement, Nico grabbed Pinkman by the front of his shirt and threw him up against the wall, holding him there. "Only cowards and thieves hide behind pit-bull lawyers who give their profession a bad name."

Fear flashed across his face as the small man lost his nerve.

Nico tensed as someone stepped in next to him. Avery Specter. He should've know—Pinkman rarely sought out a battle without reinforcements.

"And only fools push back when the law is not on their side." Specter grabbed Nico's arm. "Let him go."

Nico waited a moment, then did as Specter suggested.

Pinkman ducked away, adjusting his shirt. Once out of reach, anger and arrogance again hit Pinkman's eyes, replacing the fear. Pinkman threw his shoulders back and disappeared inside the restaurant.

Nico, his anger under control, turned to Specter. "You need to rein in your *partner*. I don't know the textile business or whatever it was you did, but I do know you'll find that pushing your weight around in the wine business will make you more enemies than you can handle."

LIKE A SOFT SPOTLIGHT HIDING subtle flaws, the light, muted as the sun dropped toward the horizon, enhanced the lush greens of the grapes on the cusp of harvest and dark deep reddish-brown of the soil. In contrast, Sophia seemed under a cloud. She couldn't shake the feeling that she had failed her son, failed herself, failed them all. They needed the house, the grapes, a place to heal, a dream to build on. As Sophia drove, Trey stared out the side window, the silence between them a yawning chasm.

Sophia dove into the abyss. "Life has a way of slapping you upside the head sometimes. I don't know why exactly, maybe to teach you something, maybe to push you in a direction you need to go but don't want to, maybe just to open your eyes, who knows? But I do know that looking backwards hasn't been the best path to the future. We need to make new memories rather than clinging to the old ones like a life raft. Going back is rarely the path forward."

Trey didn't interrupt, but he didn't look at her either. Sophia could tell he was listening even though he half-pretended not to. The funny thing was, she didn't know who she was giving the pep talk to.

While the sun cast a bucolic glow to the surrounding vineyards, it did little for Regina's house. Like a harsh light on an aging beauty, it amplified the dilapidation. If he noticed, Trey didn't comment. Sophia wondered what he was thinking, but she didn't ask.

The nails had popped loose again on the end of two steps. The boards creaked under their weight. Sophia took a breath and raised a hand to knock. The door flew open.

"Your mother's in a state." Mrs. Pettigrew adopted an air of quiet confidence, but worry lingered in the creases of her face, the arch of her painted-on eyebrows that curved higher than normal over wide eyes. A lumpish woman in a housecoat and slippers, her gray wiry hair loosely corralled in a bird's nest on top of her head, she oozed comfort like an overstuffed couch. Her face, unadorned yet sporting a natural flush, relaxed, folding into a worried smile when she saw Trey. "Oh, Mr. Trey. She'll be so glad to see you. She's a bit angry at your mother." Mrs. Pettigrew opened her glance to include Sophia. "She thinks you stole her car."

Sophia ran a shaky hand through her hair. "I didn't..." She paused and started over. "She couldn't..."

A keening wail cut her off. Regina, dressed in a robe, its satin collar and facing torn by the torment of time, hair flying free as if loosed by thoughts and memories as they fled, charged into the room. Her eyes wild, her gait the staggering lurch of an over-served lush, she made straight for her grandson. Her eyes were empty, except for the panic that clouded them. Her make-up smeared, her lips an angry red, painted by a two-year-old who couldn't stay within the lines; her cheeks wrinkled, her skin sallow under the mismatched colors. She'd tried to re-create the outer, but it was as jumbled and tangled as the inner.

Trey's face relaxed into a smile, and in his eyes Sophia saw the kindness, the hurt, the all-knowing wisdom of the sensitive old soul he used to let her see. Regina grabbed Trey, circling his waist with her frail arms, clinging tightly. Resting his chin on the top of her head, he hugged her back. "Nonna."

Without loosening her hold, she leaned back and looked up at him. Adoration burnished her features, but a question lurked there as well, as if she knew the picture but couldn't figure out how the puzzle pieces fit together.

"We need to run away, to get away from here," she whispered. "I have my things."

Sophia followed her mother's furtive look over her shoulder. Several large plastic bags, filled to overflowing were piled in the middle of the living room.

Standing in the shadows, Mrs. Pettigrew wrung her hands. "She went a bit manic. I couldn't calm her. Even her favorite ice cream from Gott's wouldn't stop her. There wasn't much to do other than let her be. She emptied her dresser and some of her closet."

"You did the right thing," Sophia said, not knowing whether that was true or not but not knowing what else to say. Like a swimmer encountering a swift current, she felt helpless, as her mother's rapid decline swept her along and tossed her into the unknown and the unimaginable.

"Of course," Trey soothed as he rubbed his grandmother's back. "Where should we go?"

"Back to the farm. Mamma and Bobbo will be worried. I've been gone a long time, and the grapes are almost ready." Regina shot a wild-eyed look at Sophia. "But don't let her come. Bobbo likes her better, but, really,"—Regina lowered her voice to a stage whisper—"she's not very nice."

A sad smile creased Trey's features, but a hint of light shone in his eyes as he looked at Sophia over his grandmother's head. "Oh, she has her moments. But, Nonna, the farm is a long ride from here, and you look tired. Perhaps a nap would be nice before we head off." Softening his voice, he raised his eyebrows encouragingly. "Would you like a nap?"

Regina's face fell as she let go of her grandson. "A long way?" Her face closed into a frown, more confused than angry. She looked to Sophia, who confirmed with a nod. "I thought we were close. How can it be far? It seems so close." She rubbed her thigh as she darted looks between the three of them. Finally, she seemed to wilt in resignation and acceptance. "My leg hurts. If we have a long journey, then perhaps a rest would be good."

SOPHIA EASED THE TRUCK TO a stop behind her mother's car, which was angled into the curb in front of the fire station. One of the fire trucks was out, the bay left open. She pulled Regina's keys from her pocket and tossed them to Trey.

He snagged them with a reflexive stab, a third baseman catching a line drive. "Thanks, Mom. I've got some errands to run, okay? I'll find you later."

"Sure." Sophia tried to adopt a casual tone, but emotions had her strung tight. "Could I talk you into dinner at the house? I'll invite your sister, maybe some of the usual suspects. What do you say?" She held her breath, hoping, pleading with all of the lesser gods and any other deity who would listen.

With his hand on the door handle, Trey turned, giving her his full attention. "That'd be nice, Mom, real nice."

Sophia started breathing again. "Good. Good." She glanced at her watch. It was already late, another day dipping toward nightfall, but she only needed a few hours. "Say seven-ish?"

"Sure. Anything I can pick up while I'm out?"

"No, thanks. Going to the store to see what inspires me." She narrowed her eyes at him. "Are you really my son?"

Trey grinned. "Feeling more like it every minute. Why?"

Sophia could tell he knew the answer. "You're not strong-arming me into cooking lasagna. I'm surprised."

"You've got enough on your plate and that's an all-day gig."

Sophia narrowed her eyes but not her smile. She felt her heart open with the bantering. "Okay, what have you done with my son?"

Trey laughed. "Perspective, it's a dangerous thing. Besides, I'm sure you've got something else to do."

Something else to do? Sophia wasn't sure.

Trey put a hand on the truck door, leaning toward the window. "How long has Nonna been like that? I'm used to the cut-to-the-bone old ..."

"Be kind." Sophia's voice held a slight warning, but she felt the same way, not that she didn't feel guilty about it. If Regina Otero had been anything, it was difficult.

"She could be pretty harsh, especially to you." A note of faraway softness, of remembered emotion, deepened his voice. "As a kid, I used to want to hit her."

Sophia leaned to get a better look at him. "Hit her? Whatever for?"

"She was hateful to you. Always telling you what to do, and denigrating your choices, your dreams ... if you had any left by then." He shrugged under the embarrassment of emotion. "I just..." His voice broke. "I loved..." Words abandoned him. Sophia squeezed his shoulder, resisting an almost overwhelming urge to wrap him in a bear hug, hold him tight, and never let him go. Trey took a deep breath. When he looked at her his eyes were clear. "You were my mom. I saw you dying inside and I couldn't save you."

"Oh, Trey." Emotion trumped constraint. Sophia reached for

him, pulling him to her, squeezing him tight. "It wasn't your job to save me."

Trey relaxed into her, hugging her back, clinging with a ferocity Sophia hadn't felt from him in a long, long time. "Good thing. Cuz it turns out, I can't save anybody."

Sophia kissed his head and stroked his hair. "Honey. You've got to save yourself before you can save anybody else."

SOPHIA THOUGHT ABOUT THOSE WORDS as she watched Trey settle himself behind the wheel of Regina's car. He stuck his arm out the window, giving her a jaunty wave, which Sophia suspected was more for her benefit than an accurate reflection of the songs playing in his heart right now. Pain, the catalyst for change. The reality of that little nugget of wisdom hit home, leaving Sophia unsettled and compounding the fact that not being needed anywhere left her at a loss. Contemplating her next move, Sophia moved the truck forward, then watched as Trey backed out then turned toward the highway. The recent earthquake of emotion had left her standing on quicksand. She had no idea what to do about any of it. Not her home. Not her mother. Not her son. Not Nico. There was only one thing to do.

Cook.

When life beat you up, the Oteros beat a path to the kitchen.

She turned left out of the parking lot, heading north. With a party to plan and dinner to cook, she'd start at Safeway and work her way south to Dean & Deluca.

Food therapy wasn't any good without sharing it. Even if it was for the last time, Sophia needed to fill her home with family, both by blood and by choice. She needed to hear laughter permeating every corner, filling the darkness with light.

CHAPTER TWENTY-FIVE

NICO WAS THE FIRST TO ARRIVE, his out-of-time engine heralding his progress up the mountain. He didn't bother to knock. Instead, with one hip he knocked the door open, his hands filled with several bottles of wine. When he stepped inside, he seemed to fill the room, leaving Sophia fighting for air, and composure.

Like a kid with a trophy, he hoisted the wine. "I scored a bunch of bottles of Arnot-Roberts for the red drinkers—there's more in the truck. Of course, the white is chilling out back—a half-case of a smooth yet complex blend—a thing of sublime beauty from this new winery I've heard about, S.O.S." Setting the bottles on the sideboard, he eased in behind Sophia who tended a pot on the stove, catching her in an embrace.

She giggled as he nuzzled her ear. "Don't get too complacent. We've got grapes to drop later."

"That's later." He peered over her shoulder. "What is that incredible smell?"

She turned her head to accept a quick kiss. "Dean & Deluca had some Prosciutto San Daniele, from Friuli, near my grandparents' farm. So I decided to do a whole menu of the foods I remember eating in my grandmother's kitchen. Before she died, my Nonna gave me this." Using the spoon, she pointed at a book with lined pages, each stained and well used. It lay open to a list of ingredients written in a flourished cursive, old and elegant, befitting of the original Italian.

"Her recipes."

"It was all she had and everything she was."

"I didn't know you could speak Italian." Nico gave her a look that Sophia couldn't read.

"I spent enough time in the Old Country, God knows. I can read it better than speak it." She dipped a fresh spoon into the pot. "Here." She held the spoon out to him. "Try it. Friuli cuisine isn't what most think of as Italian. Because of its proximity to the Slavic countries, its food is heavily influenced."

Nico took a tentative sip, then blew on the liquid a bit before taking all of it. "Delicious. What is it?"

"Jota. A pork stew. Perfect for the wines you brought. We'll have a ham and asparagus gratin to start." Sophia talked as she grabbed a towel and reached to open the oven. "Followed by an apple strudel."

Nico groaned as she placed the strudel on the sideboard to cool. "I love a woman with a perfect strudel."

Sophia raised an eyebrow in amusement.

He looked like an overgrown kid, with his hair across his forehead tickling his eyes, his white T-shirt straining to contain his shoulders and chest, his narrow waist, strong legs, and silly, bashful grin. "Hey, it's been a long time since I tried to flirt with a woman. Cut me some slack."

Sophia thought she'd already cut him about as much slack as her doubting heart could stand, but she didn't say so.

Noise upstairs startled her. Footfalls. Someone was up there, and they weren't being quiet.

"Who else is here?" Nico asked, suddenly serious. "Trey's was out front but you said he'd taken your mother's car."

"He did." Sophia shrugged—she had thought she was alone before Nico arrived. Someone had been there all along. She tracked the movement across the ceiling, then down the stairs. "Must be one of the kids. Probably Trey, although I didn't notice a car."

Despite her casual air, her heartbeat accelerated. Nico adopted a defensive position by the door. The steps got closer. Sophia held her breath, frozen, fixated on the door. Trey pushed into the kitchen, his head bent in concentration over the sketchbook he held in his hands. "God, Mom, whatever you're making, it smells to die for." He looked up catching, Nico staring at him. "Hey." Trey didn't seem surprised to see him standing there.

Sophia recognized Trey's distraction—he'd been drawing. When he was little, he'd spent hours in his room working on his sketches. When she'd call him to dinner, it would take him time to reenter the real world and get up to full velocity. The family had learned to give him space.

"Trey, you gave me a start. Where's your grandmother's car?"

"What?" He looked at her a moment, his eyes straining to focus. "Oh, yeah, the car. I left it down at the station with Drew. It was making some weird noises and the steering was loose. Drew gave me a ride home. He's going to call when it's ready, but it could take a while. They haven't made parts for that car since the Dark Ages." Tapping a pencil on the drawing pad, he continued. "I've got some ideas here I'd like you to look at." He spread the book open on the kitchen table. "You, too, Nico, if you would. I'd like your opinion. After all, this concerns you as well."

Trey pulled several sheets of paper from the book and arranged them so the others could see. "If you're going to make that wine, and actually bottle it and sell it, you need a label. I know custom labels can be expensive, but, hey, you're going for broke as it is, so why not."

The mention of labels got Nico's attention, and he flipped to all-business mode as he bent over the drawings.

Sophia was stunned, and amazingly touched. "Honey, when did you have time to do all of these?"

"After I left you at the fire station, I went straight to the art supply store. Been up in my old room ever since. I figured this is important to you, so it's important to me, too."

With emotion choking off her words, Sophia resorted to giving him a squeeze.

Looking a little discomfited by his mother's emotion, Trey turned his attention to Nico. "I don't know your style, what you're looking for, so I tried a few different things. Since time is short, I didn't do any four-color labels, just stuck to the basics. If you really like any of these and you both decide to make more wine in the future under this label, we can develop the branding strategy a bit more fully."

"These are good," Nico said, but he didn't look up. "I like the way you think. Clean, simple, unique."

"I've always been drawn to the wine business." Trey's voice was quiet.

Nico gave him a long look, then returned his attention to the labels. "You have a knack."

"The way I see it, yours and Mom's wine will sell itself."

"Perhaps. Once people try it," Sophia said.

"Exactly. And that's where the label comes in—it's like a cover on a book, designed to make people pick it up, turn it over, read about it."

Trey gave his mother a smile over the top of Nico's head, still bent over the table. He motioned her to join them, then he, too, focused on the drawings. Nico remained transfixed by the sketches, pushing some away and moving others aside according to his liking. He muttered as he did so, making Sophia smile.

Sophia held back just a little, watching her son and her... whatever. She had no idea how to classify Nico. Perhaps partner was the most accurate. Yes. Her partner. She could swallow that. Baby steps. She needed baby steps. The men, their two heads bent together, one dark, one lighter, both intense, focused on each drawing in turn.

Nico culled three from the lot. "These would be my choices."

Trey remained passive, his face stoic. Even his mother couldn't tell what he thought. And he used to be an open book.

Nico reached back and pulled Sophia next to him. "Come on. This is your baby. Tell us what you think."

Her shoulder touched his; the heat startled her. Trey's face remained blank, but his eyes betrayed him. His mother could see the joy, the need, the fear. This is what he'd wanted to do for as long as she'd known him. Wine. The business of wine had been his passion ... until his dad had died. It was as if the light that had burned inside of the boy had died that day, too, starved of fuel by pain and loss. Sophia gave him a nod. The drawings were each wonderful—distinct, imaginative, yet simple enough to be iconic and easily recognizable.

Sophia took her time, giving each her undivided attention. On the first pass, she eliminated half, including one of Nico's choices. He didn't say anything, letting her think. After a bit more time, she winnowed it down to two, one Nico had chosen, one he hadn't.

The one Nico had chosen was a small skiff, de-masted, adrift, with an arm hanging over the side holding a bottle of wine. He had a good eye. Sophia focused on each drawing in turn. Which one was elegant simplicity? Which one could become iconic? Which one made a statement?

Which one hit her on a visceral level?

The second drawing, the one that hit Sophia each time her attention returned to it, was simply a heart, a bold red brushstroke. Sophia tapped it with her finger. "That one."

Trey stepped around to stand at her shoulder. "Why that one?"

Sophia stepped back, one arm circling her waist, a hand pressed over her heart. "It works on two levels for me. It's beautiful—and I do hope we can get the red printed in time; that just makes it pop. And it's simple; yet it perfectly captures what this wine is to me, perhaps what I think wine should be. Passion. Art. A work of the heart."

Trey gave her a knowing look. "I know. That's what I was going for."

When she looked into his eyes, she saw her son—the son she had nurtured and raised to manhood—the son she had lost. And somehow she knew everything would be all right. She didn't know how, or when, but the knowledge deep in her bones that it would all work out was enough.

"You got it." Nico pushed the chosen label into the middle of the table where it caught the most light as he gathered the others into a stack. "Yep, it's really good. And, Trey, if you want to design more labels and work on the branding thing, just let me know."

"Thanks. I've engineering school to finish."

Nico weighed his words before he spoke. "That'd be a waste. Life's too short. You spend the bulk of your life at work. By God, make it something you love to do."

"Do you love making wine?" Trey asked Nico, a fair question in light of Nico's comments.

"I'm conflicted about it, to be honest. Wine was something that was forced on me." He shrugged in self-recrimination. "I let it happen. I took up the yoke of being the oldest son and fulfilling my father's expectations and all of that. So I resent wine sometimes. But it has given me great satisfaction. And the times shared with my brother are priceless. I wouldn't have had that if it wasn't for wine."

"You're good at it."

Nico looked over Trey's shoulder through the window at the vineyard beyond. "We'll see."

In that moment, Sophia understood Nico in a way she hadn't before. His fears. His sadness. And she loved him for his vulnerabilities.

The three of them looked at the label. The red heart seemed to beat with their shared passion.

Maggie and Annalise arrived at the same time, each with a man in tow. They chattered like good friends as they pushed into the kitchen, followed by the men who both looked a bit uncomfortable.

"Oh, my God, what is that amazing smell?" Maggie ignored those gathered in the kitchen, rushing over to the pot burbling on the stove. Sticking her nose in the steam, she inhaled deeply. "This isn't your lasagna."

Sophia glanced at Nico and they both rolled their eyes.

Annalise set a basket on the table. Baguettes peeked out of the blue-and-white-checkered cloth that wrapped them. "I thought these would go well with your stew." She introduced her man around, referring to him simply as Antoine.

Remembering her manners, Maggie hooked her arm through her escort's. "This here is Devlin."

Lean, lithe, and carefully sculpted, Devlin had an easy smile but wariness in his eyes. Thrown in with new folks, he kept his easy manner. While he might live on a farm, Sophia had the sense that he hadn't been raised on one.

She welcomed everyone then put them all to work, assigning each a task. Conversation and the comfort of friends and family mingled with the savory aromas. Preparing a meal for those special to her, feeding them in the sanctity of her kitchen, gave Sophia a satisfaction she found in few other places. In the embrace of a loved one. In the solitude of her vineyard where memories and hopes pressed around her. An intimacy of love, sustenance to feed the body and the heart.

Dinner was ready to serve, and Dani had yet to arrive. Sophia tossed a worried glance at Trey, who shrugged. Stepping in next to Nico, she asked, "Did something come up at the winery that would be keeping Dani? When I spoke to her earlier, she didn't mention she'd be late."

"Not that I know of."

CHAPTER TWENTY-SIX

WIPING HER HANDS ON HER APRON, Sophia stepped onto the porch. As she reached for the phone she saw headlights darting through the trees as a truck climbed her hillside. Stepping to the edge of the porch, Sophia waited.

When she dropped out of the truck, Dani lacked her normal energy. And she didn't look happy. She gave her mom a tight hug and put a smile firmly in place.

Sophia wasn't fooled. "What's the matter?"

"It'll wait." A hint of her normal fire sparked in her eyes. "I hear my wayward brother is here." She pushed past her mother, leaving her alone in the dark.

Sophia tried not to let Dani's attitude worry her as she followed her daughter inside. Trey turned as his sister launched herself at him, staggering him slightly as he caught her. They clutched each other, clinging with the ferocity of kindred souls, lost to each other for a time.

Sophia caught the looks of her friends as they all watched. Annalise smiled softly in understanding. Maggie grinned, but Sophia could tell the display touched her heart as well.

Trey put the leaf in the kitchen table. Sophia rubbed her hands idly over the fresh wood that still shone with a bright finish. They had never had much use for it, having been only the four of them. Now there were more. Sophia felt her heart swell, despite the loss of the one who was missing. Daniel would be proud of his children, and proud of the life she'd made for them. Hopefully, he'd be happy to see she was embracing her own life anew, but Sophia wasn't as clear on that. But he wasn't here and he no longer got to choose.

With the kitchen filled to overflowing, Sophia didn't want to interfere as merriment mingled with savory aromas. So for the first time ever, she stepped back and let her family pitch in. Amazingly, the table got set, everyone got seated and the food served as conversation flowed as freely as the lovely red Nico had brought. The white, her white, would wait.

Sophia noticed Nico positioned himself at her side but close enough to Trey to engage him in conversation. Dani separated the other two couples on the far side of the table. A smile curved her lips but her eyes remained dark and brooding. She still didn't look happy, but she participated in the conversations swirling around her.

Intent on remaining present and appreciative of this moment, Sophia closed her mind to her problems—food and friends were a good panacea to lessen the sting of worry. When Nico opened the white, everyone appropriately ooohed and ahhed. Sophia took a special note of the care with which Antoine approached the wine. He seemed to like it—appreciating fine food and drink was his specialty and, one would assume, his passion, after all. The only awkward moment of the evening came when someone asked Antoine what line of work he was in. He'd said he was in journalism, a freelance writer—a practiced dodge. Everyone bought it, and his true identity as the most famous food critic in Northern California remained hidden.

Secrets. So hard to keep. Facades, so hard to maintain. Sophia should know—the more she opened her heart and her life, the more she realized how hidden away she'd been, and for far longer than five years. Just now she was beginning to see hints of the girl she used to be, beckoned from hiding by dreams of her own.

With plates empty and bellies full, comforted in the presence of friends both old and new, dinner wound to a satisfying ebb. With a shared questioning look at their mother, Trey and Dani excused themselves, but only after Sophia's nod. They had precious little time together just the two of them, and it would do them both a world of good, so Sophia let them go.

Nico pushed his chair back. "Come on, Sophia. I'll wash if you dry."

Maggie jumped up, positioning herself between Nico and the sink. "No way, big guy. You brought the wine. Sophia did the heavy lifting. The rest of us have the clean-up duty. That's how it rolls around here."

So tired her bones ached, Sophia wasn't about to argue. Nico surrendered with a good-natured laugh. Devlin and Antoine hadn't needed prodding and were already chatting companionably at the sink as Devlin ran the water and Antoine stood at the ready with a stack of fresh dishtowels. Annalise busied herself clearing the table, while Maggie bent down to root through the lower cabinet, pulling out Tupperware for the leftovers, leaving Sophia and Nico with nothing to do.

He nudged her with his shoulder. "You know what they say about too many cooks in the kitchen."

She giggled like a schoolgirl. "I think that refers to the quality of meal preparation, not the clean-up."

"Still, our sentence has been commuted. Hanging around only increases our chances of being indentured to manual labor. I don't think we should chance it." After topping their glasses, he grabbed them, and with a quick tilt of his head he motioned for Sophia to follow him out onto the porch. Leaning against an upright, he handed her a glass, then looped an arm around her shoulders drawing her close. Side by side, they looked out over the moonlit vineyard. The night was still. Sophia felt wildly alive in a way she couldn't remember ever feeling and she didn't know whether it was Trey being home, her grapes, the man pressed to her side, or the wine. She suspected a combination—a heady mix like the rush of speeding headlong down a steep hill, with only an illusion of control, the world a blur as it rushes past, disaster just an eye-blink away. Will you make it or will you crash and burn?

Nico breathed deeply of the perfumed air. "Nothing prettier." He paused as he let his breath out slowly. "Well, maybe one thing." He brushed his lips against hers in a kiss that was quick, fleeting, yet enough to set Sophia's nerve-endings tingling. "Who have you been hiding from on this mountaintop these last five years?"

Sophia took another sip of her wine—her second glass and one past her limit. The question was odd. Nobody had asked her that before. "I really hadn't thought I was hiding. Healing, perhaps." She thought a moment. "But I guess I was hiding, too."

"From whom?"

"Myself mostly." Sophia surprised herself with her openness. Most days she wasn't all that honest with herself, much less with a practical stranger. A warm flush spread through her body. Okay, he wasn't a stranger, but he had been until just a short while ago. And curiously, letting him into her bed had been far easier than letting him into her life ... or her heart.

"If you live in the past, you miss the present," Nico whispered against her hair. "And forfeit the future."

Maggie and Annalise pushed through the door and into Sophia and Nico's reverie. "Enough of that, you two." Maggie dried her hands on a dishtowel as she stepped in next to Sophia and took a long look at the vineyard. "Those grapes make really primo juice." As if noticing too late she'd opened an unpleasant topic, she segued right into, "So what'd you think? Devlin is smokin', isn't he? Just gettin' a sniff of him makes my juices boil."

Nico uncoiled himself from Sophia. "That is my signal. I have nothing to add to this conversation, so I'll leave you three to dissect that perfectly adequate member of my gender." He wandered back into the kitchen with a big, "Anybody got a beer?" which would get him shot in most of the finer establishments in the valley, but Sophia's was a bit more accepting of fringe tastes.

When the door banged shut behind Nico, Maggie whirled on the other two. "So? What do you think?"

"I think being friends first, before you run him into the ground, would be a good plan," Sophia said.

"Yeah, like you did with Nico," Maggie scoffed.

"I'm older than you, and, while it's doubtful I'm wiser, I have made a bunch more mistakes and have learned what I need as opposed to what I want."

Maggie deflated. "Dang. I knew you were going to say that. And it sounds pretty wise to me, which is sorta pissing me off."

Annalise put a hand on Maggie's arm. "If you want to have the dance, you must let the man lead."

Maggie looked at her sideways. "But he's not the boss, right?"

"But of course not." With pursed lips, Annalise gave her a little shrug, almost a shiver of distaste, as only a Frenchwoman could do. "We simply let them think they make the rules."

"Okay. Okay." Maggie sounded like an athlete psyching herself up before a big match. "I come on pretty strong, I know that."

"You must weave a web of mystery." Annalise gave Maggie an apprising look. "Perhaps we try for the subtle first."

Lost in the nuances of the art of the chase, Maggie didn't seem to notice the jab, or she didn't care. Or perhaps she'd developed a heightened sense of self-awareness in the last twenty-four hours, but Sophia doubted it. She hid her grin. "Devlin seems lovely, Mags, and pretty taken with you. Let him get used to the idea. Get your mind out of the gutter and your hands off his ass. No sex, just friends... for a bit."

Maggie looked a bit crestfallen, but she was listening. This Devlin must be important.

Sophia turned her attention to Annalise. "So how are things with Antoine?"

Annalise gave her a narrow-eyed look. "Actually, I'm really enjoying his company."

"And he seems to think you're a tasty tart as well." Sophia clamped down on her smile, but her attempt at self-control was too little, too late. She felt her smile blossom.

Maggie rewarded her with a guffaw.

Annalise even managed a smile. "By the way, I phoned Nico's mother. She sounds lovely and was excited at my interest in trying out her skills in the bakery."

Sophia was pleased—perhaps that would work out for the both of them. "I really can't speak to her skills, not from a professional perspective like yours, but if it's passion you want, she's got that by the gallons. And her coconut oatmeal cookies are the stuff sin is made of."

Maggie tucked the dishrag in the waistband of her jeans, then tapped Annalise on the arm. "Come on. Let's round up our fellows and beat it." She held up her hand. "You eliminate sex and everything becomes laden with innuendo. I didn't mean that in the vernacular sense. Well, I did, just not the sexual sense. Man, I don't know what it is with you guys but it's like verbal booby-trap." She clamped a hand over her mouth. "See," she mumbled through her fingers.

"You have an overabundance of the hormones," Annalise said.

Maggie let her hand drop as she giggled. "Damn straight. You try living on a farm where everything is fucking constantly."

Sophia and Annalise looked at her wide-eyed.

"Just sayin'. Anyway, you and me," she gave Annalise a direct look, "let's boogie. Sophia looks like the walking dead, and she has a long night ahead of her."

At Sophia's raised eyebrow, Maggie squelched a smile. "Your kids have pulled out all the photo albums and are settling in for a serious trip down memory lane."

SOPHIA FOUND DANI AND TREY huddled in the middle of the living room floor, two tiny human vessels adrift on a sea of old photographs. Pausing in the doorway, she let snippets of time wash through her. A memory reel that she didn't need, not right now anyway, filled her heart as happiness and pain collided. After family dinners, Daniel always decamped to the leather chair by the fireplace. His legs crossed, his feet on the ottoman, he'd pretend to read the paper while he reveled in the children playing in the spot they now occupied, heads bent together as now, in shared concentration. Games or homework, minor squabbles or benign acceptance, Daniel had refereed while Sophia finished up in the kitchen.

To Sophia's recollection, Daniel was the last one to have sat in his chair. The leather looked rough and cracked with disuse. Sophia crossed her arms and leaned her head against the doorjamb. Dani sat back on her heels, a photograph clutched tightly, her face crinkled with emotion. "Remember this?" She thrust the photo at her brother, who glanced at it.

"Sure. Dad had just taught you how to ride a bike. You'd fallen a bunch, bloodied your nose as I recall. He wouldn't let you quit."

Dani's face softened. "No, he wouldn't let me quit." When she looked at her brother, her eyes were bright, her expression intense.

Trey squirmed under his sister's gaze. "What?"

"You look like him, you know."

"That's ironic, actually." Trey seemed pleased at the comparison.

Dani's hands, still clutching the photo, rested in her lap. "Why do you say that?"

"We butted heads over just about everything. He wanted me to play sports; I wanted to draw. He ran through life not caring who he knocked out of the way." Trey glanced up and caught his mother's eye. "Or ran over."

"Trey, that's awful. I don't remember him that way." Dani seemed to sense her mother there. "How do you remember Dad?"

"I remember him well. No one is perfect, Dani. Sometimes memories gloss over that or they amplify it, but our own memories are for our own purposes. We need to remember certain people in certain ways, so we do."

"Is that good or bad?"

"Neither. It just is." Sophia pushed herself from her resting spot.

Nico was in the kitchen behind her, polishing the glasses and putting them away. He didn't notice her standing there, so she took a moment to watch him. Measured and efficient, he whistled softly as he worked. Long and lean, dark and emotional, he was so different than Daniel with his lightness, his compact body, his breezy way of gliding over the currents and eddies of life. Nico wouldn't let her hide in the background as Daniel had. No, he'd thrust her into life whether she liked it or not. Although that scared her, it thrilled her in ways she had yet to understand.

When he sensed her presence and turned, Sophia motioned him to join them. "Come sit with us."

"Are you sure you don't want to be alone with your kids?" he asked as he let her draw him close.

"This might be a good time to get a short course in the Stone family. It's still early. You can run for the hills."

"I don't scare easily." Nico pulled chairs for each of them to the periphery of the scattered photos. From there they could lean over and pick and choose.

Normally energized by his presence, Dani shut down when Nico expressed interest in the photographic safari. Sophia ignored her, refusing to let her behavior cast a pall over the first family gathering in a long, long time. Trey and Sophia pawed through the pictures as Dani scooched back, her knees drawn in to her chest, her arms holding her legs. They paused over an occasional find, sharing a quick story with Nico, laughing over a shared silliness.

At the insistent jangle of the phone, Sophia's smile faded. She glanced at her watch. The call was most likely from her mother. She debated ignoring it, but then, with her mother's mental health teetering precariously and Ms. Pettigrew in the line of fire, she realized putting her mother off was no longer an option.

She rocked back on her heels and went to answer it. The night had cooled. Stepping onto the porch, Sophia shivered as she reached for the receiver. "Yes."

"Umm, Mrs. Stone?" A voice, deep, masculine, and definitely not her mother's or Ms. Pettigrew's. From the surprised hitch in his voice, he clearly was a bit taken aback.

"I'm sorry. I was expecting my mother." Sophia wiped a hand across her brow. Bone weary and barely standing, she mustered her tattered wits. "I'm Mrs. Stone."

"I'm so sorry to bother you. I know it's late." He sounded tired ... and young.

"Who is this?" Sophia's heartbeat accelerated. Late-night calls rarely brought welcomed news.

"I'm sorry. This is Dr. Fisher. I'm a resident at Queen of the Valley Hospital. And, oddly enough, I'm calling about your mother..." he trailed off as if searching for the right words.

Sophia, her legs weakening, reached for a chair behind her. Pulling it closer, she lowered herself, perching on the edge afraid of the brittle wicker seat. She'd been meaning to get it re-woven. "Yes?" Sophia's voice, strangled by fear, came out as a whisper.

"They brought her in a little bit ago. Her femur... her thighbone ... snapped. She was in quite a bit of pain, but we have her resting now. We'll be doing some tests. Her friend who was staying with her gave us your number. She was too upset to call. Besides, it was best that I did."

"And you drew the short straw." Seeing stars, Sophia realized she hadn't been breathing. She sucked in a deep lungful of crisp air. Although not a religious person, she also tossed off a quick thank-you to the Virgin Mary on the off chance it might help—remnants of a Catholic upbringing seared on her soul, but not in her heart. A broken leg. At her age, her mother ought to be glad it wasn't her hip—Sophia had heard that was like a death sentence.

Dani, her face serious, paused in the kitchen doorway and stuck her head out. "Is everything okay?"

Sophia pressed a hand over the phone. "Your grandmother broke her leg, but the doctors are handling it. No need to worry. Go on back inside." Dani ignored her mother and remained lurking in the doorway.

"The short straw?" the doctor continued, his tone a hint lighter. "Well, perhaps. Your mother is ..." He trailed off either searching for a kind way to phrase his assessment of her mother or at a complete loss for words.

Sophia didn't need him to connect the dots. "Yes, she's all of that and so much more, trust me. You're sure she's okay?"

"As I said, we've just had a chance to get her settled and manage her pain. We're running some further tests, and I'll know more when I get the results back. But, at her age, osteoporosis can be quite advanced, causing bones to spontaneously fracture. Most folks think broken bones in the elderly are usually the result of a fall, but, in my experience, it's usually the other way around."

"I had no idea." Sophia made a mental note to get her bones checked, then rolled her eyes at herself. With her schedule that might happen toward the end of the century.

"I will tell you, though, we, ummmm—we had to sedate your mother. She bit one of the nurses. You wouldn't know if she has any communicable diseases, would you?"

"She bit her?" Sophia didn't know whether to laugh or cry.

"Him. Drew blood." The young doctor sounded more relaxed. He even allowed himself a chuckle. "She's a force, isn't she?"

"You have no idea. But, if I were you, and if you have any notion of restoring her consciousness, I'd either restrain her or have a stun-gun at the ready. Although a broken femur might slow her down."

"Seriously?"

"No." Sophia waited until she heard the young doctor laugh. "I'm on my way." In the background she heard something metal clatter as if thrown. Then raised voices.

"I've got to go." The doctor took a ragged breath. "And, Mrs. Stone?"

"Yes?"

"Hurry. She has the entire nursing staff terrorized."

Re-cradling the phone, Sophia let her hand rest there a moment, as if keeping the connection open. Life was coming at her so fast that she didn't know what to do. So many problems. So many changes. So many questions. So few answers.

"Mom?" Dani's voice was soft, scared.

Sophia found her brave face. That was her job, after all: to keep her head while all of those around her were losing theirs. But, for a weak second, she wondered how many more blows she could take. Sophia ushered her daughter inside, out of the cool night air. "I need to go check on your grandmother—she's taken a fall. The doctor didn't seem too worried, so we shouldn't be either."

"I'll go with you."

Sophia reached and brushed a hair from her daughter's cheek. "No, thank you. I'll be fine. You have work tomorrow. I don't." Just saying it made Sophia feel lighter, like a condemned man taking a call from the Governor.

"You're going to have *him* take you." A statement from her daughter, in a cold tone as she glanced over her shoulder.

"Dani, I don't know what's gotten into you."

Dani lowered her voice, her eyes darting toward the doorway. "I have something I need to tell you. Something I found."

Sophia's heart sank. She wasn't sure she could handle any more bad news. "Is it a matter of life and death? You're okay, right? Parts aren't falling off; you're not bleeding out?"

Dani's face closed. "No. It's not as important as Grandmother. It can wait."

"Good. While the doctor wasn't alarmed, he asked me to hurry."

Dani glanced over her shoulder once again then stepped in close to her mother and grabbed her arm. "But don't do anything until you talk to me."

"There's nothing I can do that would make anything any worse. As soon as your grandmother is out of the woods, I'll find you. You can tell me then."

"Mom. Promise me."

"Dani." Sophia stared down her daughter, then relented. "Okay. I'll get Nonna settled then come straight to you. But, honestly, I don't think I can deal with anything else at the moment."

CHAPTER TWENTY-SEVEN

"I WONDER WHY THEY BROUGHT NONNA HERE?" Trey asked, his voice quiet as he turned Sophia's truck into the parking lot in front of the emergency entrance. He flicked his gaze to her mother. "St. Helena hospital is closer."

"I don't know, honey." Sophia had been mulling the same question, but she had no answers. The closer they had gotten to the hospital, the harder it had been for her to concentrate. With each mile, memories constricted her chest like steel bands squeezing tighter and tighter until she thought the pressure would still her heart. Daniel had died here. Clinging to life from the accident site on Highway 29, he had let go, lost his battle, here, in this emergency room. Before she had been able to get there to say goodbye. She'd rushed as fast as she could, but he was gone when she got there. Sophia hadn't been back since.

Dani had been sixteen, Trey two years older. One glance at her son and Sophia knew he was reliving his own memories of that night. Sophia gave his hand a squeeze. It was cold as ice.

"This sucks, Mom."

"Death is a part of life."

His eyes saucers, Trey looked at his mother.

Sophia lifted one side of her mouth in a tremulous grin. "Okay. Even I can't believe I said that. You're right; this totally sucks."

The air held a damp chill. Unusual for September, although in the town of Napa in the southern part of the Valley, tendrils of fog from the Bay to the south often snaked through the low places, seeping into the vineyards, enveloping the vines in a cool mist. Pinot Noir and Chardonnay climate, thought Sophia. Glad she had grabbed a light sweater, she shrugged into it and pulled the thin fabric around her. Trey had parked the truck at the edge of the lot—the spaces were small. This being California, the zoning folks who drew the lines on the parking lot apparently thought everyone in the Valley drove a Prius. A noble goal, but those who worked in the fields needed vehicles that were a bit more robust.

A toxic witch's brew of ammonia and fear hit Sophia the minute the automatic doors opened and they stepped inside the emergency room. Sophia fought the urge to run as she swallowed the bile that rose in her throat.

Flashes of memories, visual, visceral, nipped and bit, like coyotes weakening their prey.

Blood. There had been so much blood. Daniel's body crushed, bruised and broken. They let her stay with him only long enough to make a positive identification. There was no time to hold his hand, stroke his hair. No moment to say a final goodbye. Only the memory of his jaunty wave and quick grin as he threw a leg over his bicycle and headed off to meet his riding group. As if life had been paused, like one would a television show to grab a glass of wine from the kitchen, then plop back down and pick up where they'd left off. There were days Sophia half-expected to see him riding back up the hill.

But Daniel wouldn't be coming home.

Joe Patterson, Trudy and Alex's son and all of seventeen, never saw Daniel, who was leading the pack. In an instant, one life was lost, one irretrievably altered, and others bent and torn as pain rippled through the families and friends like waves of destruction following an earthquake, reducing once formidable structures to rubble. Trudy and Alex had split. Last she'd heard Joe was in his third college, still trying to pull the frayed edges of his life back together. There'd been no charges. Just lingering horror at how quickly life can turn.

Sophia had almost broken. Had she not had the kids ...

A part of her heart died that day. Numb even to the joy of her children, Sophia lost those first few months in a haze of pain and anger, and alcohol. Thankfully the kids had stayed with their grandmother and hadn't witnessed their mother bouncing off rock bottom.

Slowly she found her footing, bartering with life, trading future penance for present happiness. Someday her account would come due, and she would be alone with her fears, her deflated hope, and the silent mocking of what could have been.

"Mom? Are you okay?" Trey's voice in her ear sounded worried and half-sick. "We made it through that; we can make it through anything."

The world spun back into focus as Sophia glanced around, trying to make sense of where she was and why. Everything was familiar, as if nothing had changed since the night Daniel died, the nurses in purple scrubs; the doctors in their blue scrubs, shoulders bent under responsibility, faces haggard with lack of sleep; the clock on the wall above the check-in desk—the clock Sophia had watched tick off endless moments of hope. The place where lives are lost, families broken, horrible, unspeakable things happened on a regular basis, seemed benign, almost welcoming with its comfortable chairs, coffee and snack station in the corner, and the daily bits of drivel the stations now passed off as news humming from the televisions in the corners. But the faces of those who waited, drawn with worry, their smiles wan as they clung to hope, eyes sick with fear but flaring with expectation at the intrusion, told a different story.

Trey gripped her arm, squeezing tight. "It's going to be okay."

"Or not," Sophia said, surprising herself. The words bounded like hellhounds from some dark, deep place. "Let's go find Dr. Fisher."

Amazingly enough, Dr. Fisher proved fairly easy to find. He actually was where the nurse at the information desk who had buzzed them through the doors said he would be—at the nurses' station, a U-shaped desk encircled by a circular hallway. Cubicles, some of them with draped entrances, fronted the hallway. Equipment beeped and whirred from behind the curtains, as nurses ducked in and out as quietly as ghosts.

Dr. Fisher sat at the left arm of the desk, leaning forward, squinting at a computer screen, his right hand manipulating a mouse, pointing and clicking with lightning speed. Periodically he would flip his hair, dark, wavy and a trifle long, out of his eyes. With a square jaw, trimmed mustache, broad shoulders, and blue eyes, which Sophia caught when he looked up, he wasn't what she expected— except for the ever-present beleaguered look, which most doctors wore like a sweater their grandmother had knitted, ill-fitting but obligatory.

"Dr. Fisher?" Sophia asked, although she was pretty sure of the answer—he wore a lanyard around his neck and Sophia could see the first few letters of his last name on the tag clipped to it.

"Yes." He pushed himself back and stood, extending his hand. "You must be Mrs. Stone."

"Sophia, please." As she took his hand and pumped it once, she motioned toward her son. "And this is my son, Trey."

The men shook hands quickly, then Trey stuck his in his back pockets.

Sophia could see the effort it took for him to remain calm and brave. As a parent, all she'd wanted was to protect her children from the harshness of life. Not a realistic goal, nor, perhaps, even a good one. Regardless, she had failed and was left to watch life ripping through her children, powerless to stop it. There were days Sophia hated God. And for that she figured she'd be punished anew. But if God didn't understand, who would?

"My mother? How is she?"

Dr. Fisher smiled, but his cheeks drained to pale and his eyes lost their warmth as if he retreated to a place safe from the horrors of his world. "Resting comfortably. We've run some tests and should have the results back soon. You're welcome to see her, if you like. She's awake, but in and out." He stepped from behind the desk and motioned down the hall. "Third door on the right. She's been asking for you. I know she'll be glad you are here."

Thinking back to the last time she saw her mother, Sophia thought his enthusiasm a bit optimistic.

Pausing in front of the curtain to her mother's cubicle, Sophia took a deep breath, bracing herself, then swept back the curtain and stepped inside. Trey hovered behind her.

Both of them gasped at the frail figure buried under mounds of blankets, her leg elevated in a sling. The same horror had hit Sophia when she saw Daniel's body. Robbed of its life force, it was but a shell, a crumpled costume his spirit had worn then tossed aside in a heap. But, unlike her son-in-law, Regina Stone hadn't left, not yet. Sophia sensed her mother clinging with her normal rabid tenacity.

Speaking softly in her mother's native Italian, she stroked her hair. Worn short and died unnaturally dark with a deep red undertone, Regina's hair was mussed and clumped in oily tufts. A thin line of silver showed at the roots, as if her soul was oozing out through her pores, taking the color and vibrancy of life with it. Someone had scrubbed her face. Gone was the red lipstick, the heavily penciled brows, the meticulously colored lids and powdered cheeks. Regina Otero looked like a pale image of herself, as if the angels had taken an eraser to her, diminishing her with every stroke. If the angels were left unchecked, soon her mother would be gone, lingering only in half-remembered snippets, the melody of her favorite song, her recipes, the treasured bottle of Chanel No. 5.

Sophia bent down, her mouth close to her mother's ear. She didn't even smell like herself. "Mama."

Regina stirred, moaned. Her eyes fluttered open. Pale grey, they locked on Sophia then drifted to Trey behind. A smile, like a happy thought, flickered then faded and was gone. Her eyelids lowered, her features slackened.

"She's been sedated to keep the pain down. She'll drift in and out." Dr. Fisher's voice startled Sophia; she hadn't been aware of him standing there. "There isn't much you can do," he said to both of them.

At her son's stricken look, Sophia gave him a hug. "He's right. Why don't you go home, *mio caro*. You have a lot on your plate, and you need some rest."

"What about you, Mom?"

"I'll stay a bit."

"There's nothing you can do, like Dr. Fisher said." Trey looked worried.

Sophia glanced down at her mother who mumbled a bit, too low and garbled to make any sense of. Sophia stroked her hair. "Perhaps not. But I can be here when she wakes up." She looked around Trey to the doctor who still waited. "She seems agitated, in pain."

"We're doing what we can to keep that under control."

"It seems a bit much for a broken leg." Sophia watched the doctor carefully.

His eyes didn't meet hers. "She broke her femur, the largest bone in the body. People's tolerances are different. And it's especially hard on someone her age. We'll know more soon."

As Trey looked between his mother and his grandmother, his warring emotions showed in his expression.

"Go on home," Sophia urged him. "I'll call if I need anything."

"How will you get home?"

"I'll call or take a cab." She put a hand on his arm in reassurance. "I need to be here."

Trey's eyes softened, and Sophia saw the understanding born of a survived hurt. How had she let him go? He nodded and stepped back.

She stopped him with a hand. "Are you okay?"

Trey nodded a couple of times. "Yeah. Yeah, I am." He gave her a wisp of a smile. "I've been thinking ... a lot. This place, our house, the grapes, they're all a part of who I am. I'll think I'll give Rebecca a call. We need to talk."

"Will you call your sister, tell her what's going on?"

"Sure. I'll call her first."

As she watched him walk away, pulling his phone from his back pocket, Sophia felt the oddest thing. Somehow, amid all the chaos, life was coming back together.

DESPITE THE NOISE AND EVER-PRESENT parade of orderlies and nurses taking her mother's vitals, checking on her comfort, emptying the trash bin, refilling the untouched water pitcher with ice, Sophia had managed to doze. Time lost all meaning in the windowless environment as one twelve-hour shift merged into another, an old day into a new. The faces changed but little else as Sophia held vigil.

A moan from her mother brought her out of a light sleep.

"Mom?" She cradled her mother's frail hand in her own. Blue veins ran under skin so white and thin, a milky translucence the only barrier between life and death. She detected a hint of hope in the thready pulse, but just a hint. "Mom?"

Regina moaned again as her eyes fluttered open. Wide-eyed, she glanced around, looking lost.

Oh, please let this be one of the times she is lucid and herself again. I need to know what she wants me to do. Sophia leaned forward. "It's okay. You're in the hospital. You've broken your leg. I'm here. Everything's going to be okay."

"Awful lot to promise," her mother mumbled.

Sophia smiled as she stroked her mother's hand. If a black cloud drifted anywhere in the sky, her mother could find it. Sophia said a silent prayer of thanks. She had her mother back, for how long she didn't know, and Sophia felt the tyranny of time, of the precious moments left. There was so much to say. "You know me, Mother, dream big."

Even in her weakened condition, Sophia's mother managed a harrumph—a good Italian put-down. "Dreams." Sophia's mother started to say more, then shook her head slightly. Taking a deep fortifying breath, summoning an inner strength, this time when she spoke, her voice was stronger. "Don't be me, *cara mia*."

"What?"

Her mother, her eyes closed, writhed as if tortured by ... what, Sophia didn't know. "Mother, let me get you something for the pain."

"No." The word carried force—it was not a suggestion.

Sophia smiled through her worry.

"When you were born," Regina said, her voice surprisingly strong and clear, "you were so brave. So filled with wonder at all life had to give. Not like me at all. I had no idea what to do with you."

Sophia thought about her own children, about Trey, so different from herself. "You always told me God had a sense of humor."

"We have much to talk about, Sophia. I need to tell you things. I didn't know them myself until recently. Funny how life teaches you ..." Color rose in her cheeks as Regina tried to muscle her way higher in the bed. She sucked in sharply as she moved and braced against the pain.

"Mom, you shouldn't be moving. Your leg ..." Sophia tried to press her mother back gently.

Regina, driven by something far more powerful than the pain, perhaps prodded by the press of time, pushed at Sophia's hands. Her eyes had cleared, her features sharpened. "Child, we haven't much time." Her voice held the conviction of certainty.

Sophia stopped fighting her mother.

Through sheer will, and perhaps with the help of something otherworldly, Regina pressed herself up and back until she was eye-to-eye with her daughter.

Dr. Fisher pulled back the curtain, startling them both, and the moment was broken. Stepping inside the cubicle, he let the cloth drape back into place shrouding them from view. His presence filled the small space, creating an uncomfortable closeness. Or perhaps it was the tickle of fear that made Sophia nervous. Or the fact that Dr. Fisher hadn't looked her square in the eye, preferring instead to focus on his patient. Sophia stood, then stepped back, letting him move in close to Regina.

"How are you feeling, Mrs. Otero?"

"Who are you?" Regina demanded, her voice surprisingly strong.

"Dr. Fisher. We ... spoke... last night."

Regina gave him the eye. "Why don't I remember?"

"You were in a lot of pain."

Regina's brows furrowed as she tried to remember. "My leg?"

"Yes." Dr. Fisher swallowed hard. "About that."

"Yes, why did it break?" Sophia asked. Frustrated and scared, she crossed her arms and tried to summon courage.

Dr. Fisher stepped to the edge of the bed. Reaching out, he moved to put a comforting hand on Regina's shoulder but pulled back before he made contact. "I'm not sure how to tell you this..."

Regina gave him a steady stare. "Dr. Fisher, I have buried my parents, my husband, a son-in-law—I know death, and I know when it is near. There are worse things than death, remember that." Her gaze flicked to her daughter. "Bad news is the first to come."

Sophia interpreted for the young doctor. "Old Italian proverb." Sophia squeezed her mother's hand and gave her what she hoped was a brave smile. With all this odd talk of death, she wasn't feeling very brave. "Mother, stop talking like that. You're going to get better, and I'm going to get you out of here. Right, Doctor?"

If it was possible to watch someone visibly age, then Sophia was witnessing Dr. Fisher mature. His face slackened, the lines and fissures deepened, giving him a gravity, the look of one who has seen more suffering than they should. He shook his head. "Mrs. Otero, I'm really sorry to have to tell you this. I was hoping we were dealing with osteoporosis. I was almost sure of it since you didn't complain of a great deal of pain. I went over the tests multiple times, hoping they were wrong." He paused and captured them both with his sad eyes. "Your bone didn't break so much as become eaten away until there was little left."

"Eaten away?" Regina asked, her features sharp, her eyes intense.

"You have bone cancer. I'm so sorry."

Shock rendered Sophia's body stiff and numbed her mind. She reached for the chair behind her, and willed her body to bend in the right places as she lowered herself to perch on the edge. "Cancer," she whispered. Such an ugly, horrible, vile word. "How bad?"

The doctor looked down. "I'm afraid it's quite advanced."

"Has it spread?" Regina's voice was surprisingly strong.

"Yes." He flipped up the top page of the chart he had carried in with him. "Throughout the spine, your other leg." He let the page drop back then tucked the report under his arm. "There are also small spots in multiple places that we suspect are cancer, but haven't confirmed."

Sophia leaned forward, her hands clasped in a ball in her lap. "Treatment? There's a treatment, right?"

"We are referring her to the Cancer Center at UCSF. They're the best."

Silence fell like a pall over the room as Sophia tried to process reality.

"No." The single word from her mother carried the force of an edict.

"Mother, you can't be serious. Let the doctor do what's best."

Regina's hand fluttered over the bed railing, seeking her daughter's. When she found it, she held tight. "Child, I am an old woman. Tired. I have felt the burden of pain of my family tortured by loss. I watched my parents die and then your father. I watched you and yours tortured by loss. I watched the Patterson boy and his family, broken by the consequences of a moment, an accident that could've happened to anyone. But it didn't. It happened to us."

"I know, but ..."

Her mother shushed her. "No more pain. It's my time." She shrugged with that irritating Italian air of acceptance hammered into her DNA by centuries of a Catholic belief that God was pulling the strings. "I've felt myself being pulled away. Sometimes I am living more in the haze of history than in the present. They are calling to me. It's time I go."

Tears trailed down Sophia's cheeks.

Sophia had a more American view of things: life should be clung to with unwavering tenacity. "You've got to fight, Mom. The doctor thinks it's best to go to UCSF." She glanced at Dr. Fisher, looking for support, a hint of hope. Remaining stoic, he didn't offer any.

"Sophia, he is a doctor, yes, but barely out of diapers from the looks of him. He is not the one to say what is best for me. Allow me that last dignity."

Dr. Fisher bent over Regina; two fingers found that sweet spot on her wrist even though her heart rate beeped on the monitor above her head. "How's your pain?"

She waved him away. "Please. I need to talk with my daughter."

With a nod, he backed out of the cubicle.

Regina sighed and settled back into the pillows Sophia bunched behind her. Her face paled; the effort had drained her.

"Mom, you need to rest."

"Not just yet. There'll be time for that." A thin smile lifted the corners of her mouth. "A long while, and that's not a bad thing, Sophia." She nestled back even more and let her eyes drift closed. "It's funny, actually. We spend so much time and effort worrying about how we are going to die." Her eyes opened and sought Sophia's. "But do we ever spend as much effort worrying about how we are living?"

Sophia rubbed her mother's hand between hers, willing the warmth to return. "I don't know how to answer that."

"I know. And that is more my fault than yours." Regina silenced Sophia's rising questions with a flutter of her hand. "Let me talk. I need to tell you things. You see, I've made so many mistakes." Regina looked at her, a tortured look on her face. "I never thought I would hurt you."

Stunned, Sophia sat up straight. "You haven't hurt me." Sophia didn't understand any of this. The only explanation was the morphine.

"Don't argue, Sophia." Regina's voice strengthened. "You live up there alone on that mountain, a ring of forest to hide behind. The house hasn't changed; you haven't moved Daniel's things. You cling to the past, afraid of the future."

Sophia didn't argue—her mother's words rang with a truth Sophia had only begun to glimpse.

"Child, that house, that place, those grapes, they are all a monument to what was. But the past is nothing more than the only thing in life that cannot be changed. It changes us, yes, but the past itself is immutable." She grabbed Sophia's hand and held tight. "Let it go. It has you tethered to people who are gone and dreams that aren't yours."

"But, if I don't have their dreams, I don't have anything." A sad truth Sophia had come to embrace. She couldn't remember her own dreams, the ones before Daniel, before her children, before death stole her heart.

Regina shrank into herself, her eyes hollow orbs in sockets too large. Pain sallowed her skin, cutting deep grooves. Not her physical pain, but pain of deep regret too long buried and allowed to fester. "Pride, it's such a horrible thing, destructive not only to those around you, those you love who deserve your kindness and your apologies, but to yourself. It's a worm, deep inside, gnawing at tender flesh until ropes of scar tissue, ugly and tough, bind your heart. Life has a way of rubbing your nose in your mistakes, until it beats you, weakens you, and you learn."

Sophia moved her chair closer to her mother's bed so she could still hold her hand as she leaned back, her body wilting under the emotional overload. "Mother, I can't imagine what you have done that haunts you, or who you've so wronged that it pains you still. I'm sure they have long forgiven you, although I doubt they've even recognized the transgression."

"Have you, Sophia? Have you forgiven me?"

"Me?" Sophia couldn't contain her shock. "Forgive you? For what?"

"For trying to keep you safe and, in doing so, clipping your wings." Regina's voice weakened as she closed her eyes. "I don't have your courage. I should have let you fly."

Sophia squeezed her eyes tight against the flood of emotions. Her mother had never been this open. Just when she found her mother's heart, she was going to lose her. The cruelty of life stole her breath. "I'm a grown woman, Mother. I can make my own choices, chart my own course."

"Yes, but sometimes perspective is gained only after a lifetime of missed chances. Courage, Sophia, you must be brave—you were before I took it from you. In trying to be the parent, I shaped you in a way I did not intend. As a child I was afraid. My parents had no money. I never was sure where the next meal was coming from. I did not want you to know that fear. But ..." She smiled a sad, faraway smile, as if hearing words spoken by someone only she could see. "I know, *Bono*, a life without dreams ..."

"Is only half-lived," Sophia whispered. She, too, could hear her grandfather's words, the resonance of his voice. He was close. Time was short.

Regina's grip weakened. "You must fight, child. Fight hard. For yourself. For the respect you deserve. You grow grapes your grandfather only dreamed of."

"But his grapes are what make the wine."

"No! It is you. You will make wonderful wine from any grapes. You know how to get them to give you their best. It is a gift, Sophia, your gift ... among many. You have raised your children well. Dani is a warrior. Trey is a good and gentle spirit, an old soul. Now it is time for you. Fight them. Fight yourself."

"But I am afraid."

"We all are. Every day."

Sophia gasped. Regina had been feared and respected—a force. If she had been afraid, she had hidden it well.

"Yes, even me ... especially me," Regina continued as if reading her daughter's thoughts. "Courage is going forward in spite of the fear. Find your courage to live. Unfurl your wings. Demand respect, from yourself and from others. You will be surprised. And then you will be free."

The toll the conversation took on Regina was tangible. Sophia sensed her spirit leaving, could see her body wither as death pulled the energy from her. Sophia leaned over the railing and stroked her mother's forehead, smoothing her hair. "Don't go. I need you."

"You don't need me, Sophia. You have everything inside you. You'll know what to do."

"Mom, please. Fight."

"No, I'm tired. And the call is strong." As Sophia moved to stand, Regina grasped her wrist in a surprisingly strong vise. "Open your heart again, Sophia. Love is worth the risk. But never let the man choose your path or your thoughts. Follow your heart and your gut. They are good and wise."

Sophia swiped at her tears and took a deep settling breath. She needed to call the kids.

CHAPTER TWENTY-EIGHT

REGINA STAYED LONG ENOUGH TO say goodbye to her grandchildren.

Numb, immobilized by loss, each lost in their own sadness, Sophia and the kids made their way home in the darkness. Dani drove. Sophia sat in the middle. Trey held her. All Sophia could think about was how much had happened, how so totally life had changed, and the new day had yet to dawn—only a few hours had passed.

The life-altering moments didn't need much time. Like bullets, they hit with surprise, ripping and tearing the soft flesh of the soul. And the only shield was to sacrifice life, to hide, to not risk. Yes, Nonno was right; to limit the lows, one must sacrifice the highs. Now Sophia understood what a huge price that was.

Such a gift her mother had given her. Opening the doors of her heart, her soul ... her self.

Trey's arm was strong around her shoulders, his grip tight on her hand. Dani's tight on her other hand. "We're going to be okay, Mom. All of us."

"I know." Sophia squeezed her children's hands and looked at Trey. "Have you spoken with Rebecca?"

"She's on her way, bringing the kids. I think we're going to be okay." He sighed. "I hope we're going to be okay. I don't know what I'd do without those three. There's lots to talk about, decisions to be made, compromises, but at least, for the first time in a while, we're talking, and listening, taking time for us. The twins can be all-consuming. It turns out all she needed was to talk, and for me to hear her. Why didn't I know that?"

"We all get lost in our own pain sometimes, and we don't see the hurt in those we love. For that I am sorry—I did that to you both after your father died."

Startled, both Trey and Dani looked at her. "No you didn't," they said in unison.

"Dani, eyes on the road!" Sophia's heart started. They didn't need another disaster, even though they had the road to themselves at this time of night. "But I couldn't fix your pain."

"No one could, Mom." Trey's voice was soft.

Dani nodded in agreement, but kept her yes facing forward. "We each had to make peace with Dad's death in our own way, on our own terms."

"And now death has brought us back," Sophia said with a bit of wonder. She thought about adding "and set us free," but the kids wouldn't understand that. Maybe Trey would, but not Dani, not now. If Sophia had anything to do with it, neither would have to grapple with the concept, not now, not ever.

The darkness deepened as they left Napa behind and started winding their way toward their mountain. "It's almost like the sun is reluctant to rise and face this day, too, isn't it?" Trey's question was rhetorical. "I can't believe how much has happened in one night."

"We've still a few more hours until sunrise," Dani noted. Sophia could tell, with her arm out the window she was marking temperature and humidity—something she herself used to do when she had grapes to worry about. But now she was curiously detached—her grapes weren't hers and Pinkman's grapes were his problem. She had a whole binder filled with notes on each lot, its peccadillos, and how to coax the juice into the grapes, but she'd be damned before she'd turn that over to him. Fear had softened her backbone for far too long. She felt like she was reinhabiting her skin, filling it out in a way that was but a faint memory—wearing herself like an old coat. And it felt good.

"Are you sad, Mom? I know how difficult Nonna could be," Dani asked, her voice reverberating in the wind's buffet.

"Of course, I'm sad. But before you two came, Nonna told me that there are worse things than death. I think she was telling me she knew about her mental decline, felt it, feared it. And she wanted me to let her go. With that comes some peace. So I'm not sad for her, but perhaps a bit for myself, though. It's so hard to say goodbye, even when it's the best path. I don't know how I'll get by without her calling to tell me all I'm doing wrong." Sophia smiled despite the ache so deep she felt it in her bones.

Dani steered through the switchbacks up the mountain with practiced ease. She stopped at the edge of the clearing. Lights blazed in the house—a beacon of warmth, of safety, of family. A spear to Sophia's heart.

Charlie had sold it out from under her.

How dare he? With the little emotional control left, Sophia seethed at the thought. Without a word of warning. Without so much as the kindness of an opportunity to bid. The bastard had sold her heart. And, while she wasn't sure his transgression really deserved a special place in Hell, she knew Butchy Pinkman's did, and that ass Avery Specter.

Dani let the truck idle up the last slight grade then killed the engine at the front steps. The night quieted. They didn't move. Three shell-shocked, life-weary soldiers, immobilized by the reality of what just happened.

"I think we all need some sleep," Sophia said, stating the obvious but not having anything else to offer. "Anybody want some warm milk?" Sleep would be elusive. Perhaps a gentle nudge would help. Regina had always thought so. Her tears long shed, Sophia drew a ragged breath and elbowed Trey. "Come on. We can't sit here all night."

"Warm milk?" Trey shuddered. "Good God, no. That stuff is horrible."

Sophia looked at him wide-eyed. "But I thought you liked it?"

"You wanted me to drink it, so I did. But I wasn't above putting some Hershey's in it when your back was turned."

Sophia turned to her daughter who nodded, siding with her brother. "Well, how about some hot chocolate then? Or perhaps some nice herbal tea?"

As the three of them trudged arm-in-arm up the steps, Sophia felt the weight of reality drop on her shoulders. Caught up in the hospital paperwork, with decisions to be made, papers to sign, arrangements to be at least set in motion, the adrenaline had kept her distracted. Now the awful truth sucker-punched her.

Her mother was gone. And life was diminished.

They all were gone—those that came before. Now Sophia was the last defense between her children and the Great Beyond, or whatever awaited them all. Scientists said that belief in life after death was just a cascade of chemicals that triggered memories and happy thoughts, making people think their loved ones were waiting for them. The body's way of protecting the heart. Sophia preferred to think her mother was now with those she had lost, resting peacefully, released from the pain and fear—the debility that would've been an insult to Regina Otero. To think anything else would cause her heart to break.

Trey gently pulled the keys from Sophia's hands as she fumbled with them. "Here, let me help you, Mom. It's not locked." He pressed the handle and opened the door. "See? I always loved that about you—your undying belief that people are good and if they're not, well, they just needed whatever they took more than you did." He helped her inside.

Dani followed them inside, a few steps behind, her hands stuck in the front pockets of her jeans. Once in the house, her face closed, her pain drawing the skin tight over her high cheekbones, like sinew pulled that of a drum taut. Sophia knew her daughter suffered inside. Still holding Trey's hand, she looped an arm around Dani, pulling her close. Her daughter laid her head on her mother's shoulder. Sophia could feel her shaking. She looked at her son's stricken face, felt her daughter's pain, and something deep inside burned harsh and desperate. She'd been wrong. People weren't good. Pinkman. Specter. Even poor Charlie. None of them had even one noble thread. Life wasn't fair. And there were no knights in shining armor. No, if you wanted it, you had to get it yourself. She knew that now. But she'd made so many mistakes. Mistakes that now would leave her family without the heart of their home, the talisman of their remembered happiness to see them through.

As if by rote, they wandered to the kitchen. Dani opened the fridge and stuck her head inside, blank eyes staring and not seeing. Normally Sophia would've scolded her. Not tonight. Trey stood beside his sister. He glanced at her quickly, then reached in and piled a few containers in his arms. With his free hand he snagged a bottle of wine, his mother's wine. With a hip he moved his sister out of the way then shut the door.

Sophia stood in the middle of the kitchen needing to do something but at a loss as to what. Nervously she picked at a loose button on her shirt and made a mental note to fix it. Trey thrust the wine at her. "How about some glasses?" Thankful for a direction, Sophia did as asked, arranging the table. The leaf was still in it, so she clustered everything at one end.

Dani fidgeted, then her eyes cleared, and anger replaced sadness. She sidled around toward the cookie jar. Sophia could've told her it was empty, but she didn't have the energy. Dani lifted the top and pulled out some papers.

Charlie's letter was the last thing Sophia remembered stuffing in there. "What are those?" The murderous look on Dani's face jogged a memory. There was something she'd discovered, something she wanted to talk about.

"Nothing." Dani stuffed them in her back pocket.

Sophia extended her hand and gave her daughter a look.

Dani didn't budge. "No, this is not the time. We can talk about this some other day."

Sophia kept her hand extended. "You know how I hate having an unknown hanging over my head like the Sword of Damocles. I'll never have any peace until I know. Besides, I don't think those papers are going to make life any worse."

"That's where you're wrong."

Sophia lost her patience, what little she had left. "Dani, this is my house, my rules. Obviously, those papers involve me, or you wouldn't be so circumspect. Hand them over."

Dani didn't move for a moment, glancing instead at her brother. He nodded once. Not looking at all happy about it, Dani pulled the sheaf of papers out of her pocket and handed it to her mother. "Mom, I really wish you wouldn't read those. I don't know what they mean, and I'm really sorry I took them in the first place."

"You took them?" Sophia scanned them. The world focused. The haze of pain fled on the cold wind of murderous fury. Her blood pounded through her veins. She started again at the top of the page, this time reading more slowly. While she didn't know a lot of technical Italian, she knew enough to get the drift. Yes, she'd read it correctly the first time. Fisting her hand she crumpled the papers. "What do you know about these?"

For a moment everybody remained rooted to their spots, then Trey broke the tension. "Well, whether it's the time or not, it looks like we're going to discuss whatever is in those papers." The food forgotten, he poured the wine and they clustered together at the table.

Sophia took a deep breath, then another, but nothing would stop her shaking. Unsteady, on the ragged edge, Sophia lifted her glass, ignoring the wine that sloshed out, and drained the glass in several long gulps.

"Mom." Dani, put a warning hand on her mother's arm, but snatched it back as if scorched by her mother's heated look.

Catching Trey's eye, Sophia nodded at her glass. He hesitated but relented when she reached for the bottle. This time Sophia took it more slowly, and each of her children visibly relaxed. Neither of them had witnessed their mother's battle with alcohol; they'd heard about it of course, but the years had thinned the message until it seemed an exaggeration or a half-truth, so neither was particularly wary. "Where did you get those?" Sophia asked Dani with a nod at the papers.

Dani looked out the kitchen window even though darkness cocooned them. "When I was leaving, I went to find Mr. Treviani in his office—I had a harvest report for him." Her eyes met her mother's. "He wasn't there. I left the report on his desk. When I did, I saw those. I didn't know what they were, but they looked important and the name "Otero" caught my eye. So I tried to read them; my Italian isn't the best. But they seemed to be legal papers having to do with our family farm in Italy."

"They are," Sophia said in a murderous tone.

"I'm in the dark here. *Our* farm?" Trey said, then took a sip of his wine. He shook his head. "Really great stuff, Mom. I can see why you want to make it, even if it's only one vintage."

The thought of making that wine. Making it for *them*. Fury coiled around her heart. But Sophia remained composed. "Yes, it is good wine." She poked at the papers that she'd left in a wad on the table in front of her. "These papers are, as Dani suspected, legal documents from Italy." She drank more wine, a healthy swig, but that was all. Then she looked at her children. "They transfer ownership of what is known as the Otero Vineyard in Friuli." Trey's eyes grew to the size of saucers.

Dani's mouth drew into a thin line. "But I thought you said the vineyard is overgrown; no one is cultivating it."

"As far as I know, that is true. But the grapes, they have grown wild and strong. They still live there."

"Oh." Dani leaned back in her chair and contemplated her wine. "Why doesn't our family still own it?"

"I don't really know." Sophia thought back but found herself lost in an emotional tangle that made little sense. "After Nonno, no one else wanted to tend the farm, to work with those stubborn grapes." Sophia shook her head. "I was here raising you two. A vineyard in Italy wasn't in the cards."

"Who bought the vineyard?" Trey's voice held a surgical edge, like a knife poised over a heart.

"Avery Specter." Dani's eyes flicked to her mother's as if she knew what was coming. "And he had a local partner, one with Italian connections."

"What does this mean?"

"It means that not only will the bastards own the grapes I cultivated here, but they will own the source grapes. That's all there is. We have nothing left of them."

Trey's eyes turned hard. "They effectively eliminated any competition, any future cultivation of Great-grandfather's grapes."

Sophia nodded. "By anyone other than Pinkman and his gang." Her brain shut down; she was unable to really process the information. She had no idea what to do next short of homicide, which, while attractive would only trade one set of problems for another.

Slumped back in her chair, Dani remained quiet.

Trey thought for a moment, then his eyes latched on to his mother's. "And the local partner is?" He looked like he knew what was coming.

"Nico Treviani."

243

THEY'D SAT AWHILE, the children polishing off the wine. Knowing her well, they hadn't tried to make her feel better—words would not stitch a wound this large, the loss of her mother, the loss of something vital, made putrid by the complete betrayal, the utter contempt of Nico Treviani. Sophia had sat stoically, turning inward, searching for hope, for understanding ... for answers, but she found only the seething coil of anger, tightening like a constrictor needing to feed. Rage had flared, then died, leaving clear thought and staggering emotion. For the first time Sophia understood how people could kill.

Sagging under the burden of too much emotion and too little sleep, Trey and Dani had finally relented and let their mother force them upstairs to bed. Precious little night remained as it was.

Sophia had promised to follow them, a promise she had no intention of keeping.

Right now she didn't need sleep; she needed to talk to her grapes. Perhaps they could calm her; they always had. Pausing on the porch, she reached into the wine cooler and grabbed the closest bottle. She didn't even look to see what it was. She pulled the cork and headed into the vineyard, bottle in hand. She didn't bother with a glass.

The cool air sizzled off her skin like water droplets dancing in a hot skillet. Burning with rage, sadness, fear, and not a little bit of self-loathing, she staggered to the center of the small patch and fell to her knees. After taking several long gulps from the bottle, she slammed it into the soft dirt, which held the bottle upright. Sitting back on her heels, her hands on her knees, she sucked in air, breathing deeply, seeking comfort in the sweet aroma, searching for solace from the tumescent grapes hanging lush and ready from the vines.

They were perfect grapes. Bold and ripe, they had trusted her and given her their best.

And she had betrayed them. Too long the innocent, she had let scoundrels and thieves take it all. Soon the grapes would be theirs. A ragged breath; another long swallow of wine. The wine warmed her, seeping into the dark places. Anger, hate, regret, bitterness all danced like evil spirits around the fire, conjuring the devil of hopelessness.

Her mother was gone. Her son, the child whose return she'd prayed so desperately for, wanted to come home ... needed to come home. But their home was gone—or would be soon. And she was to blame—her stupid, naïve, gullible saunter through life, as if the darkness couldn't touch her, wouldn't touch them. Talk about burying her head in the sand! Her children needed her and she had failed them.

Half the bottle of wine was gone when she lifted it again to drink deeply, hungrily. Slamming it once more into the soft soil, the soil that had nurtured her grapes, her dreams, she felt the crushing weight of defeat, like a cement necklace as she took the last long step off the plank.

"God damn them all." Shackled by emotion, defeat tightening her body like an overwound spring, until even her voice was constricted, Sophia couldn't shout. Way past caring, she took another long pull on the bottle. This time she kept her hand fisted around its neck, her knuckles white as her thoughts turned murderous.

Nico Treviani.

She'd trusted him, opened her heart, even invited him into her home and her bed. *What a fool you are, Sophia Stone. What a silly, addle-pated fool.* She'd known not to trust him, but she had. She'd happily danced right past every sign, every twinge in her gut, every transgression. Had she really been that desperate? Sophia's self-loathing reached a new high as the truth that she'd handed them everything sucker-punched her, leaving her light-headed, sucking for air. Pummeled from all sides, she reeled. Pushing to her feet, she staggered, then planted her feet. Her world on tilt, she narrowed her eyes and tried to focus.

The grapes.

She stoked the nearest vine and its clusters of liquid gold—the vessels of dreams. Everything she had, everything she hoped, everything she dreamed nestled inside the delicate skin of each ripe berry.

Never again would she be so stupid, so gullible. Not ever.

Her heart shriveled. Her stomach clenched. Like the devil making a deal for a soul, they'd steal these, too.

An idea, horrible and yet perfect, birthed by anger and hate, and tempered by cold logic rose from the seething fire of her loathing.

Her cultivating shack wasn't far. She threw open the door, and as her hand closed around the cool wood of the shaft, she knew what she had to do.

CHAPTER TWENTY-NINE

THE FIRST STROKE WAS THE HARDEST.

Gasping with emotion, both hands curling around the handle of the machete with a vise-like grip, Sophia raised the blade high over her head. She didn't pause. Curling her body, pulling her arms, she brought the blade down on the nearest plant. Newly sharpened, it sliced easily through the shoots like a scalpel through flesh. The trunk was more difficult. Her hands slipped, searing skin, as the metal stuck in the tough wood, the lifeblood of the vine. With a downward motion, then a pull, Sophia jerked the blade free. She staggered back, her arms swinging.

The second stroke severed the stalk.

Broken and ravaged, driven by a frenzy of bitter emotions, Sophia hacked and raged. Oblivious to the effort, the pain, she could only see one thing, hear one voice. It sounded like her grandfather's. Or maybe her own.

Damn them to hell. Damn them all to hell.

Bits of plant flew; juice soaked her jeans and dried to a sticky sweetness on her skin, like blood from a mortal wound flung by a heart pumping its last. Tears flowed, mingling the salty with the sweet—the taste of bitterness and revenge on her tongue. Numb to what was left of life, Sophia didn't think, didn't feel. Driven by a need, primal and fierce, she fought. Hacking, gasping ... taking, plundering what should be hers but was not.

If she couldn't have the grapes, then no one would have them.

"SOPHIA?" A hand jostled her shoulder. "What the hell did you do?" The voice low, confused ... sad.

Nico Treviani. Sophia's anger flared, and her eyes flew open. Daylight speared through her, a white-hot poker through her brain. She recoiled at the pain. Her head throbbed. Her hands burned. She moved, trying to ease to her knees, but her muscles, tight as steel bands, weren't quick to respond. Memories flooded back, hot steel cauterizing her heart.

On her knees, her head in her hands, she opened her eyes.

Carnage lay around her. Her once beautiful vineyard reduced to browning, shriveling shreds. Ugly brown sticks jutted into the air. The air was sick with juice souring in the heat. Dead, the grapes were dead. The vines would give her nothing more. And Sophia knew the woman she was had died.

The birds seemed to be in mourning as silence shrouded her hilltop. Even the bees were quiet, reverent to their loss. Sunlight new and fresh caressed her face, a sweet, hopeful touch, bright with promise ... too bright.

"Who did this?" Nico sounded sad.

Funny. She was expecting anger, not sadness. "What are you doing here, Nico?"

"I told you I'd come back, remember? You left for the hospital, and I had to go check on the girls. You told me to call off the crew ... that we'd drop the grapes tonight. I told you I'd be back this morning."

Sophia didn't remember.

"How's your mother?"

Sophia laughed, a choked, gurgling sound. The question struck her as odd, all things considered. "She died."

"What? I'm so sorry." Nico moved to hold her, but the look on Sophia's face stopped him cold. "Jesus."

Sophia looked around like a general surveying the aftermath of a horrible battle. Curious, apprising, but feeling little. That surprised her. The grapes, she'd nurtured them almost as children, and, like children, they'd become stitched to the fabric of her being. But, the wounds of the last few days had toughened her skin, steeled her heart.

Narrowing her eyes, shading them with one hand, she met Nico's gaze. "Who did this?" Sophia snorted. "I did." Stretching out the other hand, she sought his help getting to her feet. When Nico grabbed it, she gasped in pain. Blisters peppered her palms. Her legs screamed in agony. Her back felt like it would break if she twisted at all. Tentatively she tested the boundaries of movement.

"Why?" Nico's voice caught. "Why this?"

Nico stood next to her, but he felt worlds away. Curiously, Sophia wasn't angry anymore. As pressure converted coal to diamonds, action had molded her anger into resolve. She'd fight, like her mother told her to. She might not win, and that didn't matter nearly as much as putting up a battle.

She turned to study Nico.

He looked haggard, world-weary as if life had sucked him dry. Dark half-moons hung below his eyes. He rubbed his hand over the two days' growth of beard on his cheeks and chin.

"Was it because of your mother that you did this?"

"No. Because of you." Stray strands of hair tickled her nose as the slight breeze pushed them about.

"Me?" Nico seemed genuinely surprised. "Why?"

A little doubt crept in around the edges, but Sophia had seen the papers, read them herself. "So you and your friends couldn't have them. These were my grapes. If you want them so badly, you'll have to grow them yourselves."

"I thought you wanted to make the wine."

"I did. And it about killed me that we'd made it perfect, but it wasn't going to be ours. That I'd be turning over grapes that dreams are made from to men who wouldn't appreciate them, who wouldn't be awed by the once-in-a-lifetime opportunity to make this wine." Exhausted, hanging on by her fingernails, Sophia drew a ragged breath. "I thought you were that man. The one who could really understand the love, the dreams, the work, the heartache that went into creating these varietals. I was wrong. It's just a great financial opportunity for you. And a chance to prove to the world you don't need anybody; you can stand alone and make brilliant wine." She made a sweeping gesture with her arm, flinching against the pain. "Go ahead, have at it."

"Me? You think I want to take the grapes from you?"

She leveled her gaze and her voice turned icy. "I found the papers."

"Papers?" Confusion clouded his features as he looked at her. Then they cleared and darkened. "Searching my desk now? That's a new low."

"Secrets. Hard to keep."

He slapped his thigh and rolled his eyes. "Dani. I should've known."

That pricked Sophia's mama-bear, and her temper flared. "Different rules don't apply to you, Nico Treviani. I don't care who you think you are, how many awards you've been given, how special your wine is, how many in the Valley bow and scrape when you walk by. You crawl with the snakes, you eventually become one."

"I see." His face shut down, his eyes turned dark and cold. "I'm glad to find out now just how little you think of me. That saves us both a bunch of heartache in the future." A mask of anger settled over his features. "Goodbye, Sophia. Good luck." He turned his back and stalked to his truck. With practiced ease he settled himself behind the wheel, then slammed the door. Nico fired up his truck and spun out, his truck fishtailing as he stomped on the accelerator. The tires caught. Sophia watched until he disappeared from sight. He didn't look back.

Sophia watched him go. A part of her went with him. Her heart broke. *Oh, God.* With a shaky hand, she swiped at the hair tickling her eyes and angrily lodged it behind one ear. Then, with the back of a hand, she wiped away the tears that flowed, despite her squeezing her eyes shut to hold them back. With Nico she had felt whole, complete, appreciated in a way she'd never experienced before.

Just a day or two ago there had been such warmth, such sweetness and hope, such heat, between them. And now there was nothing but ugliness. Had any of it been real? It had felt real. Oh, God it had felt real. She had thought that saying those words, confronting him with his sins would feel good, that she would feel vindicated and powerful. Instead she felt somehow... less. When dreams die they take a bit of your soul—at least that's what her grandmother had said.

Soon there was silence. And pain. Deep, numbing pain that strangled her heart.

Trey was in the kitchen when Sophia pushed through the screen door. "You look like you need this." He handed her a mug of hot coffee. "I ought to make you take those clothes off on the porch like you used to do to us when we'd show up covered in dirt. You're making a mess."

"Too tired to care." Sophia cupped her hands around the mug, absorbing its heat. Her blisters stung, but she didn't care. Then she took a long, bracing, swig. "I smell bacon," she said after the caffeine trickled into her veins.

"From the looks of you, I'm taking it you slept in the"—he glanced out the window—"former vineyard. You might have been a little aggressive with the pruning. And wearing half of the vineyard is not a look you should cultivate. Pun intended."

Sophia gave him the smile he was looking for. "I just couldn't sit back and let them take our grapes."

"I get it. I just wished you'd come and gotten me. I would've helped." He turned back to the stove. "Sit. I've got some bacon in the oven, a couple of slices of Annalise's country bread in the toaster oven, and I'm working on some eggs. Scrambled soft, right?" he said with a knowing smile.

Sophia was stunned. "You would've helped?"

"Like I said at the hospital, I've been thinking. Coming back here really focused things for me. My dreams lived here. When I left, I took Dad's dreams for me and I lost my way. I made not only myself unhappy but my wife as well. I hope I can fix that."

"You can. Rebecca loves you."

Trey looked a bit pained. "I'm not sure I deserve it."

"That has nothing to do with it. Sometimes we all are very appreciative that life doesn't give us what we deserved."

"True." Trey turned his attention back to the butter sizzling in the pan on the stove as he continued. "I think, and you can tell me if I'm right, that those grapes out there were your grandfather's dreams. And while you enjoyed tending them, they connected you to him but not to yourself."

Sophia shook her head. "And so the student becomes the teacher. I didn't even know that until the last few days when all of this hit the fan."

Trey cracked a couple of eggs. "Now's your turn, Mom. But, at the risk of widening an open wound, I assume you told Nico about seeing the deed."

"Yep." Just hearing his name hurt like a knife to the heart.

"What'd he say? If you don't mind me asking?"

"Not much. He shut down. He was furious."

"At you finding the papers?"

"He didn't say." Sophia took a sip of her coffee. "What else would he be angry at?"

"He's a guy, Mom." With spatula in hand, Trey turned and looked at her. "Do you really need me to spell it out?"

"Ego?"

Trey gave her a look. "You didn't trust him."

"But I saw the evidence." It had never dawned on Sophia that there was even a hint of a chance Nico wasn't guilty as hell. "I gave him a chance to explain."

"Did you? An accusation isn't an invitation to explain."

Sophia rubbed at her pounding temples. "You do know it's really irritating when your children know more than you do."

Trey laughed. "Tell me about it."

Sophia tried to remember through the haze of her hangover. "I don't know, really."

Trey shrugged and turned back to his eggs. ""I admit, it looks really bad. But I sure would like to know exactly what he was up to."

"I'm pretty sure I know," Sophia growled.

Trey slid some eggs out of the pan, splitting them between two plates. Adding a piece of toast to each, he set one plate in front of his mother and the other next to her, then went to retrieve the bacon.

When he'd picked up a fork, Sophia changed the subject. "Have you talked to Rebecca?"

Trey brightened. "Yeah, we had a long talk last night."

"Do I need to get the extra bedroom ready for the twins?" Sophia couldn't think of anything more therapeutic, more life-affirming, than having to chase her two-year-old grandchildren around for a bit ... not forever, but a bit would be just the tonic her soul needed.

"That would be great. She was at her parents' house in San Luis Obispo. I told her to stop at home, put the kids down, and get some rest herself. She'll be here by noon or so, I should think, although I haven't heard from her yet this morning. They didn't get to bed until almost two. She called me when she got to the house." Trey second-guessed his mother's need for a refill.

"Thanks." Sophia glanced through the window at what had been her vineyard. "Does Rebecca know about your grandmother?"

"Not yet. I'm not going to tell her until she gets here. I don't want her thinking about it on the way up. Driving with two screaming heathens in the back is distracting enough."

REGINA OTERO'S FUNERAL TOOK PLACE under the trees on a beautiful early fall day. Harvest was still underway, and the air was sweet with promise. She would've liked it that way. She was laid to rest next to her husband, and Sophia liked to think of the two of them together again, dancing around another living room to Frank Sinatra or, better yet, Regina's beloved Dean Martin.

After the burial, everyone gathered at Sophia's house. From the looks of it, half the valley had shown up. Of course, no one wanted to miss a party and they knew the food would be fabulous and the wine unparalleled, just as Regina would have demanded. As Fate would have it, Sophia had had the bulldozers in to pull out the rest of the vines. They'd graded the top area and that's where they put up the tent to accommodate everyone, parking the cars on the lower slope. To Sophia's way of thinking, having friends and family gathered here was sort of fitting—a good place for goodbyes.

Stepping back from all of the activity for a moment, Sophia found a quiet corner of the porch where she could watch and breathe for a bit. Watching everyone mingle, the twins running, Rebecca chasing, Trey bartending, Dani serving, and Maggie and Annalise ordering their men around and overseeing the caterers, Sophia realized the fullness of life. Yet, there was sadness, too, thoughts of those missing.

Of course, her mother wasn't there.

Even with her physical presence gone, Regina's impact could still be felt, in the bright sunshine, the blue sky, the joy of her family, and in the comforting peace that muted any strident notes and amplified the sweetness. Birds, their wings spread in supplication, let the thermals carry them higher and higher as if carrying souls to Heaven. The bees were back, busily rushing from flower to flower, their harried buzzing a welcome normalcy.

Her mother could be a handful, had been for most of Sophia's life. Sophia had found peace with that in the last few years. Human frailties—Regina Otero had had her share, even if she never admitted it, or at least didn't admit it until the end. Sadness gripped Sophia, sadness that her mother was gone, but especially sadness that Regina had found it impossible to be the mother she needed until the end. Perhaps perspective was earned only through mistakes. Regardless, Sophia believed she had been a better mother as a result of enduring her own mother. And that was a great blessing. No matter how hard one clung to the clarity of what was, life moved resolutely into the future, hazy with promise. And that's as it should be, thought Sophia. A high-wire act with the net of friendship and family, of love, to save you from a misstep.

Love.

Nico.

Even though she'd known him such a short time, she had loved him, perhaps loved him still. Once you give your heart, that stays with you. Some relationships are long, some short. But each of them takes something and gives something in return. His absence burned a hole through her. What a comfort holding his hand, feeling him near would have been. The memories ached deep inside. While she could make peace with her mother, she found it impossible to reconcile Nico's betrayal. The pain still pulled at her. Yet, understanding eluded her.

Olivia, tall and regal, radiating a comforting happiness, separated herself from her post at the dessert station. She stopped to comment to Trey's twins who darted past, then offered a sympathetic smile to their mother who rushed behind them. Catching Sophia's eye, she offered her a soft smile. Pausing, one foot on the first step to the porch, her hand on the rail, she lifted her eyes to Sophia's, holding them with her direct, unwavering gaze. "May I?"

"Of course."

On closer inspection, weariness muted her normal brightness. Sophia motioned to the wicker chair. Olivia didn't need a second invitation; she sank into it with a groan. She massaged her calves as she looked out over the gathering.

Sophia felt an awkwardness that saddened her. After all, things with Nico had ended badly. At the thought, tears sprung to her eyes. Olivia's presence eroded her resolve, conjuring memories of the night at the river, when dreams seemed so close.

"I'm very sorry about your mother." Olivia relaxed back in the chair. "We served on several committees together. I loved her fire."

Sophia's sadness at her mother's passing had evaporated, and she could now think of her mother with fondness and clarity, something she hadn't done in years. Maybe it was the knowledge her mother had escaped an earthly prison. Maybe it was the key provided by her mother that had opened her own cell door. Either way, Sophia felt an unfamiliar lightness, a peace. "She had passion. Some of it misdirected, but no one can fault her for being uncommitted."

"I see a lot of your mother in you, Sophia."

Her arms crossed, Sophia leaned against a post. She didn't look at Olivia. "Thank you."

"You're strong and have conviction." Olivia lifted her eyes to take in the scene below them. "Look what you've built. That, all those people, are here for you, and that says so much."

"For me?" Disbelief coursed through Sophia, but she didn't want to let Olivia lead her where it was the woman was going. Not today. "I thought they were here for the food."

That got a bit of a laugh. "Okay, I get it. Enough for today." Olivia rubbed the muscles in her thighs, then wiggled her feet, rotating them first one way then the other. "Thank you for mentioning me to Annalise. To be honest, I never would've thought of it, but working with her is perfect, a dream I never dared chase. I'm self-taught with no fancy pedigree."

"Just like me." Sophia turned and gave Olivia a serious look. "We have what it takes, grit, heart, and passion."

Olivia nodded, and a companionable silence settled over them, the unspoken hovering between them.

Nico.

Olivia unfolded herself from the chair and stood, a bit stiffly. "It's going to take this old body time to catch up to all of this activity. I'm not used to being on my feet, bending and lifting, twisting and turning quite this much." She turned to go, then paused and looked back at Sophia. "I know it's none of my business, but I'm a mother and my son is unhappy. I don't know what happened. I don't want to know. But, if there's a chance that you've misunderstood his passion, his fire, his drive, then I need to say he's a good man, Sophia. Listen to your heart."

Sophia gasped as her hand flew to her heart, covering it.

Olivia rejoined the party. Sophia watched her go until the crowd swallowed her and she was lost from sight. She didn't know what to think, and she'd stopped feeling, or at least stopped trusting her feelings for a bit. Too much of her father's influence, she thought. Always the engineer, he believed only in what he could prove.

And Nico had proven he couldn't be trusted.

Above the happy rumble of the gathering, Sophia caught the sound of an engine, an unfamiliar throaty growl. Someone wound up the hill, someone she didn't know, or at least hadn't heard before. The engine sounded sporty, expensive—the sound of new money in the Valley. No one she knew drove that kind of car.

Low slung and exotic, the car eased from the cover of the trees like a feral animal, crouched low stalking its prey. Conversation stopped, heads turned as everyone watched the hidden driver ease the car to the top of the hill, stopping near the house. Pushing herself from her perch, Sophia stepped off the porch and went to meet whoever lurked behind the over-tinted windows. With an air-driven whoosh the doors lifted slightly out and then up like a raptor streamlining its wings for a dive on an unwary rabbit.

First a pair of legs, then the full abomination that was Avery Specter levered out of the low-slung car. He seemed unaware of the eyes that followed him, the antagonism that filled the silence as he turned toward Sophia and gave her a smile. "I'm sorry about your mother."

Her stomach clenched. "How dare you," Sophia hissed. "Get off my property."

"I understand your feelings, and I know this is not the perfect time. And for that, I'm sorry. What I have to say is important ... for both of us—I wouldn't intrude if it wasn't. Is there somewhere we can talk?" He glanced over his shoulder. "Privately."

Sophia warred with herself. She'd love nothing more than to summon a couple of guys to throw Specter off the property. Having most of the Valley as witness would make it that much sweeter. But her father had always told her to check her facts before acting on them, to try the limb before stepping out on it. She turned on her heel.

Annalise and Maggie bent over flats of cookies arranged on the kitchen table, peeling plastic wrap off one of them, and chattering amiably. They motioned for Sophia to join them. "You must have one of these." Annalise offered her a cookie. "They are, as you said, addictive. She is very good. Thank you."

"Well, you'll get no thanks from me." Maggie put a hand on her hip, and a look of exaggerated displeasure on her face. "That woman has got to be good for at least ten pounds on my butt."

Conversation stopped and their smiles fled when Specter stepped in behind Sophia.

Maggie's eyes flicked to Sophia's shotgun leaning by the door.

Sophia smiled. "It's okay."

"I am so not leaving you in here, alone, with *him*." Maggie dug in her heels.

Annalise stepped to her shoulder. "I agree."

Sophia gave them both a group hug. "I love you guys."

"I don't mean her any harm." Specter seemed sincere, which was so out of character.

Maggie broke away and took a menacing step toward Specter. "You've done quite enough already."

Sophia caught her arm. "He says he wants to talk. I'll listen to what he says. Even a condemned man gets to say a few last words."

Annalise nodded. Maggie seemed less sure, but she let Annalise pull her out of the kitchen. "Just shout if you need anything. We'll come running."

Specter watched them. When they stopped just off the porch, he seemed unhappy, but he sighed and let it go.

"My friends are very protective."

"Then you are lucky." Specter pulled a chair out from the table, then thought better about sitting. Instead, he stood there looking a bit uncomfortable. "My *friends* usually want something from me."

"You've got to be a friend to have one, but that's probably not how you roll, so I won't waste my breath." Sophia, her arms crossed tightly across her chest, her expression closed, her voice hard, leaned against the counter. "Besides, that's not why we're here. You wanted to tell me something?"

Specter wandered around the kitchen, letting his fingers trail over the table, the chairs, his eyes taking in every detail. "My mom had a kitchen like this. We called it the family war room. I always felt safe there." He tossed her a disarming smile. A nice try, but it did little to melt Sophia's resolve. "It was as if your life could be seriously on tilt, and you just walked into the kitchen, smelled her cookies baking, saw her smile, and life righted itself."

"My family feels the same about this kitchen. The kitchen you stole out from under me." His story only made her angrier. She'd been played by too many slick men lately to stomach another.

"Yeah." He pulled out a chair from the kitchen table. "May I?" He actually waited for her answer.

"Be my guest." Sophia's manners kicked in, but her words lacked conviction, surprising her with the hint of sarcasm.

Avery, impeccable in his starched button-down, creased jeans, and lacquered comb-over, looked at her with tired eyes. "I find myself in an unusual position. Being new here, I'm afraid I've made some rather large blunders, business mistakes I'm not used to making. When Butchy Pinkman came to me and told me the property next to mine up here was for sale and it was already under good vine, I jumped at it. And I let him work the deal." He paused, chewing on his lip. "I see you've done some dirt work, which was your right. But could I taste the wine you made from those grapes?"

"What?" The air rushed out of Sophia as if he'd punched her.

"The vines were unique, and the location plays quite a part in how the juice shapes up, as you know, so there will be no others just like them. I'd like to taste it."

Completely amazed at his chutzpah, Sophia was stymied. She wanted to break the bottle over his head. But, on the other hand, she wanted him to know what he couldn't have. It would take a long time to re-cultivate the property with grafts from Italy—if they could pull it off at all. Those grapes were really finicky, tough to know and tough to grow.

Sophia opened the fridge. The kids had run through the wine last night. Pushing aside some Tupperware containers, Sophia spied a bottle. On its side in the back, it had remained hidden—one of the last Nico had brought to dinner.

Nico.

She took her time opening the bottle, then pulling some glasses— she chose two of her finest.

Setting them on the table, she poured both of them a glass and watched as Specter went through the whole ritual. Normally amusing, it irritated the heck out of her today.

"You don't deserve this wine."

He ignored her, his attention on the wine. He took the first sip, testing, tasting, then swallowing and savoring. He groaned. "How could you destroy this?" He held up his hand. "Don't answer. I know how. And I deserve it." He set the glass down with measured precision, as if buying time. When he looked at her, his eyes burned with intensity. "Your grapes. How do you know how to grow them like you do? Butchy Pinkman's..." He pushed at the glass with a forefinger, "and these."

Sophia snorted. "Pink's Passion is bilious, and this wine, Nico Treviani made."

"Butchy Pinkman wouldn't know good wine if it bit him in the ass. You give him gold and he makes lead. And this wine!" He waved silent Sophia's protestations. "Sure, Nico tweaked it, but the heart, the body... the soul ... of this wine is your juice. And it's sublime." He paused as if summoning ... something. "Grow grapes for me."

Sophia was speechless. But then the words rushed forth, tumbling with anger. "You ... you." She fought for control. "You take my home, my grapes, you even lock up my old family vineyard so all the grapes are yours. And now you want me to work for you? How *dare* you? How dare you come into my kitchen and say those words to me? You think you have me over a barrel, you've eliminated all of my options?"

"I don't think that at all. You could grow grapes for anybody and be paid handsomely for it." Specter fingered the stem of the glass and didn't meet her eyes. "I know how it looks."

Almost breathless with emotion, Sophia laughed, a strange, choked, half-mad sound. "I'm sure there is a special place in hell for you."

"Probably." A self-mocking smile lifted his lips briefly. "This is the hard part for me." Specter stumbled over the words.

"The hard part? For *you*?" Sophia fought for control. If she lost it, she didn't know what she'd do.

He caught her with his eyes. "You see, I was wrong. And I'm never wrong."

He seemed bewildered, by the concept or the reality Sophia wasn't sure.

"Wrong to take a widow's home? Isn't that how you people do business?"

"Some people," he admitted. "Maybe most. But not me. I never meant to steal from you. I was wrong."

Her heart lurched. "Wrong," she whispered, afraid to move. Her body vibrated with the effort to remain still.

"I didn't know anybody here, not really. And Pinkman is wildly successful, though not in the way I hope to be. I trusted him. Turns out I cast my lot with swine. I was an arrogant fool, and I've made a mess out of a lot of things."

Sophia didn't trust her legs. She pulled out a chair and sat.

"I had no idea about any of this. Hell, I didn't even know about this wine and the grapes until Nico brought it to me a couple of days ago. I had no idea about you, the deal, and its impact on you. Oh, I knew you could grow grapes like no one else. I'm sure you find that hard to believe, but I never intended to take anything that was yours. If I succeed at this game, at this pursuit of wine perfection, I want to do it fair and square."

"Charlie owned the property; he had the right to sell it at any time to anyone he wished."

"Yes, but this isn't about the property. This is about the grapes. Pinkman wanted to take them, force Nico to make the wine, and then claim it as his own. Even if you have the law on your side, that doesn't necessarily make it right."

Sophia leaned back. She raked her hair off her forehead with a shaky hand. "What are you saying? You won't buy the property?"

"That depends." Specter steepled his fingers as he looked at her.

"The grapes are gone."

"The grapes weren't the important part; there are other grapes, perhaps not as unique, or as sublime, but it will be fun to see what you can coax out of them. And we can take cuttings from the farm in Friuli, if you let us. You see, you're the key. It's your knowledge, your heart, your passion, that brings out the best in the fruit. It's you I want. You can grow whatever the hell you want as long as I can make the wine."

"Me?" Sophia's mind reeled. If she let them? What did that mean?

"I'll make you a deal you can't turn down."

"You want to hire me?" As Sophia said the words, even she couldn't believe them.

"You can live here if you like."

"So nothing changes, but everything is different," Sophia whispered, hoping her mother could hear. She looked out the window at the celebration that had resumed after Avery Specter's interruption. She looked around the kitchen. A monument to what was, isn't that what her mother had called it? But, it was home—a bridge to the future. "I'll have to think about it, talk to my children."

"Sure. Your call." Specter nodded, looking pleased.

Sophia raised an eyebrow, stilling him with a stern look. "Don't count your deal done, Mr. Specter. We've got a lot of negotiation to do."

"And I suspect you will push me to the limit." He looked pleased. "If you don't value your skills, you're not worth my time."

Sophia could feel her mother rubbing her nose in that little bit of philosophy. *I got it, Mother. I got it.* "What about the property in Italy? What is that all about? A really low-down underhanded deal, if you ask me. That was my grandparents' home."

Avery Specter's face sobered. He pulled some folded papers out of his back pocket. "Nico Treviani asked that I give these to you."

CHAPTER THIRTY

NICO'S HOUSE HID ON A slight rise in the middle of a lush vineyard, an unmarked mailbox the only hint that someone lived up the narrow road. Two wheel ruts with a grass-covered mound separating them, the turn-off eluded Sophia not once but twice, even though Olivia had given her the landmarks. And he'd accused *her* of hiding. As Sophia eased the truck through the narrow path, careful not to damage any of the vines that crowded the road, she thought he should know. The walls we erect, the prisons we build. They both had built castles on a hill.

A dishrag and a plate in his hands, Nico stepped out on the porch at the sound of the truck. His hair hanging limp, his face drawn, he didn't smile when Sophia stepped out of the truck. His eyes angry and dark, he watched her, saying nothing, as she stepped to the edge of the porch and looked up at him.

Nervous, fidgeting from one foot to the other, Sophia felt her heart crack at the sight of him. How did he have the power to affect her so? She pulled the papers from her back pocket and held them up. "What do these mean?"

"They mean you were wrong." He turned on his heels and banged through the door, disappearing inside the house.

Dishes clattered—it sounded like one broke. Sophia hesitated for a moment before taking the steps two at a time, following him inside. Nico stood over the shards of at least one platter, his head bowed as he worked for control. Sophia stopped inside the doorway as the twins skidded into the kitchen from the opposite side. Wild red hair, peaches-and-cream skin, bright eyes, Sophia didn't know which led and which trailed.

They looked between their uncle and Sophia with owl eyes. Finally Nico sighed. "Girls, you remember Mrs. Stone."

The first girl stepped across the room with a smile at her uncle and a glint in her eye. She extended her hand, "I'm Brooklyn. Nice to see you again."

Sophia gave her hand a quick shake. "Yes, lovely to see you." She looked at the other twin who hung back, a wary, protective look on her face. "You, too, Taryn."

The girl acknowledged her with a nod as her sister hurried back. "Come on. We need to leave them alone." Brooklyn ushered her sister out of the room, leaving Sophia at a loss as to where to begin, how to crack Nico's shell. She reached for a broom that leaned in the corner.

"Don't," Nico barked. "It would be best if you left now."

Sophia jerked her hand back as if she'd touched a live wire. "Can't we talk?"

Nico grabbed the broom and started sweeping. After a few mad passes, he stopped. Resting both hands on the top of the broom handle, he gave her a long hard stare. "I can't tell you how much men love that phrase. It usually means we'd better prepare for a verbal lashing. You obviously came here for a reason, and I suspect you won't leave until you've said your piece. So, go ahead. Say what you have to say, and then leave."

Sophia recoiled, a physical reaction to the verbal blows. "I'm sorry. I've made a huge mistake, jumped to conclusions, and I've insulted your integrity, which, I know, is unforgivable." Sophia tossed the papers on the counter. "I should've listened to my heart."

"Too late for that now."

"Nico, why didn't you tell me?"

His jaw working, he looked away, refusing to look at her. After a long moment, he said in a voice equal parts pain and anger, "Why didn't you trust me?"

NOT WANTING TO GO BACK to the gathering at her house, Sophia wandered, feeling lost and untethered. Family and friends, warm memories filled her heart; yet, somehow they left a hollow place. The unknown that lay in the future both thrilled and terrified her. She'd wanted to share it with Nico. But perhaps it was better this way. For far too long she'd relied on others to tell her what to do, to bolster her confidence, to keep her safe. And somehow, in the process, she'd lost herself. Her fault, yes, and only she could solve that problem. So better to soldier on alone. But somehow that just didn't seem right.

A parking space along Main Street in front of Sophia's favorite restaurant yawned, and Sophia took it as a sign. At this time of day, with French Blue's famous happy hour, there usually wasn't a space to be had for blocks. With practiced ease, she nestled the truck to the curb.

The restaurant, with its large windows, cozy glassed-in porch that led into a large, high-ceilinged room with wooden floors and whitewashed walls, felt both warm and cool at the same time. The open kitchen curled in behind a half-moon bar in the back, drawing her with its bustle of activity and mouth-watering aromas. Happy hour was only served at the bar. Sophia straddled the stool farthest around to the right, next to the wall, and peered into the kitchen.

She loved to watch professional chefs at work, marveling at their precision and attention to detail when plating the food—focused quiet in the chaos that swirled around them as orders were taken, dishes prepped, and food set to cook. The happy hour menu was short, the list of wines available shorter still. Sophia settled on duck biscuits, the chef's version of Tater Tots and two fingers of Single Barrel.

Life had been a whirlwind lately. Caught in the eye, Sophia had glimpsed it swirling around her, carrying bits and pieces of what had come before but obscuring what came next. But the clouds were lifting, things settling out. Trey had found his way home—that was the most important. The rest, keeping her house, a new job, new opportunities, were all very satisfying, but holes still remained. The loss of her mother would take time. But her mother had lived life and faced death on her own terms. And now it was time for Sophia to find the fullness of her own life.

Nico found her staring into the bottom of an empty glass, her food cold and virtually untouched. "Leave it to you to not hit any of your regular haunts the one time I had to find you." He sidled onto the stool next to hers. His hands on the bar, the fingers of one hand tapping out a nervous rhythm.

Her eyes roamed over his face. Several days' growth of beard did little to detract from the effect he had on her. She let her gaze fall to his hands. It was his hands she loved the best. Long and lean, artist's hands. Yet masculine, like the rest of him. She loved the way they looked, their feel, the things they'd once done to her. She tamped down on that thought and motioned for the bartender to fill her glass.

"I'll have what she's having." Nico frowned as he looked at the food. "But twice as much. And while you're at it ..." Nico stopped and turned to Sophia. "May I order you some more food? Yours looks cold and, knowing the day you've had, you probably haven't eaten much."

A smile ticked up one corner of her mouth as she gave him a quick nod.

"I'm not trying to tell you what to do," Nico continued, sounding earnest and contrite. "And I know you don't like people making decisions for you. In fact, you do really rash things when provoked. I may be an ass most of the time, but sometimes I'm trainable. Not perfect, but I try."

Sophia nodded. She didn't trust herself to speak as she fought the hope that swelled in her. Finally, she found the words. "I'm really sorry, Nico. I should've trusted you."

"And I shouldn't have tried to steamroll you. Forgive me?"

"You're not angry anymore?"

"That was ego, my precious male ego. But when you walked into my kitchen, anger and ego melted away. I just wanted to hold you, to see you smile at me, to hear you laugh and know I did that. I almost grabbed you."

"Why didn't you?"

"Pride. Fear." He looked at her from under lowered eyebrows, trying to hide the flash of humor in his eyes. "And I had to park the girls with friends down at the pizza place—your friend, Annalise, has my mother on a short leash today. When you didn't come back, I came to find you. So can you forgive me?"

Something warm and rich blossomed in her core. "If you can do the same."

He shrugged. "Nothing to forgive. I'm sorry about the grapes, though. Not that we won't make that wine, but that you felt you had to... do that. Are you okay?"

Sophia pursed her lips and nodded. "Yeah. I thought I'd feel sad, and maybe I do, a little. Where we come from is important."

Nico looked like he understood. "As long as it doesn't keep us from where we need to go."

"And the grapes really didn't." Sophia took a bite of a duck biscuit and sighed. "Oh, my God." She stared at the morsel and marveled. "It's smooth, yet with some crunch. Sweet, with a hint of savory tang. And a bite at the end. I could seriously embarrass myself with these things." With one hand cupped underneath, she extended it to Nico. "You've got to take a bite."

He complied. His eyes widened as he chewed and the flavors hit him.

"I know, right?"

Nico motioned to the waiter. When he could talk, he said, "More of those."

"How many?"

"Just keep them coming until we surrender."

Sophia popped the last bite in her mouth. It was every bit as marvelous as the first. "You know, you're wrong about flavors diminishing through the experience." She grabbed another biscuit. "Here."

Nico concentrated as he chewed. "Okay. But why, then, do we think the flavor lessens?"

"Because whatever we're eating or drinking doesn't capture us anew with each bite or sip. I want our wine to be the equivalent of this."

"A tall order."

"I think we're up to it." She gave him his first full-wattage smile. "It'll be fun chasing it anyway, won't it?"

Nico put his hand over hers, capturing it. He gave it a squeeze before letting it go. "Fun doesn't even begin to describe it."

Sophia's heart opened, love, excitement ... hope .... bursting inside of her. Life was now full, the holes filled.

"You do know I never wanted to take your grapes. I wanted you to have them, no matter what." Nico's voice, low and earnest, reverberated with sincerity.

"Even if it cost you your job." It wasn't a question—Sophia knew the answer.

Nico waved that away. He chuckled, a low rumble. "You should've seen Pinkman when he found out Specter and I had stolen that property right out from under him."

Sophia tried to look angry, failing miserably. "That's the one thing in this whole mess I'm still mad at you about."

Nico shot her a look and realized she was kidding.

"That man has been a thorn in my side for a long, long time. He so had this coming; I just wish I'd been there to witness it."

"Oh, you'll get your chance. He's still apoplectic. I'm sure we haven't heard the last from him." Nico took a swig of the bourbon. His eyes watered as he fought a choke.

"Pansy," Sophia chided. "So tell me why you didn't bring me into the loop on the property in Italy."

"It wasn't a done deal. Specter had reamed Pinkman a new one after he realized we kicked you out of house and home and were taking everything you'd worked for, so I figured the ass would try another tack. He sure wanted your grapes, don't know why. Oh, they're great and all, but still, to mortgage your self-respect, your soul to get them?"

"Butchy Pinkman has no soul."

"I'm beginning to understand that. Anyway, I called my cousins in Venice. One of them is a lawyer and they jumped on it. It turns out the property was still in the family, some distant relatives of yours. They loved the whole American family thing, and they figured you would take care of the family legacy, restore it to its original glory."

Sophia gave him a wide-eyed look. "With what?"

"I have no idea, but one problem at a time." Nico gave her a grin. "We've gotten this far, haven't we? So I let them sort of buy that story. My cousins knew how to sweeten the pot so everybody felt good about themselves—I think we're sending them several cases of each vintage we produce or something. The Italian sort of eluded me.

And I was in a hurry—I would've promised them almost anything if I thought there was a chance I could actually deliver."

Nico had missed his calling, thought Sophia. He should've been a storyteller. There was more of his father in him than he probably was willing to admit. "Mr. Specter's money was the grease?"

Nico darted a look her direction, but he didn't lie. "I didn't have any choice. I figured, if he turned out to be the swine we all thought he was ..."

"He did sort of cultivate that image."

"He did." Nico nodded at the bartender as he set another drink in front of him. "Thanks. So, if he turned out to be as bad as he wanted us to believe, then we really were no worse off. Pinkman was going to get the property anyway."

"You saved the farm," Sophia said with a smile. "You always wanted a farm."

"It's a bit of a commute." Nico paused, a thoughtful look replacing his grin. "Specter. Interesting guy. I had him pegged as a dick from the get-go. Turns out he's a ruthless businessman, and he is compelled to win, but not by breaking the rules. He's got a code, and he sticks with it. He told me that was the only way to keep his self-respect. If you have to cheat to win, what have you won? His words."

"Can't argue with that." Sophia pursed her lips as she contemplated the sea of duck biscuits the waiter put in front of them. "I hear it's really pretty in Friuli this time of year. Now that you have a farm, I think a visit is in order."

"I could be convinced." Nico chose a biscuit, then held it up, rotating it as he picked the perfect bite. "But you need to read the papers more carefully—the farm isn't mine."

"Whose, then?"

Nico squeezed her hand. "Yours."

"What?" Sophia swiped a tear that threatened to trickle down her cheek.

Nico shrugged. "Well, you do have to sign a few papers and such."

"My grandparents' farm, I can hardly believe it." She reeled as reality hit her. That farm had molded her, shaped her in ways she only now was beginning to see. A special place, perhaps her most special place, now it could be shared with those she loved. The kids—Trey especially would burrow in like a tick on a dog. If there was a place in the world that would fill his soul, that farm was it. And Dani, she'd love the grapes, the wine, although Italians were notoriously lazy when it came to making difficult wine. Maybe someday she could cook in her grandmother's kitchen, feeding her family, watching grandchildren run and play. And Nico could bring the girls, his mother, his sister, and he'd have his farm.

"Sophia, my girl, you earned that farm, but you still have to pay for it," Nico said with a grin. "Better get busy." He took a sip of the drink. "Smooth. That whiskey has some age on it."

"Damn straight. My father taught me, if you're going to drink, don't drink cheap swill." She sobered. "How much do I have to pay for it?"

"Drive a hard bargain with Specter. He wants you bad. A word to the wise, get a barracuda to negotiate for you. Specter loves the game. Don't ever forget how good you are."

Sophia's face creased into a frown. "Got it."

Nico laughed. "Don't look so serious. I'll help you with the barracuda, and, if you weaken, if you forget how amazing you are, I'm here to remind you."

"I can live with that." Sophia could live with a whole lot more, but she wasn't sure what Nico was offering, if anything.

"So," Nico took a bite, then chewed while Sophia waited. "What do you think about the grapes? Are you going to work with the vine in Italy or do something new?"

"The grapes. My grandfather's grapes." Sophia shook her head. "In the end they actually gave me what I needed but not what I wanted, or thought I wanted."

Nico looked confused. "You're going to have to give me more than that. You're talking in riddles."

"The grapes were actually the thing that made me different. They taught me what I loved, what I was good at. All along I thought it was about finding the right blend that would showcase my grandfather's grapes. But, really, the grapes were my way of finding me. Of discovering my heart." She turned a wide-eyed look at Nico. "It never really was about the grapes, was it?"

"Nope. It was about you. And you had to destroy them, the thing you thought the most important, the thing you clung to so fiercely, so you could learn that."

"Seems a waste."

Nico looped an arm around her shoulders and drew her close. "A small price. Most folks are never so lucky, or so brave."

"I wasn't brave; I was out of my head."

"Sometimes it takes that." He lightly brushed her hair with his lips then let her go. "Are we going to grow those grapes again?"

"Maybe, but only the best varietals. I've been thinking about scrounging around for some of the lesser known Northern Italian whites. I think it's time to shake up this business, show them some new brilliance. What do you think?"

"I think you are the most intriguing woman I have ever met."

The waiter, hovering nearby grinned and gave an appreciative nod to Nico.

"We'll be back," Nico said to the waiter. "Don't touch a thing." He grabbed Sophia's hand. "Come with me."

She slid off her stool then let him pull her along. "Where are we going?"

"Outside. I need to kiss you."

"Oh." Need uncoiled and seeped through her, taking her breath and starting her heart.

A few early diners and several of the wait staff glanced at them and smiled.

Nico pulled her out the door and around the side of the building. A bank parking lot, now empty, where they had a perfect view of the sun dropping toward the mountains.

Nico stopped and pulled Sophia to him, taking her in his arms. She snaked her arms around his waist, wishing she could crawl inside him.

Nico pressed his forehead to hers, gathering himself. Finally, he drew back and looked her in the eyes. "I know what's between us has been quick and a hell of a ride. But even when things were bad, all I wanted was to be with you. Nothing was right when you were gone. It's as if somehow you center me."

Sophia reached up and stroked his cheek but let him talk.

"I know I've made some mistakes. I tend to roll over people, or so I've been told. And I know I hurt your trust in me. But I love you."

Sophia gasped.

"I know," Nico said. "Such a short time, but love is like wine; you don't know it in your head, your feel it in your heart. And, Sophia Stone, you are in my heart. I don't want to press you, and I'm not expecting you to love me back. I'm just hoping that someday, if you let me try, I can earn your love. But, if you say no, I understand, and I'll walk away. All I want is the very best for you. If that means giving you up, so be it."

Sophia waited a beat. "If you don't kiss me now, Nico Treviani, I don't know what I'll do, but it won't be pretty."

"I've seen what you can do when you get upset." With a question still in his eyes, Nico ran a thumb up her jawline, a smile teasing his lips. His hand cupped her neck and pulled her to him, his mouth seizing hers.

Deep and sensual, plundering, consuming, his kiss held the promise of everything Sophia had ever wanted, on her own terms, with a man who loved her, really loved *her*. She pulled back and looked at him. "I'm giving you fair warning, I'm a handful."

Nico relaxed a little. "I'm willing to risk it."

"Mixing business and pleasure, it's not easy," Sophia said, as if she had a clue what she was talking about.

"Nothing worth doing is." Nico pulled her tight. "Christ almighty, woman, what are you saying?"

"I love you."

Nico sighed and buried his face in her shoulder. And he just held her. She could feel the slow, steady rhythm of his heart.

Sophia thought she could stay like that for a long, long time. "Nico, our food's getting cold."

He pulled back and looked at her. "What? You're thinking about food?" He looked a little deflated.

"I want to feed you, then take you home." She frowned. "Maybe we better go to your place. There's a Celebration of Life still going on at mine."

"My place. And then what?"

She looked at him with a benign look. "Up to you."

He laughed. "Oh, I do love you. Let's settle up and head home."

As she walked back into the restaurant at Nico's side, Sophia thought, right now, this place, this man, this life, she could want for nothing more. And how odd that sometimes one had to give up what they thought they wanted to get more than they could've ever imagined.

THE END

Thank you for checking out Sophia and Nico's adventure in Napa. For more fun reads, please visit www.deborahcoonts.com or drop me a line at debcoonts@aol.com and let me know what you think. And, please leave a review at the outlet of your choice.

DEBORAH COONTS

OTHER BOOKS BY DEBORAH COONTS

THE LUCKY SERIES

"Ivanovich....with a dose of CSI"
—*Publisher's Weekly* on *Wanna Get Lucky?* A Double RITA(tm)
finalist and NYT Notable crime Novel

WANNA GET LUCKY?
(Book 1)

LUCKY STIFF
(Book 2)

SO DAMN LUCKY
(Book 3)

LUCKY BASTARD
(Book 4)

LUCKY CATCH
(Book 5)

LUCKY BREAK
(Book 6)

LUCKY NOVELLAS

LUCKY IN LOVE

LUCKY BANG

LUCKY NOW AND THEN
(PARTS 1 AND 2)

LUCKY FLASH